I ACCIDENTALLY HIRED A SHADOW WALKER

USA TODAY BESTSELLING AUTHOR
JESSICA CAGE

Contents

Dedication

To the woman who struggled to trust.

Trigger Warning

First there were rotating dicks, split tongues, and food play.

Then there was bloody vampire sex on the ceiling.

Let's see what those shadows do...

Does this count as a trigger warning?

I think so.

Also...butt stuff happens.

Enjoy!

I

Bathwater

"**Y**ou said you'd drink my dirty bathwater." I slid the glass cup full of foggy liquid over to him. "So do it."

Deonta's lip quivered, and the bead of sweat that had been clinging to his hairline rolled down his forehead as he looked at me like a lost child. "What?"

"Did you lie to me when you said you would? You said you would do anything for me." A disinterested sigh left my lips as I found myself in the mirror's reflection behind him. It was time to get my hair touched up. Those pesky grays wouldn't stop popping up—as if I needed another reminder that my forties were just around the corner.

"I would never lie to you, Jericha." Deonta looked at the cup and swallowed hard, like he was trying to work up the nerve to do what I asked. His hesitation annoyed me even more.

"Good. Because there is nothing I hate more than a liar." I nudged the cup again. "Drink it."

The clock on the wall counted down the minutes until I would start a call that could change the trajectory of my business, and there he was, wasting my time with his incessant begging. I liked my men submissive, but sometimes I pushed too hard and broke them. They lost everything that made them attractive to begin with.

Deonta was a broken man, which meant I was done with him. He served no purpose other than filling up my inbox with unwanted requests for dates.

Five more seconds ticked by as I fluffed my afro and waited. He knew I meant what I said, and I wouldn't repeat myself. With slumped shoulders, he picked up the cup and gulped down the murky water. When he lowered the glass, his top lip glistened, water dripping down his chin.

"How does it taste?" I leaned back in my seat, satisfied he'd done it but instantly disgusted by the sight of him.

He choked back a gag before responding. "Delicious." Deonta lowered the glass to the table before looking at me with the most ridiculous puppy dog expression I'd ever seen. "Now, can we please keep seeing each other? I miss the taste of you, your skin, your lips."

I chuckled at the thought. "You think I would ever kiss someone who drinks bathwater?"

"I—" He glanced at the cup. "But you told me, I mean—you wanted me to do it."

"There has to be a limit, Deonta. You have a safe word. You could have used it." I stood and pointed at the door. "Leave and don't come back."

"Jericha, please." He continued his groveling as he stood.

He dropped his head, still speaking, but I couldn't hear a word he said. Thoughts of the balding spot on top of his head muffled every other sound. It had gotten bigger since I met him. In that short amount of time, what started off as the size of a pea had become the size of a quarter. It was as if the more he begged, the larger it got.

"I'm done here. You're boring me, and I need to get back to work." I walked around him, opening the door. "Leave out the back. I don't want anyone to see you looking so pathetic."

"Jericha—"

I lifted my finger to my lips to shush him. "You're no longer allowed to use my name."

Deonta said nothing else. He nodded, grabbed his jacket, and left as requested. It wouldn't be the last time I heard from him. It never was. Typically, I had to ignore at least fifty messages and missed calls before the rejected party finally got the picture. Deonta would be no different.

Just as I made it back to my desk to sit, my phone buzzed against the glass top.

I picked it up to see a message flash across the screen.

Deonta: I'm here if you ever need me.

I opened the contact card, changed his name to Bathwater, and turned to my computer. There were twenty minutes before the start of the call that would catapult my business. With the development of the new film studio just outside of town, businesses were clamoring for a way in. Yes my chances were slim, but I'd put my best business owner hat on and landed the opportunity to provide security for their upcoming productions. Being one of the few women-owned firms in my field made this a landmark event, a true testament to my perseverance.

The initial contract would be a deal guaranteeing me the right to provide security for all productions for the next six months. That contract would get me in the door, and my work would keep me there. This would mean years of business to help fund my company's expansion. My dreams were big already, but they grew each day.

"He actually drank it?" A soft gag accompanied the question.

I looked up from the monitor to see Natalie's head poking through the door. She pointed at the empty cup on the table, her braided bob swinging around her frowning face.

"Of course he did." I waved at her to come in.

Natalie was my assistant. Without her, I wouldn't have been able to run my business as well as I had. It was a hard lesson to learn for a person who likes to do everything herself, but I realized I needed someone I could trust to hold the spare keys.

I'd gone through five assistants before I found her, and as far as I was concerned, I would never let her go.

"I've heard people talk about drinking bathwater, you know. It's a popular saying, but never did I think someone would actually do that!" she gawked.

"You can get a man to do just about anything with the promise of pussy." I tapped my chin. "Hell, you don't even need to promise it. As long as he thinks there is a sliver of a chance you might one day spread those thighs, he will do anything. Men not even worthy of licking the sole of your shoe will lay their lives down for you."

"You're a badass!" She pointed at the cup. "But I have to know: was that really your bathwater?"

I laughed. "No, it wasn't. It was dishwater from the kitchen. As if my bath water would ever be that murky! I'm pretty sure there were food bits floating around in there!"

"I dream of being like you one day." Natalie beamed as she crossed the room, bringing papers and her trusty tablet with her.

"Stick around, and I'll teach you all my ways." I eyed the documents in her hand. "What do you have there?"

"The finalized contracts came in this morning." She handed the papers to me. "I took the liberty of printing them out. I know how you like to review important documents in physical form first."

"This is why I love you. You just get me!" I flipped through the pages and smiled as I recognized the well-placed tabs. She'd marked every point I'd highlighted in the previous copy.

"They made the amendments you requested and legal reviewed it. They said it's good to sign as soon as you're ready." Natalie tapped the screen of her tablet.

"Thanks. I'll look it over after the call." One thing I wasn't doing was signing any contract without reading it through.

"I can't believe you're going to be working on such an extensive project." A wide smile spread across Natalie's round face. She had the kind of smile that made you stop and appreciate the moment. "I remember when you opened this place. I wasn't old enough to work, but I hoped to be able to work for you one day, and now I get to be here to celebrate such a huge accomplishment!"

"There's a solid six months of hard work ahead of us." I smiled. "And if we do well, it's going to open so many more contracts just like this. The rep already mentioned two other productions. There may be possible overlap at the end of this round."

"We can do it with you as our leader!" She saluted me. "The new recruits are coming in, and we are right on track to have them complete their training just in time for the contract to kick off."

"I appreciate the vote of confidence." I took a deep breath. "As soon as this is done, we'll have to get on top of ordering supplies and making sure our vendors can keep up with the demand. I also want to triple our on-hand supplies. New recruits always mean lost items. We don't want to get caught with our asses out.

Look into secondary suppliers just in case. Those transmitters we got last time all burned out within three months. I don't want that headache again."

"Yes, ma'am." She tapped the screen then looked at me again. "It's time for your call. I'll step out and give you some privacy."

The call with the production team lasted exactly one hour as we reviewed the schedule and projected time consumption. This was the main reason I had to increase hiring. I couldn't have my staff tied up on one contract. We also discussed the dates for the five special team meetings that would happen throughout the six-month contract. This would require increased security as the bigwigs came in for the meetings. They would each need coverage while in town. It seemed like overkill to me, but I wasn't going to question the added income.

Just before the call ended, Von, the head of the production team, mentioned a launch party deal. Even though I felt like I could do a cartwheel, I kept it cool.

"That sounds like a wonderful opportunity. I look forward to this collaboration. Natalie will send over the start-up procedures once the contracts are executed by both parties."

"Great, I look forward to it. We'll get the contracts executed, and we'll see you soon!" Von clapped, and the others on the call followed suit.

I kept a cool smile on my face until after the call ended and I fully closed the video chat app. As soon as I was sure it was closed, I clapped and stomped my feet under the desk in a quick praise dance.

After my solo celebration, I leaned back in my chair and reached out to the vines hanging from the planter above my head. I twisted the vine gently around my finger and smiled as the leaves perked up along the stretch of it.

An hour later, I finished reviewing the contract, opened the digital signature portal, and shot off my approval. Two minutes after that, someone knocked on my door.

"Come in," I called out cheerfully.

Natalie entered with a cup in her hand that spelled disaster. It was black with a red rose vine on the side. Anytime there was a problem ready to blow up in my face, Natalie would appear with that cup filled with lavender and passionflower tea. The fragrance filled my office, and my breath caught in my throat.

She lowered the cup to the desk, locked eyes with me, and laid it on me. "Mitch just turned in his letter of resignation."

"What?" I clutched the armrest of my chair.

"And he's taking his original recruits with him."

Natalie had ripped the Band-Aid off the same way she always did. I hated long drawn-out reveals. If it was bad news, just tell me! And she did—she dumped it on my lap in a blaze.

"Son of a bitch! I knew he was going to screw me over!"

"You did?"

"The asshole was trying to get the contract behind my back. Von told me about it." I picked up my phone and scrolled through the contacts. "I'm just glad she didn't hold his disloyalty against me. Could have cost me everything."

"So what now?" She looked at the papers in her arms. "That's a quarter of our people gone overnight and no one to train the new recruits. What are we going to do?"

"There is someone I can reach out to. I was hoping I wouldn't have to do this, but it looks like we don't have a choice." As a punctuation to my statement, a chime sounded from my computer, alerting me that all parties had signed the contract. "Damn, that was fast."

"What was?" Natalie asked as I stood, grabbed my jacket and purse, and headed for the door. "Where are you going?"

"The contract is finalized. I need to get this locked down before we're forced out."

2

Ain't no way

"**S**uck it up, Jericha." I told myself as I drove from my office. "This is a necessity. No, it's not what you would prefer, but future you will love what you're about to do."

Of course, it wasn't the ideal situation to drive into my former friend's office and ask for her help. It was hard enough thinking about the way our friendship fell apart. Most days, I avoided it altogether. How do you look someone in the eye after they stole your dream?

When we were fresh out of school, I told Rose everything I planned to do for my business. It was going to be a hard sell trying to get funding, but she was so encouraging, I gave her all the details. I told her my name, my logo, my design, my message, my themes, everything. I was so excited, I even gave her an early version of my business proposal.

And you know what she did? She took that proposal to her rich father, who gave her the money to start her business. Yeah, she didn't need to go begging banks for loans like I did. Before I even had my first meeting, Rose had taken every single detail I had slaved over for years, curated for *my* business, and started her own.

And then, the bitch presented it to me like I should be happy about it. She actually took me to the front doors of her new establishment and said *look at this*! I guess she expected me to cheer and scream, "Oh my God, how wonderful! I'm so happy for you!" Nah. That's not what happened at all.

I went the hell off!

Because what the hell else was I supposed to do? Here I was, looking at the woman I thought was my best friend for the last six years of my life, and she had stolen my dream, one she never wanted for herself. Rose's problem was her low self-esteem. Cash doesn't create confidence. Even with all her family's money, she was still a girl who lowkey hated other women. If she could snatch up the thing that made you shine brighter than her, she damn sure would!

Women like Rose often took a girl's girl and turned them sour. Not me. She just made me learn a hard lesson. Keep the goal and the plan to myself. Let the world see it when it's done, when it's established and no one can take it away from me.

What made the situation worse was that Rose, for whatever reason, ran around making me look like the bad guy. She spun a story that basically swapped our roles. *I* was the friend who wasn't happy for her. *I* was the friend who had secretly been jealous and hated her for so many years. She was the innocent rich girl who had opened her heart to my poor, fat ass.

Because of what she did, I lost so many connections in my life I knew I would never get back. But they were people who I decided I didn't need in my life. As vocal as I was about my dreams, I didn't understand how so many of them could believe her. The truth was, they were just as fake as she was. They knew she was lying, but they didn't want to lose proximity to the supposed value she could bring to their lives. You know, access to Daddy's wallet.

Fast forward three years later, and Rose's business was failing. You know what she did when that happened? She came back to me apologizing and asking for my help. And what did I do? Because apparently, that lesson hadn't been engrained hard enough, I foolishly helped her. I gave her the advice to turn her business around.

I told myself it was a good idea to help her, because it meant a potential ally. That was the Band-Aid thought that kept me from kicking myself. But that turned out to be the truth, because of a dumbass named Mitch. With such a short time until the kickoff of the contract, I had no other option but to go to Rose and ask for her help.

Only this wouldn't be a handout—this would be a business proposal. I had heard rumors about Rose's business. It happened when you were in the same industry. At the last two conventions, Rose was nowhere to be found. Once again, the woman who bribed her way through college wasn't doing so well. At the very least, this collaboration would put money in her pocket and give me the manpower I needed for the short term.

"That's exactly what I need!" I slapped the steering wheel before flipping on my turning signal, indicating I wanted to turn into the gas station. No, I didn't need fuel for my car. What I needed were those little strawberry glazed donuts! They were my weakness, and most days, I avoided them because it meant an extra hour in the gym, but they also brought me joy. Shoot me, I'm a comfort eater.

As I maneuvered the car into the lot, a black car, top down, whipped in front of me. I slammed on my brakes, narrowly avoiding hitting the man with long dreadlocks that spilled out over the side of the car when he sped by me.

"Son of a bitch!" I yelled out, but he didn't acknowledge me. He parked, hopped out of his car, and headed inside.

I parked next to him, stopping myself from slamming my door into his. I was an adult, and I could handle big emotions! It didn't matter. I would have those little donuts soon, and they would make everything better.

I hopped out of the car, adjusted my skirt, and made a beeline for the last aisle in the store, where I knew I would find those tasty treats. My heart warmed, and a smile spread across my face when I saw the last bag sitting on the top rack. It was meant to be. Just as I reached for it, just as I was inches away from having the thing that could make my day better, a disgusting man's hand snatched it from me. And who stood in front of me with green eyes and a wide smile that made me want to punch him in the face? The same asshole who had cut me off!

"I was about to grab that," I said, trying to soften my voice. Maybe if I was nice, he would give me what I wanted.

"Oh, well, maybe they have more in the back." He shrugged. "Gotta be quicker than that, huh?"

And then, his goofy ass walked away from me.

"Seriously?" I scoffed. "Fucking men!"

"You have a problem with men?" he laughed.

"Generally, yes, but currently, I have a problem with one man—specifically you." I pointed at him. "First, you cut me off, and now, you won't even let me have my snack?"

He held his hands up in defense. "I didn't cut you off."

"You definitely did." I looked out the window at his car. "You in that little black exclamation of your manhood. I had to slam on my brakes to avoid hitting you."

"Is there a problem?" a woman called out from behind the register, her dark painted lips pursed in annoyance.

"Do you have any more of these?" He waved the donuts at her but kept his eyes on me, as if I would try to steal them.

"No, sorry, we're all out, and our supply order is delayed." She shook her head. "That's the last one."

"Damn. Well, better luck next time." He winked at me and headed for the register.

My intrusive thoughts took over. Infuriated, I speed-walked by him and stuck my foot out. The fool went flying when his foot met my ankle. Locs flailing, he slid across the floor and came to a satisfying stop, x marks the spot. I kept walking, stepping over his back. "Damn, you should really watch where you're going."

A better version of me would have made sure he was okay. Hell, she wouldn't have tripped him to begin with. But if I couldn't have my treat, I was leaving with something. The joy of his face planted on the floor would have to be enough. I winked at the cashier, who gave me a nod of solidarity, and walked out the door.

"I'll have to make sure she has no contact with anyone on the studio side. If she does, she'll find a way to snake me out of any future deals." I went over my game plan as I parked the car in front of Rose's building and immediately noticed something was off. The sign above the door had been removed. "Damnit! Am I too late?"

I hadn't heard anything about her doors closing. Maybe she was just having the sign replaced. If she had gone out of business, maybe I could convince her to give me her contact details for her staff. Hell, that would be even better than having to partner up with her. Just as I took out my phone to call her, hoping her number was still active, I saw someone walk inside the tinted double doors.

Maybe they were just remodeling. It was too bad she had all the windows darkened. I couldn't see what was going on inside. After another deep breath and a curse about my donuts, I grabbed my purse and stepped out of the car.

When I walked inside, I found a tall woman standing next to the front desk. Her arms were so toned that I almost asked her what her upper body routine was. At first, I thought she might have been a part of the security team—until she turned to me and greeted me with a bright smile.

"Hi! Welcome to RVC Securities. I'm Jasmine. How can I help you?"

I wasn't surprised to find a new secretary greeting me. It was typical. From what I remembered the last time I helped Rose, she had a high turnover rate. Apparently, she was as great a boss as she was a friend.

"Yes, thank you. My name is Jericha Brown. I was hoping to sneak in a meeting with Rose Connors. Is it possible for her to make time in her schedule for an old friend?"

"Oh, I'm sorry." Her expression changed from hopeful to slightly aggravated. "Rose doesn't work here anymore."

"She doesn't?" I frowned; she said it as if Rose was just another employee, not the owner.

"No, she sold the company about three months ago. We're under new management."

"Ah, I see, but you're still in the security business?" I asked. It wasn't unlike a buyer to come in and change the entire business structure.

"Yes, we are." She smiled. "We still offer private and professional security services."

"Perfect. I'm here to talk about a potential deal." If I failed to keep the relief from my face, Jasmine didn't let me know about it. "Would it be possible to have a meeting with your new owners?"

Jasmine's expression warmed again as the smile spread across her face. "I'll check. Please have a seat and I'll call him."

I took a seat in one of the gray chairs just beyond the entrance while Jasmine made her call. She spoke too low for me to hear, so I had to wait for her to come to me to confirm any potential meeting.

"Ms. Brown? I spoke to Mr. Statton. He said he will be here shortly and has agreed to meet with you before he starts his day." She smiled. "Can I get you anything while you wait? Coffee? Tea?"

"No, I'm fine, thank you. I'm glad to hear he can take the time to meet with me. Thank you for calling him." I nodded, keeping my thoughts about him starting the day so late to myself. It was me who needed the favor, so I had to keep it cute.

Where I was sitting, I could see my car parked just outside. I watched a bird flying above it and prayed it didn't use it as target practice. The relief when the bird flew away was a short-lived experience. Because just then, the little black convertible with the big, Black asshole owner pulled up right next to mine. He sat in his car, chomping on my donut!

When he was done, he tossed the wrapper onto the ground, got out of the car, checked his reflection in my car window, and headed for the entrance. That was when my stomach sank.

There is no damn way this is the same guy!

He waltzed in like he owned the place and greeted the woman at the front desk. It was without a doubt a nightmare in the making.

"Oh, shit," I muttered to myself. "Please don't let that be him."

"Mr. Statton. Good afternoon!" Jasmine spoke to him cheerfully.

"Fuck." I sighed.

Might as well pack up my shit and get the hell on!

I was so caught up in my thoughts; I missed when Jasmine directed him to me. He turned, looked at me, and started laughing. "Oh, this is just perfect."

"I'll see myself out." I stood, prepared to eat my foot...literally.

"No, no. You're here to talk business, am I right?" he asked as Jasmine looked between us, confused. "I won't let a simple accident impede a potential deal. Let's talk." He opened the door to his office and waved me in.

I swallowed my pride and reminded myself why I was there.

Huge contract, girl. Major. Big money. Years of success and industry connections. Suck it up and get it done!

It took an extra bit of effort to continue my path as I passed him and smelled the sweet scent of strawberry glaze on his lips. Salt, meet wound!

The wound burned a lot less after I stepped into the office and saw the stack of papers on the edge of the small coffee table by the window. They were all in Rose's name, and most had those alarming red stamps across them. "Past Due!" If ever there was a perfect confidence booster, that was it. He might have purchased the business, but it looked like it was still struggling.

"How can I help you?" He paused. "I'm sorry. Because of my surprise at seeing one another again, I don't believe we were formally introduced. I'm Raymond Statton, the new owner of this wonderful establishment."

"It's nice to meet you, Mr. Statton." I gave him a firm handshake and took pleasure in the shock on his face. It happened every time. Men never expected it. And yeah, I laid it on a little thick for them, really leaned into the grip.

"It's nice to meet you, Ms. Brown. That is your name, right?"

"Yes." I nodded. "Jericha Brown. I own JLB securities."

"Oh, yes. Now I know where I remembered the name from. I came across your business during my research before acquiring this company." He pointed to the chair, offering me a seat before he sat down. "So, what brings you here today?"

"Rose was an old friend of mine, and I had come to offer her a short-term partnership," I explained. "I realize she is no longer a part of the company, but I would still like to potentially discuss that deal with you if you're open to it and have the capacity."

"Sounds interesting. What are you thinking?"

"We have a large contract approaching, and I need additional manpower," I explained. "I'd need some of your men to join my team for a temporary sub-contract."

"And you chose this company for that?" he laughed.

"You find that funny?"

"Not to speak bad about your friend, but she was horrible at this business." He leaned back in his chair and pointed to the stack of papers I'd noticed when I first arrived. "Looking at current numbers and her historical reports, I'm not even sure why she ever opened it."

Because she was a backstabbing ho!

"I'm sorry to hear that. Forgive me, but it had been a while since we spoke. I didn't know things had gotten so bad." I stood. "Maybe I need to look elsewhere."

"I didn't say that. I'm running the show now. However stressful it may be, this still needs to be a successful endeavor. I had hoped to offload this place quickly—it's what I usually do—but I need to take more time to build it up before it even looks remotely enticing to a buyer."

"If it's so bad, why did you buy it?" I waited for his answer with a raised brow.

"I like a challenge. Unfortunately for me, your old friend is a tremendously good liar." He sucked his teeth. "She lied about how bad things really were. Did some fantastic masking of the financials too. If I could find her, I would sue her."

"She's missing?" I frowned. I had been out of the loop for a while, but it seemed unlikely I wouldn't have heard about her going missing.

"Deposited the check, transferred it offshore, and no one's heard from her since." He tapped the desk with his finger. "I have a private detective working on it now."

"Wow." I shook my head. "Never thought it would get that bad for her. Surprised she didn't just ask her father for help."

"She would have, I'm sure, but her father is the one who pushed for the sale." He reached under his desk and pulled out a bottle of water. After taking a long sip, he looked at me. "So, what's the proposal?"

"I'm sure you've heard about the new studios built just outside of town?"

"Yes, of course. Talk of the town." He paused. "You got the contract? So many people were clamoring for that. If I had been around sooner, I would have tossed my hat in the ring."

"Yes, I got it, and it kicks off soon. I secured contracts to provide security for them for the foreseeable future. But, as luck would have it, I recently lost my lead guy. I need someone to help me train the new hires, and if you have any staff currently in need of work, I'll gladly use them to fill the slots."

"I definitely have guys, and they'll be thrilled to hear about guaranteed work." Raymond scratched his chin. He sure was a fidgety man. "A few of them are muttering about joining someone named Mitch. Apparently, he has a new start up, and he's offering great rates for the guys."

"Damnit, he works fast."

He grunted at my outburst. "You know him?"

"My lead guy who left," I answered. "That would be Mitch."

"Oh, so you didn't just lose a guy. You've been backstabbed."

"I assume it has something to do with Rose's company crumbling." My mind went to work solving the riddle in front of me. "He sees an opportunity for himself. If he can undermine me and sneak in the backdoor with a ready-made team, I lose everything. I understand that now."

"It would seem like, in a way, Rose has screwed both of us." He fiddled with the bottle of water.

"It looks that way." I nodded.

"Well, of course, we will need to discuss the details further, but it looks like this is a way to help us both out."

"Might be." My shoulders relaxed. I could tell by the way his eyes darted over to the stack of bills, Raymond was a smart man. He had bills to pay and wouldn't shut down a perfect opportunity for petty reasons.

"How long do you need the deal to last?" He asked.

"Initially, six months," I reported. "After that, we can revisit things."

He scratched his chin. "I can hang around for that long."

"Hang around?" I inhaled sharply. *The last thing I need is another man running off and ruining my business!*

"Like I said, I'm always moving." He folded his hands in front of him. "This was supposed to be a sell and dump situation. Unless you have the cash to buy me out now, I'm going to have to stick around."

"That I don't." I shook my head.

"It looks like we got a new partnership on the horizon."

"Great." I picked up a card from the desk with his information on it. "I'll have my assistant send over everything you need for your full consideration."

"Oh, and one more thing." Raymond tossed his locs over his shoulder. "Try not to trip me again?"

I chewed my lip for a second then shook my head as I turned to leave. "I honestly can't promise that."

"Not even if I let you have the donut?" he called after me as I walked out of his office.

3

Maybe there's hope

I left his office feeling both relieved and confident this arrangement would work out. In a way, my issues with Rose had turned in my favor. Would I forgive her for stealing my concept to begin with? Probably not. But this wasn't about her, or the past. This was about the future—and the future was looking great.

Considering how well the meeting went, you would think I wouldn't need that sweet treat. But as I left his office, I found myself craving it. Maybe it was the smell of it on his breath. Maybe it was because the conversation hadn't eliminated all my stress. Regardless, I drove straight to another store, found a pack of those little pink donuts, and ate them on my way back to the office.

"You're back already." Natalie met me at the door. "I didn't think I'd see you again today. I was just about to call and ask if you wanted to reschedule the interviews."

"It turns out my first instinct was the correct one, and we may have a solution." I handed her the card I took from Raymond's desk. "I'll be writing the proposal. Once I'm done, I want you to proofread it then send it over to him. No need to get legal involved yet. Copy me on communications, please."

"Absolutely." She nodded. "And the interviews?"

"I'll still do them, now is not the time to ignore any prospects. We need to get all the talent we can right now."

It took me about two hours to draft up the proposal I wanted to send to Raymond. In it, I detailed everything from scheduling and inventory to staffing and training. I tried to address every concern. If I could be as thorough as possible, it would make things move a lot faster. I had little time to go back and forth on deal notes. Of course, our lawyers would get involved before we signed anything official, but if we could come to the initial agreement quickly, that would be great.

After I finished the proposal and sent it to Natalie for proofreading, I headed to workout. On the second floor of our building was a full gym. It was a perk for both me and the team who worked for us. They could come in at any time to use the facilities because I wanted them to be in peak condition. It was an investment in the happiness and well-being of my team.

Of course, Natalie and I both used it whenever we wanted to. Just as much as I needed them in shape, I had to be in shape. It wasn't uncommon for me to have to jump in and take someone's place on a contract. Outside of my fitness concerns, I used it whenever I needed to burn off some extra energy. It was amazing how great punching a dummy in the chest one hundred times could make you feel.

I was one of those people who had what they called a sleeper physique. To the eye, I appeared soft and fluffy. I looked like I might struggle to lift a chair, let alone be able to toss a man across the room. But underneath the surface was muscle—strong, but still soft to touch.

Lifting the heavy weight, I watched my form in the mirror; the weight pressing down, each muscle flexing and rippling beneath my skin. I could feel it more than I could see it, but it was still a beautiful sight.

"Damn, you look good." I blew a kiss to myself in the mirror before dropping the bar loaded with two-hundred and twenty pounds at my feet. "Nearly back to my college days. Twenty more pounds, and I'll be back!"

That was a personal goal. In college, I maxed out at two-forty. I could never get past that. The dream was to hit it before I turned forty. I wanted to stay as strong as possible for as long as possible. Though I could have spent another hour in the gym, I remembered Natalie's comment about the interviews. After putting things away, I headed to the private shower in my office.

A quick shower, fluff of my hair, and spritz of my cashmere vanilla perfume, and I was ready to be seen. I sat at my desk and hit the little blue button that summoned Natalie. A moment later, she came in.

"You ready?" Her head poked through the door before she stepped inside holding a fresh cup of iced ginger tea. It was my perfect after-workout drink.

"I am." I nodded as she placed the cup down. "Thank you."

"You have seven today. Four of them are promising. I've color-coded them for you."

"Perfect, as always." I gave her a small round of applause.

After a long sip of my tea and a quick read of the first résumé, I started the rounds of interviews. It was the same conversation over and over. After seven men and women, I had approved five to move on to the next stage. This was a skills check. I had to make sure they were in the right physical shape and could do the things they claimed they could.

It was shocking to see how many people would claim to have black belts but couldn't perform a simple roundhouse kick. The crazy thing was, most often than not, those skills rarely came into play. We could teach things like that, but one thing I wouldn't do was hire a liar.

"Great job today, boss!" Natalie entered my office. The sunset cast a soft pink glow through the windows that made her cheeks rosy.

"Thank you." I stood and took a bow before checking the clock on the wall behind her. "You know, you could have gone home. You don't have to stay here just because I do."

"I know, but this is an important time, and there are things to get done. I organized more interviews and set up the skills checks for the people you chose today. Did my check-ins for all active contracts, and terminated the former guys in our systems so they can't access anything." She tapped the folder in her hand. "Also, I sent off the proposal as requested, and put a call in to the vendors for back up on supplies."

"Did we lose any contracts to Mitch?"

"Only one, but it was his uncle's water park. I figured that would be an easy steal for him." She nodded. "They were behind on their payments."

"It's a good thing. That man was more of a headache than he was worth, and it frees up Mya for this deal. She's one of the best we have. Please tell me she didn't go with Mitch?"

Natalie scoffed at the idea. "I doubt after kicking him in the nuts for his dirty comments about her breasts she would jump at the chance to go work for that man."

"I can't believe I forgot about that." It was an incident that cost me a pretty penny. I had to hire a person to come in and talk about interoffice relationships. I pointed at the documents in her hands. "What do you have there?"

"I've printed off the proposed schedules the production company sent over." She handed the docs to me. "I figured you would want another look at them. They look the same as previous iterations, but there are a couple of markers in there I didn't recognize. Those are highlighted."

"You're a godsend!" I praised her. "Alright, enough work for the day. Let's get out of here. After the day I've had, I'm going to need a nice, long soak in the tub."

"Enjoy it." She rubbed the back of her neck. "I might have to do the same."

Thanks to the terrible traffic, it took me nearly an hour to drive from the office to my home on the outskirts of town. Typically, it wasn't that bad. My home was in the perfect spot when I bought it—close enough to town to get to everything I needed, but far enough that I had an actual yard to build my own little oasis.

My home meant so much more to me than just a place to lay my head. It was security, something I hadn't had for so long in my life. I grew up in this system, moving from foster home to foster home for most of my youth. I could have ended up like so many other statistics of that system. I could have fallen into drugs. I could have become a young mother.

Trust me when I say there were plenty of people giving me that exact prediction for my life, but I refused to accept that as my truth. And so as soon as I could, I got a job; I worked my ass off and saved every penny I got my hands on. Fortune turned in my favor just after my fourteenth birthday, when my case worker placed me in the foster home of a woman who treated me like I was her heart and soul.

Lavon was a light in a world that felt suffocatingly dark. The first night I met her, she pulled me into her arms and said, "Welcome home!" With other foster parents, I was always reserved. I never let my guard down. But within a week, I cuddled up to her. I lay in her bed watching movies and joined her in the garden. Lavon truly felt like home.

In my years living with her, Lavon taught me all the things about life I had struggled to learn on my own. She taught me about saving, about finances. She took the time to show me the ways of being a woman. She taught me how to take care of myself, and the importance of that. When I failed at something, she didn't ridicule me like others had. Lavon showed patience and explained why these things had to be done a certain way.

If it wasn't for her, I wouldn't be in the position I was in. When I went to college, it was her who helped me. She'd always wanted a daughter of her own but was never able to have one, and in all the years of having her foster care home, she only had boys. I was the first girl, so the money she saved for her future daughter, she gave to me.

That, combined with the money I had saved over the years—she never made me pay for a thing—was what I used to pay my way through college. The year before I first opened my doors, she died. When I went to her funeral, I didn't expect much. I knew her family; they knew me. I expected everything to be cordial. What I did not expect was to be pulled into a room by an attorney, who gave me an envelope.

In that envelope was a letter. *To my daughter.* She hadn't written *foster* daughter. To Lavon, I *was* her daughter. That was how she saw me. In over a decade of knowing her, she had become the mother I needed, and I realized as I read her words that she was my mother. She was my heart. I'd cried so hard, the letters on the page smudged so badly, I couldn't finish reading it.

The attorney then handed me a second envelope. Inside was a letter that began: *Now that you've cried through the first letter...* It went on to say how she wanted me to be okay, that everything that was hers was now mine. She'd known she was sick and her time was coming to an end, so she was leaving me her estate, a house she wanted me to sell and a bank account.

Then, the attorney handed me another envelope that contained an account ledger. It didn't have millions of dollars in it, but it had enough for a nice down payment on a new house, and some seed money for my business. That was more than I had ever hoped for.

Around my home were touches of her. I noticed it every time I thought about her. I decorated in the same way. I grew the same plants, and used the same scents in my diffusers. She loved patchouli. I even had incense in the house, though I never burned them because I hated the smokiness. Instead, I loved to pick them up and sniff them because they reminded me of her.

There was a time in my life when I'd envied others. I envied the relationship they had with their mothers, the connection,the bond, because I felt like I would never know what that was. But she had given that to me. I was grateful for it every day, because it taught me what it meant to be loved by a woman; allowed me to experience girlhood.

I stuck to my usual nightly routine: visiting my garden. As soon as I stepped through the gates, I kicked off my shoes. I loved the feeling of the soil on my feet. I danced through the grass, throwing my hands in the air, praising the space I had. I visited the flowers, sniffing their fragrance and smiling when they perked up at me, even though there was no sun to encourage them. As my final task, I sprawled out in the middle of the ground, grass against my skin, hair splayed out around me. This was my happiness. This was what I worked so hard for; to come home and lie in the grass and feel at peace.

This was my welcome home and my rejuvenation.

After laying in my garden, I entered the house, dropping my clothes at the door so as not to track dirt inside. I stripped and went to the bathroom. Another glorious part about living alone was the freedom to walk around butt ass naked. If I had been born in another life, I would have been a nudist. I would have had a beach somewhere secluded by myself, where I could just run around in the buff underneath the sun.

I hated clothes. They felt suffocating, which was why, most often than not, you would catch me in a short pencil skirt and a loose blouse. If it wasn't that, it was something like booty shorts or a tank top. If I could have my skin as free as possible, that was all I needed. Unfortunately, sometimes, I had to cover up, especially in my line of work. I had to make sure my body was covered for protection, of course. Safety was first, fashion second.

As my bath ran, I took care of my hair. I shouldn't have laid in the damn grass before covering my hair. I usually pulled my bonnet out of my purse, but the day had been stressful, and I was out of my mind. So much for letting my hair last a few more days. I sprayed it down and detangled the coils with a wide-tooth comb. The second I thought of skipping the wash, a blade of grass fell onto the sink in front of me.

"Fine, I'll wash it!" I fussed and applied the hair mask I always used before washing my hair.

While the water filled the tub, I moved through the house, tending to all the potted plants inside. These were my babies. Other people had pets or actual children. I had my plants. I talked to them, nourished them, cared for them, loved them when they flourished.

But my plants had secrets I could never share. They were more powerful than they looked, and there was one that held more power than all the others. No, I wasn't just a crazy plant lady—kay, maybe a little bit—but there was something special about it.

I walked to the large potted plant by the window, a second smaller pot sitting inside it. I had to cut out the bottom of the pot and plant it inside the bigger one because this plant got pissy when I tried to swap it entirely.

"You can stop pretending now." I tapped the potter with my fingernail then stepped back to watch.

In the same dramatic fashion, what looked like a simple vine plant with pink flowers moved. The long vine pulled back, coiling into a tight ball. Then, those petals shifted, moving to form tight scales across a long, slender body. Moments later, her head popped out of the dirt, and she shimmied to knock the soil away from her.

"There you are." I smiled, reaching out so Kaa could nuzzle my hand. "How was your sleep?"

She looked up at me, and the petals around her face spread out, creating a pink mane.

"I assume it was a good day." I lowered her small body to the floor and, as always, she went off to survey the area. For the next hour, she would slither through my home, a mythical guardian. Her presence made me feel safer. As she slid across the floor, pink and silver and giving off her magical aura, I headed back to the bathroom.

Kaa had been with me for over twenty years. I called her a gift from the universe, because I found the seed that formed her soon after my own powers first emerged.

It was shortly after I turned fourteen, though I didn't realize it. It was nothing significant, and mostly just made me paranoid. The first few times it happened, I noticed how nature shifted and responded to me. I told myself at first I just had a wild imagination, that I needed to focus more on education and planning for my future. The only thing that mattered was getting ahead in life.

But then, I met my foster mother.

It was during my time working in her garden that I understood it wasn't just something happening in my mind. A year and a half after moving in with her, I had a dream of standing in a weird cave. As I walked deeper inside, I saw a woman standing by a pool of water. I gripped the scarf I wore around my neck—my favorite, green with pretty gold spirals along the edges.

I remember her taking me into the water, telling me to relax, to understand a message was waiting for me. And then, I woke up, and at first, I couldn't remember much other than that, but as time passed, I remembered the words I'd heard in that pool. I understood something was awakening within me.

Now don't get me wrong, I never believed that dream actually happened, though I remembered dropping that scarf in the cave and never saw it again. Still, I do believe it triggered something inside me, and over the years, I slowly accepted that this was part of my life.

It was also something I could tell no one about, but it was part of me, and that was why I loved to be near nature, to feel the dirt on my skin, the wind, the grass, all of it.

When I was seventeen, Kaa came into my life, but she was nothing like her current self. I was out on a hike when I tripped, which is unusual, because typically, I'm very surefooted, but when I looked over, I saw this weird orange and blue seed just sitting in the dirt. Typically, when I'm out like that, I touch nothing foreign to me. I'm not crazy, but something inside me screamed to take the seed home and plant it.

My mother taught me to listen to my intuition, so I did. When it was time to move away from home for college, I finally bought a pot and planted it. I promised my mother I would take the best care of it. Three weeks after I planted the seed, Kaa emerged.

From the moment I saw her, I felt the connection, something beyond explanation. She understood me, and I should have been scared of this plant that turned into a snake, but I wasn't. Hell, I didn't even like snakes—still don't—but

Kaa was different. She was a part of me, like if someone sliced off a piece of my soul and made it real. That was Kaa.

To me, Kaa was sweet and gentle and made sure I was okay. There were many times, especially during finals, when she comforted me. To others, she was a bit more aggressive, but more often than not, no one ever saw her. I had very few friends who knew about her. She remained hidden in her plant form whenever we weren't alone. But whenever we *were* alone, I would tap the side of the pot she lived in, and she would come alive.

The most I would ever get were comments about how exotic the plant looked. Some green thumbs would even ask about water and lighting needs, growing irritated when I wouldn't allow them to propagate from Kaa.

My go-to excuse was that I found it at some random nursery I couldn't remember the location of, and everyone seemed to accept that as truth.

My home was a welcoming oasis, full of plants that brought a smile to my face.

The first thing I did after buying the home was remodel it. It had good bones but was an eyesore. I put in more windows for natural lighting and access to sunlight for my babies. I had natural planters built into the walls. It gave my plants access to rainwater, and all the drainage went outside, so I didn't have to worry about root rot.

I went with a cozy cottage feel—exposed brick, lots of natural wood furnishings, and stone flooring and countertops. Entering my space felt like going to a spa. At least, for me it did, especially with the heated flooring. My feet were always nice and toasty.

With the tub full and the water hot, I slid into the bath and let the water do its thing. Maybe it was because I was a Cancer and had spent most of my time in the water as a kid, but I loved a good bath. It did something to me. No wonder I had dreams of odd women in caves with magical ponds.

I had been thinking of that dream more often, but I couldn't figure out why. It felt like a deeper intuition was trying to yell at me, but I had no idea what the hell it meant.

As I soaked, I drew my fingers across the surface of the tattoos that covered my body. My first was the vine that wrapped around my arm that I'd got on the second day of college. Since then, I've gotten ten more, all nature themed. And yes, I was itching to get another one. The plan was to extend the vine that wrapped around my right leg up my body and across my chest to connect it to the one on my left arm. That would take a lot of time, money, and pain. Yes, I loved them, but I'm not one of those girls who claimed they didn't hurt. I just liked the pain.

The vine was like a map of my inner self. Every time I reached a new level in life, maturity, power, I would add to the vines. Each leaf had a name, a purpose. It was the traces of my former self. I spoke a quiet thank you to that past version of myself for being so resilient.

Hair washed, body scrubbed, and skin moisturized, I wrapped my robe around my body and headed for the kitchen. As I passed, I made sure to give extra attention to any of my plants that looked a little down. After a quick hello and a gentle touch, they always perked right back up.

As I plucked a grape from the bowl in the fridge, my phone buzzed. It was still in my bag, discarded on the floor by the door. I retrieved the phone and found a text from Mack.

Mack: Hey, are you still coming over?

"Shit," I muttered. I had forgotten all about his ass. Mack was my new flavor, a man with broad shoulders and strong thighs.

Just as I was about to send an affirmative response, Mack committed the ultimate sin. The phone buzzed in my hand, and a moment later...dick pic! Yep. And the worst fucking kind: dick in hand, toes in background.

BLOCKED!

I slammed the phone down, and then, a moment later, it buzzed again.

"I know damn well..." I picked up the phone, expecting a text from Mack, but I found an email notification.

It was from Raymond. I opened it to find one line.

This looks great. I look forward to working together.

4

Dammit, Deonta

I drifted off to sleep, Raymond's face in my mind's eye, only to be jolted awake by the insistent ringing of my phone. Curses on my lips, I reached over to pick up the device and saw his name flashing across the screen.

"The hell?" I frowned, cleared my throat, and answered the call. "Hello?"

"Are you just getting out of bed?" he asked, as if he was an old friend.

I had to check my attitude before I responded. "Can I help you? Did you need something?"

"Yes, actually." His voice came through the phone in a smug tone. "I would like to come see your facilities today. The proposal looks great, but I think it makes sense for me to see things before I completely sign on."

"That sounds fine. Our team doesn't really do much in office besides using the gym to train." I sat up in bed, wiping the sleep from my eyes as Kaa slithered across the foot of the bed. "We don't have them come in unless there are assignments."

"That's understandable. I don't need to meet the team. This is more so an opportunity to get to see your day-to-day operations and understand how we can work together to make this partnership a successful one."

"What time would you like to come by?" I asked, already done with hearing the man's voice before I even had my morning tea.

"It would have to be late in the day." He paused. "I have a few meetings to attend. If you're okay with it, I can head your way around 4:30."

So why the hell are you calling me now? I rolled my eyes, again pulled the annoyance out of my tone, and then responded.

"That should be fine. Please shoot me an email with the confirmed time and copy my assistant, Natalie, on it. We'll accommodate you."

"Thank you," he responded, and then, in an antagonizing tone, said, "Have a good rest of your morning, whenever that begins for you."

And then, he hung up, giving me no time to tell him to kiss my ass. I stared at the phone and realized this nutcase had called me at five-thirty in the damn morning. This had to be a power play, because the sun wasn't even up yet. Who had business calls that early in the morning?

"Crazy son of a bitch," I muttered, tossed my phone to the nightstand, and turned back over. I was not letting that man make me lose any more sleep.

After waking me up at the ass crack of dawn, Raymond was nowhere to be found! Not a call, text, nor the requested email to confirm what time he was coming. Throughout the day, as I checked my open contracts, followed up with potential new hires, and confirmed new appointments, my mind kept drifting back to him—that was exactly what he wanted. Raymond was a typical man, wanting the world to revolve around him.

"This man will not distract me!" I fussed after looking at the clock. It was after four, and he still hadn't checked in, not even after Natalie sent him an email requesting a confirmed appointment time.

"Still no word from Mr. Statton." Natalie entered my office. She wore an adorable baby-doll shirt that made her look far more innocent than I knew her to be. I mean, the girl frequented raves and often dated men with motorcycles and gang affiliations.

"That's fine. Maybe this is a sign I shouldn't be working with him." I shrugged. It would be difficult finding a solution to the staffing issue, but I never backed down from a challenge. Even with the pending agreement with Raymond, I had already put out a few other feelers with other companies. Unfortunately, I had yet to hear back from any of them, but these things could take time. I knew that.

"There will be better options," Natalie attempted to reassure me.

"Sure." I paused, deciding I wanted to change the topic. "Wait, your birthday is coming up! What are we doing this year?"

"Honestly, I'm turning thirty, and it should be a big deal, but it doesn't feel like it." She pulled up a seat to sit on the opposite side of my desk. "It's supposed to be more impactful than this, isn't it?"

"What do you mean?" I leaned back in my seat. "Impactful how?"

"Theres no excitement. My life is monotonous, and all my friends have moved away—I mean, besides you. And it's weird that I see you as a friend, because you pay me. I just always imagined my life would be so much more adventurous. When I first met you and figured out your secret, I thought that was a sign it was all about to get real fun, but honestly, not much has even come of that."

"First off, we *are* friends. I can cut you a check and still be your friend." I laughed. "And your life will only be as exciting as you make it. You're still young. You have no kids or responsibilities outside of yourself. There's nothing stopping you from making your life the adventure you want it to be."

"You're so wise." She shook the braids out of her face. "This is why I look up to you."

"We can find something fun to do. We still have a few weeks to plan. I'd suggest a trip together, but with this contract, it's not a good time to leave town."

"We can save the trip for when you sign the next big deal!" Natalie clapped her hands. "This is only the beginning. There's so much more greatness coming for you!"

"Spa day? How about that? I'll plan it! Besides, you deserve it after all you've done around here." I looked at the clock. "Actually, you should head out now, start the celebration early and go take yourself out for a few drinks. What about that guy you were interested in? Maybe he's available for dinner. I'm not typically a fan of women asking men out, but exceptions can be made."

Natalie's nose turned up like a dog had just taken a massive shit in her lap. "Ugh, If I could make him drink bathwater, I would."

"That bad?" I straightened, always ready to trash talk a man.

"We were supposed to be on a simple date that turned out to be his family reunion! He introduced me to his mother as his fiancée." She gawked. "Can you believe that? I stood there, no ring on my finger and panic all over my face."

"Wait," I laughed. "You only knew him for like two months, right?"

"Yes." She shook her head. "He expected me to go along with it and even called to curse me out about how much it embarrassed him when I ran the hell up out of there. I mean, I might have played along if he told me about it ahead of time. I'm all for fooling a pushy mother, but that wasn't cool."

"Natalie, what did you do to that man?" I laughed because I knew there was more to the story.

She looked down at the tablet in her hand and tapped the screen, as if she had something important to do. "I have no idea what you mean."

"You put a little something-something on him...didn't you?" I pointed at her like I found the key to an unsolved case. "That spellbook you found!"

"Okay, maybe I experimented with a spell, but it was just supposed to make him want me, not jump to marriage." She shrugged. "I even used half the recommended ingredients, like when making pancakes. I never want six. Three is more than enough."

"I keep telling you to stop playing with magic you don't understand. That's not how any of this works. You're going to get yourself in a lot of trouble if you don't stop while you're ahead."

"We can't all be like you. Your natural abilities work for you." She pouted. "I have to try my best to learn and grow my own witchy powers."

"Did you ever figure out who owns that grimoire?" I asked her. "Seriously, if it's the property of someone evil, it's going to bite you in the ass."

"No, but it vanished a while ago." She rolled her eyes. "I only got to copy a few simple spells out of it before it did."

"Good. You don't need access to that anyway." My shoulders relaxed. At least we didn't have to worry about her being cursed because she refused to listen to reason. The day she told me she found it after taking her hardheaded ass to a party meant for magical beings, I told her to get rid of it. Of course, I couldn't force her to do anything. She was a grown woman, after all, but I did ban her from bringing the damn thing anywhere near me.

"I could be a lot better if you would just take me under your wing." She waved her fingers in front of her face. "Teach me your ways, sensei."

"How many times do I have to tell you, I don't know anything about that type of magic? I don't use spells to do what I do. But even if I did, do you think I would teach you a damn thing knowing how reckless you've already been? Playing around with love spells is so dangerous, especially using one on a man you barely even know. That seriously could have backfired on your silly ass. You should be happy that man didn't try to kill you."

"But think about how exciting it would make my life!" She tucked the tablet under her arm and put her hands in a praying position.

All the prayer in the world won't make me dare mess with love magic. That shit never works out the way you want it to!

"Turning thirty isn't that damn bad." I laughed. "Now get out of here and find something safe to do!"

Just as Natalie stood to leave, a notification sounded from her tablet. She checked the message then looked at me. "It's Mr. Statton. He said he will be here in an hour. I can hang around."

"No need." I waved her off. "You can get going. I still have some papers to review. I'll wait for him. He just wants a tour of the place."

"Are you sure?" she double-checked with me, as always.

"Yes. I didn't do a love spell on him, so I won't have to fight him off." I teased her.

"Funny." Natalie mockingly rolled her eyes then left. "See ya!"

It was never my intention to tell Natalie about my abilities. Actually, I wanted her to be in the dark. Foolishly, I thought that would make things easier for me. But three months after she started working for me, she found out, and I couldn't have been more relieved.

It was innocent enough. I thought I was in the office alone and hadn't yet figured out how much Natalie liked to overwork herself. There was a potted plant in my office, a gift from an old friend, and it was dying. One thing about me—I'm going to revive a plant if I can. This one just needed a little pep talk, and just as I stuck my finger in its soil to revive it, Natalie walked in.

I could have tried to lie, but honestly, I was relieved not to have to tiptoe around her. She freaked out but not nearly as much as you would think. After I explained my abilities, Natalie seemed a lot more relaxed around me, and that was because *I* was more relaxed. Not having to hide a part of myself all damn day made it easier for us to work together.

It also made it easier to keep her long-term, considering the few supernatural clients we had. There weren't many, but sometimes, they caused more trouble than they were truly worth. With Natalie in the know, she could better handle those clients when they came into the office.

The problem that created was the more Natalie learned about the magical world, the more she wanted that power for herself. Soon, she was stalking magical beings to find her way into their world, which was exactly how she landed in a party to find the unattended grimoire. She said she found it, but I wonder if Natalie didn't treat herself to a five-finger discount.

She was lucky this time that the owner of the book didn't come for her silly ass, but it wasn't uncommon for witches to cast protection spells on their own books. Once Natalie started using the spells from its pages, the owner would have been able to locate it and call it back to her. I only hoped they didn't change their mind and decide to come smack her upside the head about messing with their magic.

After Natalie left, I did one more walkthrough of the office before settling again in my seat behind my desk. One hour stretched to nearly two before Raymond arrived, and just after seven, I marched to the front entrance to let him in.

The contract isn't signed yet. Keep it together, girl. This is important!

I wiped the agitation off my face before I swung the door open to greet him. "Hi. Glad you could make it."

"Sorry about it being so late." He grinned as if he hadn't wasted enough of my time.

"It's fine. Let's make this quick." I stepped aside to let him in. "I don't mean to rush, but I haven't had dinner yet, and it's been a long day."

Raymond followed me closely as I marched through the office. I showed him where my office was and, of course, the waiting room. Then, we walked through the storage space, which was about the size of a four-car garage, before heading to the second floor to the full gym. I showed him the equipment and the specialized training schedule.

"I like to make sure all our guys are in the best shape possible... and have access to learn anything they may be weak in," I explained.

"That's brilliant." Raymond looked around the equipment. "Not something we currently do, but I'm sure that will be a practice shift for us as well. If you don't mind me stealing your idea."

"I'm not the first to do it, and besides, it's better for your men if they have every possible advantage when it comes to their job."

"That's true." He nodded.

"Well." I clapped as I led him back to the front entrance. "That's everything."

"The facilities look great, and I can tell you take great care of your staff here," he complimented.

"My people are my top priority." I nodded and reached for the door. "I find the happier they are, the better job they do."

"That makes you a brilliant leader. Not enough people understand that. Unfortunately, the ones who don't are usually the ones in leadership roles."

"Can I take that to mean you're good with working together now?"

"Not quite." He rubbed his thick beard with his hand. "How long have you been running this business?"

"Didn't you say before that you had done your research on me? I'm surprised something as simple as that hasn't come up."

"I said your name came up during my research," he corrected me. "I never said I remembered anything pertinent."

"Ouch." I nodded. "I guess I deserve that, but to answer your question, I've been in business for about a decade now. I got things going a few years after Rose did. Actually, I had shared my ideas with her, and you can say she took inspiration from my notes."

"Did she take inspiration, or did she steal your idea?" He raised a brow at me.

"I never said that."

"You don't have to. Actually, I know a lot more about you than I let on." The long locs swayed at his sides as he leaned back on Natalie's desk just outside my office door. "Rose had a whole folder on you. It contained your original plans for your business, and a few notes about your encounters after you both got started."

"A folder?" I took my hand off the door and walked over to him. "What else was in this folder?"

"Articles about your success. She kept up with everything you had going on, but I think you know that. I assume that's why you guys weren't that close."

"How did you know we weren't close?"

"Jericha, you didn't even know she had sold the business." He laughed. "It's not that hard to figure out. Actually, I'm surprised you called her your friend when you came in. She's more like a snake, if you ask me."

"What can I say? I was in a desperate position." I shrugged. "The things we do to make our business a success."

"Been there before." He sighed. "When I first started this path, buying and selling businesses, it was a hard start up. But in just a few years, I've managed to make good headway for myself."

"You've been in desperate positions? How desperate?" My eyes narrowed.

A dry chuckle escaped him. "Desperate enough to ask for help from someone I knew stabbed me in the back before, just like you."

"Happy to hear I'm not the only one. So, what do you think? Is this gonna work out?"

"Everything you sent over looks good. The facilities are great, much better than the ones we're working with. So, if you don't mind, we'll be using this more so than mine. I'm not really trying to build up that business. I just want to make the books look good enough so someone wants to take it off my hands." Raymond switched into business mode, and I could already see why he'd been able to garner the success he boasted about. "There are a lot of things there that we can pull over here, inventory and such. If there was one thing Rose liked to do, it was buy things she didn't need. Actually, if we could put that into the contract, I'll sell all of it to you at a discount."

"What about your other clients?" I questioned. "If you move everything here, won't that make it difficult for you to do what you need?"

"Our other clients don't require nearly as much stuff as she purchased. Honestly, I'm not even sure why she has half of this stuff there. I think Rose got so caught up in trying to look like she was successful, she forgot to actually do anything to secure success for herself. From the outside looking in, that business is doing great, but when you get into the paperwork, it's just a bunch of inventory, very low sales, and a team of people who are ready to walk out the door. Actually, I already reached out to a few of our guys and asked if they would be interested in this partnership, and they're looking forward to it," he reported. "That's what took me so long to get here today."

"You talked to your team before meeting me?" I raised a brow.

"Hey, you just had half your team walk out the door, right? What good would it do either of us if we sign a contract while my team is on the way out? I had to make sure we could do what you needed."

"Smart. Thank you."

"I did question why you would come to Rose instead of one of the other firms in the area. I mean, there are a few, not major ones. Honestly, you're probably at the top of the list in terms of size and capacity. Surely one of them would have been a better fit for partnership."

I shrugged. "They're all owned by men. I was only the second woman to open the round here, and I would have been the first had it not been for Rose. Actually, because of Rose, I had to work about ten times harder than I should have just to solidify my name in this space. She screwed over a lot of people, and, because we're both women, everyone assumed I would do the same thing. I made a lot of enemies because of Rose since she allegedly name-dropped me to so many people she screwed over. When I finally got into the room with them, they didn't trust me." I sighed. "So, my first thought was Rose. She's not that great at business, she'd be less of a threat to try to steal my contract from under me, and, well, she owes me."

"Look, I'm in if you are." Raymond stood, unbuttoned the sleeve of his shirt, and rolled it up, revealing the tattoos on his arms. They reminded me of my own, but where I had vines, he had what looked like smoke trails. "You said you haven't eaten. Maybe we can go to dinner together to celebrate."

"Dinner?"

"Yes, unless you were lying about that just to try to rush me out of here."

"I would never do that," I lied. "Actually, I—"

Just then, there was a knock on the door. For a moment, I thought I'd been saved from having to cover my ass, but instead, I turned to see the man now known as Bathwater standing outside the door. Great, now I go from trying to avoid dinner to explaining why a stalker is at my door.

"Are you going to let that guy in?" Raymond asked.

"One moment." I flashed a quick smile before heading to the door.

Please don't let this man cause a scene and cost me this deal!

I took a deep breath, channeling my most professional self, then unlocked the door. As soon as the damn thing opened, Deonta started the most pathetic display of begging I'd ever witnessed from a man.

"Please, Jericha, you won't answer my calls or anything." He clutched his hands together as if pleading for food. "Tell me what to do. I'll do anything you want. You know I will."

"This is new," I muttered.

I'd never had a man actually come to my job before, and if it hadn't been for his ass following me, he wouldn't have even known where I worked. The one thing I made sure of was to never let a man know where I laid my head or made my money. Hell, most of them didn't even know my real name. I always went to them, and I always made sure to keep meetups at least ten miles from home. It was just my luck that when Deonta followed me, I was going to the office and not to my house.

"Stop this." I lowered my voice to talk to him. "I'm not interested in continuing anything with you. Accept the rejection and go away."

"I need you. How am I supposed to exist now?" He placed his hand on the door to stop me from closing it. "Do you know how much you've changed me? I can't do anything without thinking about you. I crave you, Jericha. What do you expect me to do now?"

"Therapy is a suggestion." I rolled my eyes. "I really don't have time for this right now, and all this begging doesn't make you look any more attractive. You get that, don't you?"

"Jericha…" I could see the panic in his eyes as he searched for something more to say, but there really wasn't anything he could possibly say to me to make me change my mind.

"Is there a problem?" Raymond's voice sounded in my ear at the same time I felt the heat of his body against my back.

"I—" Deonta looked up at Raymond, who was at least four inches taller than him. It was like he hadn't even realized I wasn't there alone, even though he had been well within view.

"No, there isn't," I answered for the befuddled man. "He was just about to leave. Weren't you, Deonta?"

"You're with someone else already?" Anger flashed across his expression. "It hasn't even been a few days since I last saw you, and you've already moved on. Did I mean so little to you?"

"That is none of your business." I refused to entertain whatever it was he was imagining. Deonta wasn't my damn man. I owed him no explanation.

"Look, buddy, this looks bad." Raymond moved around me, placing himself between Deonta and me. "You realize that, right?"

"I don't care. This is what I want." Deonta had the most pathetic expression on his face.

Even though I was ready to knock the man upside the head, Raymond kept his cool. He put his arm around Deonta's shoulder and casually moved him away from the door, giving me a quick, reassuring glance. "Now, I don't know you, but

I *know* you're better than this. You gotta be. What man comes to a woman's place of work and begs for her attention like this? Trust me, I know, Jericha has a way of getting under your skin. She makes you think about her when you don't want to. And then, she has that attitude that should make you hate her, but instead, you find yourself more intrigued. You want to solve the riddle that is this woman. Right?"

"That's exactly it," Deonta responded, as if relieved someone finally understood. "I can't get her out of my head no matter what I do. I try my best to move on, but I can't."

"Trust me, take a long vacation, drink plenty of water, and you'll flush that flu right out of your system." Raymond patted Deonta's shoulder and once again looked back at me, this time with a wink that made me want to slam the door in his face. "But you have to be strong here. Don't show her your weakness, especially if you want any other woman to ever be attracted to you again. That type of desperation sets in under the skin, and it stinks. Women smell that stink, and they go running in the other direction. You feel me?"

"Yeah, thanks, man." Deonta looked over at me once again. I could see the question in his mind. Could he convince me to give in? Apparently, he told himself the answer was no, because instead of asking me another time, he shook Raymond's hand. "Good luck with her. I hope she gives you a better chance than she did me."

"You know what? I have a feeling I'll need it. Thanks." Raymond shook Deonta's hand then sent him on his way. He watched closely until he got back into his tiny sedan and drove off.

This isn't good, I thought to myself as Raymond turned to me. The smile stretching across his face told me he would never let me live this moment down.

"What was that?" I asked as he made his way over to me, shit-eating grin still firmly in place. "I'm a flu he has to flush out of his system?"

"That was me diffusing the situation without it coming to blows." He clapped. "Tell me something, Jericha: am I going to have to do that often? Do you have a slew of men vying for your attention, just hoping you will choose them?"

"No. Usually, my stalkers don't come to my job." I lifted my chin. "This one slipped through the cracks."

"Stalkers as in plural, you have more than one?" He raised a brow. "So that's what you do in your free time? Gather up all the crazy men?"

"Well, they're not typically crazy when I meet them." I tapped my chin with my fingernail. "What can I say? I'm addicting. I drive them wild."

I stepped aside, allowing him to enter the office again. Just as he passed, his chest close to mine, he leaned in, looked me square in the eyes. "I'll be the judge of that."

5

Dinner with the pest

It took a week to get the contracts settled and then another week to train our teams. Between the new hires we settled on and the contracted men from Raymond's service, we had more than enough personnel to get the job done. The relief I felt was akin to seventeen orgasms! All that was left was the final in-person meeting with the studio, then we would be off to the races.

Natalie and Raymond attended the meeting at the studio with me. I needed Natalie because I knew she would pay close attention to all details, and it made sense for Raymond to be there, since he would effectively be my second-in-command for the initial contract. As a final amendment, we'd agreed that for all intents and purposes, Raymond would be an employee, since he was planning on phasing out his company at some point. It would just make things easier for me down the line not to have to dissolve the official partnership or contend with new owners.

"Jericha, it's so good to see you again!" Von greeted us just outside the conference room. "All those video calls are so impersonal."

"Von, great to see you as well." I shook her hand.

"And this must be Natalie. Your face matches your voice," Von said before turning to Raymond, who stood at my other side. "And Mr. Statton?"

"It's a pleasure to meet you." He greeted her friendly.

"Wonderful! Let's head inside. I know we're all eager to get things settled."

Inside the conference room was a long table. On one side sat five members of the studio team, three empty seats for us on the other. Von joined the side with the other studio members.

"Everyone, this is Jericha Brown, her assistant Natalie, and her partner, Raymond Statton," Von made the introductions.

The first man, an older gentleman, stood. He was shorter than me, and from my vantage point, I could see the bald patch forming at the top of his head.

"Hello, it's nice to meet you. I'm Mr. Watson." He held out his hand—not to me, but to Raymond! "Happy to be working with your firm."

"Actually," I placed my hand in his and shook it with a firm grasp, "I'm the owner. It's a pleasure to meet you."

"Oh, my apologies." He nervously glanced at our connected hands as if I was hurting him. "I shouldn't have assumed."

"That's quite alright." I smiled politely. "I understand there are few women in this space, but I'm happy to be working together and look forward to a blossoming partnership."

I let his hand go and looked at the others. One woman, who wore a blue suit, nodded approvingly. She clearly appreciated my skillful correction of Mr. Watson's behavior.

"Shall we get started?" I suggested. With masterful skill crafted through many years of proving men wrong, I ran the meeting. Every detail of our partnership was laid out, including scheduling, team changes, inventory needs, and even uniform requirements for team members. Raymond remained quiet, Natalie took detailed notes, and by the end of it, Mr. Watson had no questions.

The meeting ended later than I expected, so I sent Natalie home. There was more to do at the office, but there was no need for her to waste another night babysitting me. I parted ways with Raymond in the parking lot, and headed to the office. On the way, I stopped at a gas station and got myself a treat—those little pink donuts.

When I arrived at my office, Raymond was standing by the door. He leaned against the wall and waved at me.

"It's about time you got here," he teased as I approached the door.

"What are you doing here?" I tried not to sound as annoyed as I felt.

He looked at me like I had lost my mind. "Am I wrong, or did you say there was more work to do? I'm clocking in, boss!"

"Work for *me*." I frowned as I unlocked the door. "There's nothing for you to work on here."

"Wait, I'm supposed to be your second-in-command, right?" Raymond stood at attention. "I take my role seriously! So, here I am, reporting for duty!"

"Are you trying to take over my job?" I narrowed my eyes at him. Why the hell was he trying to be cute? "Is this a ploy to get me to let my guard down?"

"Seriously?" His shoulders slumped as he followed me inside. "This is because of what Mr. Watson did, isn't it? I'm being punished for another man's ignorance."

"Oh, you mean mistaking you for the owner of *my* business?" I stopped walking and turned to him. "No, couldn't possibly be because of that. Didn't bother me at all!"

"That was real convincing." He chuckled and rubbed his beard. "Well, you know I'm not here to take over, so relax. One foolish man isn't changing my mind."

"I'm perfectly relaxed." I held up the donuts. "I have these! The cure to all my problems in cute packaging!"

"Did you have to trip a man to get them?" He pointed at the donuts. "I hope they don't have to file an insurance claim like I did."

"You did not!"

"How else do you expect me to recover from the knee injury?"

"Well, now you're just being dramatic." I sighed. "Are you really going to hang around here?"

"Of course. Besides, you might need saving again."

"Saving?"

"You have stalkers, woman!" He waved his hand as if we were surrounded by the aforementioned offenders.

"Shut up." I rolled my eyes and marched into my office.

Yeah, I tried to work. Computer on, files open, contracts ready for mark-up. For about thirty minutes, I pretended to be productive while Raymond sat across from me, feet on the edge of my desk, fingers tapping on his phone.

"Is this what you call being helpful?" I reached across the desk and knocked his feet down.

"This is what I call waiting for directives." He smiled.

"I already told you, I have nothing for you to do here."

"Right, and it doesn't look like you're getting much done either." He pointed at the paper in front of me. "You've been looking at the same page for at least ten minutes now."

"It's hard to work when someone's sitting across from you playing on their phone while propping their dirty shoes on your desk. Do you know how many germs are on those things?" I pointed to his shoes.

He inhaled deeply, a scrutinizing expression on his face, brows pushed in tightly, lips twisted. "What I'm hearing is that you need to get away from the office."

"I'm not sure how the hell you took that from what I just said." I folded my hands in front of me. "What I need is to be left alone so I can focus."

"You're hungry. Let's go."

"Are you just ignoring the words coming out of my mouth? It's like I'm talking to myself. What the hell do you mean, let's go?"

"We need dinner. I know I do." He stood and stretched. "Those little finger fruit things they gave us at the meeting weren't nearly enough to satisfy me. I'm a big, strong guy. I need food."

"You're a big, strong pain in my ass," I fussed as I rubbed the tension forming at my temples.

"You know, ever since we finalized that contract, you don't sweet talk me anymore."

"Sweet talk?" I cackled. "You do need to eat, because clearly, you lose your mind when you're hungry. I've never done that!"

"Are you saying those little donuts were enough for you?" Raymond shifted the focus. "I need dinner. You do too. Let's go."

"You're not going to drop this, are you?"

"No, I'm not." He stood and moved to the door to open it for me. "Grab your bag, woman. Let's hit it!"

I sighed, looked at my computer monitor, which had already gone to sleep from lack of usage, and gave up on getting anything done. Instead of continuing to fight him on the topic, I grabbed my bag, locked the computer, and headed for the door.

"You better have something good in mind," I fussed. "Don't you dare ask me to make a plan when this was your idea."

"Yes, ma'am!" He saluted me as I passed him.

When we made it outside, Raymond marched to his car as I locked up. He held open the passenger side door and waited for me. I promptly walked right by him and headed to my car.

"Seriously?"

"I am more than capable of driving my own car." I frowned. "Lead the way, and try not to drive so recklessly. I'd like to make it home in one piece tonight."

I drove closely behind him as he led me fifteen minutes away from the office. He must have taken my comment about his driving to heart, because the man drove five miles under the speed limit the entire way. If I had known where he was going, I would have left him in the dust.

"You're insufferable," I said as he opened my door for me. I stepped out of the car, shaking my head at him. "Did you forget where your gas pedal was? Why were you moving like a damn snail?"

"I only did what you asked." He held back his laughter. "Safe driving only, remember?"

"You're petty." I wagged my finger in his face as he shut the door. "I see now. You're just here to drive me crazy."

"Correction, I'm here to drive you crazy and have dinner. I hope you like Italian!" Raymond sidestepped me and headed into the restaurant.

The food was great; the service was fast, and an hour later, I sat in front of an empty plate. The creamy Tuscan salmon had melted in my mouth. It was so good, I was considering ordering a second serving to go.

While we were out, I tried to keep our conversation focused on business, but over the past weeks, Raymond had been trying to learn as much as he could about me, as if Rose hadn't provided enough information in that creepy ass folder of hers.

"What are you doing?" I asked after he'd asked me about my childhood.

"Attempting conversation." He sipped his water. "Why are you so resistant to that?"

"You're being nosy. We work together. Why would you need to know about my childhood?"

"I don't *need* to know anything, Jericha," he corrected my wording. "I *want* to know. We're going to spend a lot of time together in the foreseeable future. Should we spend none of that time learning more about each other? Ask me anything. I'm an open book."

I waved off his suggestion. "No, thank you."

"This is a control thing for you, isn't it?" His brow rose as he examined my expression.

"I'm not sure what you're talking about," I said.

"From the moment we met, you've been trying to take control of the situation." He spoke as if he was solving a case.

"How could you say that?" I crossed my arms over my chest. "I was nothing but polite when I proposed we work together."

"You know that's not what I'm talking about." He nodded. "The gas station. You nearly bit my head off for not letting you have your way. And then you tripped me!"

"You falling had nothing to do with me. Clearly, you're a klutz."

"I'm sure they still have the security footage." He pointed at the cars parked outside. "We can go ask them to run it back."

"What's your point, Mr. Statton?" I asked.

"Mr. Statton?" he laughed. "You're not going to make any of this easy for me."

"Things will be easy *if* you remember boundaries." I raised a brow as the server returned to set the check on the table between us. *Right* in the center. I looked at it and then at Raymond, who chuckled.

"So this is the one thing you don't want control over?" He grabbed the check and then pulled his wallet from his pocket. "Interesting."

"You invited me here," I reminded him. "Why should I pay? If not for you, I would be in my office working."

"Something you should be thanking me for. You work too much," he fussed. "Natalie is a competent assistant, and yet you send her home while you do menial paperwork."

"I want to make sure it's done right."

"Are you saying you don't trust her to do it?"

"Are those the words that came out of my mouth?" I removed the napkin from my lap. "I trust her. I—"

"You like to be in control." He finished my sentence for me. *Incorrectly*, might I add.

"Is this about earlier today?" I asked. "Look, I'm not going to just stand aside and let someone take ownership of my stuff."

"And there it is!" He handed the check back to the server, who'd at some point returned.

"What? Are you reconsidering working with me now?" I lowered my voice.

"No, not at all." Raymond leaned onto his elbows. "I'm not the kind of man who backs down from a challenge."

"A challenge?"

"Yes." He smirked. "You need to release some steam. You look tense."

"Please don't tell me you're trying to push up on me now." I leaned away from him. "I only had water, remember? There will be no shenanigans to blame on liquor later."

"Actually, I figured we could do some sparring." He raised a brow. "But interesting that your mind went to sex when I said the word 'release'."

"Shut up." I drank the last of my water.

"I will if you join me in the gym."

6

Time for sparring

After some debate that led to me really wanting to punch this man in the face, we headed back to the office. This time, I didn't drive behind him, so when he tried to go the slowest speed possible, I zoomed by him, and out of my peripherals, I saw him laugh at me.

I beat him back to the office, parked, and waited for him by the door. As he pulled into the parking lot, he slowed down even more before I crossed my arms and huffed. I watched him ease into the parking spot, put his car in park, and then sit there pretending as if he was looking for something. When he finally got out of the car, I just rolled my eyes. He then went to his trunk and pulled out a duffel bag, which I assumed had his training gear in it.

"See? We could have just driven together," he said as he casually strolled over to me.

"Don't tell me you honestly think I would have been able to ride with you." I pointed at his car.

"But I drove so safely." He pretended to pout. "Isn't that what you wanted from me? Now I see why Deonta was so upset. I don't know how to please you, woman. Jericha, I'll do anything to please you!"

"Ugh, I'm going home." I moved toward my car. "Spar on your own."

"Don't be that way." He grabbed my arm and stopped me from storming away. "All right, all right! I'll stop. I'm just joking. Can we get this done now? I drank some pre-workout on the way here. I'm ready to go!"

"Apologize," I demanded.

"Seriously?"

"Yes," I pursed my lips, imagining the pre-workout making him itch without exercise because that's what it did to me. "Apologize for teasing me and then we can go inside."

He hesitated, considering if he really wanted to give in to me. Then, after the frustration sparked by my stubbornness kicked in, he apologized.

"Ms. Brown, I apologize for teasing you about your crazy stalker." He fluttered his eyelashes, making me notice those green eyes. "Can you please find it in your heart to forgive me?"

"Yeah." I waved him off. "Quit your pathetic begging and come on."

Raymond headed straight upstairs to get started in the gym while I went into my office to change. I always kept a few spare outfits for working out in the closet. I took my time getting ready. He had made me wait for his slow ass driving; he could wait while I made the hard choice between my purple fit or my turquoise. And what shoes would I wear? I had a few options—of course I had to give it ample thought. When I made my way up to the gym dressed in the purple workout set—a pair of shorts, and a form-fitting tank top—he was already doing some stretches and warming up, so I joined him.

"What's your style?" I asked him as I stretched my calves. They had been giving me some issues, and I wanted to make sure I didn't catch a cramp while we worked.

"My style?" He raised a brow.

"Hey, you asked me to come spar. What kind of sparring are we doing? There are different styles, you know—wrestling, taekwondo, karate..." I mimicked each as I listed them off.

"How about some basic grappling? Does that work for you?" he asked. "We can see where it goes from there."

"If you want to keep it simple, that works for me."

"Right..." He trailed off, raising a brow. "You're going to try to hurt me, aren't you?"

"I would *never* do that." I finished stretching then got into my starting position. "Come on, make your move."

"I think you should go first. I don't want to hurt you." He winked. "This is supposed to be friendly, so show me what you got. I'll adjust to it."

"Just like a man." I rolled my eyes. "You think I can't take you? I run this business, remember? I know what I'm doing, so, come on."

He came for me, and I proved my point quickly. As he reached for my shoulders, I dropped down, initiating a double leg takedown that landed him flat on his back. He hit the mat hard, and I smiled as I heard the air escape from his lungs.

"Oh, shit." He coughed as I got up, giving him room to breathe. "You're stronger than you look."

"Not the first time I've heard that." I stepped back, readjusting the tie around my hair. "Don't go easy on me, big boy." As soon as he made it to his feet, I punched him in the jaw.

"You want a fight, huh?" he laughed. "What happened to friendly sparring?"

"Hey, you said I needed a release." I shrugged. "That's how I get it."

"As long as you promise not to hold it against me if you get hurt." He grinned. "I mean, I wouldn't want you being upset with me."

"I can handle myself. Let's go!" I got into a fighting stance.

Raymond didn't hold back that time. He rushed me, lifting me from my feet and slamming me to the ground in one, swift move. *Payback*.

"Damn!" I shifted my hips, put my foot into his chest, and kicked him away from me.

"You said not to go easy." He shrugged.

"And I meant it!" I did a kick flip up from the ground, took two rushing steps, and kneed him in the gut. I followed up with an elbow to the spine.

From there, it was a full-on fight. We both launched our attacks, meeting most with skillful counters, but now and then, a hit would land. The longer we went, the less the big guy held back. Before I knew it, he was tossing me around the gym like I was a grown man, just the way I liked it.

Eventually, he got the advantage over me. I was strong, but I still had to hold back. Sure, I could have used my ability to give me an advantage, but that wouldn't have been fair. So, I tucked those magical abilities into my back pocket when he went for a move that once again landed me on my back.

Instead of quickly shifting into the next move, Raymond lingered. His breathing was quick, sweat dripping from his brow. He looked down at me, and *boom*. There it was: that tension everyone expected when two grown adults of the opposite sex claimed they're just friends. When my eyes met his, green and consuming, I felt my body respond.

Oh, hell no! The thought flashed through my head just as that heated look reached his eyes.

I shifted my weight; the muscles in my legs burned, but I was determined to get out of the compromising position. The shock worked in my favor as I flipped him, grabbing his arm and locking in a tight armbar. While I had caught him off guard, it wasn't enough to stop his instinctual response. I hadn't had the submission hold long before he displayed strength I hadn't seen in a man before. With me still locked on his arm, he lifted me in the air and crossed the room. His locs slapped me in the face, adding salt to the wound as he slammed me back down onto a stack of mats.

Cushioned blow or not, that shit still hurt. Once again, I tried to shift my weight to escape what was basically a pin, but he overpowered me.

Girl, get the hell out of this!

My mind screamed at me to flee while that lower brain was saying, *no, don't stop him*! I listened to the mind led by logic. This was a man I worked with! I couldn't be having moments edging on sexual tension. I ignored my increased heart rate, told myself it was because of the workout and not my raging hormones. It took some doing, but I slipped from his hold and pushed him across the room. Once again, I repeated an earlier move.

The moment he was away from me, I leaped to my feet, ran to the opposite side of the room, then turned and headed back toward him with a jump, knee aimed for the face. Raymond caught me midair and slammed me down again. This time, he had me on the floor, all his weight pushing me down as he grinned.

"You want another one?" he asked through heavy breaths. "I can keep slamming you all night. Just say the word."

That time, I tapped into my power, just enough to give me the strength to lift him from my chest. I rotated beneath him so our bodies were crossed then lifted my leg, slamming it into the side of his head. Raymond rolled away, popped back up, and tackled me. We rolled around, shifting between different holds, slams, and sweeps.

In the last move, I ended up on top of him, my legs straddling him. I used the strength of my thighs to lock him in place beneath me. I held his shoulders down and grinned.

"Gotcha!" The sound of joy that escaped me surprised both of us.

"Yeah, you did." He chuckled, and then I felt his hand move. He could have knocked me off, but he didn't. He placed his palm flat on my back as his eyes glanced down at my position on top of him. "You want to keep going?"

And there was the instant response from my lower half. My walls tightened, Kegel style, and I squeezed my eyes shut as I hopped off him.

"No, I think I'm done!" I raced out of the gym, leaving him on the floor. I didn't shower or even lock up before I left. He knew the protocol. I headed straight to my car and raced home before I did something I would regret.

I made the drive from my office to the house with the windows wide open. The cool air was supposed to help me calm down, and at first, it did. That was, until the chill reached my nipples. After that, every bump in the road sparked a jolt in my bra. I squirmed in my seat, and tried my best not to break any laws.

Make it home. All I had to do was make it home, and then I could fix this. The problem was the scent. A mixture of his cologne and his sweat was all over me. The smell filled my car even with the windows open. It was like a cloud hanging around me. I touched the top of the jar that hung from my rearview mirror. It was full of scented oil that coated my fingertips, and I rubbed it beneath my nose to try to mask the smell.

As soon as I pulled into my garage, I hopped from the car and started stripping my clothes away. Before I hit the bathroom, I was fully naked. Fuck waiting for the water to reach the prime temperature. I turned it on and stepped right into the stream. The shock of the water worked, but again, it didn't last. I scrubbed my body clean, trying to avoid my nipples, stopping myself from lingering between my legs.

"I cannot do this!" I fussed at myself. "No! I refuse to masturbate while thinking about that man. I will not give him that power over me."

Maybe it was a silly superstition, but I had a rule. I never pleasured myself while focusing on one man. To me, it felt like casting a spell I wanted no part of. Sexual energy was powerful, and to think of a man, to send that kind of energy to him for him to claim over me, was something I would never do! But there was no way I could orgasm that night without thinking of Raymond.

Out of the shower, bonnet snatched from the warmer, I headed to bed. I could just sleep it off. Close my eyes and wake up to a new day not full of sexual tension. All I had to do was avoid direct contact with Raymond for a few days, and everything would be fine.

I laid on my bed and forced my eyes shut.

And just as my mind quieted, the phone buzzed. I looked over to see the message on the phone I'd tossed on the floor.

Don't look at it! You know it's him!

Did I listen to myself? Of course not. I picked the phone up, and yep, it was him.

Raymond: I locked up the place. Next time, I won't hold back.

Without responding, I put the phone on the charger and climbed back into bed. Thanks to my foolish decision to check the message, Raymond was fresh in my mind. I'd washed his scent from my flesh but could somehow still smell him when my eyes closed.

I can keep slamming you all night. His words echoed in my mind. I grabbed my pillow and covered my face. *You want to keep going?* There his voice was again, teasing me with innuendo.

"That's not what he meant!" I fussed aloud.

Yes. I wanted more, so much more, but I couldn't let him know that. I couldn't let him know how my body responded to him or how I went from wanting to punch his face to wanting to sit on it.

And running out of there like a fool was a great way to keep my cover!

"Breathe, girl!" I rubbed my hand over my chest, but even that soothing action just made matters worse. I imagined it was his hand on me, and he wasn't trying to calm me down. Raymond wanted to excite me.

"Dammit!" I ripped the covers away, exposing my naked flesh to the cool air. "This is exactly what he meant to do! Get me all riled up! Why did I let this happen?"

My heart rate was already quickening as my flesh won the war against my mind. My hand slid from my chest, inching down my skin with determination. I shuttered as my own hand felt foreign to me, moving across my stomach and pausing just above my pussy. Did I really want to do this right now? What would it mean if I did?

You like to be in control, don't you?

The echoes of Raymond's voice were there, challenging me to continue. Though I should have rolled over and denied this mental nudge, I didn't. Moments later, my fingers gently rolled across my clit, and the shiver stretched over my body with that first contact. I bit my lip as I added a little more pressure to my touch.

Don't think of him.

I tried my best not to. I didn't want to have Raymond on my mind as I worked my body the way only I could, but nothing worked.

With each stroke of my fingers, with each catch of my breath, the vision of him became clearer—smooth brown skin, thick beard, green eyes, long locs with evidence of gray spiraling through the length. I saw his full lips, his strong shoulders, those arms sleeved with smokey ink. The image of him in my mind urged me to increase the pressure on my clit.

He was there. I could feel the weight of his body on top of me, the warmth of his breath against my neck, even drips of his sweat hitting my flesh as he pinned me to the mat. My nose flooded with the scent of him. It was consuming and overwhelming, but the image in my mind, the experience of him, encouraged me to keep going.

My fingers rolled across my clit, but that wasn't enough. I needed more, and so I reached lower, spreading my lips and slipping two fingers into my pussy. Needing more leverage, I sat up, bracing my back against the headboard with my legs stretched wide while I worked myself, but even that wasn't enough. So, I reached into the drawer, pulling out my toy.

Thank God, I had already charged it up. I hit the power, and it came to life, buzzing and rotating.

Too bad this thing doesn't come attached to a man.

I slipped it inside me, and as it moved, pulsating, rotating, coaxing me to orgasm, I gripped the headboard with my free hand to steady myself.

You want to keep going?

His question kept rolling through my mind. I wanted more, so much more. But I wouldn't allow him to give it to me. Still, I answered that question in my mind.

"Yes! Yes!" I called out as I let the tension build between my legs. I held on, wanting it to last just a little longer.

And then, against everything I knew, against my better judgment, I called out his name as I came.

"Oh yes, Raymond!"

My body trembled as the orgasm erupted between my legs. I felt my juices spray across the mattress between my legs, and then, as the shivers subsided, I heard it.

Loud and clear. Deep and demanding.

"Good girl."

I freaked out, reaching for the lamp on my nightstand.

"What the hell?" I looked around, as if expecting to find someone there, but of course, I was alone. I pulled the covers over my body and popped up on my knees.

"Damnit!"

7

Night Shift

For the next week, I avoided Raymond at all costs. When Natalie tried to schedule meetings, I created excuses so bad, even she raised a questioning brow.

"How many dental appointments are you going to have this week?" she asked after I recycled the excuse. "And why are you going after the office closes?"

"Hey, I get special treatment, and I have a serious toothache."

"Right." She gave me a side eye. "So what do you want me to tell Raymond? He seems to really want this meeting. I'm not sure why he hasn't just called you like he usually does."

Maybe because I blocked him, so all his calls go straight to voicemail.

I shrugged. "No idea!"

"Oh, you're going to need to do a fill-in at the site," she said. "Luke is sick and needs the night off."

"When?" I frowned. I had planned on doing the same thing I had each night that week: run home and hide.

"Tonight, so you might want to cancel that dental appointment." She laughed as she turned and walked out of my office. "I don't know why you're avoiding that man, but you must have a great reason!"

"Whatever!" I called after her.

Once left alone, I quickly wrapped up the rest of my tasks. The studio was a good forty-minute drive from the office, even without traffic. I wanted to get there in enough time to make sure I could relieve Sandra, the guard on duty, before Luke.

"This is good," I said after parking. I walked across the lot and headed to the post. "I won't have to worry about seeing him here."

"Seeing who?" Raymond's head popped out from around the corner ahead of me.

"Holy shit!" I skidded to a halt.

"Hey, you're supposed to be here on guard duty. Can't let someone sneak up on you like that."

"What are you doing here?" I asked.

"I got a call Luke was sick, so I figured I would fill in." He grinned.

"I'm here to do that, so you can go home."

"Now, that doesn't make sense." He ran his hand over his beard. "I'm the second-in-command. Shouldn't *you* go home?"

I shook my head. "You're the second-in-command, so you should do as you're told."

"Ah, got me there," he sighed. "Still, I think I'll stick around."

"Why?"

"You've been avoiding me. There are things I want to talk about." An evil grin spread across his face. "You're insisting on being here, so you have plenty of time."

"Fine, I'll leave."

"Oh, darn!" he shouted. "I'm not sure I remember the protocols here. I would hate to mess something up!"

"You wouldn't dare mess anything up." I turned on him. "That would look bad on both of us."

"Correction: that would look bad on you. Remember, this is a temporary thing for me. I'm not the one who needs a long-lasting reputation of upstanding service."

I wanted to stomp my foot but decided cursing was better than looking like a child. "Son-of-a-bitch!"

"Lead the way, oh leader." He stepped aside, waving me forward.

"I cannot believe you're pretending as if you don't know how to do this job on your own," I complained as Raymond followed me through the lot. Soon, we would reach the post where Sandra waited, so I didn't want to get too much into any conversation she might overhear. No matter what, we had to look professional. I would not let my discomfort or annoyance with this man ruin my business.

"I thought you would appreciate my desire to learn everything I can." He slowed his pace, but I kept going, forcing him to keep up. "What if I have to step in when you can't?"

"Isn't that why you came here?" I shot him a nasty glare. "You said you intended on doing the job, which meant you knew what you were doing, because why would you come here if you didn't?"

"Darn it, you caught me in a lie." He shrugged in that playful way that made me want to pop him upside the head.

"So you admit to lying to me." I pointed at him then dropped my finger when I heard my name.

"Miss Brown, it's good to see you. Thank you so much for coming to relieve me," Sandra called out as she stepped outside of the guard post. I kept my thoughts about Raymond to myself as I greeted her.

"Of course, you know how I am. If you guys need me, I'm here." I smiled at her.

"I've completed my rounds and everything is good to go," she reported. "They're just really getting started on the new production, so there is a little more foot traffic than over the last couple weeks."

"Thank you for the update."

Sandra grabbed her things and headed out. As soon as she was out of earshot, Raymond started up again. Apparently, I wasn't the only one concerned about keeping up professional appearances.

"Now that we're alone, will you please tell me why you've been avoiding me?" he asked.

"This again?" I huffed. "Was there something in our contract that said I had to answer every time you called? I swear that's something my lawyers would have talked to me about."

He paused, a tight frown on his face. "Did I do something wrong?"

"If this is you teasing me again, I'm going to hurt you," I threatened.

"This is me genuinely asking what I did to make you avoid me for a week." All the joking tone had left his voice. "Did I hurt you when we were sparring? Are you embarrassed?"

"No, you didn't hurt me." I ignored the second question, because yes, I was embarrassed, but no, I was not about to tell him that.

"So, what is it? Because I thought we were finally building a good relationship. I know that's not important to you, Jericha, but it is to me." He sat in the empty chair next to me inside the guard post. "We don't have to be the best of friends, but I would think if I was in business with someone and I was calling them, they would at least give the courtesy of answering me."

"You're right. It was unprofessional of me, and I should have responded to you," I relented. "You had something related to business you wanted to talk about, and it deserved attention."

The smug look of a man rarely told he was right spread across his face. "That's all I'm saying."

"So, what is it?" I asked.

"What's what?" His expression turned from pride to confusion.

"The important business thing you wanted to talk to me about so badly," I reminded him. "What is it?"

"I—um..." The man looked like he was actually panicking. "The mats in the gym seem a bit firm. I think we should probably think about swapping those out."

I scoffed. "Do you expect me to believe that's what you really wanted to talk to me about?"

"I expect you to have some compassion for my...short term memory loss and drop it." He leaned to look out the window, as if he spotted something more interesting than our conversation. "I'll give you a pass about ignoring me, and you give me a pass for letting things slip my mind."

"Raymond. This is a professional relationship, nothing more." I turned a serious eye to him. "Do you often talk to your other partners a lot?"

"Only the ones I want to talk to."

"So, you want to talk to me?" I leaned back in my seat and raised a brow. "That's what this is about? Were you lonely?"

I expected him to come back with something snarky, an attempt to put me in my place, but the damn man answered with honesty.

"Yes, Jericha. I wanted to talk to you." There it was, that challenging expression I hated so much. He was testing me. "Is that so bad? I realized I enjoy your company. I enjoyed talking shop and even sparring. That was one of the best sessions I've had in a very long while. Figured we could do it again."

His honesty caught me off guard, so much so that I struggled to respond. He enjoyed being with me? He wanted to talk to me? What was I supposed to do with that information? Sure, he presented it like he was talking about a typical friendship, but there was something in his tone and the way he looked at me when he spoke that made me feel like there was far more to the story than he was telling me.

"Well, don't." I shifted my attention away from the man who stared at me. "Focus on the contract. Getting the job done is all that matters. You shouldn't want to talk to or spend any extra time with me. That's inappropriate."

"Says who?" Raymond locked his eyes on me. "You're the boss, aren't you? You make the rules."

"Yes, and a strict rule of mine is to not get too close with my staff. It creates conflicts of interest."

"Your staff. Right." He paused. "I think I qualify as more than staff. As a partner in your business, however temporary, shouldn't I at least be allowed to get to know you?"

"Why would you want to do that?" I laughed. "I don't understand why this matters so much to you."

"To be honest, it didn't before." He leaned closer to me. "But seeing how resistant you are to the idea makes me a lot more intrigued. I need to know why you're so against it. Is there something about me that repulses you, or are you typically this abrasive?"

"Oh, I see." It finally clicked. Raymond's ego was bruised. "This isn't about me at all, is it? Let me guess: you're used to women falling over you?"

"Not just women." He winked. "I'm a people person. People like me."

"Men too?" I raised a brow. It wasn't something I expected to hear, but Raymond was an attractive man. I could see people of all types wanting to get their hands on him.

"What are you asking me, Jericha? Is that a professional question or a personal one?" He frowned. "Doesn't that go against your policy?"

"It's not a question at all." I kicked the thought out of my mind. "Forget I said anything."

He moved closer to me and whispered, "Just know, I'm the one doing the bending."

"I—" My breath caught in my throat. Had he really just insinuated what I thought he had? And why the hell was it a turn on? I mean, my pulse quickened, and I felt that familiar tightening between my thighs.

"Is that a problem?" He leaned back and propped his feet up on the table beside me, laughing when I knocked them down.

"Why would it be? I'm not asking to be bent." I cleared my throat because I knew that sounded worse than I intended. "Look, it's none of my concern what you do or who you do it with. This conversation has left the realm of professionalism, so I think it's best I excuse myself. Besides, I need to make the rounds."

"Ah, I've made her nervous. Never thought I would see the day when that happened."

"Whatever. Keep your feet on the floor, please." I pointed at the black sneakers he wore. "How many times do I have to tell you about the germs those things carry? I don't need that near my face or hands."

The illness that took Luke down had spread throughout the team. The next day, it was Sandra, and then Greg after that. Each night, there was someone we had to fill in for, which unfortunately meant I couldn't escape Raymond. Even when I suggested he cover on his own, he would pretend he didn't know what to do and play on my desire to make sure everything ran smoothly. And so, he and I would end up covering the night shift together.

"Looks like this is the last night we'll share," Raymond said after ending a call with his assistant. "Everyone's all healed up, and the new recruits are ready to step up to the plate as well."

"That's good. Everyone passed the training?" I looked up from the clipboard in my hand.

"With flying colors." The grin stretched across his face. "Sandra and Greg will move into their managing roles as of tomorrow."

"What a relief." I sighed. "Don't get me wrong, I love what I do, but this is the more boring side of things."

"You mean looking after property isn't fun?" he teased.

"I got into this business because I wanted to protect people, but the bigger contracts are more about assets. I understand that. Taking a large contract like this means I can continue offering affordable services to individuals."

"That's a great way to think about it," Raymond said. "I never asked why you chose to be in security."

"I learned at an early age I needed to know how to protect myself, and not too long after that, I realized I wanted to protect others." My throat dried as I talked, bringing up a memory I wanted more than anything to forget. "There are some actual monsters out there and too many people who are vulnerable to those beings."

"Something happened, didn't it?" Raymond asserted. "You don't have to tell me what it is, but I can see it in your eyes. Some life-changing event pushed you to do this."

"Well, yeah. That's how everything works. There's always a cause."

As I looked at him, I realized Raymond had slowly learned more about me. During the nights we spent together, I'd softened to him, each time revealing more about myself. I talked about my time in college, the decision to buy a fixer upper for my first home, and even my friendships. I was a lot like Natalie. Long-distance besties was the name of the game. Just as I was about to tell him to mind his damn business, the alert sounded on the panel.

In front of me was a full dashboard full of cameras that gave a view of nearly every angle of the studio's lots. I pressed the key on the dash that lit up, and the view on the screens shifted. The image shown was at the back of the east lot, an area that had had no activity yet. I used the controls to zoom in and scan the area, but there was nothing of apparent concern.

"What is it?" Raymond moved to peer over my shoulder. "Anything there?"

"I'm not sure. Something triggered an alert, obviously." I peered at the camera, shifting the view again. "But I don't see anything."

"Maybe it was an animal," Raymond offered. "Not unlike those things to trigger security systems."

"Maybe, but I think we should check it out, just to be sure." I stood. "Our systems are sophisticated enough to be able to distinguish between a threat and a stray. I'm going to go check it out just to be on the safe side."

"Do you really think that's necessary?" He stood as well.

"What? Are you afraid?" I laughed. "After the way you tossed me around, I wouldn't have taken you for a scaredy cat!"

"Oh, don't do that. Don't try to play on my male sensibilities." He sighed. "Fine, let's go."

"You can always stay here," I teased as he followed me to the golf cart used for transport around the lot. "I won't tell anyone about your fears."

"Always in control," he muttered.

"You think you'd understand that by now." I winked, and as soon as he sat down, I hit the gas.

We drove through the darkness to the area at the back of the studio. It was late, almost midnight, which would be when the next shift change would happen. I wanted to get there, check out things, and make it back in time to hand things off to Piper, a spunky guard with an amazing MMA background. She worked with Lucky, a guard who stood just over six feet and was built like an ox. At least if there was a threat, the two of them would be fine to guard things until the next shift.

We had three more weeks until we were supposed to have four times the staff on hand. Filming would begin, and we would need more staff onset. The last thing we needed was an issue before we even got to that point.

As soon as we parked, Raymond hopped from the cart, maybe to prove he wasn't afraid. He did a quick jog around the area, flashing his light into the shadows.

"See, I was right." He returned, putting the flashlight back in his pocket. "There's nothing here. Must have been an animal, and they're already on their way to be a menace somewhere else."

"I guess you were—" I started, but I stopped when I heard a weird sound like rushing air, though there was no wind blowing. "What was that?"

"What?" he looked around. "Did you see something?"

"I thought I heard—" I looked over his shoulder and paused. "We're not alone."

At first, there was nothing in the darkness, but when my eyes adjusted, I could just make out four figures. They stood, lined up, cloaked by the shadows. I holstered the flashlight in my hand; I could already tell by their stances that they weren't there for a friendly visit. Maybe they were there to rob the place, or maybe they thought there was something of value here. It didn't matter.

I stepped to the side so they could see a clear view of me and waited as Raymond positioned himself to see who I was talking to.

Though I kept my gaze locked on the offenders, I struggled to see them. Their bodies looked like they were phasing in and out. I blinked to clear my vision. Maybe I was tired. It had been a lot of late nights staying up far later than I was used to.

After several more forced blinks, the figures settled into men, all of them tall, bulky, the kind who landed punches that hurt like hell. Didn't matter; if it came to that, I could take them.

"Hey!" I called out. "You can't be back here. I'm only going to give you one warning. Turn around and leave!"

They didn't respond to me at all.

"Did you hear me?" I shouted. "Leave, or I'll be forced to call the police."

Maybe the threat of the law would convince them to leave, but something in my gut told me it wouldn't. Whatever they came for, they wouldn't leave without a fight.

"I don't think they care about the police being called." Raymond's voice sounded far more serious than I'd ever heard it before.

Without looking at him, I could tell we were on the same page. At least there was no question about whether we could hold our own. This would be a fight.

"Oh darn, I left the phone back in the booth." I sucked my teeth. "Guess we won't be calling the cops after all."

They must have taken that as confirmation of a fight, because no sooner had the words left my mouth, the first guy lunged forward. He moved silently, no battle cry, no verbal exclamation of his efforts. I stilled myself, ready for a fight, but before I could even move, Raymond was there.

Guess I wouldn't be able to call him a chicken after all.

Raymond took it straight to the man. I tried to see the intruder's face, but he wore a hood that hung low across the bridge of his nose. Raymond seemed sure as he charged forward, but then, a half step later, he hesitated. That hesitation cost him, because the man landed a hard fist across Raymond's face. Before I could jump into action to help, Raymond recovered. He threw two blows back at the man, who stumbled back, holding his jaw.

Hell yeah! I kept my cheers to myself; I didn't want to distract him. Also, the fight was only beginning. I couldn't celebrate yet, especially because the other three took that as a challenge to move forward.

When they moved, they split up just as I expected. The first two headed for him, joining their pal in a collective beat down. The last one made a path for me. This would be their biggest mistake. Underestimate the woman in the room and get your ass handed to you.

I couldn't be worried about Raymond. I had to trust he could handle his own at least long enough for me to deal with the guy who charged me. The plan? Quickly disarm him and go to help Raymond with the others.

I braced myself, locking in on the guy who came at me. Even as he neared, I was struggling to see him. It didn't matter; my instincts would work in my favor. When he got close enough to reach me, he sent a blow to my head. I ducked under it and hit him with an uppercut square in the jaw. The impact of my fist against his face knocked his hood back just enough so I could see him.

My heart lurched. This wasn't a normal guy. If he wasn't, that meant none of them were. His skin looked like an illusion struggling to keep its hold. My mind quickly went to those magical face masks witches used. Were they from a coven? The questions in my mind didn't interfere with my physical response.

I followed the uppercut with two sharp jabs to the gut. When he doubled over, I slammed my knee into the side of his skull, knocking him out completely. The moment he slumped to the ground, I wrapped the zip ties I kept in my pocket, standard for our team, around his wrists then turned to join Raymond in his fight.

"Son of a bitch!" I yelled as I pulled the man from Raymond's back. I was used to slinging grown men, but that guy felt like he weighed a ton. Still, I flipped him onto his back and, as his head slammed against the ground, I stomped him in the gut.

I reached for the zip ties, prepared to secure him with his buddy, but when I looked up, the guy I'd already taken down was gone.

"What the hell?" I quickly scanned the area but saw no one. That was when I heard Raymond yell out, and when I shifted my weight to look at him, I lost the leverage I had on the guy beneath me.

That one moment was all he needed to take advantage of me. After seeing Raymond flat on his back, I turned to look back at the man I had on the ground and met his fist with my face. He punched me square in the jaw, and when I fell back, he hopped up and ran away. I quickly jumped back to my feet, but he was already gone.

"How the hell are these guys so damn fast?" I rubbed my jaw, looking back at Raymond, who was alone on the ground.

At least I wasn't the only one who took a hit. I walked over to him and stuck my hand out, an offer to help him up from the ground.

"Where did they go?" I asked as he dusted himself off.

"I don't know, but we should get a few more people out here tomorrow night."

"What did they even want? They took nothing, and the lots back here have nothing of value anyway."

"They don't know that." He sighed. "Might have been trying to scope the place out and see if there was anything worth snagging. Wasn't expecting us to be here."

"Well, whatever the case, we need to file a report." I checked my pockets and belt to make sure I had everything then pointed to the flashlight he dropped on the ground. "We'll have to tell the team to be on the lookout and let the studio heads know. They should be aware. Did you see any weapons on them?"

"No." He shook his head. "One had a rope but nothing meant to harm anyone."

"Good; then we're just dealing with common thieves."

"Yeah, sounds right to me," Raymond said, but something felt off in the way he spoke, like he suspected something he wasn't telling me.

"You think it's something else?" I asked as we walked back to the golf cart. "You don't sound too sure. What are you thinking?"

By the time we made it back to the post after doing a thorough check of the grounds, our relief was already there. We gave the report of what happened and told them to keep a close eye on the back lots.

"Starting tomorrow, we will double the night shift team. Luckily, we have a few more members coming off a contract and looking for the extra hours."

"Sounds good," Piper confirmed. "I'll make sure all the team knows. Do you want me to write up anything?"

"No, I'll handle it. It should be a first account. Thanks." I shook her hand and headed out. "Where's Lucky?"

"He's about ten minutes out. There was an accident that's backing things up." Piper nodded, giving me the sign to go home. She knew I would find any reason to stick around.

I'd sent Raymond home ahead of me, but when I made it to my car, he was standing by the door.

"What are you doing here?" I asked.

"Making sure you go home and get some rest." He nodded. "I know how you are."

"How sweet of you." I laughed. "I'll go home after I file the report. Right now, I'm going to the office."

"At this hour?" He shook his head. "You're unbelievable."

"I'm sorry, I didn't know I had a curfew. Wait." I pulled out my phone and opened the calendar app, showing it to him. "According to the date, I'm a grown woman who can do what I want."

"That's very clever of you, but you should rest," he repeated. "The report can wait for morning."

"That would be irresponsible." I insisted.

"You're the boss." He held up his hands. "Who's going to punish you for it?"

"True." The smile stretched across my face. It was good to be the boss.

"Jericha, it's been a long night." Again, Raymond's voice softened in a way that made me question everything about him. "Make yourself a voice note as you drive home and write the report in the morning."

"You're being really insistent about this." I sighed.

"I am." He nodded.

"Fine," I agreed.

He squinted at me, clearly not believing a word I said. "Are you going home?"

"Yes," I blatantly lied. Anything to end the conversation. I'd never let a man tell me how to live my life, and I wasn't about to start just because one with green eyes and locs to his ass wanted me to.

I took his advice about the voice note. As I drove from the studio after he pulled out ahead of me, I recounted the events aloud, recording them on my phone to make for easier transcription later. I took the less direct route to the office, hoping if Raymond had suspected me of lying, he wouldn't see me as I made the approach. I felt like I'd gotten away with it when I pulled up to the building. There were no cars in the lot.

Then, my headlights illuminated the entrance, and standing right next to the door was...Raymond.

"Of course," I muttered as I parked the car. I guess I wasn't that convincing a liar.

8

Accidents Happen

As I got out, I scanned the area, looking for his ride, and saw the convertible parked in the lot across the street. Well played.

"What are you doing here?" I sighed as I pulled the office key from my bag.

"Shouldn't I be asking you that?" Raymond shook his head. "You said you were going home. You lied to me, Jericha."

"God forbid a woman changes her mind." I threw my free hand up. "Besides, I told you—I want to write this up while it's fresh in my mind."

"Great. I'll help." He smiled. "I really should give you my point of view to make the report as thorough as possible."

"You could always just write your own report and we can file them together." I offered an alternative that would get him out of my hair.

Raymond stepped around me as soon as the door was unlocked and strolled inside, holding it open for me. "I like my idea better."

"Of course you do," I muttered as he waved me through.

Raymond followed me through the building, shadowing everything I did, including grabbing a snack and a bottle of water from the kitchen. He hummed as we moved through the space and yawned when I finally headed for my office.

"If you're that tired, you can always go home."

"And leave you to write our report by yourself? I could never do that." He placed his hand on his chest. "That's no way for a gentleman to behave."

Inside my office, I turned on dim lighting, hoping it would convince him to go home or at least go to sleep and stop bothering me. Just as I sat down at my desk, I heard Raymond groan. I looked up to see him wincing in pain as he pulled off the jacket he wore.

"What's wrong?" I asked. "Are you hurt?"

"Just a little pain, no big deal." He winced again. "It's expected after being knocked around in a fight."

I got up and walked around the desk. "Let me check it out. If you're hurt, I need to add that to my report."

"Anything for your report." He winked at me. "Have your way with me."

"Hush and sit down so I can see." As soon as he sat, I could see the faint stain of blood through the white shirt he wore. "You're bleeding."

"Am I?" He looked back at me as I pulled his collar to the side.

"Take that off. It doesn't look that bad, but I should clean the wound and bandage it. Better to avoid infection."

"You sure this isn't just a ploy to get me out of my clothes?"

"Fine, let it get infected. The contracts are signed." I rolled my eyes. "Drop dead if you want to. It won't hurt my business."

"Harsh!" he said and carefully stripped away the shirt while I pulled out the first aid kit from my desk.

"Something about this doesn't feel right," I spoke as I poured peroxide on a cotton ball.

Focus on the task, girl, not the muscles or the tattoos on his back and chest. He's hurt. You're better than a man. Focus!

"Is it that bad?" Raymond twisted his neck, trying to see what I was doing.

"Not the cut." I grabbed his chin and turned his head back forward. "Sit still. I'm talking about the men at the lot tonight. I can't understand the motive. Even if they were there to scope the place out, they didn't look prepared to take anything. No bags, no tools. Hell, I didn't even see a car. How did they get there?"

"You're really concerned about this, aren't you?" he chuckled.

"Shouldn't I be?" I paused. "Why aren't you? I mean, our reputations are on the line here. Even if you don't plan on staying in the business, your name is attached to this. It should matter to you."

"I think it's premature to jump to conclusions now. We have little evidence, and this is a first occurrence."

"Maybe you're right." I continued cleaning his cut, then placed the bandage over it after adding the antibiotic ointment. "There, you should be just fine."

"Thank you." He craned his neck as he tried to examine my work. "Look, I get it. This is a major contract, a pivotal moment for your business, but you've been here before. You've done this on a smaller scale. If you weren't ready to handle this, you wouldn't be in the position you are."

When he stopped speaking, he looked up into my eyes. And then, every damn moment that followed felt way too intense. The moonlight pouring through the windows glinted off his green eyes as he looked at me, a strange intensity in their depths. For a moment, I forgot how to breathe. My heart leaped into my throat, and my pussy tightened.

Oh, shit!

Panic! It was time to get away from him.

"You know, maybe you're right. The report can wait." I moved away from him, quickly put up the first aid kit, and grabbed my bag to head for the door.

But Raymond stepped in my way.

He towered over me, looking down with those eyes that felt deeper by the second. "Are you really going to run away from me again?"

"I'm not running away." I shook my head.

"You're moving so fast, you left your keys on the desk." He pointed over my shoulder.

I looked back to see the key ring sitting next to the water I hadn't finished.

"Oh, right?" I reached back, snagged the key, then continued my escape. But this time, he grabbed my wrist, halting my movement.

"Wait," Raymond said. "Don't go."

"What are you doing?" I looked at my wrist, his large hand wrapped around it. "Let me go."

"Jericha,"

I pulled, snatching away from him. "I'm going home. You're the one who was insisting I rest, remember?"

"What is your problem with me?" His question caught me off guard.

"I don't have a problem with you." I shook my head.

"You shield yourself from me whenever I—"

"Whenever you what?" I cut him off. Was he doing it on purpose? Trying to get me riled up, trying to get under my skin?

"I just want to get to know you better." Raymond's shoulders dropped. "I swear it's like you refuse to just be yourself around me without that barrier you've put up. I keep getting these glimpses of you, the real you, and then you push away again."

"I don't know what you're talking about." I patted the side of my head. The tight bun I pulled my hair into was screaming for release. "Your shoulder still needs to heal. You should go rest."

"My shoulder is fine, Jericha." He rolled his neck, lifting his shoulder for me to see. Then, he did it. Raymond grabbed my wrist again, this time pulling me closer.

A gasp escaped me as he shifted our position and put himself between me in the door. *So much for a quick escape.*

"What are you doing?" I looked around him at the door.

"Nothing," he said heavily, taking a pressing step toward me.

"This doesn't feel like nothing." For each step he took, I took one back until my ass hit the desk. "Raymond, stop."

The corner of his lips twitched upward. "Stop what?"

"Really?" I narrowed my gaze.

"You want me to go?" He was right up against me. "Is that what you want, Jericha?"

"Why are you doing this?" I was damn near panting from the feeling of having him so close to me. What happened to playing it cool?

"Answer the question. Stop running from me."

I said nothing, defiantly crossing my arms over my chest in protest of what he was doing, stopping him from getting any closer. Hell, if he did, he might be able to hear my heart racing.

"You're so bold until it's just us, alone, when you can't hide from me." He took a deep breath, eyes locked on mine. "Fine, I'll go."

He abruptly turned, the scent of his cologne lingering in the air as he moved away. The idea of him leaving felt like a physical blow—a sudden, sharp pain pierced my heart at the thought of never seeing him again. So, I turned the tables on him. With a firm grip, I grabbed his arm, yanking him back to my side. Overzealous, I pulled him too hard. He spun around and I lunged forward, landing awkwardly in his embrace, my breath catching in my throat. We paused, eyes locked, and a million unspoken words hung in the air before I kissed him.

"You just wanted to be in control, huh?" Raymond smiled against my lips.

"Shut up." I pushed him away. "That was an accident."

"You accidentally grabbed me and kissed me?" He chuckled. "Never seen such a passionate accident before."

"The only thing I meant to do was stop you from leaving." I straightened. "I stumbled, that's all. The kiss wasn't supposed to happen."

"And now that you've kissed me? Accidentally, of course." He stepped closer to me. "What happens now?"

"It *was* an accident." I avoided his question. "Accidents happen all the time!"

"Oh, I'm sure it was." He took another sure step toward me, this time getting so close, he pressed me up against the edge of my desk.

"Why are you looking at me like that?" I gulped. "That wasn't an invitation for whatever you think you're about to do."

"Who said I was going to do anything?" The smirk lifted the corner of his mouth. "I'm just standing here. You want me to go? Say the word. But considering you stopped me from leaving..."

"What is this?" I didn't mean to say aloud. That was supposed to be an internal thought, but he smiled when he heard it.

"This was a budding friendship until you kissed me." He slipped his hand around my waist. "Now, it's something more."

I grabbed his arm, resisting his hold. "And what if I don't want it to be something more?"

"I have a feeling you do. You just want to be in control." He stepped back, putting his hands out to his sides. "So, Jericha, I'll give you the control you want. You say the word, and I'll leave, but hesitate, and I'm taking control."

"I—"

"Three..." He took a step closer. "Two..." Another step brought him within arm's reach. "One." Raymond ended his countdown then reached out for me, pulling me into his arms. He paused, giving me just half a second to refuse him. When I didn't, he leaned in to put his lips next to my ear and, in a voice so deep it felt like fingers in my pussy, said, "I thought so."

The next moment, his hand was on my neck, his touch both rough and surprisingly tender, as Raymond pulled me into his arms. Suddenly, his lips were pressed to mine, a soft kiss that rapidly turned into something far more urgent and electrifying.

My pulse raced as my mind flip-flopped between letting this man have his way with me and kicking him in the nuts for kissing me without my permission. After he lifted me into his arms, wrapping my legs around his waist, I decided his nuts were safe. That thought might have been driven by the fact that I could already feel his dick growing hard under me as he carried me across the office to sit me on the small couch beneath the window.

He lowered me to the couch then sat beside me, and I wanted to smack him. Why the hell was he putting space between us? I sat there, like a kid being put in time out, and waited. Was he going to stand and strip? Would he kiss me again? The man did nothing, and it was absolutely infuriating!

And then, for whatever reason, he tried to strike up a conversation.

"Jericha—"

I knew what he was going to say. That was the moment when the cocky guy turned sweet and asked me if I was sure. That was the moment he would give me another out. And if he offered it, I knew I would take it. I was stubborn that way. But I also knew I didn't want to take it.

"Don't start talking to me now." I slammed my mouth against his. If he spoke, I might reconsider everything that happened between us and run for the door again.

He didn't resist me. Raymond kissed me back, pressing his bare chest against me as he pushed me back onto the couch. My lips trailed from his lips to his shoulder and my hands met my lips just by his wound. I felt the magic pull to my fingertips but held back the energy. I could easily heal him with my magic, push the energy from the plants into him, but I didn't. I couldn't raise any suspicion. Instead, I kissed the top of the bandage gently and continued across his shoulder.

"That feels good." His voice was heavy in my ear. Then, he tugged at my shirt. "Take this off. Let me return the favor."

I removed my top, revealing the sports bra beneath it. It was the kind with double support, a zipper in the front.

"Is that thing bulletproof?" he joked.

"I gotta keep the girls secure, especially when I'm in the field."

"And how do I get the girls out of there?" He tugged at the zipper in front, and it pulled down, revealing my tits to him. "Oh, I like that."

He grinned hungrily, and then, like a competitive eater at an ice cream buffet, he went to work kissing on my breasts, sucking my nipples and biting. I might have told him to stop, but I liked it. Each graze of his teeth sent a shiver down my spine right to my pussy.

"Oh, you like that, huh?" He looked at me. "Jericha, don't tell me you're kinky."

"If nipple biting is kinky to you, I'm going to have a lot of fun with you," I said as I pushed him back across the couch. I stood, pulled my pants off, and climbed on top of him. A few quick movements later, I had his dick in my hand and my panties pulled to the side. "Be still."

"Jericha," he moaned.

I put my finger over his lips. "Raymond, I need you to be quiet right now."

He nodded.

"Condom?" I asked.

He shifted his hips, lifting from the couch and pointed to his pocket. I pulled his wallet from his back pocket and opened it to find a condom inside.

"Always prepared, I see." I winked.

Then, I unwrapped the condom and slid it onto his dick. He was already hard, ready for me, and I stroked him a few times before positioning his tip between my pussy lips.

He lifted his hips, but I pulled away. "Don't." I ordered.

"Hmm," he moaned and settled back into the couch.

I returned to the position. His head settled between my lips, teasing him. I moved lower, allowing him to slip inside of me, just enough so I could feel the heat of him and gauge his width. And then, with my pussy wrapped around the head of his dick, I flexed, squeezing the muscles around him until I saw him grip the couch.

"Come on!" he groaned. "Stop teasing me."

"Don't tell me what to do," I ordered, then slowly lowered myself onto him.

Raymond's eyes bulged, and I could feel his pulse racing beneath the hand I placed on his chest.

He tried to grab my ass, but I slapped his hand away. "Don't touch me."

"What?"

"Keep your hands to yourself," I ordered.

"Oh, okay. I get it." Raymond bit his lip and locked his gaze with mine.

I rode him, hips rocking, and sped up. This was what I wanted, not what he wanted. It was about me.

Our eyes locked, but his stare grew so intense, I wanted to look away. I refused. If I did, it would give him the upper hand, and he might think it meant he could take control. No, in this, with my body, the control would always be mine.

I remained on top of him, riding him.

I grabbed my breasts in my hands and pinched my nipples as I continued.

He was a tool I used to get me where I needed to be.

And he let me use him. Raymond gripped the edge of the couch and, despite the slight lift of his hips every now and then, he remained still. It was when I caught the movement of the plants I realized I had to bring it to a close.

I picked up my speed, rocking fast as I leaned down onto him, burying his face in my tits so he wouldn't notice anything moving.

"God, yes!" he said into my chest.

I moved faster, sliding up and down the length of him, and soon, I came. I gripped the edge of the couch and moaned as I finished.

As soon as I was done, I hopped up, dressed, and ran out of the office. I didn't know if he finished. It didn't matter. What mattered was escape. I felt victorious—that was, until just before the door slammed behind me.

Because I could hear him in my office, chuckling like a damn villain who had pulled off the greatest heist.

9

Meet me in the gym.

Kaa wrapped her body around my arm as she slipped along my flesh to wake me up. It had taken me so long to fall asleep, my mind wanted to stay there as long as possible. As my senses returned, the faint, tinny sound of my alarm clock pierced the silence.

When I looked at the phone that buzzed on my nightstand, I realized I'd already slept through the first two scheduled alarms.

"I should just stay in bed today." I pushed my face into my pillow.

It wasn't that I was too tired to face the day. The problem was Raymond. The thought of him still overwhelmed me; the moment his name surfaced, my heart pounded like a drum against my ribs.

I'd done everything to erase him from my mind before I hopped into bed, but nothing worked. Not the roll in the grass with the plants, who seemed to perk up a lot more than they ever had the moment my hands touched the soil behind my house. Not the shower that lasted so long, the hot water ran out. I thought I could wash away everything that happened, but instead, I stood beneath the stream, imagining all the things I wished I had allowed.

I planned to get up early and head to the office. There was a report to write, and staff items to address. Instead, I picked up my phone and shot Natalie a message.

Me: Hey, running late today. Please pull the staff reports and inventory tracking for me to review when I get in.

I put the phone down beside me. Before I could drift back to sleep, Natalie had already responded, confirming she received my message and would have things ready when I got there.

With that done, my mind began the daily race, building the list of items I knew I would never be able to complete in one day. Once that started, there was no way I could get back to sleep. So, I pulled my bones from my bed, and headed for the kitchen. Along the way, I scooped my laptop from my desk, and while the water heated for my tea, I powered up the laptop. This was the perfect time for me to finish the report.

The events of the night before were still fresh in my mind. The moment my fingers began tapping the keys, Kaa's small body reappeared. She loved the sound of the keys and would always dance to the beat. I smiled as she swayed, her petals moving like a dress flowing around her form.

"You look so pretty, Kaa," I complimented her, and she moved in a circle then dipped her head in a tight bow.

The kettle whistled on the stove, and I abandoned my laptop to make my cup of tea. I'd chosen a raspberry leaf and mullein blend to help with the terrible cramps I'd been having with my recent periods. I fell in love with the blend years ago, and it had become a staple in my kitchen. As I steeped the tea, flashes of Raymond passed through my mind.

"I can't believe I did that." I looked at Kaa, who had curled her body up on top of my open laptop. "How the hell am I supposed to face him now?"

She tapped the keys with her tail, as if she were actually writing a response to me. I leaned over to see a series of Rs and Ws fill the screen.

"You're no help," I fussed, and Kaa lifted her head, rolled her eyes, then slithered back over to her pot. "I didn't mean to upset you!"

She would stay there for at least two days before she let me see her again. Sensitive little thing.

I finished making the tea and grabbed the bowl of fruit from the fridge before returning to the table. While I nibbled on the fruit and sipped my tea, I worked on all the things that needed to be handled—responding to emails, filing official reports for two other work sites, and confirming four meeting requests, including one with Von. It was the first of what would be many progress reports. I wished I didn't have to report an attempted robbery, but at least they would know we were on top of our game and earning our coin.

After responding to Von's message, which had included an inquiry about Raymond, I realized I hadn't heard from him. Not a text, call, or even an annoying email. The man had been quiet.

"Maybe he regrets it as much as I do," I muttered wishfully as I closed my laptop and headed for the bathroom. Though I would have preferred to hide away for the day, I needed to go to the office.

During the first hour, I was too busy to be concerned with Raymond. During the next three, thoughts of him would creep up then quickly fade away. Five hours into my day, I became annoyed. *Where the hell was he?* No, I didn't want anything more from him, but how dare he not at least text to make sure I was okay?

"Just like every other man," I huffed as I flipped through the papers on my desk.

"Who is?" Natalie stood in front of me.

"Shit!" I hadn't heard her come in, and her voice had me jumping out of my skin. "Please don't do that."

"I knocked." She pointed back at the door. "You've been really distracted today. You even made a mistake in the inventory calculation here." She slipped the document over to me on the desk.

"I did?"

"That's at least double what we need." She pointed to the total on the page. "Are you sure you're okay?"

"I guess I am a little distracted." I leaned back in my seat. "Last night…"

"The incident at the studio?" she asked.

"Yeah," I recovered. I'd almost slipped and told her about Raymond. I glanced at the couch beneath the window, which I had conveniently buried in random items throughout the day.

"Do you want me to clean that up?" Natalie followed my gaze.

"Oh, no." I waved her off. "I'll handle it. It's getting late. You should get going. I'll correct the inventory report myself."

"You know I can do a lot of this stuff." Natalie paused then quickly blurted out, "It's what you pay me for."

"Yeah." I understood her hesitation. She didn't want to feel like she was overstepping. "I promise to hand a lot more over to you soon."

"Okay." She chewed her lip, as if considering saying something else, but she didn't.

"You okay?" I asked.

"Yep. I'll head home now." Natalie turned and ran from my office.

"That was weird." I looked at the door for a moment before returning to the work in front of me.

After another two hours of working without accomplishing much, I gave up. The entire time, I could only think of what both Natalie and Raymond had already said to me. Why was I spending so much of my time doing things I should have offloaded to Natalie already? She was more than capable, but there was something in me that refused to give up the work, some fear that everything would be ruined or worse—taken from me. What I needed was time to journal and work out my feelings. So, I cleaned up the couch, put away the documents, and headed out.

As I stepped out of my office into the waiting room, my thoughts shifted from giving up control to keeping control of myself.

"Did you have enough time?" Raymond spoke as he stood from the chair by the front door. I hadn't realized he was there, and his presence caught me off guard. Exactly what he wanted, I was sure.

"Enough time for what?" I held back all expressions of how annoyed I'd been about him not reaching out to me.

"Don't tell me you didn't notice my absence." He plastered on the fakest pout I'd ever seen. The expression looked painful on his face. "Here I was, thinking I would give you space to process what happened, and you weren't even thinking about me?"

"Sorry to hurt your feelings." I played it cool.

"I'll survive this like I have so many other hurts in the past." He walked over to me. "Nevertheless, I had to see you again."

"Listen." I held up my hand to stop him. "About last night. That was a mistake, and it's never happening again."

"Is that so?" he stopped. "A mistake? Are you sure about that? I gave you plenty of opportunities to reconsider."

He held his hands out to his side just as he had the night before, and I immediately remembered what he looked like without his shirt, imagining in full detail the muscles of his arms and chest and the tattoos that covered them.

"I'm not sure what you expect to happen, but whatever it is, get it out of your head." I pointed to his shoulder. "How's the cut?"

"See how much you care about me?"

"Only because if it gets worse, I have to report it."

"Well, ease your worries. The cut is fine. Healing up perfectly." He pulled at the collar of his shirt, a black t-shirt, so I could see the bandage still in place. "You want to examine it?"

"I'll take your word for it."

"I'm surprised you're leaving this early." He pointed to the window. "There's still sunlight."

"I need to—" I was going to say I had to clear my head but realized it might lead to further conversation I didn't want to deal with. "Go to the store."

"The store?" He frowned. "That's vague."

"Groceries. I need groceries," I blurted out, knowing damn well I didn't need to go to the store. I had just had groceries delivered two days ago.

"Perfect, me too! I'll tag along." He offered the company I was clearly trying to avoid.

"Seriously?" I asked. "How do you even know what store I'm going to?"

"What's the difference? I'm not picky." He held the door open. "Let's go."

With no other option to escape him, I sighed and headed out the door. As he tailed me from the office to the grocery store, I tried to think of anything I needed at the house, but my mind went blank. All I could think of was honey. I needed more honey for my tea.

He parked next to me and followed me into the store, grabbing a basket as we entered. Our trip turned into me playing tagalong as he filled the basket with fruits, vegetables, and other items.

Damn, he actually needed to go grocery shopping!

We had walked the entire store, and all I grabbed were two jars of honey and a pack of gummy bears.

"That's what you needed?" He raised a brow at me.

"Yep."

"You were just trying to avoid me, weren't you?" He snorted.

"No, I needed this stuff!" I held up one of the jars. "How do you expect me to start my days without honey for my tea?"

"Right." He pushed the cart. "The world would come to a fiery end."

We checked out, and Raymond paid for my items, insisting there was no need to have two separate charges when I got so little. After a tight smile at the cashier, who looked at us with a confused expression, I followed him out of the store.

"Are you going home now?" he asked as he loaded his groceries into his trunk, holding my bag hostage until he was done.

"Yes," I said and tried once again to grab the bag so I could flee, but he held on to it.

Raymond closed his trunk, walked the cart to the return slot, and then came back over to me. With my bag still in hand, he opened my door for me.

"Drive safely."

"Yeah, I will." I took the bag and slipped into the car, avoiding any physical contact with him.

Despite what I told him, I didn't drive home. I drove to a nearby park. It was close to a taco spot that was usually busy during the summer. Often, I would see a long line when I arrived. The last time I was there, I watched a woman run to her car and take off. No one else reacted, so I assumed she was a regular nutcase. But I loved the park just beyond the taco spot.

I parked my car and headed for the trail to the pond. The sun was finally setting, and there weren't many people around, but a few souls still lingered. I stood by the water, watching the birds floating across its surface.

"I thought you were going home." Raymond stepped next to me.

Though his presence shocked me, I kept my composure and continued watching the birds. "Why are you following me?"

"Maybe I was worried about you. You said you needed to shop but only got honey and candy. Then, you said you're going home, but you're here, alone and looking out at the water like you're fighting back tears. Be honest with yourself and with me. What's going on?"

"I do not look like I'm fighting back tears." I rolled my eyes. "Don't be so dramatic."

"Hey, that's my observation. Something is clearly bothering you. What is it?"

"We can't do that again."

"Do what? Grocery shop?" He shrugged. "It's not that big of a deal. People buy food every day."

"You know what I'm talking about. The—" I lowered my voice. "Sex."

"For a woman who wants to be in control, you sure are worried a lot about what others will think of you. No one in this park knows us. Why are you whispering as if it's breaking news you need to protect?"

"You know what? I'm done. Don't follow me." I stepped away from him.

He grabbed my hand. "Don't do that. Don't walk away from me like that, Jericha."

"What do you want, Raymond?" I looked down at his hand. "Why are you stopping me?"

"I want you to loosen up," he said, clearly frustrated.

"Loosen up?" I laughed. "I'm trying to be professional. What do I need to loosen up for?"

"Jericha, we have a temporary partnership. In a few months, we won't be working together anymore. Maybe what happened between us isn't professional, but I don't care." His hand slipped from my wrist to my waist. "I want more of you. And if you think I can go back to just being your partner at work after what happened last night, you're insane."

"I'm not trying to be with anyone right now," I blurted out.

"Hey, I'm not asking for a relationship." His hand flexed against my waist. "We're grown, attracted to each other, and obviously, there is chemistry between us."

"Are you trying to coerce me?" I looked down at his hand and then back at his face.

"Not at all." He leaned closer, and the last rays of the sun touched his eyes, making them glow. "I'm just telling you how I feel. If you disagree, I'll respect that."

"You say that but..." I looked down at his arm, which he slid further around me. "You're pulling me closer to you."

"Yes, and you aren't stopping me, just like you didn't stop me last night." He tugged me closer. "In fact, you took control, Jericha. Remember?"

"Yes, I remember." My heart pounded in my chest.

"Do it again," he challenged me. "Take control."

"Have you considered me walking away was me taking control?" I put my hand on his chest and pushed him back. "Like I said, what happened last night can't happen again. If you choose to leave our agreement because of that, I won't stop you."

I walked away from him, and Raymond didn't stop me. When I got in my car, I looked back to see him standing on the path. He followed me, but he didn't stop me. Our eyes met, but I was committed to my decision. I drove away, leaving him standing in the park alone.

The next day, Raymond beat me to the office.

"What are you doing here?" I sighed when I pulled up to find him standing by the door.

"I'm respecting your wishes." He lifted the tray of coffee in one hand, and two packs of the little pink donuts in the other hand.

"How is this respecting my wishes?" I crossed my arms to keep myself from snatching the donuts from him.

"We're partners, right? Technically, I work for you. So, I'll show up, work, and in a few months, I'll be out of your hair," he explained. "I'll also do the coffee run in the morning. The stuff you have here sucks, and this place near my house is too good to miss out on."

"What about things at your office?" I looked around. "Don't you have things to take care of there? You can't be here every day."

"I've already shut down operations," he replied. "I meant to tell you that before, but it slipped my mind with everything going on. This is the only open contract I have left. Once it's done, I'll move on. Oh, and if you want, we'll transfer all employee records to you. The guys have already agreed to it. Is that okay with you?"

I took the offered coffee and donuts from him. "Thank you."

From that moment forward, Raymond was the perfect employee. He spent little time talking to me, and all his energy with Natalie and the other staff members. He filled in wherever we needed help and even beat me to the punch on a few items. At the end of each day, he had status reports filed and ready for my review. He gave me no trouble.

And it was driving me crazy.

That's what he wants! I thought as I arrived to the office a week later. I called myself getting there early to prepare for our meeting with Von, but Raymond was already there.

He wants me to go crazy trying to figure out what the hell is up with him. I refuse to give him the energy. Let him be the perfect employee. Great. Less headache for me. In a few months, he'll be gone, and I'll be able to move on with my life!

"Good morning, Ms. Brown," Raymond addressed me as I entered the office.

"Raymond." I nodded. "Early again."

"Yes, of course." He nodded. "We thought we would get a head start, considering how early the meeting with Von is."

"We?"

"Good morning." Natalie stepped out of my office. "I just put your notes on your desk. Everything is ready to go, and the conference room is all set. Von emailed; she asked to move the meeting up by a half hour. I told her that would be fine, so you have about twenty minutes before she arrives."

"Great." I swallowed my comments about how annoyed I was with Raymond. "I'll review everything. Please make sure there is fresh coffee. Von likes the dark roast."

"Got it!" Raymond stepped forward, holding out a receipt for me. "I had to use my personal card. I'll need you to approve this for reimbursement."

"Thanks." I took the receipt from him and marched into my office, closing the door behind me.

Natalie's notes were thorough, as always, and by the time Von made it to the office, I felt confident about the meeting. Raymond joined us, and while I expected him to speak up, he remained a silent supporter, nodding when appropriate and taking notes whenever something important was mentioned.

"You're doing a wonderful job. Thank you so much for how thorough your report was. A lot of studios have been getting hit all over the country. I'm not surprised it's already happening here." Von stood from the table and took a long sip of her coffee. "You mind walking out with me?" she asked me.

"Of course." I nodded at Raymond, who opened the door for us but remained behind to clean up the room.

"Thank you for taking the time to meet with me," Von said.

"Of course. I'm happy to," I said honestly, because I genuinely enjoyed speaking with her. It was a refreshing break from majorly male leadership.

"I also wanted to ask you for a favor. A private contract of sorts."

"Oh?" I asked. "What are the details?"

"We're having a meeting with the executives. It will be downtown, at the Echo hotel," she explained. "One of the owners is nervous about being there without security. I was hoping you could provide your services. And of course, you will be paid for it."

"Of course. If you send the details over, Natalie will get things squared away." I smiled. "We have plenty of available team members eager to work."

"That's the thing. After looking at the report you provided..." She paused. "And this is why I wanted to talk to you privately about this. I was hoping you would do the event yourself, along with Raymond."

I glanced back at the office door and was relieved to find no one there. "You want me and Raymond to do it?"

"Is that a problem? I mean, I wanted to ask you directly because I know how uncomfortable it was before when the exec thought he was the owner and not you. I didn't want to step on your toes or make it awkward."

"No, it's fine. Not awkward at all." I took a deep breath. "Shoot me the details, and I'll confirm if it works with our schedules. I can't promise Raymond will be there, but I'll make sure I am."

"Perfect. Thank you!"

I stood outside long after Von had driven away; I could feel their eyes burning at the back of my neck. When I turned around, Natalie ran to her desk, but Raymond stood there and waved at me with the biggest grin on his face.

"Did you hear?" I asked as I walked back into the building.

"Hear what?" he asked.

"Von would like us to provide security for a private event next week. They needed the best. So, of course, she wants us."

"Great. Who do you want to assign?" Raymond pulled out his phone. "I'll make the calls and set the schedule. I assume she will send over the job notes to Natalie?"

"No, she wants us. You and me," I told him, and he slipped the phone back into his pocket. "She liked how we handled the incident the other night and wants us to be there in case anything else happens."

"Is she expecting something like that?" Natalie stood behind her desk. "What's going on with that place?"

"I think it's just a precaution. Besides, it is supposed to be an event full of execs. It couldn't hurt for us to be in the room. Maybe we'll overhear information about new opportunities to expand."

"In that case, count me in!" He straightened. "What night? I'll be sure to be there."

That was it—perfect agreement. No snarky comment about how much I needed him or wanted him around me.

"Okay, what is this?" I pointed at him.

"What's what?" He shrugged then glanced at Natalie, whose mouth was slack.

"In my office," I muttered and headed for privacy. Raymond followed me into the room, and as soon as he stepped over the threshold, I shut the door and turned on him. "Why are you doing all this? Being the perfect employee, working closely with the staff. Hell, even Natalie is referring issues to you. Are you trying to convince me to give in?"

"I don't know what you mean." He shook his head, an innocent look on his face.

I took a deep, calming breath to avoid further freaking out then pointed at the door. "Meet me in the gym."

"You want to spar?" He perked up.

"Yeah, I'm going to get changed." I wanted to knock his head off.

After quickly changing my clothes, I avoided eye contact with Natalie as I headed upstairs to the gym. With each step, I could feel her eyes watching me. And I swear she whispered something under her breath about me losing my mind, but I wasn't about to stop and ask her about it.

The space was empty. I hadn't considered that none of the staff had made it to the office yet, so we wouldn't have an audience. That was a mistake, because Raymond stood in the middle of the gym in slacks and nothing else.

"Where is your workout gear?" I pointed at his pants and bare feet.

He glanced down and shrugged. "I didn't plan on working out today."

"I see."

"We can still do this." He stretched his neck. "You need time to stretch? Wouldn't want you to pull a muscle."

"I'm good." I nodded.

We started just as we did before: simple tactics. But to be honest, I put far more power behind every attack.

"Did meeting with Von wind you up that much?" he asked as he dodged a punch. "I thought you liked her."

"I do." I went for a kick, which he slapped away. "My tension has nothing to do with her."

"Oh, I see." He grinned. "And what's the source?"

"It doesn't matter."

"I think it does." He grabbed my arm and pulled, flipping me onto my back.

"Why?" I looked up at him when he released what could have been an easy pin.

"If you're tense, you'll make mistakes. That's dangerous," he fussed.

"And you care?" I scrunched my brows.

"Of course I do." He looked down at me with those green eyes, and, for a moment, I lost my senses.

I grabbed his face and pulled him to me, slamming my lips against his. At first, he responded as I thought he would—lowering his weight onto me—but then something shifted, and Raymond pulled away.

"What are you doing?" I huffed, accidentally showing my frustration.

"I thought you would want to run away again." He glanced at the door. "Now is your chance."

"Funny." I sat up just as he moved to his knees in front of me.

He leaned in close, voice low, with a dark edge to it as he spoke.

"Jericha, if you cross this line with me again, there is no going back. I will not be the nice office boy you can order around. I'm not someone you can toy with. Trust me, I know the kind of weak men you're used to dealing with. I'm not them. Don't mistake me for one."

He got up slowly, holding eye contact for a moment, then turned and left me alone on the floor.

IO

Rooftops and Shadows

I saw little of Raymond after that. He went from an eager office boy showing up every morning with coffee in hand to keeping his distance. Every time I came into work, Natalie reported how I'd just missed him. Each time, she would have coffee, and I wouldn't. I never mentioned it. I wouldn't give him the satisfaction of knowing I wanted the damn stuff.

But he got his point across, and after the first two days of his conditioned absence, I realized he was right. I'd never been the type to go back and forth on a decision, especially when it came to men. It shouldn't have been any different with Raymond. Yes, I found him attractive, and yes, I wanted more of him, but I knew the best course of action was to steer clear.

"That man had the nerve to ask me to wait for him while he was in prison!" Natalie burst into my office, eyes red, as if she had been crying. If I asked, she would blame it on allergies.

"What?" I looked up from my phone and stared at Natalie, who stood by the couch beneath the window. She peered through it as if waiting for someone.

"You haven't heard a word I've said, have you?" She turned to me and put her hands on her hips. "I've just been wasting my breath, haven't I?"

"Sorry, distracted." I frowned; I could have sworn she'd only just come into my office. "Who's going to jail?"

"Caleb. The guy I was talking to. Our third date, and he ended it by asking if I would wait for him. *'It's only four years.'* That's what he said to me. As if I would give up four years of my life waiting for a guy I've known for less than a month!"

"How do you keep finding these men?" I stood from my desk and walked over to her. "We need to reevaluate your process."

"Dating apps." She pulled the phone from her pocket and waved it at me. "I'm on seven of them."

"Natalie. I say this with love: it's time to log off!" I laughed. "You've encountered the worst men on those apps."

"How else am I going to meet someone?" She rolled her neck. "You don't know how hard it is out there."

"Why are you so concerned with men?" I asked.

"I don't want to be alone. I want someone who chooses me every day like I choose them," she said. "The problem is being chosen by the right one."

"That's your problem right there. You need to change your way of thinking." I sighed and gently lifted her chin with a hooked finger until she looked me in the eye. "Girl, ain't nothing special about a man! You're the one who chooses! Look at you! You're beautiful, intelligent, and successful. You've given them the power. They're animals. They can smell it on you. You wanting them so much smells like desperation, and that only attracts mama's boys and jailbirds—neither of which deserve any of your time."

"I just need to be more like you. You have guys so worked up over you, they'll drink bath water to prove how much they want to be with you!"

"Ugh, don't remind me." I rolled my eyes. "Besides, what you're describing isn't what I have. The men I deal with are here for a good time, not a long time. They aren't the kind you marry. That's the problem with comparing yourself to someone else. You only see what is presented, not what's behind the curtain. I choose men I can dispose of because I don't want a long-term commitment."

"Well, maybe I'll spend a few years doing that. I'm flexible, and you said you would teach me your ways, but you haven't. Come to think of it, you haven't even mentioned a man since the bathwater guy."

"It's the new contract," I offered as a quick explanation. "I'm giving my energy to things that matter and will benefit me. Right now, that's not a man. I want things to go well, and that means putting my focus where it matters."

While Natalie looked at me in admiration, I crossed my fingers behind my back. I couldn't tell her a big part of the reason she hadn't heard me talk about any other man was because of a man I wasn't supposed to like. How could I? She looked up to me. I couldn't let her know I apparently also had a weakness, and that weakness came with green eyes and tatted sleeves.

"You could always give more work to me. It would free you up and give me something else to do with my energy." She sighed. "I mean, maybe you don't want to date, but you have other interests, right?"

"You've been talking to Raymond, haven't you?" I shook my head. "All those mornings he came in early, he was just getting in your head, wasn't he?"

"Maybe." She winked. "By the way, he will be here soon, so you two can ride to the venue together. Von said there is only one confirmed parking spot for you two to use."

"Perfect." I moved to sit back at the desk. "Thank you for staying on top of everything, and I promise, I will hand more over to you soon. Not because of Raymond, but because you deserve the opportunity to learn and grow in the company. If we continue to expand, I won't be able to keep up with everything."

"You've been saying that for well over a year now, but I appreciate the consideration," she called me out.

"That bad?" I frowned. I could have been mad, but I appreciated the honesty. That was the kind of person I wanted in my corner, and honestly, it was refreshing to see her stand up for herself.

"I still love you anyway!" She smiled.

"You better." I chuckled. "Head on home. I'll see you Monday."

Half an hour after Natalie took off, Raymond arrived. He knocked on my office door, pulling my attention from the new contract I'd just gotten from the lawyers. Business was expanding faster than I thought it would. Word was, another company was going under, and that sent clients preemptively searching for replacement providers.

"You ready to go?" Raymond asked.

I turned the computer off, and grabbed my jacket from the back of the chair as I stood. "Yes, but I'm driving. I'm not showing up in your flashy car."

"Of course you are," he muttered and headed out. Raymond waited outside while I locked up, and when I came out, he stood by the passenger door. "Ready when you are."

We drove for nearly forty-five minutes in silence, only talking when it came to the details of the evening. It was simple enough: a three-hour dinner with the top seven executives, and one person only named "X". Whoever this X was, they were the reason for the security detail.

They'd booked a suite in the hotel where X would be staying for the night to eliminate any additional travel. There was a private chef with a team of three who would serve because X didn't want to eat the food from the hotel and needed a controlled source.

We were to stand outside the room where they met and complete a perimeter check every half hour. It surprised me that they only requested two people, but from what I gathered, it was a direct request from X, who wanted to keep a low profile.

When I asked for more information about the mystery guest, Von made it clear it was information I didn't need to know. They had deep pockets and were looking to invest, and that was all that mattered.

"Were you able to find out anything else about this X person?" Raymond asked as we arrived.

"No, but I don't think it matters. This is a one-time event. Von made it sound like once this is done, this X won't be back."

"Works for me."

"You run the initial perimeter check, and I'll meet with Von to check in. We have an hour before they're supposed to start." I handed him the black bag from the back seat. "These are the cams. Try to get as many angles of the entrances as possible."

"Yes, ma'am." He saluted me and jumped out of the car.

Raymond headed off to check the area while I went inside. I already had the keycard for the elevator that led to the top floor. Once inside, I took a deep breath to clear my head, and by the time the doors slid open to reveal Von waiting by the door, I was ready to work.

"Jericha, it's good to see you again." Von seemed cheerful yet nervous.

"You as well." I nodded, holding my hand out to shake hers.

"Where is Raymond?" She looked in the elevator behind me as if the man would materialize.

"He's doing a quick check at ground level before we begin. We'll keep our presence up top, but he's also placing some visual aids for us to use remotely."

"Visual aids?"

"They're for temporary footage. Once we're done here, we will remove it. But you didn't want extra bodies, so this way, one of us can keep an eye on the ground should something happen."

"Smart thinking."

"It's what you pay me for." I smiled.

Von led me into the suite, and I took a quick walk around, checking all internal access points, noting the balcony that led outside the main room and the one off the bedroom. There was a large dining room with massive windows, which could be a threat if X was the type of person to have snipers after them. I hoped that wasn't the case.

Other than that obvious threat, which I pointed out to Von, everything looked fine. The chef and their team were already working on the meal. Von insisted there was no need to check them, as they were X's team.

I nodded and headed out of the space. Soon, the execs would arrive, and I didn't want to be in the way. By the time I stepped back outside the room, Raymond was already there.

"That was fast."

He held up the tablet and swiped through the screens showing the working cameras. "We're all set. All the cameras are up and running, and I swept the grounds. There are no obvious threats."

"Good." I took the tablet from him, wondering how the hell he'd done that so fast.

I didn't question him, though. I didn't want to start any bickering, and it was good I didn't, because the elevator slid open at that moment, and the execs all stepped out. One by one, they walked by us, nodding as they did. We gave each one a pat down and then allowed their entry.

Ten minutes later, the elevator opened again, and out filed four large men, a hooded figure in the middle. They walked to the door. Von stepped out and nodded to me. She'd already insisted we not give X the pat down.

I stepped aside, nodding at the men, but intuition screamed at me. I couldn't figure out why, but the men felt familiar. When I glanced at Raymond, I could see his tension. His jaw tightened, and he kept his eyes forward, making zero contact with the men.

X paused, their hooded head turning toward Raymond for a moment before they entered the room. As they passed me, I got a distinct smell of heat, like after running in the summer sun. It was a warmth that filled my nose and head. It was misplaced. It was warm outside, yes, but the sun had set and the temperature dropped.

"That was weird." I kept my voice low as I spoke.

"Was it? Didn't notice." He pointed to the tablet in my hand. "Look, I'll take the perimeter checks. You stay here with the tablet."

"What?"

"I think it's better if one of us stays stationary."

"You want to change up the plan now?"

"Yes." He looked at me sternly, and there was a flash of something dark in his expression. Something was bothering him. If he was upset, it was better he was not near the clients.

"Okay, that works for me." I nodded, and Raymond walked away.

Nothing happened. I stood outside the door alone, checking the tablet periodically, sometimes seeing Raymond and other times not. He returned just before the doors opened and the execs filed out, all drunk off their asses and grinning from ear to ear.

"Things must have worked out." Raymond winked at me before the four guards stepped outside the room and, once again, he tensed up.

They filed out before X, who once again had the hood over their face—I wondered if they kept it on the entire meal. They still smelled of that summer heat when they left.

Is that a special brand of cologne or something?

"Jericha, Raymond, thank you so much for being here." Von exited last. She draped a shawl over her shoulders. "You don't have to stay. The chef will keep the room for the night before returning home in the morning."

"Did everything go well?" I asked.

"Yes, perfectly." Von looked like she was ready to pass out. "And I'm sorry. I didn't know X was bringing their own security. It felt like a waste having you both here."

"An added layer of precaution." I said. "I understand, though. It would have been helpful to be in communication with their team."

"Agreed." She spoke with a long yawn. "Well, I'm going to head out. I have a long drive home. You two have a good night."

"Drive safely!" I waved as Von walked toward the elevator. As soon as she stepped inside, I relaxed.

"That was worth the money." Raymond nodded. "Ready to go?"

I returned his nod. "You go collect the cams, and I'll meet you at the car."

"Sounds good." He smiled.

Raymond called the elevator, and, when it came, he stepped inside. As soon as he was out of sight, I walked to the stairwell and headed up to the roof. It was something I'd wanted to do for a while since seeing a report about the views from the top of the building. It wasn't something any normal visitor could gain access to, but I wasn't a normal visitor.

When I reached the top, I pulled the seedling I had in my pocket and lifted it to the frame of the door. With some coaxing, it grew, stretching its vines and slipping around the sensor that would sound the alarm once the door opened. After I was sure it was safe, I picked the lock, and the door opened easily. This way, when I left, there would be no damage to the door, no evidence of my presence.

"Thank you. I'll make it quick," I whispered to the plant that aided me. When I was done, I would take it back home with me and plant it in the garden so it could live a happy life.

Once out on the roof, I took a deep breath, opening my chest to the night sky and sighed. It was as beautiful as I had imagined it to be. I leaned on the railing, looking over the city, and wondered about the lives of all the people beneath me, those who were headed to or from work, going home to families or empty houses. How many were healing, brokenhearted, or dealing with a cold?

"This isn't a part of our perimeter." Raymond's voice startled me. "What are you doing up here?"

I turned to see him standing by the door. "Shouldn't I be asking you that? You're supposed to be meeting me at the car."

"I changed my mind." He joined me by the metal railing that wrapped the rooftop and peered over the edge. "Great view up here, isn't it?"

"Yeah. Saw it on a news broadcast and wanted to experience it for myself. Besides, I needed a moment to clear my head, and this felt like the perfect place to do it."

"What's so heavy on your mind that you had to come up here to get away from it?"

"Natalie mentioned something earlier today about me giving her more work. I asked her if you had talked to her, and she said yes."

"Am I in trouble?"

I raised a brow at his question. "Should you be?"

"Look, I meant what I said. I believe you should hand over more of the workload to her. She's more than capable and eager to take it on, but I'm not here to step on any toes. Natalie told me she aspires to take on a larger role in your company, and all I said was that if she doesn't assert herself, you won't hear her."

"It's not that I don't want to do it, okay?" I ran my hand across the back of my neck. "It's just hard thinking about handing over things that I'm used to handling myself. What if something goes wrong?"

"Something tells me you've done a lot of hard things in your past. You're telling me you can't face this? It's just some paperwork, Jericha. No one's telling you to hand over the plans to your business like you did with Rose. That's what this is about, isn't it? You trusted once and got burned. I get that, but you will not get where you want to go if you don't get over that and do what's best for yourself and your business."

"Ouch. I guess you just see right through me, huh?" I chuckled nervously. He had hit the nail right on the head. My issue wasn't that I didn't trust Natalie. It was that I didn't want to be dropped on my head again. "It didn't happen once. It happened twice. Need I remind you about why we're working together to begin with? Mitch and his ploy to destroy me."

"Right, and where is he with that business? Any clients? Last I checked, the guys who left with him are all looking for other employment now," Raymond smirked. "The people who hurt you are failures. You should thank them for packing up and getting out of your way. And no, I don't see right through you. There's a lot about you I'm still trying to figure out."

"You can stop trying to figure me out."

"Oh, trust me, I plan to. I have my own things to do, issues I need to take care of. Some things have come up recently." He trailed off. "Regardless, I'm actually thinking of cutting our contract short."

"Cutting it short. What do you mean—you're gonna leave me hanging out to dry?"

"No, I mean handing over assets to you sooner rather than later. This arrangement was a good one, but I don't think it's necessary to finish it out. Honestly, I think it's time for me to move forward. I need to move on with my life. Some things are coming up, and if I stay here too long, it may cause me more problems than it's worth."

"What kind of past are you running from?"

"That doesn't matter," he said.

"Oh, so we can talk all about me,what I need to be doing, and how I'm running from my past, but yours is a secret. How is that fair?"

"I don't believe we agreed on having a fair exchange here. Besides, you don't want me around anymore. You've made that perfectly clear. All I'm doing now is offering you a way to make that happen sooner."

"I never said I didn't want you around anymore." I turned my attention back to the view of the city.

"What was that?" He turned and leaned his back on the railing so he could see my face.

"It was me correcting you. I didn't say I didn't want you around. What I said was, what we did was a mistake." I set him straight. "This is supposed to be a professional relationship, and I want to keep it that way."

He slowly rolled his tongue across his top lip. "Hmm. So should I sign the papers to hand over everything to you? That would end the professional relationship, wouldn't it?"

I could see where his mind was going and debated if I wanted to reroute him. Instead, I answered honestly. "Yeah, it would, actually."

"And would you still view what we did as a mistake if that was the case?"

"Hadn't really considered it." I shrugged.

He stood, moving to stand behind me. With his lips right next to my ear, he whispered, "Consider it now."

"Why?" I turned to face him and pushed him away from me. "You just said you're going to be moving on from here, right? You're handing over everything early so you can move to the next spot. So why does it matter if I consider that?"

"I just want to know," he said, his voice so low it was almost a breath. "Curiosity."

"For the sake of satisfying your curiosity." I paused, staring up into those green eyes, and chewed my lip. How daring did I want to be here? I thought of Natalie and the conversation about men. Raymond was the sort I steered clear of, so why was I so drawn to him now? "No, I wouldn't consider it a mistake."

"Why not?" he asked.

"I enjoyed myself. I rarely regret anything I enjoy if it doesn't have any negative impact on the rest of my life. You being gone would mean what we did no longer affects the rest of my life."

"And should it happen again?" He lowered his voice. "That thing we did."

"It's not going to." I squinted at him.

"Right." He took a half step forward, closing the space between us.

"What are you doing?" I looked down at his feet.

"You just said you don't regret it. It wasn't a mistake."

"And?" I asked, breath catching in my throat.

"You enjoyed it." His voice was low, seductive. "You enjoyed me."

"So?" I tried to sound indifferent, but my voice shook, and I knew I failed.

"Are you saying you don't want to?" The corners of his lips lifted. "Fine, I'll go."

Raymond turned to leave.

"Wait." I stopped him.

"I knew it." He turned back to me with a devious grin.

"When are you going to sign the papers?" I raised a brow, knowing I'd caught him off guard. "I want to make sure everything is done before you disappear."

"Wow, okay. Fine. I'll have my attorney send you everything you need tomorrow." He held his hands up as he stepped back from me. "It was nice to know you, Ms. Brown."

Raymond turned and walked back toward the door. I could have let him leave, and I probably should have, but once again, passion overwrote resolve. I ran after him, grabbed his arm, and pulled him back to me. We paused for a moment, our eyes locking before I reached around his neck and pulled his lips to mine.

Raymond leaned into the kiss, quickly feeding his own desire. His arms snaked around me, and he lifted me into his hold as the kiss deepened. But then he stopped, ripped his lips away from mine, and put me down.

I watched him carefully as he caught his breath, eyes dark and locked on me. "I told you not to play with me. If you do this..."

I reached up, putting my finger on his lips to stop him from talking.

"Don't play with me," he muttered beneath my finger.

With confidence and surety, I moved my hand from his face and reached down to grab his dick. Beneath the fabric, Raymond grew. "Who said I'm playing?"

He kissed me again, this time controlling the action as he backed me up across the rooftop. He kept going until the railing hit my back, and I gasped. His hands were there, gripping the rail by my sides in an unspoken promise of my safety. He wouldn't let me fall.

"Let's make this view even better," Raymond spoke against my lips before he pulled away. With one hand, he spun me around and pressed my stomach up against the rail.

Then, before I could speak, he unbuttoned my shirt and let the fabric fall open. The cold bar sent a chill through me as my stomach pressed against it. Raymond's hands were like fire in comparison to the cold air. He palmed my breasts through my bra and moaned as my nipples hardened beneath the lace.

"What happened to the armored bra?" He bit my neck. "Were you hoping this would happen?"

"Shut up," I moaned as he continued to play with my nipples. I tried to push off the rail and turn on him, but he stopped me.

"What are you doing?" I asked. "Let me—"

"Not this time." He put his hand over my mouth to stop me from talking. "Ms. Brown, always in control. This time, you submit to me."

Mouth still covered, I felt him undo my pants and then slide them down along with my panties, just far enough to gain access to me. His hand slipped from my mouth to the back of my neck as he pushed me forward and, with a deep growl, slipped his dick inside me.

I gripped the rail, holding on as Raymond took me from behind. He pounded into me, and I bit my lip, trying to stop from screaming. I couldn't be sure it wouldn't call attention to us. He lifted me, and I arched my back as he continued to fuck me and grab my tits.

"Damn, I love your breasts." He held them like handles, controlling the ride as he fucked me.

Then, as if he hadn't done enough, he slipped his hand between my legs to play with my clit.

"Oh God," I moaned.

"Remember what I said." He grunted in my ear as we both came closer to our finish. "There's no going back."

"Oh." I gripped the railing so hard, my knuckles burned.

"Say it, Jericha." He bit my shoulder then licked my neck like he was claiming his territory. "I want to hear you."

"I remember," I gasped.

He slid out of me until his head teased my opening then slammed back into me again. "What do you remember?"

I pushed back, urging him to do it again. "There's no going back."

"This pussy is mine now. Don't you ever forget that." Raymond smacked my ass and growled before picking up the pace. He fucked me faster, holding until I came, and then he pulled out, turned me around, and made me watch him finish.

With one hand on my tit and the other stroking his dick, Raymond shot his load on the ground. I should have known he was dangerous when I looked down at his orgasm splattered across the concrete roof and thought, *Damn, what a waste!*

"Everything's accounted for." Raymond put the tech bag in the back of my car. "Double checked it. No lost inventory."

"Thanks." I looked at him with a raised brow. He'd really gone from fucking me to talking about inventory.

We sat in the car together, not speaking, just existing in the moment. My mind felt fuzzy, like I'd been drinking all night, but I knew that was just the aftereffect of good sex.

"Take your time." Raymond placed his hand on my lap. "I'm going to head off. This way, you can go straight home."

"I'm fine with taking you back." I had to force a yawn back down my throat. Truth was, all I wanted was a hot shower and my bed.

"I'm a big boy." He glanced down at his lap then winked at me. "You know that."

"Don't be gross." I slapped his hand.

"Ha." He straightened his collar. "Well, yeah, I'll be fine. Besides, there is something I need to handle before I go home, and it's here in the city."

"Okay, sounds good."

"I'll speak with you tomorrow." He reached for the handle. "I meant what I said about handing off assets."

"Okay." I nodded.

I watched him walk away, admiring his ass in the pants he wore until he rounded the corner and I couldn't see him anymore. With a heavy sigh, I decided to head home, but just as I reached for the gearshift, I saw the phone between the door and the passenger seat.

"Damnit." I picked up the phone and realized Raymond had dropped it. I pulled the key from the ignition and hopped from the car. If I was quick, I might have been able to catch him.

I ran in the direction he went. As I turned the corner, prepared to call out his name, I skidded to a halt. Raymond stood just off in the distance with two of the guards who were with X. I stepped back, hoping they didn't see me, and watched.

What the hell is he doing with them?

I considered stepping forward and calling his name. Then, I wondered if this was some covert act of betrayal. Was Raymond someone I could trust? That thought was followed by a mental face palm for having fucked him without a condom. And as all these thoughts connected and cycled through my mind, I watched him closer than the others.

Raymond's head and shoulders were straight, lifted, assertive. Whoever these men were, they didn't intimidate him. Still, I could sense an imbalance in power. They weren't stronger than he was, but the person they worked for, X, was.

Then, it happened. The darkness moved—it fucking *moved*—like a curtain being opened. Behind the men, a passage appeared that wasn't there before. Then, the three of them stepped into the shadows and disappeared!

"What the fuck?" I backed away slowly, keeping my eyes locked on the spot where they vanished.

As soon as I made it back to my car, I peeled out of the parking garage and dialed the number of the one person I thought could explain what just happened. I tapped the steering wheel as the phone rang and felt relief wash over me when she answered.

"Hey, beautiful!" her energetic voice came through the speakers. "Long time, no hear! What's up?"

"Jackie, we need to talk!"

II

Jackie to the rescue

The next morning, I ignored two calls and several text messages from Raymond. It was halfway through the day when he gave up on his attempts. I didn't know what he wanted to discuss, but I wasn't about to talk to him, not until I figured out what the hell I had witnessed the night before. A man I'd let bend me over on the rooftop had stepped into the shadows and vanished, but what really got under my skin was how he didn't seem afraid.

It wasn't like those men dragged him kicking and screaming off to some unknown doom. He was comfortable with what happened and had walked into the abyss with no need for coercion. That alone had me ready to block his number. He not only knew what was happening, but he was part of it. Despite the desire to give him a swift boot out of my life, I couldn't. It wouldn't make a difference, because even if I ignored him all weekend long, he would show up to the office Monday morning, ready to talk.

I sat in the bay window, looking out at the entrance to the driveway. Jackie would be there soon, and hopefully, she could tell me what the hell was going on. I sipped the tea meant to calm my nerves, but even that wasn't working. The aroma filled my nose with every sip, and for a moment, I felt at ease, but in the next, my mind would go back to him—the feeling of his touch, the sound of his voice, the memories of that rooftop.

"Damn it!" I had to fight the urge to throw a full-on tantrum. How ridiculous would I look, kicking my feet and flailing my arms around in panic? But that's what I felt like on the inside. "Why did I let him do that to me? I knew I should have left his ass alone. A few more months, and I would have been free, none of this freaky, shadowy shit to deal with."

My gut told me by witnessing what happened, I'd opened Pandora's box, and there was no closing that bitch back up!

I'd spent the night, after talking to Jackie, scouring the internet looking for information, but of course, I only found a list of fictional books about beings who used shadows to bang fae girls. It had been a while since I'd read anything for pleasure, but some of those titles had me ready to dip my toe into the fantasy world again.

A wave of relief washed over me as the car pulled into the driveway. As I dashed for the door, the surrounding plants perked up. They always did when Jackie came around. Her energy was pure—chaotic but genuine. They loved it.

"I'm here!" she called; she stepped out of the car as I opened the door. She wore a cute pink jogger fit and white sneakers, perfect for comfy travel. "Now we can figure out what the hell is going on here."

"Please! Because I don't know. I tried looking it up and came up with nothing." I waited as she marched up the steps then gave her a big hug. "It's so good to see you."

"I've missed you too!" She kissed my cheek. "Let me guess: you used a standard search engine to look up what happened?"

"Of course I did," I chuckled. "I knew it would be a slim chance of coming up with something real, but I had to try."

"Girl, you know people like me work to keep all things magical out of sight and off the human internet. You have access to our database, so use it."

"I also know if I were to log into that thing, there would be people searching for *me* next." I tapped my temple with my fingertip. "Tell me I'm wrong."

"Okay, so that's true. There are some people out there looking for your kind." She winked at me. "We may have spotted a few others, by the way. You know, should you ever want to organize a family reunion."

"I'll pass on that." Did I want to know more about my bloodline? Yes. Did I want to sit in a room full of strangers talking about our abilities over a plate of spaghetti and potato salad? Absolutely not!

"I really thought you would want to build a community."

"You thought wrong." I pointed her to the kitchen table, where she sat down and pulled a laptop out of the bag she carried on her shoulder. "Now, you get comfy and do what you need to do so you can tell me what the hell I saw last night."

"I don't have to search for it. I brought the laptop for online shopping." She winked at me. "I already know what you're dealing with."

"You do?" I quickly sat down across from her. "Well, what is it?"

"You got shadow walkers in your neighborhood." She said it as if I was supposed to know what she was talking about.

"Shadow walkers? What the hell is that?"

"It's exactly what it sounds like. They are supernatural beings who can use shadows to cross space and time. But those are the advanced baddies." Her voice lifted with budding intrigue as she reported her findings. "Apparently, some of them can do a lot with the shadows, depending on their type and how old they are. The more they age, the stronger they get. As far as I found out, there are twelve known kinds. Most are weak, but some are powerful and can even cross between worlds."

"This is insane." I shuddered and immediately thought about the hooded figure known as X. I knew something felt off about them. Were they also a shadow walker? Maybe X was the powerful, realm-crossing kind. But if that were true, what did that mean about Raymond?

"Agreed." She nodded.

"What am I going to do?" My heart raced, and my mind created a laundry list of problems this could cause me.

"What do you mean? You saw it, they left... Move on with your life?" She paused then pointed her finger at me, drawing quick spirals in front of my face. "Unless you left something out of your little recap last night."

"Maybe I did." I chewed my lip. I hadn't mentioned my relationship with Raymond at all.

"Like what?" She closed the laptop, leaning forward like a dog begging for a treat.

"Like, the guy I saw walk into the shadows works for me." I started off light, easing her into the full truth.

"Fire him." She shrugged, always ready to throw a man away. That was why we all loved her! "Problem solved. You know, you could have told me that over the phone." She narrowed her eyes.

"Maybe." I nodded.

"Give me more detail. What happened?"

"We just finished a job, and there were four men there. They were a part of the meeting. Afterwards, well, some things happened, and he left his phone in my car. I went to chase him down, and when I made it to him, I saw him with the guys. Things looked tense, and then…"

"Then they walked into the shadows," she finished my thought. "Wait, you said some things happened… What was it?"

"Um…" I hesitated.

"You're acting like you banged one." She laughed, but when I didn't join her, she looked at me like I was crazy. "Oh, shit! You did, didn't you?"

"Well—" I continued.

"What?" She gasped. "I knew it. There's something more!"

"We may have been…intimate." I dropped my head. I refused to watch the range of shifting emotions in her expression.

"Intimate. Oh my God. Don't tell me you actually fucked the demon!" She slapped the table and started laughing. "Girl, I was just joking! Oh, this is too damn good! Jericha! How could you?"

"Demon?" I hung onto that word. "What do you mean, demon?"

"Well, I mean, that's what we have them classified as. They originate from the same place, I think."

"Okay, no. I'm gonna be sick." I swallowed the lump in my throat. "There is no way."

"Girl, you've had worse. Trust me, I know."

"Funny, Jackie." I held my stomach. Each time I thought about the word demon, my insides twisted. "I'm actually starting to feel nauseous now."

"Don't be dramatic." She winked. "Did you wrap it up, or should we expect shadow babies soon?"

"Funny, Jackie."

"Tell me all about him…and did he do anything special while you were with him?"

"No! I thought he was a normal human," I assured her. "You know I don't like to mix it up with magical men."

"What's with you?" She tapped on her laptop then sucked her teeth, clearly not pleased with what she found. "Only hooking up with human men. Is that because you can control them better with that plant magic?"

"Sort of." I chewed my lip. "Explains why he seems so damn resistant to my ability. You know how they used to call me a siren? I could play with men whenever I felt like it, and they would just do what I wanted. Raymond isn't like that. He wants me, but he maintains control." I could use the connection to the plants to do a lot more, like how the perfume I wore was a blend I created. It was hypnotic to human men and made them my play toys.

"We know how you like to stay in control of everything." She laughed. "Broke so many hearts because of that."

"Hush. I don't need you to get on my case too."

"What do you mean?"

"It's work." I waved off the question. "I'm being advised to let Natalie take on more of the workload."

"She's competent." Jackie nodded in agreement. "Why wouldn't you?"

"We aren't talking about that. Focus. Shadow walker."

"Right." She sighed. "But you brought it up, remember that. Look, if you don't want to see the man, just walk away—unless you think he will go stalker on you. Is that what you're worried about?"

"No, honestly, that's the last thing I worry about when it comes to him." I didn't mention I was concerned about him vanishing altogether. That was a new development I had yet to work through in my own head.

"So, what's the problem?"

"The problem is, he doesn't just work with me. He's a business partner—a business partner who is apparently from hell and is clearly tied up with some terrible people." I took a deep breath. "And yeah, I'm still contracted to work with him for a few more months. He talked about dissolving the contract early. Maybe this was why. He knew this shit was about to pop off."

"HA!" Jackie laughed. "That's fucking funny!"

"I forgot how much you love to laugh at the pain of others." I paused. "Help me."

"Lucky for you, I cleared my schedule to be here. It also gave me an out for a pixie problem."

"Pixies?" I shuddered.

"Yeah, you know those evil little things! They love any reason to pop off. Apparently, they have beef with some local shifters. When you called, I quickly passed that task to Miguel, who sends his regards, of course." She laughed. "You should have seen his face! I don't know why I didn't think to have my camera out to record!"

"He blamed me, didn't he?" I shook my head. "How could you do that?"

"Of course he did. You think he had the balls to blame me?" She laughed. "Said you owe him some of your special tea in exchange for his services."

"I'll get right on that." I glanced at my supplies on the counter to see if I had enough to make the blend he preferred. When I looked back at Jackie, there was only one question on my mind. "How is she?"

"Whitney?" she sighed. "I should have known you were going to ask about her. I don't think I can remember the last time we talked when you didn't."

"Yeah, I know. I can't help it. Besides, we don't talk that often anymore, so I have to catch up on everything!"

"Your sister is fine." Jackie smiled. "Don't worry. I'm still watching over her, and so is Maverick. He's gotten so big. I'm pretty sure he's done growing. It was a thoughtful gift for you to give her. He's grumpy but looks out for her."

"You think she will ever be ready to learn about me?" I asked.

"Will you be?" She challenged my question. "You know that goes both ways. Last I checked, you weren't ready to tell her about your connection."

"I don't know. She still doesn't have any abilities, right?" I sighed. "It's hard enough to say *hey, I'm the sister you didn't know about, adoption ripped us apart,* but on top of that adding, *oh, and we come from a magical bloodline, and you may or may not develop powers of your own one day.*"

"That is a lot, and no, she doesn't have any abilities. But maybe you can save that part of the conversation for a future topic." She shrugged. "Just a suggestion. But you know, the longer we keep this a secret, the more upset she's going to be, more so at me than you. Because, you know, I'm her best friend. There isn't enough sushi in the world to cover keeping a lie like this."

"I forgot about your sushi pact. That's still so weird to me." I slumped in my chair. "Damnit. Yeah, maybe I'll think about coming clean soon."

"Is that what you're waiting for?" she asked. "For her powers to show up? Do you think that will make it easier to do?"

"Kind of. Don't you think that would be easier to connect over?"

"If you say so." She stood. "I'm going to go check into my hotel. You know I don't ride sofas anymore. I'll be back a little later. We need to get food and catch up!"

As I watched her drive away, I thought about my sister, Whitney.

Jackie was the reason I found out about Whitney. We met while she was still in college and, oddly enough, Whitney was one of Jackie's roommates. We didn't figure out the connection until she came to me with her other roommate, Lena.

They were planning to cast a spell of protection for Whitney and came to me for some herbs they couldn't find. It was during that exchange I felt the energy that lingered in the hair they took from Whitney for the spell. It was a small thing, but something inside me wouldn't let it go.

When I saw Whitney, my gut told me to dig deeper. She looked like me but younger. She preferred braids while I loved to sport a fluffy afro whenever I could. We met a few times, only briefly, and I vowed to never interfere with her life, but my heart told me who she was.

I said nothing to Jackie because I wanted to be sure. So, I went into investigative mode and eventually found the original adoption agency that split us up, and sure enough, Whitney was my sister. I was happy she hadn't bounced around too many homes like I had. She was younger, more adorable, and had been adopted a full two years before me.

She lived with one family who took great care of her, and even after they had another daughter, they still cared for her the way a parent should. I didn't know if Whitney knew she was adopted, and for years, I told myself I didn't want to be the one to lift the veil on that secret. But even after Jackie told me Whitney knew everything, I couldn't bring myself to do it.

I cleared away the cups from our tea. Knowing Jackie, she wouldn't be back that night. As soon as she made it to her room, she would pass out, and I would see her in the morning. We could do brunch. There were a few new spots around town, two of them owned by Black women, so I was ready to go support!

Just as I turned to go to the backyard to pull the leaves I needed to make Miguel's tea, there was a knock on the door. I scanned the kitchen, wondering if Jackie had left something behind, but there was nothing.

"Maybe she just wants another hug." I laughed at the thought of Jackie's overt appreciation for my breasts. She wasn't blessed up top like I was, and would often sneak in a second and sometimes third hug for the feels.

I reached the door and swung it open without checking who was on the other side. "Did you forget something?" I immediately regretted that decision.

Standing on my porch wasn't my friend, arms opened for another hug. It was Raymond, jaw tight and eyes narrowed.

"Shit."

12

Yardwork

"**A**re you avoiding me?" Raymond asked with a straight face.

"Why would you think that?" I crossed my arms over my chest and peered around him, hoping to see Jackie's car. She was long gone.

"You haven't responded to a single text or answered my calls." He pulled his phone from his pocket and tapped the screen. Moments later, I heard my phone ringing from inside the house. "So your phone does still work."

"Yep. It works just fine." I looked back into the house, contemplating if I should answer it. Then, it hit me: Raymond was standing on my porch even though I'd never given him my address. "Wait, how did you figure out where I live?"

"We both work in security, Jericha. I wouldn't be good at my job if I couldn't do something as simple as figure out your address."

"That's still pretty damn creepy." I raised a brow at him. "Is that what you do to anyone who doesn't answer your call?"

"Stop deflecting. What's the problem here? I told you once you crossed the line with me, you couldn't walk it back." He placed his hand on the doorframe above my head and leaned in closer. "Are you switching up on me? And don't lie to me. Something's up, or you wouldn't have cursed when you saw me standing here."

"I was just expecting someone else. A friend." I shrugged and tried to appear as uninterested as possible. "She's supposed to come back for dinner."

"Seriously, Jericha?" He cocked his head to the side and held back a laugh. "Telling me your friend is coming back. A tactic so I won't do something to you? Do you think I plan to hurt you?"

Okay, so he saw right through me.

"Problem? Why are you jumping to conclusions?" I chose to gaslight him instead of admitting he'd caught me.

"Clearly, something is wrong." He looked around. "You're hiding out, ignoring my calls, and acting like you don't trust me."

"Well, you did find my address like a stalker. But despite that, you're wrong. I've just been busy dealing with some personal things."

"Can I come in?" he asked. "Maybe I can help."

"No." I stepped out onto the porch and pulled the door shut behind me. "It's not something you can help with. Hence why I had my friend here. I told you she was coming back so you wouldn't think I had time for a long visit, but I guess that went over your head."

"Okay." He took a step back from me. "Something is off. I don't know why you won't tell me, but that's fine. I just wanted to make sure you were okay. Also, I left my other phone in your car. I need it."

"Oh, right. I saw it...after I left. Can't believe I forgot about that." I pointed to my garage. "It's still in the car. I'll grab it."

"I'll come with you," he insisted.

Not seeing a point in stopping him, I pointed at the front of the garage. "Wait there."

"You seriously won't let me inside?" he scoffed.

"I didn't invite you over here, so no. If you arrive with an invitation, you can come inside."

I went inside, leaving him on the step. I walked through the house and into the garage from the connected door then manually opened the garage door with the switch on the wall. As the door lifted, Raymond stood there like a model posing under bright studio lights, and I berated myself for staring so intently at his revealed body. No, I didn't need to let my eyes linger on his powerful thighs or his imposing arms, but I did.

"You know this is ridiculous, right?" Raymond called out to me as the door finished its accension. "I've been inside you, but I can't come into your house?"

"Don't question my boundaries, just respect them." I jutted my chin out, challenging him to say anything else.

"Fair enough." He held his hands up and waited as I reached into the car to grab the phone.

"Damnit," I fussed after realizing the phone had slipped out of reach. The damn thing had slid in between the seat and the center console.

Damn my chubby fingers! I thought to myself as I tried adjusting the seat, hoping that would give me a better chance.

"Are you okay?" I heard his voice and could tell he'd come into the garage, but I didn't look back to confirm. "Do you need help?"

"No, I'm fine. I got it. Your phone slid under the seat. I'm trying to reach it," I fussed as I reached further. My fingertips touched the thing, but I couldn't get close enough. I leaned further into the car, scooting my ass up in the air as

I stretched my arm, trying to reach it. "If this damn seat would go back a little further, I could get it."

I paused when I felt the warmth behind me. He wasn't touching me, but he was close enough that if I moved an inch, my ass would be against his dick. I clinched my cheeks as if that would do anything to help the situation. *Yeah, girl, suck those yams in!*

"Let me help," Raymond offered again.

"Um, I got it." I wiggled some more, grunting as my efforts actually pushed the phone deeper into the crevice. "Fuck."

"Come on, don't be like that." He touched my shoulder then stepped aside to give me room to move. "I know you can do anything you put your mind to, but this is ridiculous."

"Fine," I relented and let him take over the effort. "Have at it."

"Thank you." He nodded as I moved out of the way.

I stood aside and rolled my eyes, ready to laugh at his failure. If I couldn't get it, I was sure he would have no better luck. I prepared to ogle his ass the way I was sure he had done me, but it only took him a few seconds before he had it in his hands.

"Easy." He stood and waved the phone at me.

"Great." I clapped slowly. "Glad you managed. Thanks for stopping by."

"Jericha, what's the problem?" He slipped the phone into his pocket. "I hate to keep repeating myself, but clearly, there is an issue here. Talk to me."

"I don't know what you mean." I shrugged. "Well, you have your phone now. Thanks for coming."

He closed the car door but didn't leave. Raymond stood defiantly next to the car and waited for me to give in. I would not.

"You're not going to leave, are you?" I asked.

"No." He shook his head. "Not until you talk to me."

"Fine. Then you're going to work." I looked over at the garden supplies stocked at the back of the garage. "I hope you don't mind getting dirty."

"What?" he asked.

"I got some weeds to pull." I grabbed a pair of garden gloves from the wall and threw them at him. No, I wasn't planning on doing the yardwork, but I figured I might as well get something out of the awkward situation.

"You can't be serious." He laughed. "You prefer yardwork over conversation?"

"Oh, now you're ready to leave?" I scoffed. "Just like a man. They want to be all up in your business until there is some real work to do."

"Well, that's a sexist thing to say." He sighed and slipped the gloves on. "I'm not scared of a little work."

"Great!" I turned to the door at the back of the garage that led into the backyard. "Follow me."

He stepped into the yard and gasped. "Wow, this looks amazing. It's like a little oasis back here."

"It's my place of peace." I pointed at him. "So don't mess anything up!"

"I'll do my best." He nodded. "No promises, though. Where do I start?"

I really didn't have anything I wanted him to do, but the moment he asked, I spotted a patch of weeds growing by the fence. I left him admiring the yard and walked over to the patch. They were new buds and would take little time to deal with, but I had to make him work harder than that.

I glanced back at him to make sure he wasn't looking then touched the weed. I felt the power pulse through my hand like sparklers. With each stroke of my finger, I imbued my magic into its roots, making it grip into the land stronger. More weeds sprouted up quickly and bowed to my presence. Did I need to make these weeds more stubborn to pull? Maybe not, but I wanted him to experience what I felt when he said he wouldn't leave me alone. It felt like poetic justice.

"I have some stubborn weeds here," I finally called back to him. "You're big and strong. Maybe you can pull them out for me."

"That's all you need?" He rolled up his sleeves, flexing as he did. "And here I thought you had some real work for me to do. Won't even need these gloves."

"I'm sure you'll make quick work of it." I stood. "That means you'll be able to head on home a lot sooner."

Raymond walked around me and pulled the gloves from his hands, making an exaggerated display of it as if he was trying to tantalize me. He kneeled, gripped the weed by the neck, and pulled. Veins in his arms and hands popped out. Sweat beaded on his forehead as he tugged at the weed that would not give. The man pulled so damn hard, he lost his grip and fell flat on his ass.

"Maybe you do need the gloves." I picked them up from the ground where he dropped them and waved them at him. "They'll help with that weak grip of yours."

"What the hell?" He stood and dusted himself off. "My grip isn't weak. Those weeds are fucking bionic."

"Bionic weeds, really?" it took everything I had in me not to laugh in his face. "Look, I know they're stubborn. I can't seem to figure it out. I've tried everything to pull them out of the ground."

"You sure this isn't a trick?" He looked at me. "Something isn't right here."

"A trick? Now why would I have weeds planted as a trick?" I crossed my arms in offense to his words. "Do you think I thought you were coming over here and planted this for you? Do you know how ridiculous you sound right now?"

"I don't understand how this is possible. It's like trying to pull a chain wrapped around a boulder." He kneeled beside the weeds, trying to get a better look. He did another gentle tug and grunted. "How are they so firmly in the ground?"

"Your guess is as good as mine. I was going to call in a professional to figure it out." I sighed. "Guess I'll still be doing that."

"You don't need to call anyone." He protested the thought, just as I expected. "I'll figure this out myself."

"You're not going to give up?" I bit my lip to stop my laughter again. That male ego was working overtime. It looked like even with creatures from other worlds, men were all the same.

"Do I look like the type of man who gives up that easily?"

"I guess not. You wouldn't be here bugging me if you were." I winked at him playfully. "Well, while you do that, I have some other stuff to work on in the garden, and I'll just be over here."

I watched him as he continued his sabotaged attempts at pulling the weed until he reached the point of near exhaustion. While he repeatedly embarrassed himself, I gathered the herbs I needed to make the tea for Miguel. When I was done and after I had laughed at him more than enough, I decided to give him a break. I also had to do something before he tore up my garden.

The man went into the garage and had things clattering around while he searched for something to dig with, and the last thing I wanted was him ripping up the dirt. I touched the ground, closed my eyes, and focused on my energy. The pulsing slipped from my fingertips, traveling through the ground and signaling the weeds. It was time to let up.

"Maybe give it one more try before you rip up my yard?" I offered when Raymond reappeared carrying a garden hoe.

"I—" He paused. "Okay, fine."

I was already ready to laugh as he marched over to the weeds because I knew exactly what was about to happen. And it did! With one powerful pull, the big, strong man went flying backwards onto his nice, firm ass. But that time, he held the weeds up, a hard-fought trophy.

"I told you I'd get it done." He flexed as if he'd won an Olympic gold.

"I'm glad you figured it out without tearing up my yard." I laughed and pointed at his pants, where there was a big hole in the inner thigh. "Too bad we can't say the same about your pants."

"A casualty of war." He pointed to the sky, where the sun had already dropped closer to the horizon. "And I did it before the sun set."

I clapped slowly. "Very proud of you. Now you can leave."

"You mean to tell me I did all that work and you still won't be real with me?" He stood.

"Is that why you did this?" I rolled my eyes at him. "To try to get something out of me? You should have told me that, and I could have stopped you from wasting the effort."

"This is about last night, isn't it?" He pressed.

No, I wasn't ready for it.

"What?" I took a step back from him. Did he know what I saw? Was he about to snatch me up and drag me into the shadows to protect his secret? Was I being a little dramatic? Yes to the last question.

"You're having regrets." He took a deep breath. "That's what it is, isn't it? You took it there, and now you're wishing you hadn't."

"I'm..." That was not at all what I expected from him. Was Raymond feeling insecure?

"Don't say you aren't. You're acting like a totally different person now. It's the same way you did after what happened in the gym. Look, I know I said there is no going back, but I'm not going to force you to be with me. I just don't want to play games. If you don't want this, don't chicken out and ghost me. Open your mouth and say so."

"Are you looking for an actual relationship here?" I didn't know what else to say. Yeah, I knew he wanted to fool around, but I didn't think the man was trying to build something serious, though that's what it sounded like. "I thought this was just something fun until you leave. You are still leaving, right? That's still the plan?"

"Yes, that is the plan, but—"

"But what?" I scoffed. "Look, I really don't want to sound like a bitch right now, but what exactly do you expect to happen here? Did you think I would be falling all over you after a hookup with no promise of anything more? What happened to all that talk about you not being like the guys I dealt with before? Because this is exactly how they sound."

"It's not like that. I just want to make sure we aren't about to go back to you awkwardly avoiding me."

"I didn't answer you for half a day, and you found my information and popped up on my step. That's weird as fuck, not something a man who is so secure would do. I'm starting to think that was all an act."

"Wow." He took a step back, bobbing his head like he was sorting through what I said.

"Wow, what? Am I wrong?" I narrowed my gaze. "Or is there something else you aren't telling me that would make this make sense?"

His jaw clenched, and just as his lips parted, the energy around the yard shifted. The sun dipped further into the horizon, and I felt it. The surrounding plants cowered. It wasn't their usual recoil at the end of the day. This was something more. They felt fear. Why?

"Shit." Raymond moved, pushing me behind him as he faced the fence where the trees stood, spreading their canopy and giving the yard a blanket of privacy from nosy neighbors.

"What are you doing?"

"Stay back," he ordered.

I could have tried to debate him, but it didn't seem like the right time to do so, especially as I peered around him to the area beneath the trees. The shadowed space grew darker, the air growing heavy and still, like an unseen presence was filling the void. Suddenly, it felt suffocatingly hard to breathe, despite the fact that we were standing outside. Panic tightened my chest, shallow breaths catching in my throat, each one a struggle. Raymond tensed, his muscles bunching in silent anticipation.

A static itch started in my ear, and the sound of energy sizzling filled the air. The sensation of running my fingers across the surface of an old television that had been left on idly started in my palms. Though that fuzzy sensation reminded me of a more innocent time, I knew it wasn't a good sign. Danger was coming.

Two heartbeats later, that shadowed space beneath the trees parted. It was hard to tell that it opened, but through squinted eyes, I could see layers of darkness folding back like a flower opening to the sun. At first, I couldn't see much, but then, there was movement. Outlined in gray smoke, bodies formed like sharks breaking the ocean waves.

Their forms looked mutated, large, off center. There were sharp edges and humps in places there shouldn't be. I expected them to look like Raymond, like a human, but they were nothing like him. There were no golden ratios used in the creation of these monsters.

The first body stepped out fully into view: a creature with yellowed skin. It had spikes down the bridge of a wide nose with three nostrils and thick fur that covered its bare shoulders. It grunted as it stepped aside, allowing space for the others who followed. Each one was massive, dangerous, and I quickly realized Raymond couldn't face them on his own.

The last one stepped out, the fifth in the crew. He pushed to the front of the group and locked his eyes on Raymond quickly. His mouth spread into a wide grin, allowing drool to spill down his chin.

"I'm sorry," Raymond said without looking at me just seconds before they attacked.

It was one of those moments I would have expected to slow down, but it didn't. Everything happened quickly. The first two demons charged. They targeted Raymond, ignoring my presence entirely. They weren't there for me. I fell back, watching and hoping for the best.

Raymond met them with force, never backing down. At first, he fought like a human, with fists and hands, but then, it changed. His limbs stretched and became wisps of themselves. It was as if he were becoming the shadow. I watched him throw out a punch, and as he did, his hand phased into nothing before appearing on the other side of the yard to slam against the jaw of a man. He did the same thing with every blow—kicks, punches, elbows, whatever he could to keep them from me. But it wasn't enough. They outnumbered him, and though he looked strong, I knew he wouldn't last long.

So much for keeping my secret.

I kicked the shoes from my feet and gripped the dirt with my toes to ground myself in my power. It took seconds to tap into the connection between myself and the land. Those plants that had cowered before perked up, ready and willing to aid me in my fight.

It took another moment for me to set my intention. This wasn't a gentle request. This was a brutal one. I needed to fight, to defend myself and Raymond.

As if it were waiting for such a request, the land responded with exhilaration as for the first time in years. I used my connection to the Earth to hurt another being.

But these things weren't from Earth. They were ugly and brutal and deserved to be taken down.

Just as one of the beasts turned its eyes on me, the vibration spread from my body into the ground, and moments later, vines that climbed the side of the fence shot out at the monster. They grew, tripling in length as they tied around the enemy and held it in place, its chest bared to the assault of roses. Their thorns, fortified by magic, shot out like bullets through the night and penetrated its chest. It let out a powerful roar as it fought against the vines.

I kept as much distance as I could, allowing Raymond to take up the hand-to-hand combat while relying on my magic to support him. Those same weeds he'd pulled up. I dug a hole with my hands and stuck them back in the ground. After a few strokes for confidence, they became rooted in the ground and then stretched beneath the surface, shooting up sprouts in various areas. The weeds grabbed hold of their ankles, locking monsters in place and making them easier targets for Raymond.

Even with nature on our side. I knew I had to do more. I had to fight. So, I did what I knew best. I put my fist up and chose a target. But I wasn't dumb enough to think I could do it without help. As I marched forward, a vine shot out to me, wrapping a protective layer around my hands, pulling rock and dirt with it to fortify the glove.

As soon as it was done, I clenched my fist, and magic radiated from within me, pulsing across the surface of the eco-friendly accessories. I caught Raymond's eye as I moved forward. He looked shocked, as expected, but now wasn't the time to pause and ask questions. He had his secrets, and now he knew for sure I had mine. Just as we had the night of the attack at the studios, we fought. I singled out the smallest of the demons to focus my energy on. Though the creature had hands, four to be exact, I managed my own. If I could keep it occupied long enough, Raymond could take care of the others.

My plan seemed to be working until I heard Raymond cry out to me.

"Jericha, watch out!" His voice had a frightened rasp to it that stopped me in my tracks.

I turned in time to see a pointed tail coming straight at my face. I held my hand up, hoping to protect myself, but I didn't have to. The tree next to me reached out, extending its branches and slamming down on the demon attacking me. It broke through the tail, and the demon wailed as it turned and ran back into the shadowy portal.

It vanished, but while I was distracted, the one with all the hands moved in on me. It wrapped two of the arms around my waist and grabbed my hands with the others, stopping me from moving.

That would have been smart, but bare feet left me connected to the Earth. I dug my toes into the dirt, and those same weeds sprouted up around us. They moved in between us and, with the help of the vines, ripped us apart.

"Crush it!" I called out, and the plants worked together, tightening as they wrapped around the demon. It cried out in pain as bones broke, flesh ripped, and odd-colored blood spilled from its eyes and ears.

After that, everything stopped. The other demons retreated and, as the shadowed portal snapped shut, the one wrapped in vines melted into a sickly puddle.

"Damnit. That can't be good for my garden." I frowned at the mess.

"How did you do that?" Raymond breathed heavily as he stepped next to me.

"This is my house. I'll ask the questions." I headed inside.

"Where are you going?" he called out to me.

"I need a drink."

13

I'll take Bourbon

"Tea?" Raymond looked at me sideways as I pulled out the leaves from the cabinet. "I thought you meant something stronger."

"Oh, hell no. I'm not about to get drunk with demonic things stepping out of the shadows!" I fussed at him.

"Okay, but I'm going to need something with some weight on it." He leaned back in the chair and reached his hand out. It vanished for a moment, reappearing with a bottle of bourbon.

"So you're a shadow walker?" There was no sense in beating around the information I already knew, since he was performing party tricks.

"Yes." He cracked open the bottle as I handed him a glass. "Wait. How did you know that?"

"I saw you last night." I waved him off. "You were with those men who had accompanied X. I followed you after I realized you left your phone in the car."

"And that's why you've been avoiding me." He sighed.

"Yes." I placed the kettle on the stove. "I needed time to process what the hell I saw. I've seen a lot of freaky things in my life, but never that."

"But you already knew what I was. How did you figure it out?"

"I had to phone a friend."

"The one you said was returning for dinner."

"Yep." I nodded.

"And what are you?" he asked. "Clearly, you aren't new to any of this. So, what's your deal?"

"There really isn't a name for what I am. Descendant of magical alien abilities, connected to nature and can use it at my will." I shrugged. "Call it whatever you want. Closest definition is a green witch because of my connection with nature. Except I don't really do spell work, though a lot of witches come to me for what they need. I have the best stuff."

"That explains a lot." He grinned.

"Does it?" I asked.

"I know a few others with similar abilities. They're control freaks too. They also have that same hypnotic ability over non-magical beings." He sipped his drink and smiled. "That explains why I've had to fend off that sad sap a few times."

"Who?" I raised a brow.

"The guy who showed up that night. What was his name? Deonta?" He tapped the table with his finger. "He started showing up at the office early in the morning, trying to catch you off guard. That's why I was coming in early for a while. I had to set him straight."

"That's why? I thought you were just being a pest." I chuckled. "Why would you do that?"

"Of course you did. I wanted to protect you and Natalie. He could have hurt her, since she often gets there before you. But I think he's gotten it through his thick head now." He laughed. "Now that I know about you, I realize you could have handled it on your own."

"True." I paused; I hadn't considered Natalie's safety when Deonta showed up at my office. "I have a solution for men who get a little too enthusiastic. It's an elixir I make that works like a memory eraser."

"You make them forget about you?" He scoffed. "That's a shame."

"It may be, but it's the simplest solution. It's pretty easy to do when they don't know anything real about me. Most of them never even know my real name. Deonta found a way around that."

"Damn, woman." He sucked his teeth. "You're a lot tougher than I thought."

"Anyway, we're not here to discuss all that. There are more important things to focus on." I sat at the table across from him. "Why are you being attacked?"

"Getting down to business, as always." Raymond fiddled with his cup.

"Yes." I looked out the window. "There's no time to waste skirting around the issue. Tell me everything."

"I have enemies." His shoulders lifted and dropped with a deep sigh.

"Enemies who are clearly not from this world," I commented. "I exist on the outskirts of the supernatural community, but even I would have heard about those things if they were from Earth."

"They're from the Bane," Raymond confirmed. "A long way from here."

"And what exactly is the Bane?"

"Another world often described as a hellscape," he explained. "It's where I'm from originally. Things went bad while I was there, so I left. I thought I could live here peacefully, and for a long time, I have. But it seems my problems have followed me."

"Is this the moment you're going to explain to me what drama you had going on that made you need to run away from hell? Because if, after all these years, they still want to come after you for it, I'm sure it wasn't a minor issue."

"You're right. It was a big issue," Raymond started as the kettle whistled. "Someone died."

He waited for me to return to the table with the tray I'd prepared, and as I began making my tea, he continued.

"It was someone very important, and they lost their life because of me. I made a mistake, and I knew no one in the Bane was going to let me forget it. A few people wanted to take my head because of it. If they have their way, I won't live much longer. They will end me, but not before dragging me back to hell to make sure the right people know about it."

"So you did something that led to the death of someone important, and now you're on the run for it?" I thought about his words as I added honey to my cup. "Did you kill them? Are you leaving that part out of the story?"

"No. I wouldn't do that. I've killed a lot of people in my lifetime. That's not something I'm afraid to admit. What happened was a mistake, a lapse in judgment on my part. It's something I can never take away. The wrong person lost their life, that's all I can say. And I will never forgive myself for that." He gulped down the rest of the drink before refilling his cup.

"So, what happens now? They know you're here; they're going to keep coming after you. Those things did not look like henchmen. Even if they give up, more will come. Am I correct?"

"Yes, you are. They work for someone a lot more powerful."

"X?"

"Not exactly. X is above them but still not the top of the chain," he explained. "It's a huge organization. You'd probably compare it to the mafia here on Earth, but it's so much bigger than that."

"And now they know where I live." I rolled my eyes. "Demonic mafia about to be busting down my damn doors."

"That's why I came here. I wanted to make sure you were okay. You weren't answering your phone. My mind went to the worst place. They saw us together, learned your energy signature, and they could have easily found their way to you. I was afraid they had hurt you. That's why I'm still here."

"Still here as in here in my home?" I glanced around the kitchen.

"As in, on Earth. I planned to leave. There are other places I can go where they won't be able to find me. That's why I decided to hand over everything to you.I probably should have left immediately, but I didn't. I couldn't."

"Why not?"

"Do you really have to ask that question?" He leaned back in the chair and looked me dead in the eye. "Do you not know why I would not want to leave this world? I've been here for decades and never had an issue, but suddenly, I feel tied to this place. Connected."

I ignored the implications behind his words. "How did they find you?"

"They came here looking for something else." He chuckled. "Isn't that just my luck? They came here for another demon who'd messed up, and while they were searching for him, they found my energy signature and followed it."

"Well, they know you're here. Leave," I said with naïve optimism. "Leave now, and all of this goes away, right?"

He snorted. "Do you really believe that?"

"No, I don't. Those things are going to keep coming after me to get to you. They think I'm more important to you than I really am, and that's some bullshit. Why should I have to deal with any of this? I swear to God, if I ever see Mitch's backstabbing ass again, I'm going to throat punch him."

"Mitch?" He raised a brow. "What does he have to do with this?"

"Isn't it obvious? If he hadn't screwed me over, I wouldn't have had to reach out to Rose for help, which means I would have never met you, which means

I wouldn't be dealing with any of this right now." I tied it all together while ignoring the look of increasing confusion on his face. "This is all his fault."

"Hey, as long as someone else is taking the blame for this, I'm all good." He chuckled and ran his finger along the edge of the cup. "Shit. I can't believe this is happening. I did everything right."

"Okay, what do we need to do?" My brain kicked into work mode. There was no sense in sitting around pouting about the situation. We had to take action. "How do I protect myself?"

"Now that they've seen what you can do, this is going to be a lot more complicated. Before, they just thought you were a human. They weren't worried about you. Now, they'll see you as a threat and are probably going to come back with more aggression. They're gonna want to know everything about you, and I'd be surprised if they haven't already started digging deeper into your past."

"Were those the same people from last night?" I asked. "I know you said they work for X, but are they the same guys? They didn't look the same."

"A couple of them, yeah, but the others weren't," he explained. "Most demons have to use a disguise when they come to Earth. They need to blend in."

"Damnit!" I fussed. "I can't have this demonic shit messing with my business. Wait...are you in disguise? Do you look like those things? I think I'm going to be sick."

"No, I look like this all the time. Well, kind of."

"What the hell do you mean, kind of?"

"When I'm in the Bane," he pulled up the sleeve on his arm to show me his tattoos, "these aren't tattoos. They're an extension of myself. Since I'm here, I keep them flat to my skin, but when I'm alone... Wait, I'll show you."

He stood and took his shirt off. Somehow, I kept my mouth closed; I didn't want to stop whatever he was about to do. Raymond took a deep breath, flexing the muscles in his arms and chest, and then wisps of smokey tattoos lifted from his body. They stood around his body like the aura of an animated character.

"I..." I stood from the table and put my hand over my mouth.

Then, before either of us could say another word, my forever protector jumped into action. Kaa slithered onto the table, lifting into a protective pose. She hissed and stared Raymond down.

"What the hell is that?" Raymond pointed at her.

I didn't get to answer him, because Kaa took immediate offense. I'd only seen her do the quick expansion once before, but her body grew so big, she took up half the kitchen. Her tail slapped the mugs from the counter and knocked over the kettle, spilling hot water everywhere. As I jumped back to avoid getting burned, she reached out for Raymond.

Kaa wrapped her body around him, quickly constricting. Raymond, with a look of disbelief, phased into a shadowy mist to avoid her. He reappeared on the other side of the room.

"Jericha, do something!" He pointed at me. "Get that thing under control."

Kaa, clearly annoyed by the failure, hissed and redirected her attack.

I jumped in front of her. "Kaa, stop!" I held my hand out to her. "He is a friend. It's okay."

Kaa wasn't convinced. She continued to hiss and sway her head, as if looking for a way to get around me without hurting me.

"Kaa, chill!" I raised my voice and immediately felt bad when she looked at me like I had crushed her soul. Kaa shrank back down, slowly backing out of the room as she did. "I'm sorry, I didn't mean it like that!"

"So, there is a lot I don't know about you," Raymond said as he peeked around the corner to make sure Kaa wasn't there.

"You're one to talk." I pointed at his shadow aura that still outlined his body.

"True." He pulled the shadows back to his flesh, and the tattoos reappeared.

"Ugh, she's going to be bitchy for at least a week after that," I fussed.

"What is that?" he asked. "And why do you call it a she?"

"Kaa...is my pet, sort of."

"A pet that looks like a plant but acts like a snake?" he huffed.

"You're literally from hell." I squinted and shook my head, jutting my neck out at him. "Are you telling me you haven't seen wilder things?"

"Right, sorry. That's just not something I would expect to encounter here." He looked around me to the hall where Kaa had exited. "Am I safe here, or do you have more of those things?"

"She isn't a thing," I corrected him. "And she's the only one. She's protective of me, and after what just happened out there, she has every right to be."

"Why didn't she come out?" he asked suspiciously.

"What?" I searched for a towel to clean up the spilled tea.

"During the battles, she stayed inside. She didn't sense the danger you were in? Why didn't she help then?"

"She might have been sleeping. I don't know." I shrugged. "She doesn't have a radar on me to know when I'm in trouble."

"Got it." Raymond sighed, and after a brief pause, he returned to our previous conversation. "Should we get back to trying to figure all of this out?"

"Yeah. I just wish I knew where we could start." A sigh escaped my lips as I gazed at the now-wasted tea, the faint scent of ginger still clinging to the air. "I'm good at figuring out stuff on Earth. I don't know anything about your world or those things that came from it."

"You said you had a friend, right? Who helped you figure out what I am?" Raymond put his shirt back on. "Seems like she would be a good resource right now."

"Yes, Jackie." I nodded. "She was here earlier."

"Is she actually coming back, or are you just telling me that to get rid of me?"

"She said she would come back, but Jackie is the type of person to get to her hotel and never leave again. If she's already in bed, she's not getting back out. But I think if I let her know demons actually attacked me tonight, she'd be well on her way."

"Good. Call her back over here. We're going to need all the help we can get." He looked at the broken bourbon glass and shook his head. "While you do that, I will go see if I can recruit some help of my own."

"We're really about to face off against some demons, aren't we?" I huffed. "This isn't just going away."

"Hey, I thought you'd be excited about the action. Think about it, Jericha. Me with my shadows and you with your vines." He waggled his eyebrows at me. "We could have a lot of fun."

"I'm going to choose to believe you aren't spewing innuendo right now." I waved him off. "Go do what you gotta do. I'll call Jackie and get her back over here."

"Believe what you want." He winked at me. "But the images I have in my mind aren't going away."

A shadowy wall materialized behind him, the air growing cold. With a wave, he faded into the darkness, leaving only a faint chill.

"That is not okay!" I rubbed my arms and waited for the chill to leave. I turned around to find my phone but saw Kaa. She'd returned and sat coiled on the hall floor.

"Kaa, I'm sorry, okay?" I immediately apologized to her. If she was back, it was for an apology. "I wasn't trying to be mean. I was just trying to stop you from killing our new friend."

Instead of her usual hiss, Kaa reared back and made a ticking noise that reminded me of being scolded by my mother.

"Maybe calling him a friend is a bit generous, but that's where we are right now. If we're going to survive whatever is coming next, we have to play nice." I retrieved my phone from the counter where I left it and cursed at the small chip on the screen. I could have fussed at Kaa about all the things she broke, but that would only make things worse. "There's no way I have time to get that fixed." I glanced back at Kaa, who rolled her neck like she was telling me I deserved the cracked screen.

Instead of engaging in petty behavior with her, I dialed Jackie's number, grateful when she answered.

"Look, I know I said I was coming back over, but—" Jackie started, but I interrupted her excuse for ditching me.

"The shadow walker came over and then demons attacked us." I took a deep breath; just saying the words had me ready to scream. "Get your ass back over here."

"Coming!"

The call ended, and Kaa hissed again before slithering away.

"Oh, get over it!" I fussed and went to clean the mess she'd made.

14

Jackie's Bag

"Is he back yet?" Jackie burst into my home carrying her signature duffel bag. This time, she wasn't coming to browse on the internet. She was ready for war. "Bring the shadow walker to me!"

I couldn't help but laugh at her. "Are you going to kill him?"

"If I have to. I'm not sure how to take out one of his kind." She slapped the side of the bag. "But I'm sure there is something in this bag that can get the job done. If nothing else, I'll have fun experimenting!"

"You're insane." I shook my head. "And no, he isn't back yet. Actually, I'm glad he isn't. It gives us some time to talk before he pops back in here."

"True. You can fill me in on all the details." She dropped the bag on the bench in the hall. "What do you have to eat? I was choosing to sleep instead of having dinner, but now that I'm up, I need grub!"

"They delivered sushi just before you got here," I said and had to keep from laughing when her eyes widened like I'd just presented her with a bag of diamonds.

"Oh, you know me so well!" She headed for the kitchen then paused. "Wait, what did you lie about? Unrequested sushi is for apologies. You know that."

"Nothing, but something tells me this is going to turn into a big thing, and, well, I want to butter you up ahead of time," I joked. "Besides, I know you're a lot nicer when you're well fed. I don't know what he's coming back here with, so I need to make sure we're good."

"Smart. I pop off when monsters appear. If you want me to be nice, you better have some nigiri in there!" she called back to me over her shoulder.

"Of course!" I made sure the door was locked before I followed her. "I didn't forget what you like."

By the time I made it to the kitchen, Jackie was sitting with Kaa on her shoulder. Kaa put her face close to Jackie's ear, as if she was telling her a secret. I rolled my eyes—I already knew what was coming next.

"What did you do?" Jackie snapped her fingers at me. "Why is this precious baby upset?"

I rolled my eyes. "Really? Since when is she a precious baby?"

"Since always!" Jackie fussed. "You upset her. Don't lie. That's what all this sushi is really for."

"You're both ridiculous. I still don't understand why she likes you. She hides from everyone else."

"I'm special, duh." Jackie rubbed Kaa's head with her finger. "She needs someone to love on her. Clearly, you're over here treating her like a bald-headed stepchild!"

"She tried to attack Raymond. I stopped her, and now she has an attitude. She'll get over it." I reached into the cabinet above the sink and pulled out the bottle of plant food. Kaa immediately perked up. She loved the stuff. "She's just like you, pouty until fed."

I poured a bit of the liquid food into a glass cup then added water to dilute it. When it was ready, I shook it at the drama queen then headed for Kaa's favorite pot. As soon as I poured the mixture into the soil, she was there. She slithered into the pot, rooted herself, then looked at me with that strange smile of hers. The petals around her head stretched out, an extension of her smile. She had forgiven me.

I returned to find Jackie, already done with the first tray of sushi and opening the second.

"You plan on sharing?" I quickly grabbed the second bag, pulling it away from her.

"Girl, you know you have to act fast!" She stood and headed for the fridge, opening it to find a fresh case of beer. "Oh, you really *do* love me!"

"Yeah, I do, so much that I put that nasty stuff in my house for you." I turned up my nose. It wasn't something I enjoyed, and despite previous vows to never waste my money on the stuff, I'd had several cases delivered the night before.

"Oh, to have people who understand you!" She skillfully popped the top off the glass bottle then returned to the table.

While she chugged the beer, I opened a container of dragon rolls, grabbed a piece, and popped it into my mouth, followed by a piece of ginger.

"With your fingers?" Jackie slid me a pair of chopsticks. "Act like a lady, please!"

"That's funny coming from you." I snatched the pair of chopsticks and opened them.

"So, give me the rundown." Jackie cracked open her second beer. "Tell me more about your shadow daddy."

"Shadow daddy?" I almost choked on my food. "Is that what we're calling him now?"

"You hooked up, right?" She tapped her chin. "More than once? That man has gotten under your skin. You can't deny it."

"Anyway." I rolled my eyes. "None of that is important right now. The threat is the focus."

"I'm right, I know it." She laughed. "If he wasn't under your skin, we wouldn't be talking about any of this, but I digress. You said he's looking for help?"

"Yes," I confirmed. "I told him I would call you, and he said he had some people he thought could help us. So, he went to go find them."

"Did he say what that help would look like?"

"No, and I didn't ask." I paused. "Now that I think about it, I'm not even sure where he went. I guess he could be in hell right now. You think he's going to bring back other demons?"

"It would make sense. Not like the guy from the local grocery store is going to be able to help us out here. We're going to need some power on our side."

"Right." My mind drifted off. What else would we need to be able to get through things?

"Are you okay?" She looked at me with concern. "I mean, you're usually a lot more on top of things than this, Jericha. What's going on?"

"Sorry, but the demons stepping out of the shadows kind of shook me up. It was a lot." I ate another piece of sushi. "It's one thing to hear about something. It's another thing to see it with your own eyes."

"I've watched you take down a werewolf while holding off a manic dragon pup." Jackie picked up her phone and opened my contact card. There, for the profile picture, was a photo of me and a baby dragon who nearly burned my entire afro off. "Be real. What's going on? You know I'm your friend, right? I'm not going to judge you."

I couldn't believe she still had the picture, but something about seeing that former version of myself opened the floodgates. Jackie was a safe space, as she always had been. "I'm under a lot of pressure right now, Jackie, and honestly, I'm just trying my best to keep it together. On top of business issues, staffing issues, resurfacing crap from my past, and then Raymond turning out to be a damn shadow walker just when I was—"

"Just when you were what?" She leaned in, gripping the bottleneck tightly. "What were you doing?"

"Nothing." I pulled back the confession. "I'd just gotten used to him being around, is all."

"Holy shit! You actually like this guy, don't you? I was just joking, but..." She narrowed her eyes. "You're not just tolerating him. You like him."

"Once again, I feel like you're focused on the wrong thing." I got up to grab a glass of water. "And you said something is off about me? When did you become so boy crazy?"

"Don't you dare try to deflect this..." Jackie stood, but I held my hand up to stop her when I felt the drop in temperature.

"Did you feel that?" I put the glass I'd retrieved on the counter. "The temperature just dropped."

"Nuh uh," Jackie shook her head and eyed the mostly consumed food. "You better not have fed me no damn tainted sushi. What do you mean the temperature just dropped? I feel fine."

"I think he's coming. The same thing happened when he left. It got really cold, and then the shadow appeared."

Just then, the corner of the room darkened, an unnatural shadow spreading like a stain, accompanied by a chilling sound of energy crackling. I stood with Jackie as we waited. Jackie immediately pulled a knife from her back pocket.

"Really?" I raised a brow at her.

"We don't know if what's coming through that thing is going to be friendly. They already attacked you once. What's stopping it from happening again?" Jackie slapped my shoulder. "Get it together, friend."

"You're right." I shook my head. That was why I wanted Jackie there. In moments when my judgment was cloudy, Jackie was there to bring clarity.

I slipped my hand under the table and pulled out the gun I stored there. After flipping the safety and checking the chamber, I pointed at the center of the shadow.

"Just gotta show me up, huh?" Jackie nudged me with her arm. "Bringing out the heavy artillery."

Then, Raymond's head poked through the shadow. "Jericha? It's me." His eyes widened when he saw the weapon in my hand. "We good?"

"Oh." I lowered my weapon with a sigh of relief and then placed my hand on Jackie's arm to reassure her, feeling the tremor in her muscles. She slipped the knife back into her pocket. "Just playing it safe. We're good."

"Good. I have someone I want to introduce you to. I'll be right back." He disappeared again, but the shadow remained.

"Oh, now I get it!" Jackie winked at me. "That man is fine! I'd be all out of sorts too!"

"Chill." I picked up her beer and handed it to her. "I don't know if that thing is soundproof!"

"Oh shit, my bad." She grabbed the beer and took a long sip. "I should just eat my sushi and hush, huh?"

"That would be nice."

"Okay, you didn't have to agree with me." She winked then reached for her sushi.

Jackie stood next to me with a tray of rolls in one hand and the chopsticks in the other. She happily stuffed her face while we waited for something to happen. I was ready to scream into the dark void when Raymond reappeared.

"Damn, it's about time," I fussed. "You just opened a portal in my kitchen and left it there. Is that even safe?"

"Oh, sorry about that. Time is different there. To me, I haven't been gone that long."

"Right." I sighed. "Where's your friend? I thought you said you were bringing help."

"I told them to hold back for a few so I could set the stage, so to speak."

"Are they actors?" Jackie pointed her chopsticks at Raymond. "Are they going to put on a little show for us?"

"Not exactly." He looked at my friend and smirked. "You must be Jackie. Nice to meet you."

"I'll let you know if that's mutual after your friends get here."

"Tough." Raymond nodded. "There are two others coming. The first is my brother."

Raymond reached his hand back into the shadow for a moment to signal the others. Then, he pulled his hand out and moved away. I held my breath, not sure what would follow, but I relaxed when a man who looked like him came through the shadow.

He was just an inch shorter, with short hair, but the smile, the eyes, and even the swagger were all the same.

"Jericha, Jackie, this is Cufio, my brother," Raymond introduced him.

"Brother?" I raised a brow. I couldn't remember Raymond ever mentioning having a brother.

"Nice to meet you." Cufio nodded.

"You too," I said, but I noticed how tense Jackie was beside me. "Isn't it nice to meet him, Jackie?"

"Oh, yeah, sure." She continued her assessment, looking both men up and down. "You mentioned there would be another?"

"Yeah, can we get this over with?" I added. "I really don't like that shadow portal thing being opened here for so long."

"Of course." Raymond grinned and stepped around Cufio. "Keep in mind, he prefers not to use a human disguise."

"Right." I glanced at Jackie, who was already staring back at me with a look that screamed, *What the hell is he talking about?*

Raymond stuck his hand into the shadow again to signal the next guest.

The air crackled with erratic energy as the shadowy figure stepped through the portal, leaving my heart frozen in my chest in stark terror. There was nothing to conceal his appearance; he made no effort to comfort us with a veiled expression of humanity.

His skin was the gray of weathered stone, leathery and seemingly dry to the touch. His immense size filled the room, head brushing the ceiling, three horns jutting from his forehead like wicked daggers. Two horns curled down around his pointed ears, and a third, larger horn jutted from his forehead, curving backward like a carefully sculpted mohawk, sharp and imposing. While Raymond and Cufio were dressed in ordinary clothes, his attire consisted of what appeared to be bark fashioned into waist-high trousers held up by elaborate suspenders.

"Is it friendly?" Jackie's voice broke the tense silence.

"I am not an 'it'," the demon responded.

"Oh, shit. Sorry." Jackie held her hands up.

"I agreed to help you, but I won't be insulted." The demon looked at Raymond, who whispered an apology for Jackie's comment.

"He's sensitive," Cufio joked. "Ease up, big guy. She didn't mean anything by it. Humans aren't used to seeing things like you walking around."

"This is Noville," Raymond introduced him, giving Cufio a warning glare.

"Are you a shadow walker?" The question fell from my lips before I looked at Raymond. "Is that what you really look like?"

"No." Raymond shook his head, and I could tell he was holding back laughter. "He's a stone demon."

"Like a gargoyle?" Jackie asked.

"No, not exactly, though they are mistaken often. He can control earth and stone, like an elemental." Raymond pointed at me. "Not unlike what you have with plants."

"I see." I looked at Noville. "It's nice to meet you, Noville. Thank you for coming here to help us."

"You're welcome. I owed a debt to," he paused, side-eying his friend before he continued, "Raymond. I plan to pay that off here."

"Uh uh," Jackie spoke up. "Why did you hesitate when you said his name? Is that not your real name?"

"No, it isn't. There aren't many Raymonds walking around hell. I had to choose a new name when I came to Earth." Raymond looked at me when he realized how shocked I was. "You didn't think I was a demon named Raymond, did you?"

"You gave me some of your back story but never mentioned changing your name or having a brother," I reminded him.

"You're right." He nodded. "I did leave some things out."

"You never told her about me?" Cufio placed his hand on his chest. "I'm hurt, brother."

"Cut it out." Raymond scoffed.

"What's your real name?" Jackie asked. "If I'm working with you, I'm calling you by your real name."

"Mnuktilous," he spoke with a challenging glare.

"Yeah, okay, Raymond works." Jackie picked up her beer and took a long swig.

"Glad you agree." Raymond waved his hand at the portal behind them, and it closed. "Now, we need to come up with a plan. Things in the Bane are moving quickly, and it won't be long before they attack again."

Just then, I felt a weird feeling, like pressure gripping around me, but it wasn't me. It came from the garden. I could sense the plants freaking out, like they were being suffocated. I moved to look out the window that looked out on the backyard and gasped as a man appeared almost out of nothing. Then, I realized the horns on his head shrunk until they were nothing. A demon.

"Um, please tell me that's one of your friends." I pointed out the window.

Raymond turned and looked out the window. "Damnit, what is he doing here?"

15

Meet the team

"I invited him." Cufio stepped next to Raymond. "I know you don't want to deal with him, but it just made sense."

"Am I missing something here?" Raymond tensed. The muscles in his arms flexed and his jaw tightened. "Why the hell would you invite him? He's the reason this is happening."

"He's also our best shot at getting out of this alive," Cufio explained. "I know you don't like him, but we have to think strategically here. He just faced off with the big guy and walked away alive. How many others do you know who can say that?"

"It's more than just not liking him." Raymond shot a warning glare at his brother. "That man has never been on our side, and now you want me to believe he is?"

"I've never had an issue with him. You two bumped heads, and that's unfortunate, but it's time to move past that, especially since your life is on the line, brother."

"You want to fill me in on what you're talking about?" I asked, pointing out the window. "Is that guy going to be a problem for us? If he's an enemy, why the hell is he standing in my yard?"

"Let me figure that out and then I'll let you know." Raymond looked at his brother and then headed out the door. "With me," he called back to Cufio.

"Coming!" Cufio called out then turned to me when Raymond was out of earshot. "It'll be fine. These two just have a tense history. They just need to hug it out."

"Do you actually think that will happen?" Jackie asked.

"Hey, anything's possible!" He smirked then ran out the door to catch up with his brother.

I watched them carefully as they walked out to meet the strange new guy. The murmur of their conversation was lost to me, coming through as only a frustrating hum. The newcomer mirrored Raymond's discomfort. He slipped his hands in his pockets and lifted his chin as he came face to face with Raymond. It looked like things could erupt into chaos at any moment.

"They better not destroy my garden. I already need to make up for the first fight out there." I looked over at Jackie, who joined me. "What do you think that's about?"

"Looks like bad blood." She popped a sushi roll into her mouth. "Enemies forced to work together. This is getting juicy."

"Really?" I scoffed at her. "With everything going on, you're still eating?"

"What? Should we let good sushi go to waste because demons are popping up? I think not!" Jackie winked at me. "Look, while they talk, I'm going to call some backup of my own. We need more help here. I'll be back."

Jackie left the kitchen, sushi and beer in hand, leaving me alone with Noville. We stared at each other awkwardly for a moment, and I realized he hadn't said much since arriving. I didn't know what to say to break the tension, so I turned back to look out into the yard.

"You're too kind to be with...Raymond." Noville spoke with the same hesitation around Raymond's name, reminding himself of the modification.

"Am I?" I turned back to the large demon, who looked too big to be in my kitchen. It was strange. His skin appeared rock hard when motionless, softening to normal skin as soon as he moved. "What makes you say that?"

"Your energy. It's not nearly as chaotic as his," Noville continued. "He usually surrounds himself with people who are just as wild in their spirit. People like your friend Jackie."

"Um, thank you?" I frowned; I didn't know what to think about his observation. I'd barely spoken since he'd been there, and yet he had already formed opinions about me.

Did he really just say my friend was more compatible with Raymond than I was? And why the hell does that annoy me so much?

"I hope you survive this. Most don't," Noville continued, and I immediately wanted to tell him to keep his thoughts to himself. "The shadow walkers are messy. You'd think they would be able to handle things better than they do, but their elusive nature often leads to them making mistakes because they think they can never be caught, despite all the times they have been in the past."

"You really need to work on your people skills." I sucked my teeth. "Are you trying to make me doubt myself?"

"I'm often told that." He nodded. "I prefer to be honest, but I do apologize. That wasn't my intention."

"Be honest when your honesty is requested. That should help a lot."

"Of course." He sighed.

"Can everyone in the Bane speak English?" I wanted to change the conversation but also avoid going back to the awkward silence in case he decided to share any more of his *honest* opinions.

"No, and I don't speak it either," Noville responded.

"Maybe you don't realize it, but we're speaking the same language, and I damn sure don't speak whatever is the natural tongue of your people."

Noville nodded again before opening his mouth. He reached his boney fingers behind his back tooth and pulled out what looked like a piece of bark. He held it out to me and spoke a garbled language I couldn't understand. As if satisfied with his display, he popped it back into his mouth. "This is what helps me understand you and you me."

"Whoa." I shook my head. Once again, he spoke perfect English. "So it's like a magical translator?"

"Easier than learning new languages." He shrugged. "There are many dialects and languages in our world, just like there are here. This bridges the gap, especially with new creatures coming to the Bane every day. There is no way we would all be able to communicate without it, not unless you're someone like Raymond. That guy has a big brain; he picks up languages quickly. Last I checked, he knew over four hundred."

"Four hundred?" I looked at his mouth a lot closer as he spoke and realized the movement of his lips didn't match the words I heard. It was the same disorienting feeling of watching a foreign movie that had been dubbed. "How much does something like that cost, and how can I get one?"

"This is small talk, right?" Noville chuckled. "You don't really care about this. Just trying to fill the awkward silence?"

"Okay, maybe you're better at peopling than you're given credit for." I smiled. "But honestly, in my line of work, that would come in handy."

"If we survive what's to come, I'll have one delivered to you."

"Brace yourselves." Cufio popped into the room. "The big guy is coming inside!"

"Damn it!" I shouted at him and clutched my chest. "Don't do that. Are you trying to freak me out? And why didn't I feel you coming?"

"Feel me coming? Why would you?" He looked genuinely confused by my question.

"I—nothing. Where is your brother?" I deflected, because his reaction made me second guess if I should tell him how I felt the temperature shift before Raymond appeared. Maybe there was something wrong with him. If that were the case, I wouldn't be the one to expose it.

Cufio paused, looking at me for a moment before he responded. "Raymond's bringing our special guest. He wanted me to come give you a heads up. Honestly, I think he just wanted to say something without me hearing it. Those two have a deep history."

"Oh." I looked over his shoulder out the window, where I could see Raymond approaching. "Is he dangerous?"

"Yes, but so are you, from what I've heard. But he's on our side, so you don't have to worry about him."

"Help is on the way." Jackie returned, waving her phone in her hand. "Didn't take nearly as much convincing as I thought it would. Starting to think that man has the hots for me."

"Perfect timing," I pointed out the window. "They're coming in now."

"Great. We get to meet the mysterious new stranger!" She clapped. "You think he's also a shadow walker, or something different?"

The door opened, and Raymond stepped in first, followed by a tall man with dark skin, a stern expression, and no horns. I swore they were there when I first saw him, but as he stood there, leather jacket, low collar, brimming with aura, I couldn't tell he ever had them.

"Are you going to introduce us to your new friend, or are we just gonna stand here staring at each other?" Jackie was the one to break the silence.

"I'm glad somebody said it." Cufio chuckled and leaned against the wall. "This is starting to get really awkward. You both know how I feel about awkward situations. I will pop out of here in a second."

"Jericha," Raymond addressed me and nobody else. "This is Metice. He's here to help us with our situation."

"It's nice to meet you." I reached out to shake his hand and instantly noticed the strange look he gave me. "What is it?"

"Your energy. It feels familiar." Metice furrowed his brow, conflicted by something unspoken. "Like I've encountered it before."

"Considering you were close enough for our paths to cross, you probably have," Raymond interjected. "Remember, that's why we're all here now."

"Right. Well, it's a pleasure to meet you, Jericha," Metice continued, and it felt like the house rumbled with his voice.

"Damn," Jackie commented. When I looked back at her, she was popping the last piece of sushi into her mouth. "I just know he got the demon girls going crazy over him."

"Jackie." I rolled my eyes.

"My bad. It's nice to meet you too, Metice. My name is Jackie," she introduced herself. "I'm Jericha's home girl, also here to help them clean up this little mess they've created."

"Hey, I didn't create any mess," I corrected her. "It was dropped into my lap."

"After you dropped into his lap, right?" She pointed at Raymond and winked.

"Oh, she's funny." Cufio grinned. "So, she was in your lap? You left that out."

"Don't get any ideas, shadow man." Jackie balled up a fist, ready to fight off his advances. "Just because my friend likes to play in the shadows doesn't mean I do."

"Can we get focused here?" Noville groaned. "Earth's air is making my skin itch. How do you all survive with such pollution?"

"Thank you, Noville." I rolled my eyes at Jackie for her shadow comment before returning my attention to Raymond. "Are you two good to work together? It looked like there may have been some tension out there."

"Yes. Metice and I had something to discuss, that's all." Raymond glanced at the dark man. "We're all good. For now."

"As my brother mentioned earlier, it turns out, Metice is the reason the others found Raymond," Cufio offered. "He was also coming here for a human."

"You were?" Jackie gawked at him. "Big, fine thing like you can't find something good in hell?"

"My soulmate," Metice confirmed. "She lived here on Earth."

"Maybe I need to find me a human soulmate." Cufio waggled his brow at Jackie, and I could tell he was having fun messing with her.

"I repeat, not me!" Jackie sucked her teeth. "Men. Ugh. Even the ones from hell can't catch a hint."

"Okay, maybe a different one." Cufio licked his lips and then suddenly became very serious. "All jokes aside, we aren't in the best position here. They know where you are and how to find you. I don't think we need to keep things here."

"You don't?" Raymond asked. "And where do you suppose we take things?"

"I agree with your brother. We don't want them to send more demons here. You know how reckless they are. It will only cause more drama and bring unwanted attention," Metice spoke, and all eyes snapped to him. "We've already had a few cause scenes that took a lot to clean up."

"Did you find out anything useful?" Raymond asked Metice, avoiding my question. "When you were cleaning up their mess?"

"About you? No. But after Cufio reached out, I did some digging." Metice pulled a small coin from his pocket and rolled it across his fingers as he spoke. "Nothing's changed since you left. They gave up on their initial searches when they realized you left the Bane, but you're still enemy number one. The orders to bring you in still stand. And if I were still part of the organization, I'd be following those orders now."

"So you're really out? Never thought I'd see the day." Raymond nodded, almost approvingly. "Had to be something major to get you to walk away."

"Yeah, he's been out for a while now." Cufio nudged Raymond with his elbow. "If you had stuck around, you could have witnessed the explosive events. Almost lost my head helping him, and now, I'm risking it again for you."

"I can't believe they haven't moved on after all this time. Surely there are other things to worry about, people who've screwed them over since I left."

"Maybe, but it wasn't a low-level demon who lost their life. This isn't one they can easily get over. The organization is still feeling the impact," Metice continued. "And you running away like you did only convinced them you were guilty. If not, you would have stuck around and tried to defend yourself."

"I was just doing my job," Raymond said. "It wasn't supposed to go that way."

"We know that, and they know that, but you know how this works," Cufio said.

"I don't know that," Metice voiced his opinion. "But if that's what you say, we have no choice but to believe you until it comes out otherwise. Either way, you betrayed the Order, and there is no easy way back from that."

"The Order?" I asked. It was hard enough following their conversation without them dropping names we didn't know.

"It's the organization we all once worked for," Metice supplied. "One of the strongest in our world."

"Sounds dark." Jackie huffed. "But what else would we expect? Dealing with demons and all."

"Hey, it was actually pretty chill in the Shadow League!" Cufio smiled.

"Shadow League?" I sighed. "Look, if you're going to keep introducing new entities, please accompany them with explanations."

"It's the department in the Order made up of shadow walkers," Raymond offered.

"All different variants working together and using our skills to help the Order succeed," Cufio spoke with pride, like he would happily join the Shadow League again.

"It was peaceful until Talkeen decided he wanted to run the place," Raymond muttered.

"He wanted more power, as lots of people do," Cufio spoke.

Raymond furrowed his brow. "His plans would have destroyed so much. You know that."

I couldn't take my eyes off Raymond. He was so different now that the others were there. The relaxed and easy demeanor I knew had disappeared, replaced by a man who looked like he would need heart meds soon. His jaw was hard set, his brow scrunched. He looked miserable. Was this how life was for him in the Bane? If so, it was no wonder he wanted to get away.

"I do, but again, he doesn't care." Cufio walked over to the fridge and pulled out a beer. He waved it at me, asking permission before he cracked it open. After a long sip, he continued, "And because of you, they demoted him anyway. He thought if he could take you out, it would put him back in good favor with the boss. When that failed, he ran off on his own. Now, he's trying to build his own company, one big enough to knock out the Order entirely."

"That's not going to happen," Metice muttered. "We all know that."

"Who's on his side?" Raymond asked. "Talkeen wasn't that popular before. Who would help him now?"

"Pretty much anyone who hates you." Metice smirked. "Not a short list."

"That's why I think our best bet is to go straight to the top and see if we can make a bargain," Cufio said. "You'll have to beg for forgiveness, but it's better than dealing with everyone else. If he agrees, he'll call them off, and they can't touch you without pissing him off."

"Beg?" Raymond shook his head no. "I'm not doing that."

"Raymond..." Cufio sighed. "Put the pride aside, man."

"What's this about variants?" Jackie spoke. "Sorry to back you up in this long-winded discussion, but that sounds like something we should all understand. You know, in case they come here trying to attack us."

"Shadow walkers are fundamentally the same, but some of us have abilities others do not," Cufio offered while Raymond sat down at the table. "We all share the basic skills. Our powers are tied to the shadows. All of us can enter them, but what we do while we're there is different. Like my brother and I can cross realms, some shadow walkers can barely cross a city with their abilities. I can create and leave behind shadow portals for non-walkers to use, but Raymond can't."

Cufio said it like he was bragging.

"Yeah, my brother got that little gift," Raymond said and then, to add his own show of skill, his body phased into a smokey being before returning to his solid form. "I not only create my own shadows, but I become them. It's much more intense and takes immense skill and focus."

"Lucky bastard. I still have to borrow shadows from other things." Cufio took a swig of beer and sighed. "This stuff is really good."

"I know, so don't drink them all," Jackie said then clapped once again, calling everyone to focus. "Alright, what's the plan here, boys? I have backup coming, but I need to know what we're doing so I can start strategizing."

"Unless your team plans on going with us, I'm not sure what you can do," Raymond said. "It's pretty obvious this isn't a fight we can have here on Earth."

"Exactly. You'll be in hell dealing with whatever mess you left behind," I said. "That means I'll be here. Jackie is right. We need to know everything we can. You already said your enemies won't leave me alone."

"Which is why it's better we all go together," Cufio said. "There's no way they'll leave you alone if you don't come. And I'm sorry, but I seriously doubt you have anything here that can properly defend you from beings who use shadows to attack."

"Now the shadow man is speaking French!" Jackie clapped slowly, each one echoing in the quiet room, punctuated by long, pregnant pauses. "Who the hell is *we*? You're not dragging my friend to hell!"

"It's the only way any of this is going to work," Cufio insisted. "We can't be there and protect her here."

"Um, I can protect myself. I did just fine earlier." I said, reminding them of our earlier encounter.

"Yes, with my help," Raymond added.

"So you think I should go to hell with you? I thought this was just your brother's idea, but you agree with him?"

"I think that we should stick together. If that means you coming to the Bane, then yes."

"Alright, you've clearly lost your collective minds, and I think it's time for you all to leave." Jackie pulled me back from Raymond. "Go put your heads together to come up with another plan."

"Jericha," Raymond looked at me, but there was something there. Hesitation? Maybe he wasn't sure if it was a good idea after all. "Is that what you want?"

"She's right. You should go. I need time to think about what's going on." I nodded.

"I—" Raymond started, but he stopped when a hand touched his shoulder.

"She's right." Metice tightened his grip on Raymond's shoulder. "This is a lot to ask from one woman. Trust me, I know. Jericha you should take your time. We can arrange for protection while you think things over."

"You're speaking for all of us now?" Raymond jerked his shoulder away from Metice.

"No. I'm listening to what she wants. Forcing the issue will not make this any easier for anyone," Metice said confidently. "If she comes, it needs to be on her terms."

"Wow, you've changed." Raymond laughed. "No more kicking down the door and taking what you want? I can't count how many times you dragged someone from their home kicking and screaming and took them back to the Bane."

"It's called maturing," Metice grunted. "You should try it."

"It's called having a woman wrap you around her little finger." Cufio pulled a Jackie, injecting humor into a moment that was growing more and more tense. "You know he can't act out, or his woman will kick his ass."

"I'm leaving." Metice rolled his eyes then pointed at Cufio. "I'll see you in our spot. Don't take too long. I have other stuff to deal with."

"Yeah, we'll be there soon," Cufio confirmed.

Metice nodded, and then the pressure in the room intensified. Weight pressed against my chest, and when it stopped, Metice was gone.

"Jericha." Raymond stood from the table. "Is this what you want?"

"I need time to think, Raymond," I said.

"Okay, yeah. I'll go," Raymond spoke.

Cufio opened a shadow and stepped through, followed by Noville, who sighed in relief as he left. Raymond took one last look at me then followed the others.

"They're out of their minds if they think you're going there," Jackie fussed.

"This is too much." I pointed at the empty sushi containers. "And your greedy ass ate all the sushi!"

"There's still plenty of beer!" She shrugged. "My bad, girl. I guess I was a lot hungrier than I thought. You want me to run and get you something?"

"No, thank you." I waved her off. "And you can keep your nasty beer."

"What do you need right now? I know how you usually are. You want to be alone while you think things through."

"Yes, I think I need to be by myself." I peeked out into the backyard once again. "Even if there are things lurking in the shadows, I gotta take time to process."

"Cool, I'll go back to the hotel and wait for Miguel and the others. Let me know if you need anything." Jackie grabbed her bag.

"Thanks," I said.

She started toward the front door but looked back at me. "I can't believe you're going to hell."

"Seriously?" I held my hand out in disbelief. "I thought you were on my side!"

"Hey, I might protest it, but even I see the obvious outcome here."

"Goodbye, Jackie!"

"See ya!" She waved, and a minute later, I heard the door shut behind her.

As soon as she was gone, I locked all the doors and shut the windows. None of it mattered, considering the threat, but it made me feel better as I cleaned up my kitchen and made a new cup of tea. I sat down at the table and wished I had those little donuts to pair with my drink.

Then, I felt that familiar chill in the air, the alert that someone was about to pay me a visit. I was seconds from being irritated; I had just asked the man for some time to think, but Raymond knew me well enough. In front of me, on the table, appeared a small package of little pink donuts. And before he could appear to apologize for the intrusion, I'd already forgiven him.

16

Bath time

"Are you going to show your face or just keep dangling donuts in front of me?" I called out.

Raymond appeared, standing opposite the table where I sat. "I had to make sure you were okay with me being here first."

"So much for giving me time to think." I snatched the donuts from the table and opened them. Yes, I wanted them, and yes, I'd already forgiven him, but I couldn't let him know that.

"I know. I'm sorry." He took a step back, like he was afraid I would hit him.

"Don't be. But you could have brought more than one pack."

His hand vanished, and when it reappeared, a plastic bag full of packs of those little donuts appeared.

"I figured you might want more." He put the bag on the table. "And if you decide to come with me, you'll have plenty for the trip."

"You're going to need a lot more of these to get me through a trip to hell." I pointed at the bag. "Think semi-truck full!"

"Does that mean you're considering going?" he asked hopefully.

"You gave me less than an hour to think," I huffed. "But what I'm considering is everything that will need to be managed while I'm away. *If* I go, there's a lot to consider. Like my business—who will take care of everything? And my home. I have a lot of plants here, in case you haven't noticed. They need me."

"Logical frame of mind." He sat at the table. "I should have expected nothing less."

"I don't know how else to be at a time like this."

"Natalie could handle things for a few weeks," he suggested. "That would take care of the work stuff."

"Weeks? What do you mean a few weeks? How long could this possibly take?"

"Honestly, it could take longer than that, but in the Bane, time moves at a different rate. A day there is a week here," he explained. "So even if we're only gone less than a week, it would be a month you're away from work."

"How do you expect me to stay away from my business for a month?" A searing pain shot through my chest as I tried to inhale, and the constricting feeling left me lightheaded, on the verge of collapse. "Damnit! What am I supposed to do now? I've worked so hard to build my business, and now, it's all just going to fall apart."

"Just breathe." Raymond stepped around me and put his hands on my shoulders. He massaged me with just enough pressure to make my head fall back.

I sighed as I felt the tension leaving my body, but my chest still burned with the building anxiety. "You don't know how much I put into this. I don't want to lose everything."

"Do you think you'll lose everything after taking a few weeks away? If that's the case, your business isn't as solid as you think it is. Maybe I should reconsider signing all my assets to you."

"Funny. I didn't think that was still the plan."

"Of course it is." He paused the massage. "Did you think I would go back on my word?"

"I—" Pretending to struggle to breathe was the perfect mask for hiding how I really felt. I couldn't tell him I thought he would stay, that after our time on the roof together, I expected him to change his mind and insist on continuing our partnership. Instead of admitting that, I simply said, "No."

"I will protect you, Jericha. You know that." His hands warmed against my shoulders. "If that's what you're worried about, you can stop. Nothing is going to happen to you."

"That's great for you to say, but you and I both know that's not a promise you can keep. Anything can happen when things really pop off."

"You're right," he conceded.

"Wait, why is it I can feel you coming but Jackie can't?" I asked. "And I didn't feel your brother either."

"Because my brother is rude." He shook his head, and his locs brushed against my shoulders. "I do that on purpose, like a doorbell to let you know I'm coming."

"Oh, I thought something was wrong with you!" I chuckled at the feeling of relief. "Man, I was afraid you were sick or something. Tried to keep it from Cufio just in case."

"Look at you, trying to protect my interests." He laughed. "I'm good, I promise. Now, tell me what you need to make you feel better."

I leaned back in my seat and glanced at him. What did I need? For demons to not be threatening my life so I didn't have to carry my ass to another world and for his hand to be massaging a whole lot more than my shoulders!

"A hot bath and a planner so I can start mapping out things for Natalie." It made no sense to pretend they weren't all right. I had to go with him.

If I didn't go, not only would I risk being attacked and threaten the safety of my friends, but it would put Raymond in a bad spot. Not only would he be distracted, wondering if I was okay, but if anything happened to me, he would blame himself. Or, at least, I hoped he would. Hell, he better!

"You work on the planner, and I'll run the bath." He rubbed my shoulders once more before leaving me.

While Raymond did that, I headed for my office and went to work. There was so much to consider—pending contracts, existing ones, meetings to reschedule, staff changes. Instead of just making a simple checklist, I put together an entire handbook. It was so thorough that even someone who'd never been in my company before could open it and run it flawlessly. At least, that was what I hoped.

"Are you done? I've had to run that bath three times now. I don't think you have enough hot water left for a fourth."

"Oh." I looked up from the document on my laptop. Raymond stood in the doorway, arms crossed and waiting impatiently. I hit the print button and stood. "Yeah, I think that's good. I'll need to go over it again, but I think it's all there."

"Great. Now," he stepped aside and pointed down the hall to my bathroom, "go."

"Who do you think you are, my dad?"

"Oh, you can call me daddy if you want, but I never really liked that. It's weird." He bit his lip. "I like, sir. Call me sir."

"I set myself up for that, didn't I?" I rolled my eyes.

It would be a cold day in hell before I called a man daddy! Now, sir... that was kinda hot.

"Yes, you did." He chuckled as I passed him. "Surprised you would leave yourself open like that. We both know how much you love to be in charge."

"We're talking about this again?"

"Yes." He followed me. "It's the only way you're going to grow and change. Change is good."

"I'm going to grow by being nagged?" I frowned. "That doesn't sound right."

"No, you'll grow when you let someone else take control."

I stopped outside the bathroom door and turned to him. "I'm fine with being in control. Now, you can go. I'm going to take this bath and go to bed. There is a lot I have to get done if I'm going to go to hell with you. Also, I need you to put together a presentation for me, an intro to hell so I know what to expect when we get there."

"You are something else, you know that?" He leaned against the hallway wall.

"It will be helpful, and it will give you something to do until we leave." I smirked. "Now, step into the shadows and let me have some privacy."

"You sure you don't want some company in there?"

"Seriously?" I scoffed. "Demons chasing you, and that's what you're thinking about now?"

"That's not a no. Besides, what better way to get my mind off my troubles?" He pointed at the door. "I'm sure a hot bath would help me too."

"PowerPoint presentations do the trick for me!" I pointed behind him. "Call your shadow and go."

"As you wish." The shadow opened behind him, and he stepped back, waving until it swallowed him whole.

"Tell me I can't be in control. It's my damn life," I muttered before I turned and headed into the bathroom.

Raymond hadn't just run me a bath. He lit candles, dimmed the light, and set up my towels for me. I looked around the bathroom, and butterflies fluttered in my stomach.

"Stop it!" I fussed at myself. This was not the time for fantasizing—but that was exactly what was about to happen. I could feel it at the back of my mind, a story forming about me and the shadow walker who ran the perfect baths.

It didn't take long for me to tie my hair up and slip into the tub. The water was the perfect temperature, just hot enough to where I felt like my skin might almost melt off. As the water worked on me, easing away all the tension left from the day, I closed my eyes. Yeah, he was right. They were all right. At some point in my life, I would have to learn to let go of being in control of everything. With shadow walkers and demons knocking on my door, it felt like the absolute wrong time to relinquish control of any part of my life.

Already, I was coming up with ways to prolong the situation and give myself more time to get acclimated to the idea of going to hell. I thought about faking an injury or packing my bags and running away in the middle of the night, but even if Raymond couldn't find me, Jackie sure could. And there he was again, in my head.

Raymond.

It started simple. I thought about how well we worked together, how things would be different when our partnership ended. Then, I replayed the day, how tense he looked around his brother and the other demons. How, after they were gone, he was back to the same swag-dripping guy I knew before. Then, I questioned his motives and how he felt about me.

At any moment, he could have left me, demonic threat or not, but he didn't. He stayed to protect me. But why the hell did it matter to me how he felt? I didn't want to be with him, did I? And even if I did, what possible future could I have with a man who wasn't even from the same world as me and whose real name I couldn't pronounce?

Was that the reason I cared so much about him? Was that the reason I found myself more and more intrigued by him every day? He wasn't from Earth, but neither were my ancestors. Was there a part of me that connected with, that recognized that foreign energy and bonded with him because of it?

As my thoughts spiraled deeper into the layers of feelings and confusion, a familiar, throbbing pressure built between my legs, a deep warmth spreading through me. A quiet moan slipped from my lips before I knew what was happening, and when I opened my eyes, I knew I wasn't alone anymore.

Smoky tendrils filled the space. They crossed the bathroom, moving closer to me, and as they approached, I felt the tension rising. I looked down and saw those lines of smoke converging across my chest. I couldn't take my eyes off the movement. First swirling and translucent, they turned into flesh, dark and hot against my skin. A hand formed between my thighs, and the pressure on my clit grew more intense. I wanted to throw my head back, but I couldn't stop watching as a hand, wrist, forearm, and those familiar tattoos, smokey patterns different each time I saw them, came into view.

While one hand formed between my thighs, the other appeared on my left breast. Fingers teased my nipple as warm breath moved against the right side of my neck.

Hold your composure, girl!

I tried, but the soft moans betrayed me as I spoke to him. "Raymond? What are you doing?"

The deep chuckle, a devious sound, rang in my ear. "Tell me to stop, and I will."

I should have. I should have cursed him out for appearing there, for touching me without permission. I should have screamed bloody murder and maybe even committed it. I didn't, though. Because just as I was about to let the curses fly, his arms warmed again, and the heat he generated radiated through me.

"How are you doing that?" My eyes rolled back as the room blurred, and I suddenly felt intoxicated.

"What?" His voice was another caress against my skin, further melting me into him.

"The heat," I moaned. "It feels so good."

"The perks of dating a demon." He chuckled.

"Are we dating now?" That snapped me out of the trance, and my head snapped right to look at him. "I don't remember agreeing to that."

As soon as I moved, his head turned smokey and vanished.

"Don't tell me you're embarrassed!" I laughed. "Big man can sneak into my home and touch me from the shadows, but ask him about what a relationship is, and he disappears."

Raymond said nothing. Instead, he thrust two fingers into my pussy, and I gasped, hands gripping the edges of the tub as my eyes slammed shut.

"Quiet." His voice came deeper than before, and then his fingers stretched deeper inside me, swirling and hitting every spot imaginable.

I looked down to double check it was, in fact, his hand and not something else. There it was, one hand between my thighs and two fingers out of view. So how did it feel like so much more?

"What?" I gasped, "are" my eyes slammed tight, "you" my thighs clenched around his hand, "doing?"

"Helping you learn to let go," he whispered. "I'm in control now."

"I—"

His hand moved from my breast and clapped over my mouth as the tornado of sensation continued inside my pussy. It felt like he had more fingers than his anatomy would allow, inside me, playing with my clit, pinching my nipples. The sensation was overwhelming, and yet I wanted it to continue. I looked down, and there were *more* hands. They were all over me. Two held my legs open while one continued working my pussy and the other two played with my breasts.

Holy shit!

"You talk too much." Raymond's voice dripped with a dangerous playfulness.

When he moved his hand from my mouth, what felt like a piece of tape remained. It stopped me from talking.

I know damn well he didn't just gag me!

As soon as I thought about it, the plants in the bathroom responded. The vine plant, one of my favorites, burst from its planter. I cringed at the sound of shattered clay hitting the bathroom floor but couldn't dwell on it for too long, because Raymond continued despite the attack. The vines shot out to grab him, but just as he had before, he phased into that smokey appearance, and the attack moved through him.

Still, those extra hands worked on me, but the one between my legs vanished.

"Call them off." Raymond shimmered into view, his form almost invisible save for the serious expression etched onto his face. He meant business.

But I hadn't been called a control freak for most of my life for no reason. I looked him in the eye, smiling defiantly beneath the shadow gag, shaking my head no.

He phased into smoke again before he reappeared in the tub, naked. "Jericha, call them off."

Again, I refused, and the surrounding plants grew more irate. The eucalyptus that hung in the shower spilled out and slapped the back of his head.

"Well, now you're going to be punished."

He vanished, and I felt it between my legs—fingers, no, a tongue. I looked down, and I could see nothing but his head, locs floating in the water, and those extra hands holding my legs apart to give him better access.

Holy shit!

The plants hesitated as my annoyance turned to pleasure. They pulled back as Raymond ate my pussy underwater and never came up for air. I just knew after the first orgasm, he would stop, but he didn't. My pulse raced, sweat forming on my forehead, and I fought to catch my breath as he swallowed my orgasm and kept on eating.

The second came quickly, the third he had to work for, and the fourth left my legs feeling like jelly as two more hands appeared, lifting them higher in the air. Two more appeared under my arms to keep me from slipping under the water.

"Damnit!" I cried out the moment the shadow gag vanished. "I'm sorry. Please, I can't." I tried to speak, but the air felt like a stripper teasing me with peeks of the good stuff, giving me moments of clarity then snatching it away.

I tried to grab his head, push him away before he pushed me to a painful fifth orgasm, but I couldn't. He was still smokey, and I was still in trouble, apology or not. I tried my best to avoid it, but it was no use; I came again so hard, I slapped the water, sending it all over the bathroom floor.

"I called them off!" I shouted, hoping it would be enough to stop him.

He lifted his head from the water as the rest of his body, naked and powerful, appeared beneath him. After a quick glance around the bathroom, making sure the plants were truly behaving, he smiled at me and licked his lips. "You taste like green tea and resilience."

"You're sick." I huffed as I grabbed the edge of the tub, trying to keep myself upright. All his extra hands had already vanished.

"And you're a brat." He leaned forward, bracing himself on the tub as he invaded my space. "Out there, in the world, you can be as strong as you want, Jericha. Take down the largest beast, and I'll be there to root for you. Sign as many contracts as you want, and I will round up all the men you need to make it happen. But when it's just you and me, drop the weight. Let me hold it. I got this, and I got you."

I stared at him, his words causing a building pressure in my chest. It wasn't panic, it was fear; discomfort caused by how much it terrified me to think of anyone being there for me the way he'd so passionately described. How did I respond? The only way I knew how: total avoidance!

"Can I finish my bath in peace?" My voice trembled, betraying my hope of appearing unaffected. "The water is getting cold."

"You want me to leave?" he challenged me, inching close enough to kiss me. "Say the words, and I'll go."

"I—" My eyes dropped to his lips, and the hope he would move in closer sparked a tingling in my stomach.

"Hesitation." He raised a brow, slowly pulling back from me. "Careful, Jericha. Your mask is slipping."

He grabbed the African net sponge that hung on the hook next to the tub, added the lavender soap to it, and went to work scrubbing my body from my toes up. I let him. Something about this man made me want to let him do whatever he wanted to me.

What the hell is happening?

My mind spiraled as he bathed me with careful intention. When he was done, he vanished, reappearing in the shower, where I watched him through the glass pane as he turned the water on and adjusted it to the perfect temperature. He returned to me, lifting me from the tub and carrying me over to the shower.

I remained quiet, afraid I would say something to reveal what I really felt. I'd be damned if I let him know the internal battle that raged inside my heart and mind.

He joined me inside, lifted the shower head from the rack, and slowly rinsed the soap from my body. I expected him to take it further, tease my pussy with the water, or press his dick, heavy and dripping wet, against my ass. Yes, I looked. How could I not?

But he didn't. The man showed restraint I thought was impossible.

When his gaze caught mine, I didn't dare speak. The throbbing between my thighs was only just subsiding, and I didn't want to do anything to warrant another orgasmic punishment. I wasn't sure I would survive it.

He finished rinsing me and turned the water off. We stood there, naked and dripping, for a moment as he looked my body over, double checking his work. Then, he reached out, hand vanishing for a moment before reappearing with the bath towel.

"Arms up," he ordered, and I lifted my arms, allowing him to dry my body with the towel.

When he was done, he grabbed a fresh towel and held it out. Shadows swirled around the towel, turning a slight red as they went. When they vanished, he wrapped the towel around me, and I couldn't help the quick smile that touched my lips when I realized he'd warmed it.

He caught it, winked, and vanished.

I stood alone in the shower, not sure what to do. If I moved, would I be in trouble?

Not me being afraid to move! What is this man doing to me?

A moment later, he reappeared, dressed in a loose-fitting gray t-shirt and joggers. He lifted me into his arms and carried me from the bathroom. As we left,

I could see those extra shadow hands working to clean up the water from the floor and fix the planter that broke.

He took me into my bedroom and laid me on the bed. We said nothing. I watched him go into my closet and waited until he returned with one of my nightgowns. It was soft pink with little roses along the hem, one of my favorites. He put it next to me and grabbed the shea butter from the nightstand.

Raymond unwrapped the towel as if opening a present. He bit his bottom lip, the first show of his battle with self-control, then opened the shea butter. I watched the stuff melt in his hand before he massaged it into my skin, starting with my feet and working his way up before he turned me over and repeated the work on my back, taking extra care on my ass cheeks.

I know damn well my ass ain't that ashy.

Once I was moisturized to his liking, he turned me back over. When he grabbed the nightgown, I sat up and let him pull it over my head. He picked me up, those extra hands appearing to pull the sheets back before he laid me back down. He tucked me in, studying my face in a way that made my stomach tighten with awkwardness, and then walked around to the other side of the bed.

I expected Raymond to leave me with my thoughts, allow me to lie in bed wondering what this man really wanted from me. I knew exactly where my mind was ready to go, replaying his words about us dating, revisiting the way he ate my pussy, imagining where we would go next. He wasn't even gone yet, and the thoughts were already off to the races.

Until he pulled back the covers and slipped into bed beside me.

What is he doing? What does he expect now? I can't come again. I'm still sore. Maybe he wants more. Does he think I'm his girlfriend? He said he has me. What does that mean to him? What—

Raymond wrapped his arm around my waist and scooped me into him, and every thought in my head stopped. All the worrying, the hope of controlling the narrative, it all fell silent. My back pressed against his chest, and he adjusted the surrounding cover. There were no thoughts, just the feeling of him—his breath against my neck, his lock that fell across my neck, his hand across my stomach, and soon, the soft rumbling of his snore. Raymond warmed just slightly after he slept, and that heat took away any resistance I still had.

It wasn't long until his heat and the soft rumble at my back lulled me to sleep.

17

Caught red-handed

I expected to wake up alone, ghosted by the shadow man, but he was still there, still holding me, when my eyes opened. My mind raced for half a second until I heard his soft snoring. Funny how his presence did that suddenly. My overthinking, my analyzing, my narrative making—he stopped all that.

I sighed, not knowing how much I needed the noise in my head to stop, and melted back into him.

Maybe I could get used to having him around.

He tightened his hold on me, like he could hear my thoughts, but his snoring continued. Content with spending more time there, pretending like my life wasn't imploding, I closed my eyes. Maybe I could sleep in.

Nope!

The loud chime of the doorbell snatched away my hope of peace. I reached for my phone, wanting to check the security camera to see who it was, but I realized my phone was still in my office.

So, to the remorse of every molecule of my body, I pulled away from Raymond's heat and slipped out of the bed.

On my way to the door, I grabbed my robe and wrapped it around myself. I should have checked the camera, I should have looked out the peephole, anything but swinging that damn door open like I had no sense. Because the moment it opened was the moment all sense slammed back into my head.

The shadow man is in your bed and you're just opening the door? Your ass knows Jackie is in town! Who else would it be?

And there was my friend, standing on my porch. Her happy expression quickly shifted from excitement to see me to suspicion. I could see her investigator hat forming on her head as her eyes scanned my body, searching for clues.

In an effort to deflect her pending judgement, I looked around her, ready to comment on the weather. The passenger door of her rental swung open, and my heart plummeted into the pit of my stomach as the short, muscular monster hunter stepped out. Miguel.

Damnit! This can't be happening!

"Did you bring the entire team with you?" I asked, trying to sound like I was joking and not panicking.

"Would it bother you if I had?" Jackie's right eyebrow lifted—more data being collected in the case against me.

"Some notice would have been nice is all." I pulled the robe tighter around me.

She lifted her phone and wagged it at me, and I had a flashback to Raymond standing on my porch. "I called you twice and sent you three texts about me coming."

"Oh, I left my phone in the office last night." I looked over my shoulder, more so to make sure Raymond wasn't there than anything.

Please, just stay in bed! Or better yet, pop your shadow ass on up out of here!

"Either way, it's just us. Thought we could go grab breakfast and talk over things. But…" She looked me up and down. "Now I have questions. For one, what have you been up to?"

"What do you mean?" I could feel the heat in my cheeks already giving away my secrets.

"Everything okay?" His heat was suddenly on my back. *Raymond.* I closed my eyes in shame as he spoke. Yes, she was going to give me shit about it.

"Um." I opened my eyes to see Jackie's lips twisted. She was holding it back. Thank the heavens!

"On second thought, we're going to go grab breakfast and come back here." She pointed two fingers at us. "Give you two some time to put clothes on. That work?"

"Thanks," I said simply before stepping back to shut the door and cringing when I heard her laughter.

Never living this down!

"You couldn't just stay in the room?" I smacked his shoulder. "I could have gotten rid of them without them knowing you were here."

"Why? Are you embarrassed?" He slipped his hand around the back of my neck, pulling me closer to him. "Are you ashamed of me, Jericha?"

"No," I pushed him back to get more space and let my heart slow down. "I just don't put my business out there for the world to know."

"That's one of your best friends, right?" He frowned. "Jackie, I mean. I don't know about the man, but I assumed you two were close. Women tell each other everything."

"We do when we're ready. I prefer to wait to tell my friends about the men I've been with, preferably until after I'm done with them."

"Are you done with me?" He held up his hands. "Let me know now, and I'll leave."

"Also, what was *that* about last night?" I ignored his question and focused on my own.

"What about last night?"

"The extra hands!" I pointed at his hands still up. "You had more than two of them."

"You liked that, huh?" He bit his lip seductively. "There's a lot more I can do with my shadows."

"Did I say that?" Arms crossed over my chest in a stance of defiance, I squealed when I felt a firm pinch on my ass and looked back to see one of his floating hands. "Ah! Don't do that."

"Tell me you don't like it, and I'll never do it again." He lowered his head, staring at me with a quirked brow.

"Just...don't do it again."

"Right." He stepped aside so I could walk by him.

"I'm going to get dressed. You should do the same." I waved him off. "Poof on over to your place."

I stomped by him and went to the room to get dressed. Just after I closed the door behind me, my feeling of triumph slipped through my hands as I felt a firm slap on my ass.

"Not funny!" I shouted through the door.

I heard him laugh just before I felt the chill of his departure. When I opened the door to check, he was already gone.

I stood in my closet, obsessing over what to wear. Suddenly, it felt like it mattered, because everyone would have some judgement. Wear something too put together, and I'm trying to look good for Raymond. Dress down, and I'm trying to deflect their attention. Jeans and a tank. That would have to do. I pulled the items from my closet and threw them on the bed along with underwear before heading to the bathroom. Despite the thorough scrubbing Raymond gave my body the night before, I felt the need for a shower. Flashbacks be damned—I needed something to ease my nerves.

By the time I was showered, dressed, and back out of my room, Raymond had returned and stood next to Kaa's pot. He leaned over, moving his head as he examined what looked like an ordinary potted plant.

"You're back," I said after he neglected to acknowledge my presence.

"Yes. Tell me more about her," he said, still looking at the plant who hadn't yet revealed herself.

"You're suddenly more curious about Kaa? Why?"

"Kaa? Pretty name. Did you name her that?" He glanced back at me for a moment. I nodded, and he returned his attention to the plant. "Her energy. It's not of the Earth, but I've encountered nothing like it before."

"I'm not sure where she came from. I found a seed one day, planted it, and soon after, she appeared. We've been together ever since. I don't know much more about her. I've been too afraid to ask anyone else in the magical community. They're all so greedy. If they found something of interest, they'd try to take it."

"She's bonded to you." Raymond nodded as one of his shadows lifted from the tattooed spot on his skin and reached out to Kaa like a dog. "There are etches of your energy mixed with hers. It makes her energy look kaleidoscopic."

"Really? You can see that?" I crossed the room to lean in next to him, squinting as if I would suddenly see what he did. "I've always thought of her as a soulmate."

"So that role is already taken?" He turned his head to look at me.

His question caught me off guard, but my head snapped to look at him. The moment I turned, my breath caught in my throat. Our faces were so close, a deep breath would have our lips pressed against each other, and I knew exactly where that would lead us: back to the bedroom.

Interrupting my internal conflict, Kaa took that moment to make her grand appearance. Her head appeared, lifting from between the camouflage of petals, before she snapped at him, hissing with the threatening movement.

Raymond moved away from her and me quickly and chuckled. "I'll take that as a yes."

"She's just protective of me." I scratched the top of Kaa's head, and her body vibrated, a sign she was happy with the attention she was getting.

"She's going to have to learn to share." Raymond straightened, and Kaa hissed again. Raymond hissed back, and Kaa lifted from the planter, stretching.

Before I could comment on how ridiculous they were both being, the doorbell rang. I pulled my phone from my pocket and saw Jackie and Miguel standing on the porch, bags of food in hand.

"They're back." I headed for the door, paused, and turned back to Raymond, pointing like a parent warning a toddler. "Behave."

"Exactly what do you think I'm going to do? Strip you down and eat your pussy in front of them?" He laughed. "Jericha, I have more self-control than you give me credit for."

"You need a filter for that mouth." I snapped my fingers at him. "I don't know what you'll say or do, but be on your best behavior. Remember, I'm in control now."

"Oh, so you're accepting the dynamics of this relationship?" He licked his lips. "Does that mean you won't protest tonight when I put you in your place?"

The way his voice dropped and his eyes darkened caused something sinister to stir in my stomach, but I pushed that energy back down. If he wasn't going to act like he had some sense, I had to, pussy quivers be damned. I had more important shit to think about than riding his face while those extra hands held me up. "Shut it."

"Yes, ma'am!" He straightened and gave me a stiff salute.

Hormones quelled, I marched to the door, Raymond following behind me. When my hand touched the doorknob, I took a deep calming breath then opened it. Just as I expected, Jackie stood there, a goofy smile plastered on her face. Behind her, Miguel's face looked flushed. He was a short guy but had a powerful build and a great smile beneath a head of loose curls.

He was also Jackie's shadow and secretly in love with her, though she pretended not to notice. It was the best thing for their working relationship. They were monster hunters and often in tight situations. Mixing business with pleasure could mean risking their lives...literally.

It wasn't bad enough that he had cheeks as red as my favorite rosy lip tint, but then painfully, his lips lifted into the most awkwardly forced smile I'd ever seen on a grown man. It looked like his face hurt!

How embarrassing. She definitely told him everything. Big mouth ass!

"Food acquired!" Jackie lifted the bags, and Miguel mimicked her, lifting trays of coffee. "Wasn't sure how you liked your coffee, Raymond, so I got black and had them throw in creamers and flavors on the side so you can make your own concoction."

"That's very thoughtful of you. Thank you." Raymond reached around me to grab the bags. "Miguel, right? Let's go in and set this up. Give the women time to talk about us."

"Sounds good to me." Miguel shot me a nervous glance and then stepped around to enter the house.

"He seems a lot friendlier today than yesterday." Jackie stuck her tongue out at me when the guys were out of view. "You put it on him, didn't you? Got that mood adjustment." She swirled her hips then humped the air with mimed thrusts.

"Hush!" I pushed her back and stepped out onto the porch, closing the door behind me.

"What's with you?" Jackie laughed. "Since when are you so uptight, Jericha?"

"Jackie, this is already a difficult scenario. Please. And did you have to tell Miguel everything? I can see by that stupid look on his face that you did. Usually, he tries to look all debonair, but now, he just looks like he got caught with his hand in the cookie jar. I can't take this. It's too—"

"Yo! Chill out!" Jackie grabbed my hands, which were flailing as I spoke, and pinned them to my side. "This isn't the woman I know. Why are you all over the place?"

"I..." I took a deep breath. "Girl, I don't know. This man, that demon. He's all up in my head, and I can't get him out."

"Damn. I was just teasing you, but this is serious." She sucked her teeth. "I have never known any man to get under your skin. You're the prototype for all my hype woman shit. Who am I going to tell my people to model themselves after if you start falling apart now?"

"Thanks for adding the pressure here. And yes, it is serious, which is why I'm so annoyed you told Miguel."

"Girl, I didn't tell that man anything." She rolled her eyes at me. "He saw Raymond. The man ain't blind. And he is smart enough to put two and two together. You guys were in your pajamas looking all disheveled. Anyone with half a sense would come to the same conclusion. Boots were knocking."

"We didn't have sex." I told what couldn't officially be called a lie. No sex was had—I mean, Raymond had a feast, but there was no penetration...by his dick.

"Either way, he doesn't care. And neither do I..." she said. "I see how you look at Raymond. And now that I see how you're physically responding to the man... Look, as long as he doesn't hurt you..."

"Stop it." I held my hand up. "Don't give the protective sister speech. This ain't that."

"Tell yourself whatever you need." She let my hands go and rolled her eyes. "I don't understand why people choose to cling to their delusions."

"Because they're safer than reality." I offered her the only explanation I could think of.

"Yeah, whatever. Now, can we get in there before my eggs get cold?" she fussed. "I hate reheated eggs!"

Fifteen minutes later, we all sat around the table with food in front of us. Awkward sounds of forks scraping against plates, glasses clinking, and chewing noises filled the kitchen. I avoided looking directly at anyone in the room by becoming overly concerned with my plants. The succulents looked a little wimpy. They definitely needed some love. How hadn't I noticed?

"So...demons. Those are real, and they're attacking. Wild, huh?" Miguel held up a piece of toast like it was a microphone.

Jackie elbowed him in the side. "Great ice breaker."

"Hey, it's better than sitting here listening to everyone chew." Miguel dropped his toast. "I'm sorry, but there is an enormous elephant sitting in this room, and I feel like its ass is in my face."

"Not the imagery I need in my head right now." Raymond looked at Miguel over the brim of his cup.

"He could have been less vulgar, but he's right." Jackie leaned back in her seat. "As delicious as all this is, we're here for more than breakfast. What's the plan?"

"We talked it over last night." I glanced at Raymond. "I'm going to set up Natalie so she can handle things for the company while I'm away, and then I'll go with Raymond to...hell."

"You're setting up a training plan?" Jackie smirked. "Really? Is this the time for that?"

"Look, demons be damned, I'm not messing up my business. According to Raymond, a day in hell is like a week on Earth. I can't be away for that long without making sure everything is good here. When all this is done, I still have employees to pay, a mortgage, and clients who depend on me."

"We can buy some time," Raymond spoke up, looking at Jackie. "It makes sense to get things in order here before leaving. I'll get the guys together, and we'll coordinate our efforts with your team as well."

"How long will you need?" Miguel asked. "We have men here, but we can't keep them for weeks or months."

"Just a couple of days to get Natalie trained."

"I can hang around after you leave." Jackie nodded. "Just to keep an eye on Natalie and the place until you return. It will be easier for me to move my operations here for a while than trying to keep our field men here. But they will stay until we're sure the heat is off."

"Once we leave, no one will be interested in coming here," Raymond confirmed. "And if they do, they'll follow our energy signatures back to the Bane."

"What happens once you're there? How will we know if you're okay?" Jackie asked. "You're taking one of my best friends to hell. I need to know what's going on."

"There's no cell service in the Bane." Raymond sipped his coffee.

"Do you want to take a moment and come up with a better answer? You better find a magical solution to this problem," Jackie fussed. "Use your damn shadows. I don't know, but figure out a way to let me know what's happening."

"I will do my best." Raymond took a long sip from his coffee. "Actually, Noville, he may have some ideas. I wonder if there is an implant we can use."

"Implant? In who?" My head snapped up. "You're not implanting anything in my ass!"

"What about the one with the vanishing horns?" Jackie asked after laughing at my response. "He seems pretty smart. Maybe he knows something, considering you all said he had a girlfriend on Earth. How do they keep in touch?"

"Looks can be deceiving," Raymond grumbled. "I don't know what he knows, but I'll ask."

"Touchy subject, that man. What was his name?" Jackie tapped the table with her nail. "Metice, right?"

"Is there anything else we need to consider before I head out?" Raymond asked. "It will take a while to gather everyone. I'll need at least the rest of the day."

"Nope, I think we're good. We can reconnect in the morning. Get a security detail up and running for the next couple of days until you leave."

"Good." Raymond stood and touched my shoulder. "I'll be back."

Without addressing any of Jackie's comments, Raymond left. That familiar chill lasted only seconds after he vanished.

"You need to find out what's up between him and that Metice." Jackie snatched the piece of bacon Raymond left untouched on his plate. "There's something there, I'm telling you."

"Why?" I shook my head. "Does it matter?"

"Because I want to know! Since when do I need reasoning for wanting tea? Something tells me whatever is brewing between them is piping hot!"

"Be careful, or you'll get burned," Miguel chimed in. "Wouldn't be the first time either."

Jackie and Miguel hung around after Raymond left. The three of us hadn't been together in years, and with what was happening, we didn't want to miss the chance to catch up. I laughed as they recounted their adventures and tallied their kills. It was always a competition between the two of them.

Jackie updated me on Lena and Whitney and showed me her growing social media platform and business. I gave her a few of my marketing contacts I thought would be able to help her further expand when she spoke about a product line she was thinking of launching.

While the conversation continued, I worked on finishing up the tea blend I owed Miguel and tripled the recipe. He deserved it, especially with having to deal with Jackie, who was more energetic than ever before. Part of me wanted to call her out about Miguel like she had me about Raymond. How quick would she be to curse me out if I pointed out that she clearly liked the man?

We also talked about her staying at my place once I was gone. Someone would need to take care of Kaa and the other plants. Jackie eagerly volunteered for the role. They liked her energy, and I trusted her not to give them dirty water or forget to rotate the potted plants for adequate sun exposure.

When they left, I went to my office, busying myself with finishing up the training materials for Natalie. I shot off an email letting her know we would start a new training schedule the next day.

After eating the food I'd ordered, my favorite burger and fries, I took a brief shower and headed to bed.

As my mind drifted off, I thought about Raymond and how much I wanted to have him next to me. Just before I could get frustrated by those thoughts, the chill was quickly replaced by the heat of his body. Raymond was there.

"I got you," he whispered into my ear as he pulled me into his body.

How was I ever going to sleep comfortably again without him?

18

From across the room?

As expected, Natalie was all too eager to receive more training. Her eyes were so wide, they looked like they hurt when I presented the new manual and told her it had everything she would ever need outside of banking details. I didn't expressly say I was going to be gone for a long time, just that I wanted to prepare her. She suspected nothing, considering how much she and Raymond had been on my case about letting her take on more work.

And the girl showed out. Honestly, by the end of the second day, I could have handed her the keys confidently. But also, by the end of the second day, I realized that meant I would then have to carry my ass off to hell, so I made the brilliant decision to stretch things out a bit. What would it hurt if I just took a couple more days to make sure she was truly going to be okay on her own?

The problem was, after the first day, Jackie started shadowing me. She watched everything I did with Natalie and could clearly see how competent the young woman really was. On the fifth day, Jackie called me out on my shit.

My head snapped up from the notes in my hand as Jackie, dressed like she was ready for the battlefield, burst into my office. I eyed the combat boots and wondered if she wore them to kick me in the ass.

"What are you doing?" She stood there, her expression twisted in judgment,arms crossed over her chest. Oh, she meant business.

"Going through paperwork. Is that hard to tell?" I gathered the files I had splayed out in front of me and held them up. "There are four more prospects I want to reach out to."

"Jericha, you're dragging this out and you know it." She snapped her fingers at me. "Those dusty ass folders haven't been touched in how long? Why is it so important for you to reach out to them now? You're so worried about doing bad business, but you're going to start new conversations before running off to hell?"

"Jackie," I gasped and pulled the folders closer to my chest. "How could you say that? These clients are just as important as any of my other ones."

"Look, I wouldn't want to be in your position either, but you can't keep running from this." She grunted at me. "While you sit up in this office thinking of more ways to keep your ass here on Earth, we're out there fighting off more attacks."

"What attacks?" My breath caught in my chest. No one had mentioned anything about attacks to me.

"Girl, you have to know what's going on." Jackie leaned over and snapped her fingers in my face. "Wake the hell up! My people and your shadow man's team have been keeping the threat at bay. I don't care what Raymond or that other demon has to say about it anymore. I'm not going to keep coddling you, because the threat is only growing."

"You've been hiding attacks from me?" I put the files down, standing from my seat. "Why wouldn't you tell me? I thought everything was okay."

"Raymond's idea, not mine. I'm done with this. I broke two nails in that last fight!" She held up her hand, displaying her ruined manicure. "I can't get them fixed until I go home, and I can't go home until you take your ass to the Bane and deal with this shit."

"You've been really wanting to say that to me." I pointed at her fingers. "And you held it back. That's not like you."

"No, it's not. I did it because he asked me nicely and promised me food." Jackie sat in the guest chair next to my desk. "But this is getting ridiculous, and I can't keep my team here forever. There are other assignments, other threats we're supposed to be keeping the world safe from."

"You're right. I know it."

"What's the problem?" She pointed at the files in my hands. "This place and those crusty old files will be fine. I already agreed to hang around here and help Natalie, process payroll and manage the big contract issues, take care of your home and pets. What more do you need?"

"Jackie, we're not just talking about a trip overseas or something. This is hell! I know I'm strong and typically not afraid of much, but come on. Even you would be afraid to do this, right? Don't treat me like I'm crazy." I took a deep breath, hoping to calm myself, but it didn't work. "I'm terrified of what I'll see when I get there and afraid I won't make it back to tell you all about it."

"Girl, I won't sit here and lie to you. The idea is crazy, and there is no amount of money that would convince me to trade places with you, but the point has already been proven. Those things will come here to get to you and Raymond." She softened as she continued. "The problem is, we're not equipped to keep them at bay for much longer."

"And if you were in my place?" I asked.

"I'd already be gone." She shrugged. "Prolonging it changes nothing, but it puts everyone around you in more danger."

"So what you're saying is, I'm a selfish ho?"

"A ho, no. But selfish?" She pinched her fingers in front of her face. "Yeah, you are a little."

"You always give it to me straight. Thank you for that." I pushed the files away from me.

Jackie was right. There was nothing of use in them. They were prospects I had ruled out time and time again, the files I picked through whenever I felt desperate.

"Look, how about we have one more night out?" Jackie offered with a big grin on her face. "And then you pack your bags and take your ass to hell."

"How do you possibly make that sound like more fun than it is?" I shook my head.

"It's a gift!" She mimed a small bow. "Just make sure you pack plenty of moisturizers. You know how dry you get. I can't imagine you won't be a piece of ashy toast down there."

I sucked my teeth at the thought. "Have I told you how hilarious you are?"

"No." Jackie fluffed her pixie cut. "It would be nice if you did, though. I'm not lacking in self-confidence, but compliments are nice either way."

"You're right, but I wouldn't want to lie to you." I stuck my tongue out at her then called for Natalie.

"Oh, so *you're* the comedian!" She leaned across my desk picking up the document left there. "To Conjure Love. What are you doing with this?"

"It's the new production at the studio we're contracted with. No one is supposed to know about this, so don't tell anyone."

"Oh, I already know about it." She waved her hand at me. "The announcement isn't out, but I have an inside tip, of course. I can't wait for the big party!"

"How do you know about this?"

"Lena… The name didn't look familiar to you? That's our Lena!" she shouted. "Our girl is a star!"

"What?" I picked up the document. "Oh shit, how did I miss that?"

"Miss what?" Natalie asked as she entered.

"Um, nothing." I quickly changed the subject because, as much as I loved Natalie, she had a problem with gossip. "Natalie, I've been training you over the last few days to take on more responsibility around here, and you've done an amazing job. Which is great, because I've been training you for a reason."

"Thank you." She grinned. "What reason? Am I getting a promotion?"

"Something like that, yeah." I nodded.

"Your boss is taking a much needed…vacation," Jackie offered. "And you're going to be running this place for her. I'm sure that leads to a promotion and a pay bump of some kind."

After a sharp side-eye to the woman promising raises she wouldn't be paying for, I offered Natalie more explanation. "I'm going to be going away for a few weeks, starting tomorrow. I understand if this is too short of notice for you to—"

"No, absolutely. I can handle it." She waved her hands to stop me from speaking. "You sure you don't want to leave now?"

"You're that ready to get rid of me?" I chuckled. "I thought you liked me as your boss."

"Oh, I didn't mean it that way." Natalie scratched her neck nervously.

"Yes, you did, and that's okay." Jackie sucked her teeth. "She needs to back off! This will be great practice for her. Besides, I'll be here if you need anything. Jericha has downloaded everything about this business into my head. So, she can go away and completely disconnect. Also, I'll be the one processing payroll or any other financial things."

"Jackie, you're supposed to be on my side," I butted in.

"I'm on the side of the greater good. It's all I can do, since I'm not funny enough for my dream career in standup comedy." She stuck her tongue out at me.

"I'm just going to get things wrapped up here, and then we can go." I moved to clean up my desk but was cut off by Natalie.

"Let me!" Natalie offered eagerly. "I'll be in control for a few weeks anyway, right?"

"True." I glanced back at the desk, longing for the safety of overworking.

"Okay, well, I'll handle things tonight, and then you can let me know how I did tomorrow."

"Brillant idea, Natalie." Jackie clapped. "See, she's already running this place like a pro!"

A few minutes later, Jackie pushed me out the front door. I took one last glance back to see Natalie standing with her tablet in hand, grinning and waving. I imagined she did a cartwheel and danced around the office the second we were out of view. Okay, the cartwheel might have been overkill, but she would have definitely done a celebratory shuffle.

"What are we going to do now?" I asked as Jackie drove me away from the office.

The woman was clearly planning to kidnap me, because Miguel was there to drive her rental. He followed us closely.

"First, we need to pack your bags," she said. "Then, we're going to a party. Nothing major, just a last hurrah for you before you leave."

"You want to have a party now?" I twisted in my seat to look at her. "A room full of helpless humans doesn't sound like an open invitation for demons to you?"

"Who said anything about humans? Look, I'm all for protecting them, but parties are way more fun when they're not around. I reached out to some of our old friends. It's going to be me and you and a room full of magical creatures who can kick those demon's asses if they even think about spoiling our fun."

"You're serious, aren't you?" I shook my head. "I don't know, Jackie. This seems risky."

"Yes, I'm serious." She rolled her neck as she spoke. "You've been working your ass off, and now you're going to another world. How many times have you said you wanted a break or to reconnect with old friends? Hell, we've talked about meeting up for months now, and it never happened. So tonight, before you take off and go fight demonic entities, we're going to let loose and celebrate everything you've accomplished and all the good that's coming. Tonight, all our magical buddies are coming to town, so get your elemental ass ready for a party!"

"Elemental. I forgot that's my official classification." I smiled.

"Well, alien isn't one we wanted to explore, remember?" She glanced at me. "Anyone who takes that on is bound to be probed!"

"True. I'll gladly opt out of having anything put up my butt!"

"You mean Raymond hasn't..." She looked away from the road to waggle her brows at me. "I thought you liked that."

"Get it together, woman." I slapped her arm. "No, he hasn't... Well...at least not yet." I stuck my tongue out, and she laughed.

"Girl, you're still just as kinky as ever." Jackie shook her head. "Can't believe I used to try to keep up with you. Does he know?"

"I have a feeling he does." I chuckled. "But let's stay on topic. Really, the classification, however questionable, is oddly comforting right now. I never expected that."

"It means you belong with us." She winked at me. "Not to get too sentimental, but you were a foster kid. Your entire life, you've had to choose your own family and find a place that felt like home. With us, you're home. So, make sure you survive this thing and come back. And when you get back, we won't take so long to hang out again. Promise?"

"I promise." I inhaled deeply as I realized just how much I needed to be around my girls and quickly thought of the other friends I'd been neglecting while building my business. The first thing I'd do when I got back would be to call them all and catch up.

"Okay now, you know if you're lying, you're going to owe me so much sushi!" she said, as if she hoped I was, in fact, lying.

We went to my house, packed several bags, one almost completely full of skincare, heavy on the moisturizer, and got cute for the party. After pre-gaming with street tacos, Jackie drove us to the event hall she'd booked. I'd expected a few friends, but she had gone all out, and when the doors opened, the faces of people I hadn't seen in years met me.

"Ta-dah!" Jackie waved her hands as she presented a party hall decorated in my favorite colors: rosy reds, soft lavenders, and forest greens. There were fake vines and twinkle lights tracing the walls, with various strings of petals falling from the ceiling. They swayed softly overhead. It was like walking into a summer garden party, and it made my heart feel instantly full.

Jackie was right. I needed a proper sendoff. I just had to keep reminding myself that this wasn't sending me off to my death. It was Jackie's way of telling me she loved me and distracting herself from what was to come.

As I walked into the space, greeting old friends and sipping the fruity drink that someone handed to me, my mind went back to our college days, when we were mostly carefree and had our entire futures ahead of us. Jackie had dragged me to more parties than I could count, even after I'd graduated and she was still in school. She was one of the few friends who refused to let me walk away from her when I shut down after Rose's betrayal.

I spent the next few hours dancing and being grateful for healthy knees, singing, and avoiding the werewolf who still blamed me for his hair loss. Failed tonic...long story. I added way too much poinsettia sap, and he lost every hair on his body. Hairless werewolves are a terrifying sight. As far as I knew, he still hadn't grown it all back nearly fifteen years later. My tipsy brain toyed with the idea of asking him to shift so I could see what he looked like, and that was exactly why I never drank.

As the hours ticked on and the drinks continued to flow, I felt like I would pass out, but I refused to end the night. The longer I could stretch it out, the longer I could avoid the inevitable. But the inevitable wasn't planning on avoiding me. As I danced in a corner with Christa, a witch who used the luck of others to feed her spells, I spotted the shadow forming across the room.

I know damn well this heffa didn't take my luck!

As I side-eyed the woman who started to shimmy away from me, he appeared: the man I had seen very little of since he went on security detail. The man whose presence made my temperature rise despite the chill that accompanied his arrival. Raymond.

He spotted me quickly, and when our eyes locked, a voice inside my head said *run, girl!*

So, I did. I hurried over to another group of women who were talking about rumors of a witch who had put an actual spell in her fictional book. I thought I heard them mention Lena, but I couldn't be sure. I was too busy trying to monitor Raymond.

He stopped approaching, but why?

I looked at him closely, squinting my eyes, because his face looked off. Everything was fine except his lips. The more I tried to focus on his usually full lips, the less I could actually see them. It was like looking at them through a piece of plastic. I could almost make out the shape.

"You plan to run from me all night?" I heard his voice like he was speaking into my ear and jumped. The women looked at me like I was nuts, and how could I blame them? I'd moved into their conversation, added nothing to it, and was acting weird as fuck.

"Got a chill, sorry." I played it off with an awkward laugh.

But he wasn't done—far from it. As I stood there, trying to appear normal and clutching on to my purse like it would save me, he upped the ante.

Fingers, his fingers, materialized between my thighs. They radiated a deep heat that went straight to my clit, and I bit my lip, eyes darting to him. His lips were clear as day and lifted into the smile of a man ready to drive me insane.

I looked at those strings of flower petals hanging above his head and wished they were real. I would use them to tie his ass up while I ran for it.

I felt the heat growing between my thighs and pressure parting them, like the shadows created extra space there. I looked at him, and his hand was in his pocket. Raymond raised his left brow and cocked his head to the side, as if daring me to say or do anything. I didn't. Instead, I took a couple of steps back from the women and scanned the area, looking for an exit.

I can't believe this is happening...but damn it if it's not sexy!

Okay, maybe I was a little tipsier than I thought, because my heart was racing and my mind only grew more curious about what he would do. The game was on, and I was eagerly participating.

And then, he did it. My panties slipped to the side, and one, no, two fingers moved inside my pussy. I gasped...loudly, and too many eyes turned to me. I had to get out of there; I knew what he was doing. There was no way I would let this man make me come in the middle of my send-off party!

So, I ran. I ran for the exit, and when I found the sign for the ladies' room, I made a beeline for the door and whined when I realized it was locked. I jiggled the handle until an annoyed voice shouted, "Occupied!"

"Damnit." I stomped my foot then fell against the wall as Raymond continued working his fingers inside me. I wouldn't be able to hold it together much longer.

Then, I saw it: my freedom. The coat closet.

"Wherever you are, I'll find you." Raymond's voice was a joyous sound as another finger appeared. It flicked my clit softly, teasing me.

"You're having fun with this, aren't you?" I asked aloud, thankful I was in the hall alone.

"Yes. I am. Keep running, little mouse." The deep chuckle vibrated in my ear and sent shivers down my neck into my stomach.

I'm supposed to be in control. I take the lead. Why am I enjoying this?

As my internal conflict continued, I made a dash for the closet. Inside, a soft yellow light flickered, giving off a gentle buzz. I closed the door behind me and leaned against it. I didn't want anyone coming in and finding me there.

As my back touched the door, I finally let the deep moan building inside me out as that first sweet orgasm came to a head. I gripped the wall as my panties became drenched. Fun fact: voyeurism and squirting, not a great combo.

Then, I was alone. For a moment. I could feel the shift in energy. Raymond had left me to myself. It was a moment, just long enough for me to compose myself and reach for the doorknob. My thoughts? Find Jackie and get the hell out of there. He wanted a chase? I would give him one. Ninety miles an hour across town!

Well, that never happened. Because the moment I thought I had a chance, those hands were there. As the first one appeared in front of me, shadowy and waving, I backed up, and the light went out.

"Shit." I reached around for the light switch but couldn't find it. "What are you doing?"

I called out to him and hoped he would respond and give me more time to get out.

"No more running," Raymond responded. Only his voice was there, his voice and his hands. In the dark, I felt his hand slowly move through my hair and slip around my mouth as his voice returned. "Shh. You wouldn't want anyone to hear you, would you? You asked about my hands. Let me show you what I can do with them."

One hand was on my left thigh, another on my stomach, another on my neck, and another grabbed my right breast. I stood there, covered in his hands, and my pulse quickened. They were firm, but they didn't hurt me. This was a game, and Raymond called the shots. I'm not sure when I decided I would let him. Probably when I first saw him appear across the room, that devious expression on his face. As the sixth hand appeared, pulling up my skirt and slipping into my panties, I gasped. My head fell back and landed on his shoulder.

"Got you," Raymond said, and I realized he was there with me in the dark corner as his many hands strummed every sweet spot they could find.

"This isn't fair," I said when the hand over my mouth moved away. "I'm supposed to be in control now. You said in the real world, I'm in control."

"You're right. Let me fix that." His lips pressed against my neck as something in the darkness shifted; a chill wrapped around me, fought off by his heat. Then, we were no longer in that coat closet.

19

Raymond's Place

The darkness enveloped us, clutching us tighter as the moments went on. A sudden, overwhelming feeling of dread gripped me. My heart hammered against my ribs, sweat slicked my skin, and the feeling of spinning threatened to send me tumbling into unconsciousness. The strange crackling sound, sharp and persistent, was the only thing that kept me cognizant.

That feeling of eating a bowl of Rice Krispies. Snap. Crackle... Before the pop, tingles spread from my mind all across my body, like feathers being passed over me again and again. The blanket of strange energy moved quickly, shifting with the cold of the darkness, but there was warmth there, against my back. Raymond.

Raymond.

Raymond.

I repeated his name in my head because it was the thing that kept me sane in the strange moment. He was there with me, his body against mine, his arms around me. The more I thought of him, the more of his warmth I felt. It was like an anchor bringing me back to my body, keeping me grounded.

Raymond.

When the darkness pulled away along with that crackling chill, we stood in an unfamiliar room.

Tall ceilings and walls painted a dark burgundy left me overwhelmed. Long black curtains hung over arched windows partially opened, letting the moonlight filter into the space. The room felt like a contradiction to the smell of oak, cedar, and smoke. My eyes said opulent, my nose said simple cabin in the woods.

My heart continued to race, pounding in my chest as I catalogued the space. To the right of us was a plush red sofa draped in a soft cream throw. Just ahead, left of the window that let moonlight wash over my face, were two large paintings of strange landscapes that looked familiar and yet not.

The tall plants sitting in the corners of the room brought me comfort. I could feel how healthy they were. Their leaves bowed to me like a greeting. They were happy in this home. The last thing I could see in my peripheral was the bar to the left of us. The light of the moon glinted off the glass bottles that lined the shelves above it.

This act of cataloging the space made me feel better, but a question still hung in the air.

Where was I?

"Relax." Raymond lowered his lips to my ear as he spoke the simple command.

I realized how tightly I'd been holding my body. The lower half of my face was already beginning to throb with sharp pains as a direct result of my jaw being clenched so tightly. I took a deep breath, again inhaling that woodsy scent, and let the tension fall away.

"Where are we?" I asked, not moving away from him. I felt safer in his hold.

"My home," he answered, tightening his arm around my waist, as if he knew exactly how I felt.

"This is where you live?" My mouth fell open. "Not at all what I imagined."

"What did you imagine?"

"A pigsty," I joked.

"Funny. Either way, we're no longer in public." His voice lowered to a rumble in my ear. "So, who's in control now?"

That was enough to snatch me out of the semi-thawed state fear left me in. I pulled away from him and turned on him to put my finger in his face as I scolded him.

"That's not fair," I fussed. "You can't just kidnap me to get your way!"

"Who said I played fair?" He walked away from me, heading over to the bar.

"Jackie is going to be worried about me," I spoke as he went to work making a drink. "She'll find me. She has ways. And when she does, she's going to kick your ass."

"No, she isn't. I already told her I was taking you home." He winked at me.

"And she just let you?" My mouth fell open. There was no way Jackie had agreed to this.

"Why wouldn't she?" He continued working on his concoction. "I never thought you were the type to let someone else fight your battles for you."

"I'm not."

"Sure." He finished the mixture, dropping a slice of lemon in it and handing it to me. "Drink this."

"What is it?" I realized then that I hadn't paid attention to what he was putting in the glass. "I'm not thirsty."

"Something to prevent you from having a hangover tomorrow." He stared at me. "We have a long trip ahead of us, and I don't need you getting sick along the way."

I put the cup to my nose and inhaled an earthy scent. "What's in it?"

"Nothing toxic." He smirked.

"You know, that's not exactly the best way to convince someone to drink a suspicious liquid."

"Fine. Let's find another way to convince you." He stepped around me, and I followed his movement with my eyes, but my tipsy brain lagged for a moment when he lifted his hand in the air.

Whack! His hand landed firmly against my ass.

"Drink it," he said after I jumped from the impact.

"Oh!" I looked back at him. "Are you serious right now?"

"You need another?" He rubbed his palms together, squinting as he focused on his target. "How many will it take?"

"You can't just spank me and make me do what you want." I protested.

"Let's test that theory." He pulled his hand back, targeting my left cheek.

"Okay!" I said, stepping away from him and quickly chugging the drink. It tasted the way it smelled: earthy. A frown creased my face as the thick, cool liquid coated my tongue with a chilling, almost violent descent to my stomach.

"That wasn't so bad, now was it?"

"That tastes like dirt." I stuck my tongue out at him. "Why would anyone drink that?"

"Just wait for it." He moved to sit on the stool next to the bar and watched me.

Moments later, I felt it: the energy surge just beneath my skin. It moved from my toes up to my head and, like a magnet to metal, pulled away the intoxication left behind by many fruity drinks. As the seconds passed, I felt surer on my feet, my mind cleared, and the slight nausea went away. And then, I was...sober.

I felt like I had just woken up from the best night of rest. Even my skin felt clean, like I'd showered for an hour. How the hell could a drink do that?

"Woah." I looked at the cup as if the secret to what I experienced would be written inside it.

"Do you feel better now?" he asked with raised brows that told me he already knew the answer.

"That's absolutely amazing. How does it work and where can I get more?"

"Do you need more?" Judgment laced his question. "Since when do you drink like that?"

"Since I'm planning to leave the planet for a new world where I might die." I put the cup down on the bar. "Something like that will push a woman to do strange things, like knocking back six suspiciously fruity drinks."

"Interesting." He stood, sliding the cup into the sink behind the bar. "So what you're telling me is you become reckless when you're afraid?"

"That's not what I said," I defended myself. "I let loose one night. Do you think I'm not allowed that? This coming from the man who keeps trying to convince me to stop being in control of everything. Isn't that hypocritical?"

"You could consider it to be, but when I tell you to stop trying to control everything, I mean, let other people do things for you, not put yourself in a spot where you can be hurt," he scolded me. "There are demons after you. They will take any opportunity they can to hurt you."

"I considered that, and I let Jackie handle it for once." I started to defend myself then stopped, because I didn't have to justify a damn thing to anyone. "Wait. I didn't do anything wrong. Why do I feel like I'm in trouble?"

"Because you've been a bad girl, Jericha," he said in a forceful yet playful tone before phasing out and appearing again behind me. "Bad girls have to be punished."

Punish me!

"Bad girl?" I shook my head; why the hell was I excited about the idea of being punished by this man? "I haven't been a bad girl."

He smacked my ass again, holding on for a moment before rubbing the spot where his palm met my ass. "Don't lie to me."

"I'm not lying. What do you think I did wrong?"

"You told me you were okay when you weren't." His hand slipped around my neck. "Jackie talked to me. She said you're afraid. Why didn't you tell me?"

"I'm going to kill her," I muttered. "Since when is she so open to men? She hates y'all."

"It took some convincing." I could hear the humor in his tone. "And about five hundred dollars' worth of sushi. I have never seen anyone inhale fish so quickly. It's concerning, really."

"I'm glad you two got close."

"Now." He tightened his hold on my neck. "Tell me why you lied to me."

"Because I'm not used to feeling this way." I squeezed my eyes shut, imagining I was driving down the highway, ranting to the universe like I often did. "Everyone keeps telling me how I'm supposed to be. Loosen up, pull back, delegate. None of you are thinking about how incredibly uncomfortable that makes me feel. It's strangulating to think of having anyone else take care of things. If they mess up, it's on me. I have always had to be prepared for everything. I couldn't mess up because there was no one there to catch me if I fell. I have no family left, and all my friends, while I love them, have their own burdens. I never want to lean on them too much because I'm afraid that will break our bond. So, I prepare. I over-plan and I double check everything. But how could I have ever prepared for something like this, Raymond?"

"Again, I ask," he spoke, "why didn't you tell me? What makes you think you couldn't share that with me?"

"You're acting like I purposely hid something from you." I pulled away from his hold, and he let me. "It never crossed my mind. Honestly. I handle my own shit, Raymond. You know that."

"If we're going to survive this, if we're going to be together, you have to drop that." He moved closer to me, bringing a fresh wave of that woodsy scent with him. "You're going to have to consider me."

"Be together?" I swallowed. "Suddenly, this feels like we're talking about something very different."

"I told you; I got you." He pulled me to him, my chest against his. "I meant that, in every possible way."

"I—Raymond. That's a much bigger topic. I think…"

"None of this works unless you stop acting like you're alone and trust me," he cut me off. "From now on, I expect you to be honest with me about what you're thinking and feeling, especially when we get to the Bane."

"I just really think…" This time, he cut me off by pressing his lips against mine. Every protest in my head silenced the moment our lips met. My back arched, and my arms slipped up around his neck as the kiss deepened. When he pulled away, a part of me ached.

"I'm taking you to hell with me." He looked deep into my eyes, his breath steady as his hands found my back. "You can't run anymore."

"I'm not running. I already explained things to Natalie, and I talked to Jackie. Everything is set for us to leave tomorrow night. I've even packed my bags."

"Good." His right hand slipped from my waist to my ass.

"Does that mean I don't have to be punished now?" I asked playfully, partly because I didn't want to get back to the part of the conversation that focused on our relationship status. Yes, it required more thought, but honestly, that could wait until after we made it back from hell.

He tightened his grip on my ass then gave it a small smack. "What do you think?"

"I think you should reconsider."

"Interesting." He let me go, stepped back, and scratched his chin. Then, he pulled off the gray shirt he wore, revealing his chest and arms. I watched in awe as the tattoos on his flesh moved, and the shadow around his form spread. "I don't think I will," he said, and those shadows reached out to me. They wrapped around my waist and arms and lifted me from the floor.

"I'd like to play a game," Raymond said and then turned and walked away from me. The shadows carried me behind him.

"If you had more plants in this place, I swear I would use them against you!" I threatened.

"Why do you think I didn't take you to your home?" he laughed as we continued through the house.

We went down a short hall, up a large staircase, and into a room with double doors. The room felt like him—open, spacious, dark. There was a massive bed, a bookshelf cluttered with books, and a large armchair just beneath the window. That was it, simple and to the point.

The shadows held me floating in the center of the room while Raymond took a seat in the armchair. It moved, positioning him just right so he could watch the show.

When he was ready, the shadows did the work for him. They pulled away the dress I wore, removed my bra, and left me levitating with nothing but my panties on.

"Are you afraid?"

"No," I spoke as a chill crossed my skin, quickly followed by the warm touch of his shadows.

"Good." He stood and made a path around me, examining my body. "Damn, you look good." He smacked my ass again, and a soft moan crossed his lips in appreciation of the recoil.

I felt slight pressure on my back as his shadows bent me over. Raymond had the perfect view as he rubbed my ass, slow circles on each cheek before his thumb brushed across my asshole. I moaned and heard him chuckle, like he'd received confirmation of something.

"Something else you like, huh?" he asked as he continued his path around my body.

Still bent over, I turned my head to look at him. "With the right person."

"Hmm." He returned to his seat in front of me. "Have you found the right person?"

"Are you asking if I've ever let someone fuck me in the ass?" I asked.

And that got me a shadow slap right across my rear.

"Have you?" His voice sounded strained, like the thought alone upset him.

"If I say yes?" I couldn't help myself.

Smack.

"Have you?" he repeated, eyes darkening as he watched me.

I bit my lip as I considered the strain in his voice and what it meant. I knew it; the sound of possession. Soon, this man would try to claim me. Would I let him? Instead of pushing him again, I answered simply. "Yes."

SMACK!

"What was that for?" I lifted my head to look at him defiantly. "I answered you."

"Never again." His jaw tightened. "You belong to me now."

"I belong to no one," I said, even though I knew what the result would be.

SMACK!

I winced but thought about saying it again. *It hurt so damn good!*

I kept my eyes on him as his shadows worked my body. Soft caresses covered my ass before they spread across me, over my back, stomach, breasts, all the while keeping me bent over in front of him. I lifted my head again to see him sitting in front of me.

Raymond maintained his focus. His eyes carefully watched me as he directed his shadows, and the longer it went on, the more his dick grew. That was where my eyes were, focused on that area tightening beneath the fabric of his pants.

I froze when I realized he caught me. I was damn near salivating, imagining him without those damn pants. When I expected a smack, another punishment, he surprised me. Raymond phased out of view for a moment, and when he returned, he was completely naked. He sat in front of me, legs spread, dick hard and in full view.

The shadows carried me closer to him—so close, I could almost touch his dick with my tongue.

Raymond grabbed a handful of my hair and lifted my head so he could look me in the eye. "You want it?"

I bit my lip.

SMACK!

"I asked you a question, Jericha." When he spoke, his voice felt like another set of hands, drawing every letter of my name across my flesh.

"Yes," I moaned.

A moment later, I floated back from him. The shadows held me in the same position: bent over, forced submission. It felt like a challenge. If I protested, there would be more of his special...punishments. Something told me the smacks on the ass were introductory. I wasn't ready to find out the next level.

Just as that thought moved through my mind, Raymond stood. He opened his hand, and slowly, a paddle board formed. Made of shadows, it had little studs along the face of it.

Can this man hear my damn thoughts or something?

"Tell me your safe word," he instructed as he took slow steps around me.

"Honeybee," I responded calmly.

"I knew it." He stopped just to the right of me. "You really are a naughty girl, Jericha." His hand rubbed my ass. "Let's find out how naughty."

I took a deep breath, the best way to prepare for what came next. The first smack of the paddle hurt more than I expected. It stung a little but wasn't too bad. The second came soft. The third was even harder than the first. He continued, and I let him.

Fifteen. That was how many times the paddle made contact with my ass. Fifteen painfully sweet smacks across the ass, and I imagined how red I was, but I never said the safe word. I never felt like I was unsafe.

After he finished, the shadows moved across my flesh, cooling the sting left behind like aloe to a sunburn.

"Good girl," he hummed approvingly. And then, the shadows stood me up. His hand was there, caressing my ass as he kissed my neck and shoulder. "And what do you say?"

I'd been in this situation before, though never on the receiving end. Still, I knew what he expected. "Thank you, Raymond."

"Let's continue," he whispered, and then the shadows lifted me in the air, flipping me on my back to look at the ceiling. My legs were open, and when I looked down my body, Raymond's face was perfectly positioned between my thighs.

He's going to eat my pussy while I'm floating?

How the hell could I not be excited about that? My head fell back as he started. The first stroke of his tongue against my clit had me vibrating. I turned my head to the side and saw him stroking his dick with his hand, and my mouth watered again.

He caught me, once again, looking at his dick. He stopped eating my pussy and licked his lips, which were lifted in an inquisitive grin. "You want that?"

"Yes," I said, eyes moving back to his dick, which faded away. There he was, looking like a damn ken doll, all smooth in the crotch. "What the-?"

"Look up," he instructed.

I did, and there, floating above my face, was his dick, big, imposing, and throbbing.

"Holy hell." I can't lie, I cringed a little. It felt like the dildo in the back of my closet had crawled out of its box and attacked! Damn me for preferring the one that vibrates!

"Open your mouth," Raymond said firmly.

I glanced down at him, nervous. All I could think about was his dick sliding so far down my throat, I couldn't get it out. How would that sound? Here lies Jericha Brown, death by swallowing an entire dick while in a floating shadow hammock.

"Trust me." He tapped my ass lightly.

Hesitantly, I opened my lips and watched in a strange mix of horror and anticipation as his dick slowly slid into my mouth, just the head. The tip of his dick touched my tongue, and I salivated. He tasted of sunbaked earth and cool, clear water, like the flavors of a warm summer day.

My nervous ass just floated there, mouth open, dick just sitting on my tongue as I catalogued the flavors like it was a wine tasting.

"Suck my dick, Jericha." I felt him shift his weight, and his dick moved in and out of my mouth carefully until I responded.

I wrapped my lips around him, feeling the veins pulsing against my tongue, and sucked. It was slow at first, but he encouraged me with each thrust. He reached deeper into my throat until I gagged on his length. When he went too far, I put my hands up to push him back, and though I couldn't see him, I felt him. I noticed then that my hands had partially vanished. I stopped sucking and looked down, and I could see my palms against his thighs.

After that, knowing I could control his thrust, I went in, sucking, slobbing, pulling him deeper into my mouth. I reached my arms out, moving through the shadowed void, and grabbed his ass as I controlled the motion. His hands gripped my sides, and I felt him seizing. The smokey taste of his cum, drips that told me I almost had him, filled my mouth.

"Damn it!" he cried out, and I continued. "You want this cum?"

"Yes," I mouthed around his dick then went into vacuum mode.

"Fuck!" His hands found my tits, and he held them like handlebars as he unloaded down my throat, trembling until the last drop. Then, his dick faded from my mouth.

I swallowed the smokey flavor happily, a triumphant smile on my face quickly replaced by shock when Raymond tested me again. His hands were back on my ass, his mouth on my pussy, and then one finger slid into my ass. I knew what it was. He wanted to know if I would let him.

I gave him the silent cue and pushed my hips back, thrusting my ass against his hand, encouraging him to explore my body more. He responded with a low chuckle against my pussy before he stopped licking me. He stepped away as the shadows that held me in the air flipped me back over and carried me to the chair by the window.

The shadows placed me on the chair knees first so my ass was in the perfect position for what he wanted. I looked back at him in anticipation of his approach. With each step, he stroked his dick, and it once again grew to attention. When he reached me, he placed his right hand on my ass, still stroking himself with his left. His thumb slipped into my pussy first and then found its way back to my asshole. He smiled when a moan escaped me.

"You want it?" he asked.

I nodded.

"I can't hear you." He stuck his thumb in deeper. "I want to hear you say it, Jericha."

"Yes, I want you," I said.

I prepared myself for his dick to slip into my ass. That was clearly what he wanted, but he didn't go for it. Instead, he thrust into my pussy, deep and fast, then remained there for a moment before starting a slow and steady stroke. He kept going, thumb in ass, dick in pussy.

I gripped the chair, arching my back as much as I could. I pushed back, meeting his thrusts, helping him move deeper inside. Then, he stopped, and his hand found my throat to lift me. His mouth next to my ear, he growled.

"Tell me I'm the right one," he spoke, and my pussy quivered around his dick.

I knew exactly what he wanted: permission to enter. I said nothing, wanting to know what he would do if I denied him. He pulled his dick out of my pussy, just to the tip, then slammed back inside me. He waited, and I said nothing. Two of those shadowed hands appeared in front of me. They moved to my breasts and pinched my nipples. I had to keep the smile from my face; I liked it, but I wouldn't let him know it.

"Say it," he demanded.

"Say what?" I looked back at him.

"You want to play those games?" The hands on my nipples heated, and I squealed as my head snapped forward. I looked down to see the fingertips slowly glowing red.

"Okay," I said, and they cooled instantly. "Damn, you didn't even give me a chance."

"That was just a warning." He kissed my jaw. "Let me hear it."

"You're the one," I said as his lips moved to my neck.

"The only one," he instructed between kisses, and the shadowed fingers warmed a little, a warning that I should do as he asked.

"You're the only one."

His hand slid from my throat to cover my mouth. "Spit in it."

I spit in his hand then waited as he pulled from my pussy and covered his dick in my spit. Extra lube for his entry.

He placed his hand on my back and pushed me forward. My stomach clinched in anticipation, and I had to remind myself that clinching was *not* the move. So, I took a deep breath and relaxed.

He pressed against my asshole for a moment then slowly entered. I inhaled sharply when he first pushed inside. I couldn't remember the last time I'd let anyone do it. The pain of adjustment faded fast, and then there was pleasure, pure and intense.

I slipped my hand between my thighs and rubbed my clit. The combination of his hands on my hips, dick thrusting into my asshole, and my own fingers rubbing slow circles on that special spot quickly had my legs shaking. But even that wasn't enough, because I felt the heat of those shadows working for him. They moved across my back, up to my shoulder, down my arm, across my hand. They danced around my fingers before slipping inside my pussy. Moments later, that heat, that tingle that followed, found my G-spot.

"Fuck!" I cried out, gripping the chair for dear life. "I'm coming."

"No. Not yet," he said, and it was like everything stopped. The shadows pulled back as he lifted me from the chair and carried me over to the bed.

He disappeared while I lay there, on edge and highly irritated. When he returned, he had a towel in his hand and stood in front of me, cleaning off his dick, and the shadows returned. They moved in and out of my pussy, slow and unnerving, just enough to keep my body humming.

I realized what he was doing, and those hands appeared again, pulling my legs apart.

Did he just clean his dick before entering my pussy? Okay, consideration!

Raymond climbed into the bed, positioning himself on top of me. Then, he kissed me. His lips captured mine, stealing my breath as his dick slipped into my pussy. He fucked me slow and deep, each dive a targeted effort. My body seized beneath him. My nails dug into his back.

"Please," I moaned. I couldn't believe it, but I was asking for his permission to orgasm.

He had me. He knew it.

The deep chuckle rumbled in his chest, and then he whispered in my ear, "Let it go, baby."

And I did. I came.

"Good girl." Raymond remained on top of me until my legs stopped trembling. He kissed my lips, my chin, my neck. "I'll run you a bath."

He stood from the bed, and as he walked away, the shadows appeared with a blanket to cover my body. The heated cover felt like heaven. I smiled as I pulled it closer to my face, snuggling into it, then groaned when the alarm sounded in my bag. I lifted my head, wanting to check the alert but refusing to get up.

Raymond chuckled and nodded, and the shadows brought me the phone.

I tapped the cracked screen and frowned. "Oh no."

"What is it?" He stopped at the doorway. "Is everything okay?"

"The alarm at the job." I opened the app to view the cameras. There was nothing outside, no evidence of a break-in. I assumed it was a false alarm and entered the code to avoid the call to the cops, but something inside me said *check the other cameras.*

So, I did. Everything looked fine. The gym, kitchen, front office. It was all good—until I opened the camera in my office. The harsh glare of the lights illuminated the chaos: papers were strewn across my desk, broken pieces of the planter behind it. I quickly opened the previous recording stored in the cloud.

Natalie was there, standing in the office. "What was she doing there so late?" I narrowed my eyes as I watched her organizing items on her desk and doing a happy little dance.

I tapped the screen preparing to fast forward the video but paused when I saw the movement in the corner behind her. Something was there. I sat up, fear constricting my chest like a vise as the video's edge dissolved into an ominous black. Out of the shadows came a figure, its shape vaguely human but with an unnatural stillness that spoke of something otherworldly.

It grabbed Natalie and, as terrified as I knew she must have been, she fought that fear and did the smartest thing she could. Natalie hit the silent alarm, the button just beneath the desk. Then, the shadows swallowed them both.

20

They done took the wrong girl!

"Jericha, what is it?" Raymond crossed the room in what seemed like one step and grabbed the phone from my hand. He watched the video replay as I stared at my hands, clutching the blanket that covered my naked body.

"They got her. It stepped out of the shadows, and it took her." The words felt like daggers in my throat. Natalie. That demon, that monster who was likely there to get me, took Natalie instead. "How could I let this happen?"

"Don't do that, not now." He disappeared and returned quickly with clothes from my closet. Sweats, a t-shirt, and gym shoes. I dressed quickly while he made several calls on his phone. As soon as I was done, he was there. "Let's go."

Raymond held his hand out to me, and I took it without hesitation.

"Stay close." He looked at me as the dark opening appeared in front of us.

Raymond went through first, pulling me behind him. My instinct was to hold my breath as I stepped into the darkness and onto the narrow path. I glanced back, but his bedroom was already gone. As we walked, I forced myself to breathe and focused on his footsteps ahead of me, placing my foot exactly where he had.

The path we were on glowed slightly and gave just enough light for me to see Raymond ahead of me but nothing beyond him. I wasn't sure I wanted to see what else was out there, because there were noises in the darkness, painful wailing and an eerie wind that gave no breeze. I also had an unnerving feeling of being watched.

I clutched my fingers tighter around his hand as we moved; it was the only thing that kept the panic at bay. Don't get me wrong, I'd never been afraid of the dark, but this was different. I felt suffocated by the darkness, its weight was a tangible pressure against me. A constricting feeling pushed at my skin, making each movement stiff and unnatural.

"You're okay." He kept his gaze forward, but I heard his reassuring words as if he was speaking right into my ear. "Almost there."

After a few more awkward steps, a light appeared ahead of us. I tried to look around him but decided not to risk it. Raymond led me off the darkened path into the light of my office. As my foot touched familiar ground, I skipped forward, moving as quickly away from the shadowed path as I could.

"Ugghereisere..." The random sound fell out of my mouth as I shook my arms and legs, trying to relieve the strangulating feeling.

"What sound just came out of you?" Raymond laughed as the dark opening disappeared behind his head.

"That felt horrible!" I fussed. As soon as I was out of there, it was like all the panic I pushed back burst out of me all at once. "It was hard to move or breathe, and what the hell were those sounds? You could have warned me."

"It's better this way. If I made some big speech warning you about how it will be, you'd overthink it. Happens every time." He shrugged. "Better to just get it over with and talk about it later."

"Yeah, right. Lots to talk about." I slowed myself down, taking several deep breaths as the jittery feeling of panic eased from my body. The world felt real again, not icky and constricting.

"She fought." Raymond moved around to the desk behind me.

We stood in the center of my office, the scene of Natalie's struggle. He was right. I hadn't noticed it in the video because I was so consumed by the sight of her being swallowed by the shadows. She did more than just hit the alarm. She fought, clawed even. Drops of green were on the floor. Raymond bent down to touch it.

"Blood."

"Hers?" Fear struck me, worried my human friend had a not so human secret.

"No, demon." He looked around and found the pen on the floor just beneath the desk. He lifted it, and the sharp tip dripped green. "Smart girl."

"You're right. She is smart. Smart enough to keep herself alive until I get there." I pulled my phone from my pocket and pulled up Jackie's number, but Raymond's hand covered the screen before I could initiate the call.

"I already called Jackie. She's on her way here now," Raymond said. "And she's bringing backup."

I looked up from the phone at him. "You're in my head, aren't you?"

"Just anticipating your needs." His eyes locked on me. They were deep, consuming, and left heat on my flesh I couldn't comprehend.

"Tell me what I need now?" I didn't mean for it to sound like a question or for my voice to tremble the way it did.

"To find the demon who did this and remove his head." There was no question in his voice. That was exactly what I wanted.

"You really do know me, don't you?" I lowered my phone, and his full lips dropped as I moved my hand away from him. I hesitated before I searched the office for more clues. "How could this happen?"

"They've been targeting this place for days." Raymond picked up the chair that had been knocked over. "Maybe one of them thought they got lucky with everyone away."

"You think it was an accident?" I looked at him.

"Possibly." He looked around. "Yeah, I think so. If not, they could have gotten her anywhere. Why here? Why in your office?"

"They came for me." My stomach hurt just thinking about it. It was the first thought I had after watching the video. Natalie was in danger because they were there for me. "I should have left days ago. This wouldn't have happened."

"Don't beat yourself up. You couldn't have seen this coming."

"I should have!" I smacked the desk. "I was so busy worrying about losing my business, I didn't see it, the obvious threat to her."

"We should have had guys watching her as well." Raymond tried to take some of the weight off my shoulders. It didn't help. Natalie was my responsibility.

His words didn't take away the mounting guilt, but they activated something else in my brain, the part that was pissed about not knowing about the security details they had in place. He reminded me I was actually upset with all of them for not telling me the demons were attacking to begin with. I turned that anger into action. After a long breath, I shook away the part of myself that had been frazzled by Raymond. I needed the "get-shit-done" Jericha.

"Regretting past actions won't change them, but we can learn from them. That is the last time you hide something like this from me." I looked at him with a serious expression, but before he could defend himself, I continued. "I understand why you did it. You don't have to explain it, but no reason is good enough. It might have been hard for me to hear, but I'm a big girl. I've been taking care of myself for a long time. And while I am bending the rules here, allowing you to help me, that doesn't mean I don't need to know everything."

"Understood." He nodded. "Won't happen again, I promise."

"When Jackie gets here, I'll tell her everything. She can run things while I'm gone. She's already offered anyway. I know we planned to leave tomorrow, but after I hand everything off to her, we'll leave tonight."

"Are you sure?" He crossed the room and placed his hands on my shoulders.

"Of course I am." I looked up at him. "That thing took my friend. Natalie must be terrified right now, and she's the only one of us who can't even begin to protect herself in a situation like this. She's not magical. I can't waste any more time here, not when she's in trouble now."

"Good." He pulled me closer, his hands tightening on my shoulder as he did. Then, he kissed me. In the middle of the chaos in my office, with demon blood spilled on the floor, Raymond kissed me.

Everything went quiet as our lips pressed together. This wasn't like our other kisses. It wasn't one of lust or challenge. It was gentle, the kind of kiss that touched something so deep inside me, I forgot it existed. The kind of kiss I never let a man give me. My heart fluttered and my stomach tightened as his lips trembled against mine.

Then, the thought, like hot iron, pressed into the back of my mind. Was he afraid? Is that why he hadn't forced me to go into his world sooner?

When his lips lifted away, his forehead pressed against mine. I stared at his lips, afraid to look up into his eyes. I could feel his gaze on me, heavy, intense, wanting. What would happen to me if I did? Would that flutter in my chest grow?

I stepped back from him, placing my fingers on my lips as I turned my back on him. I couldn't look him in the eye. I had to keep my mind on the task in front of me. Natalie.

"We wait until Jackie gets here." A guttural sound, heavy with grief, escaped Raymond's lips as he spoke, reiterating the plan I'd already laid out. I flinched at the sound before he cleared his throat, and his voice returned to that usual smoothness. "Let her know what's going on, and then we leave. Tonight."

"Okay." I took a deep breath before I turned to face him. He was there, the cool guy I knew before that moment, and the tightness in my chest eased.

I was about to ramble. The need to just fill the space with words to avoid talking about that moment bubbled up in me like an unwatched cauldron. Luckily, my incoming rambles were interrupted by the sound of approaching tires. I moved to look out the window and saw the familiar car pulling up. A moment later, Jackie stepped out of the passenger side.

"She's here."

"I'll let her in," Raymond spoke quickly, and before I could look back at him, he'd already left my office.

Moments later, Jackie entered the office ahead of Raymond, who was trailed by Miguel.

"Are you okay?" Jackie ran straight to me. She grabbed me and looked me over like a mother whose child had just fallen off the park swing.

"I'm okay," I choked out as she crushed me in an unexpected hug.

"You tell them everything they need to know," Raymond spoke over Jackie's shoulder. "I have some things to take care of. It won't take long. I'll be back to get you."

My heart stuttered as I looked at him, and though my brain said to respond, my lips did nothing. That heavy awkwardness was still there.

Say something!

"Uh, um, o-kay." I cringed; what the hell was that?

He nodded. Chill covered my arms, and the shadow appeared behind him. A second later, Raymond was gone.

"What was that about?" Jackie let me go. Her eyes darted to the spot where Raymond had vanished then back to me.

"I-I don't know, but now isn't the time to try to process it. They took Natalie." I pointed to my desk where Natalie had been snatched.

"He told me on the phone," Jackie said. "Where's the video?"

I pulled up the video on my phone. She watched it then handed the phone to Miguel so he could inspect it.

"You mind if I plug in?" Miguel pulled the laptop from the bag that hung from his shoulder. "I want to see if I can pull anything else from the video."

"Sure." I nodded.

"Look, I hate to ask you this but," I looked at Jackie, "do you think you could stay here and watch the place while I'm gone?"

"I got it here, Jericha." She scoffed. "I already told you I would do that for you."

"Are you sure? I mean, you have so much to do. Running your own business and the monster hunter stuff. I hate to lean on you like this."

"Girl, don't make me pop you. I got it. And I have that damn manual you put together to make sure I don't mess anything up."

"And I'll be here with her." Miguel handed my phone back to me. "I've moved some things around so I can stay to watch her back, just in case."

"Thank you," I said, relieved things would be in good hands without me.

Jackie pulled me to the side while Miguel busied himself looking around the office.

"Girl, what is going on with you?" She lowered her voice. "And don't tell me it's nothing, because I've known you long enough to recognize when something's not right. You look pale and nervous, which means there is something bothering you. Now, typically, I would mind my business and wait until you're ready to talk, but this is different. I can't let you leave like this."

"He kissed me," I blurted out. She was right. I had to talk about it. I just didn't know how.

"So?" she shook her head. "You two have done a lot more than kiss."

"No, this was different. It wasn't just a kiss, you know? There was more behind it." I nodded slowly until her eyes widened with recognition.

"Oh," she sighed heavily. "I get it now."

"Yeah, like the kind of kiss that makes you want to have that 'what are we' conversation." I shook my head. "Jackie, I don't want to have that conversation with him or anyone else, for that matter."

"Damn, well, I mean, what *are* you two?" She knocked the question at me like a volleyball, like I hadn't *just* said I didn't want to have that conversation.

"Jackie! I—" I was going to tell her I didn't know what Raymond and I were. We were intense, passionate, hot, and opposing, but we were also magnets, and I felt his pull growing stronger every time I was near him. I was going to lay it all out because Jackie was a safe space, but that icy chill returned. It licked the back of my neck, and when I turned around, he was there again, that magnetic force already pulling on my chest. I wanted to run to him, have him wrap his arms around me and kiss me the way he had before. Instead, I stood there, mouth and eyes wide open like a deer in headlights.

His eyes met mine for a fleeting second in silent acknowledgment before he turned and walked to Jackie.

"This is for you." He handed her a small leather pouch.

She took it, opening it to peer inside. "What is it?"

"You asked for a way to keep in contact with her." He walked over to me and lifted another pouch. I held my hand out, expecting him to give it to me, but he didn't. He opened the bag and pulled out a necklace he then placed around my neck. I stilled. "It wasn't easy to get these, but you threatened to kill me, so I made it happen."

"How does it work?" Jackie held up the matching necklace.

"Hold the pendant in your palm and close your eyes." His eyes dropped to my face as he spoke. "You do the same."

I watched as Jackie did what he said. As soon as her eyes closed, her face relaxed, as if she'd immediately fallen into a deep sleep. After another glance at him, I did the same. When I closed my eyes, the sound of my own heartbeat transported me to a space made of fuzz. My skin tingled and my eyes itched, and then, it cleared away.

Jackie appeared right in front of me. It was just her head and shoulders floating there like a weird balloon, slightly distorted.

"Oh, shit!" She swiveled her head, and when she spoke, it sounded like static. It reminded me of old radio recordings, where the audio had strange pops and fizzles. "This is pretty cool."

"It is." I smiled, and relief washed over me. I was going away, but I would still be connected to her.

"Do you think they can hear us?" Jackie asked. "How secure is this thing?"

"I don't know." I chuckled; she always surprised me. There I was, my head full of sentimental thoughts, and she was analyzing the connection. It was what I should have been doing, what I *would* have been doing before he entered my life. Raymond. That man had changed me. In just a short while, I was becoming someone else.

Jackie's face suddenly vanished. I felt something warm on my shoulder and looked down, but there was nothing there. I relaxed my hand, releasing the cool stone, and the fuzzy space pulled back, leaving me looking at Raymond's hand on my shoulder.

"So you didn't hear me at all?" Jackie spoke to Miguel.

"No," Miguel said. "Just looked like you dozed off. Might want to be sitting down the next time you use that thing."

"Perfect." She examined the stone again. "I don't need you eavesdropping."

"As if I would do something like that." He frowned. "Wait, do you have something you don't want me to know?"

While they bickered, I looked at Raymond. Our eyes met, and it was like Miguel's question belonged to Raymond. Was there something I didn't want him to know?

"Hey, shadow man," Jackie snapped, her fingers drawing his attention away from me. "Explain how these work. I need more information. Is it a secure connection? How long do the calls last? Can anyone use them or just us?"

"Um, yeah." Raymond dropped his hand from my shoulder. "The connection will last up to ten minutes, but it might be shorter once she gets to the Bane. I haven't been able to test that out. It will work, though. The connection is secure. No one can hear what you say to each other while you're in there, and it's coded to both of you, but anyone can use it if they have something of yours, like hair."

"Hair?" Jackie touched the short cut on top of her head. "Seriously?"

"It could be anything you own, but a part of your physical being works best," Raymond said.

"Right." Jackie glanced at me with frantic eyes as Raymond continued talking.

"Hold it for more than fifteen seconds, and the other will pulse, letting them know you want to talk."

"That's pretty cool," Miguel spoke as Jackie wrapped her stone in her hand. Fifteen seconds later, I felt the pulse against my chest.

"It works." I looked down at it.

"You also must promise not to share this with anyone." Raymond looked at Miguel when he spoke. "No picking it apart or trying to study it. The device will disintegrate if you do."

"That's some advanced fail-safe." Miguel frowned. "Would have been cool if I could see the inner workings of it."

"This world is not ready for the magic of my home." Raymond warned. "Trust me."

"Got it," Jackie blurted out. "I'll keep this to myself."

"Are you ready?" Raymond asked me.

"Y-yes," I said after some hesitation.

He held his hand out, and the darkness appeared behind his head.

I shot one last glance at Jackie and wished like hell I could tell her everything I didn't get a chance to, but time was up.

"Be careful," she said in a voice smaller than I'd ever heard from her.

"I will. You be safe while I'm gone. Don't let this place fall apart." I crossed the room to hug my friend then returned to Raymond, who still held his hand out to me. I placed my hand in his and followed his lead...into the darkness.

21

Take me to the Bane

I didn't know how long I thought it would take to walk across the path to a new world, but I definitely thought it would be longer than forty-five seconds. Yes, it was forty-five seconds. I counted. I followed behind him, and as I moved, placing my footfalls exactly where he had, the mental counting was the only thing that drowned out the eerie wailing around us.

Just as I had before, I gripped his hand tighter with each step, and Raymond responded, squeezing his around mine, letting me know I would be okay. He would keep me safe. Only this time, I didn't hear his voice in my ear as we moved, just the counting in my head.

One. Two. Three.

Step. Step. Step.

Seven. Eight. Nine.

And then, ahead of him, there was light. It had a strange turquoise glow to it, like walking into the center of a jewel. I followed him because I trusted him, and I knew wherever that light led, I would be safe with Raymond.

A gentle breeze brushed across my skin as I took the last step from the darkness into that turquoise light. Then, my senses were completely overwhelmed. As my eyes adjusted to the brightness, a strangely sweet scent like pear filled my nostrils. My ears rang as they adjusted to the pressure of this world, and then I could hear the lapping sound of nearby water. In the distance came the strange calling of a bird I couldn't see.

"Are you alright?" Raymond asked me, and I turned to see him standing by me, his brows bunched, his eyes stared at me as if he was waiting for something. "Breathe, please."

"I am breathing." I laughed at him, and his jaw relaxed. "Sorry, this place is just nothing like I expected it to be."

"I told you it wasn't the fiery pits of hell you were imagining." He chuckled. "The Bane is a beautiful world full of terrible beings, but we care about our home, and we treat it as precious as it is."

"It's beautiful, and it smells so," I took a deep breath, "fresh."

"There are worlds that exist without pollution." Raymond smiled, proud of his home. "Noville wasn't trying to be rude when he asked how you live there. Most newcomers to Earth find your world suffocating."

"Does it hurt you like that to be on Earth?" My chest tightened thinking Raymond suffered like that in my world.

"No," he tapped my chin with his finger. "Don't worry about me. I'm made of tougher stuff."

"Where are we?" I looked around the area. We stood on a small hill, in a simple plain of grass, but I could tell even by the landscape we weren't on Earth. The trees looked...happy, their branches lush with leaves, waved in a praise dance in the distance. There were also small fuzzy plants at the base of each tree, like something I would have seen in a children's' book, soft and purple.

"This is a safe space, but not exactly where we need to be. I used to come here whenever I needed to clear my head." He looked around. "To be honest, I've dreamed of this place for so long, almost every night I've been on Earth until recently. It felt like the perfect spot for you to get acclimated before being thrust into the chaos of the coming days."

"This is your spot." The statement sounded more intense than I meant. This was a special place for Raymond, and he thought to share it with me. He turned to me again, those eyes carrying words he wouldn't, or maybe couldn't, speak.

"Yes, it is." The corner of his mouth lifted just a bit.

"Are you okay?"

His hand returned to mine. "Why do you ask that?"

Damnit! I have to say something. This is too heavy to let it hang out there between us.

I took a deep breath and then let the words fall free. "Because something's different between us. I know it, I feel it, and I know you do too. Whatever we're about to face together, we need to be open and honest about how we're feeling."

He paused, glancing off into the distance before his eyes returned to me. "How are you feeling?"

Okay, I could go first.

"I'm scared. Borderline terrified right now. I'm worried about Natalie. And I'm hoping I make it back home." My honest words filled the space between us.

"I—" he started, but I put my finger up to stop him. I had to get it out while I still had the nerve.

"But I'm happy you're here with me. It's strange right now with what we're facing, to have this underlying feeling of happiness. I don't know why I'm telling you now, but I think I need you to know. You make me feel safe, like my feet are on solid ground. Facing this...I'm glad that you're here with me."

"You wouldn't be facing any of this if not for me." He hardened. "You wouldn't need me to keep you grounded if I hadn't walked into your life to begin with."

"To be fair, you tripped into my life." That brought a smile to his face, and something in me softened a little more. "Besides, with my luck and with the way Natalie likes to play with magic, something like this was bound to happen anyway."

"She does?" he frowned. "You never mentioned it."

"I didn't really have the time to. She found a grimoire, but the witch called it back. I'm sure nothing will come of it." I shrugged. "It wasn't even the first time. I'll tell you all about it when this is done."

"Jericha, I'm sorry," he said in an even tone.

"For what?" My stomach twisted into a knot.

"For all of it. For keeping a secret from you this big, for risking your life by staying around you. I'm sorry I had to bring you to this world, and I'm sorry for everything you're going to learn about me while you're here. I hope that on the other side of this, you still feel happy to be around me. But I will also understand if you don't."

"Okay, just stop all that right now." I shook my hands between our faces. "That's the wrong thing to be thinking about. I don't want to talk about us...I mean this...falling apart. I get it, this is dangerous, and you have a life here I know nothing about. I won't hold any of that against you."

"Jericha, I need you to face something for me. Seriously, think about it. At the end of the day, I am a demon. What you would consider a demon, anyway. To you, I may be the good guy, but to everyone else? I was a horrible person." He pulled my hands back into his. "I did terrible things for terrible people. And being back in this world means all of that is going to come rushing back at me."

I grabbed his hand. "And I'm here with you, holding on."

"Yeah, you are." His eyes dropped to our hands, linked between us. "But I won't hate you if you decide to let go."

I can't explain why I did it, but it was something in the way he looked at me that made my heart flutter and my head spin, and suddenly, I felt like I actually wasn't breathing. I pulled him closer to me, lifted to my toes, and I kissed him.

And once again, it was a kiss that changed things between us. It wasn't one that would lead to sex, or to flirtation, or to passion, or to any of those superficial things. This was so much deeper. It touched every part of me, and it made the world, his world, seem so much bigger and yet so much smaller all at the same time.

"Why did you do that?" Raymond breathed against my lips.

"This is your happy place." I tightened my fingers around his. "It's the place you go when you want to smile, right?"

"Yes. It is." He nodded, pressing his forehead against mine.

"So we should keep it that way." I looked up into his green eyes then moved my hands to push his locs back over his shoulder. "I like when you let your locs hang free like this."

He pulled me back to him again, this time pressing further into the kiss. His right hand slipped around me to the small of my back before he lifted me from my feet, and I wrapped my arms around his neck. For a moment, neither one of us had any problems. The sweet scent of his world mixed with the smokey taste of his kiss, and suddenly, nothing mattered. There were no demons chasing us, there were no friends in trouble, no worlds colliding. It was just him and me, and it terrified me with how perfect that felt.

"I want to keep you here, in this moment, forever." He sighed. "But we have to go."

"We do." I huffed.

"Are you sure you're okay?" He pulled back to examine my face. "Feeling well?"

"Yes." I scrunched my nose. "Why wouldn't I be?"

"Good." He kissed my forehead. "Not all humans can acclimate to our world."

"You forget, I'm not entirely human." I winked at him, and then my stomach twisted, and that newfound worry must have been written all over my face.

"What is it?" he asked.

"You said humans don't adjust well to being here." I shook my head. "I'm not all human, but Natalie is!"

"Shit." As the word crossed his lips, that shadow wall opened behind him. I expected him to put me down, grab my hand, and lead me through the shadows.

He didn't. With me still hanging around his neck, Raymond carried me through the shadows.

This time, it was quick. A few steps, and we were out of the darkness again.

When we stepped out, we were inside what looked like a modern condo with large windows overlooking a strange world. I looked out the window to see a bustling city landscape in the distance. I admitted, I expected something different, like caverns and archaic architecture, but there was none of that. Inside the apartment, there was sleek furniture, most of it stone and leather. I could imagine Raymond living there.

"Is this your place?" I looked at him.

"No, not exactly." He sighed before a new voice greeted us.

"You're here!" Metice stepped into the room. "Just making sure everything is all set for you."

"Yes, thank you for letting us stay here," Raymond greeted him.

"No problem. I haven't used this place in years, since before I left the business. It's the perfect place for you to hold up." He looked around. "You just missed Rayna. She really wanted to meet you, but she had to run back to earth."

"Sorry I missed her." I smiled. "Thank you for letting us stay here."

"When this is all over, we can double date." Metice smirked. "Rayna will probably insist on it."

"A date?" The question slipped from my lips before I glanced at Raymond. I couldn't even be mad at the way his jaw tightened.

Girl, you were just hanging from this man's neck, kissing on him and telling him you wanted to make sure he was happy! And now you're freaking out that someone suggested you go on a date? Get it together!

Metice quickly turned and headed for the kitchen. Because who the hell would want to stand there in such an awkward situation? I braced for Raymond to say something, but he didn't. He turned and walked away, following the other demon.

I thought about saying something, apologizing for my outburst, but just then, the necklace pulsed around my neck. It was Jackie reaching out to me, and without a second thought, I wrapped my hand around the stone and closed my eyes.

"Thank God!" I blurted out when I saw her face. "Is everything okay?"

"Yeah, I mean, mostly. Why are you thanking God? What happened?" Jackie's eyes widened. "Are you hurt? Because I promised Raymond I would kick his ass if—"

"I, um, nothing happened. You just saved me from an awkward conversation." I spoke quickly to calm her down. "Wait. Why is everything mostly okay? What's wrong?"

"Well..." Jackie chewed her lip. "We have a minor problem."

"We do?" My heart raced. "Did someone get hurt? Did the demons attack you?"

"I can't find Kaa," Jackie said, and my panic eased.

"What do you mean, you can't find her?" I asked.

"I've searched this house top to bottom, and all plants are accounted for except the one that can slither away."

"She might just be hiding. Maybe she's upset that I didn't come there to say goodbye before I left. Just leave out some of the liquid plant food. Usually, that works, and she reappears after a day or so. She'll be fine. How was everything else?"

"Everything is wonderful," she reassured me. "You still have a business. Have you found Natalie yet?"

"No, we've only been here a little while. We just got to the place we're staying."

"Okay, well, at least we know these things work across the realms. Sound quality is not as good, but it works. Let me know as soon as you find out anything more."

"Yeah. I will."

"Are you sure you're okay?" she asked. "I know you were trying to tell me something before Raymond came back. Do you want to talk about it now?"

"So far, I'm all good. But no, I don't think this is the time to talk about it." I shook my head.

"Okay. I'm here." She winked.

"I know." My lips lifted in an appreciative smile.

That static in my mind increased, and Jackie's voice faded.

"I think the connection is failing." I sighed. "Love you, girl."

"Love you too!"

And she was gone. I opened my eyes and removed my hand from the stone. I looked at the doorway to the kitchen. In clear view was the counter, and next to it, Raymond's back. Damn it, if I didn't want to run away.

"Jericha! You're here!" the cheerful voice startled me from behind.

I turned around to find Cufio standing behind me, and behind him, stepping through a portal, was Noville. I didn't think it was possible, but the big guy looked relaxed. His shoulders were loose, and his dark lips lifted into a smile as he nodded.

"Yeah, we made it." I smiled.

"Is the mean one with you?" Cufio's eyes darted around, looking for someone.

"The mean one?" I frowned then caught on to what he meant. "No. Jackie isn't here."

"Hmm. I thought she would force Raymond into taking her along for the ride, but never mind. You're right on time!" He clapped, and as he did, Raymond and Metice came out of the kitchen. "Brother, it's so good to have you home finally."

"This isn't my home," Raymond bristled, and once again, he hardened.

I glanced at Metice, who was right behind him. Something was definitely up with the two of them. It was like Raymond put on a shield the moment he got around the guy who had his horns proudly displayed atop his head now.

"Well, no. They burned your place down after you left, but you know what I mean."

"What do you have for us?" Metice asked.

"Good news. We know exactly where Natalie is." Cufio inhaled sharply. "Bad news is, she's in the last place we want her to be."

"Where is that?" I asked.

"Klougus has her," Noville answered, saying a name I didn't know. He looked at me and offered the explanation I needed. "The guy we all once worked for."

"Oh," I said, quickly glancing at Raymond, noticing his worried expression.

"Fuck." Raymond grunted. "Guess we're headed there sooner than we thought."

"Yes, but we need to make another stop first," Cufio added.

"Why do we need to make another stop? We're here to save Natalie. That's what matters," I spoke up.

"She wants to see her," Cufio said to Raymond, not me. "It was a part of the deal for making those charms."

"Does this have to happen now?" Raymond looked at me then at Metice.

"You're seriously asking me that question?" Metice laughed. "I told you how she was with me. That woman doesn't like to wait; she'll deactivate those stones just to be petty."

"You're right. Let's go."

"Better if you two go alone." Cufio winked. "Let me know how the water is."

"Shut up." Raymond moved to me and held out his hand. "Come on."

"Where are we going?"

"It's better if you see it. Trying to explain it will take too long."

"Okay." I placed my hand in his as the shadows opened.

On the other side of the path was the opening to a cave. We stood there together, and I felt that tingle of intuition. Something inside me told me I knew this place, but how could I? I was in another world, far from anything I'd ever seen or experienced. But still, that feeling of déjà vu was there.

"You ready?" Raymond asked me, his eyes looking straight ahead of him at the opening.

"Do you expect me to say yes?" I laughed nervously. "I don't even know what's in there."

"No, I don't. Let's go."

We entered the cave, first walking through a narrow space before we came to a wider space with curved walls that reached to an impossibly high ceiling. And then, it hit me: another wave of familiarity. I *had* been there before. Confusion washed over me as I saw the dark pool of water, its surface moving with soft ripples.

"This isn't possible!" I frowned, pointing at the water. "How is this here?"

Raymond looked at me, his eyes wide. He gripped my hand like he was about to snatch me up and carry me out of there.

"You're here. Finally," a cool, melodic voice sang out.

Our heads snapped to the back of the cavern where she appeared. Her skin glowed, and those eyes, soft pink orbs, found my face.

The woman I'd dreamed of all those years ago.

Wrapped around her neck was the scarf I'd left behind.

22

Oh, Hey, Likosa!

"This can't be real." I backed away from the woman who approached. "There's no way."

"What's wrong?" Raymond moved with me, his body tensing like he was preparing to defend me.

"She...she—I—" I couldn't find the words to answer him because I was completely freaked out. Standing in front of me was a woman I'd dreamed of all those years ago. There was no way she was real.

"Oh, Jericha, welcome back." She smiled at me like we were old friends.

"What?" He looked at me. "You've been here before?"

"That was a dream." I shook my head. "None of that was real. It couldn't be."

"That was no dream. You were here." She held up the end of the scarf and waved it at me. "You left this here. See? I kept it all this time because, well, because it's pretty and very soft, but also because I knew you would need it again someday."

"You're real." I relaxed as I looked at her face, realizing she had, in fact, changed my life for the better. I didn't know if it was self-regulation or some magic she worked on me, but I suddenly felt at ease. All I could think of was how many things had shifted in my life after that dream. For years, I attributed everything good in my life to that moment. "You're like an actual living, breathing person, or demon, or I'm sorry, I don't really know what your classification is here."

"That's alright, take your time." Her lips lifted in a soft smile as she glanced at Raymond then back at me. "And I'm not a demon. I'm actually not even from the Bane. This is a second home for me."

"How? How did any of that happen? Why did you bring me here, and why did you send me back without telling me anything more? You brought me here." I pointed to the pool of water behind her. "And you took me into the water. I heard things, things that took me a long time to understand. Why?"

"To help you. You were one of the first I found from your bloodline. I let the rest of them come to their discoveries on their own, but you, I knew I had to do more. You were alone, the first one I found who was entirely on your own." A heavy sigh escaped her lips before she continued, her voice thick with a blend of worry and concern. "I watched you for a while, bouncing from home to home as a girl. And when you found your foster mother, I realized she could help you. She was magical in her own right, though I'm not sure you ever knew."

"She was?" My throat suddenly burned as I thought of the woman who took me in and cared for me like I was her own. "I never knew she had magic."

"She might not have known it either. There are plenty of humans in that world who have inherent abilities but never truly unlock them." She sucked her teeth. "A shame, really. Imagine how amazing your world would be if not for all that suppressed magic. But if you hide your gifts for too long, they become dormant."

"Couldn't you have awakened hers like you did mine?" I asked.

"Not exactly. Yours were genetically suppressed, needing a key to unlock them." She mimed turning a key. "Hers were not; they were there, just unused. Also, while magical, she wouldn't have been that powerful. I found it fascinating how her abilities aligned so well with yours. Think of the way she taught you how to take care of the Earth, how to bond with and care for your plants. Your power is based on the element, so it made sense for me to help you unlock that side of yourself so you could learn from her and really appreciate what she taught you."

"Anyone want to fill me in on what you guys are talking about?" Raymond looked at us. "It sounds touching, but I'm starting to feel like I'm missing a pretty significant piece of information about my...you...and I don't like that feeling."

That hesitation. What was that about? What was he going to call me?

I shook the thoughts from my head to explain what he hadn't known.

"When I was a young girl, I had what I thought was a dream here, in this cave, with a woman with pink eyes. She told me I was special and took me into a magical pool." I pointed at the water behind her. "When I was in there, she cast a spell. When I woke up, for a long time, I felt uneasy about that dream. I kept trying to remember the words I heard in the water. It took a while, but I did eventually remember it. I thought the dream was just somewhat of a prophetic moment. I thought it was my powers unlocking themselves, but it was really you. I'm sorry, I don't know your name."

"Likosa." She smiled. "It's nice to meet you officially. Our last encounter was brief. I wanted to keep you here longer, but I couldn't risk it."

"So you brought her to the Bane to unlock her abilities and then sent her back?" Raymond recounted what I told him, but there was a suspicious tone in his voice, like he recognized something in the information I hadn't.

"Yes." The simple word fell from her lips like a bird's morning song.

How does she do that?

"Why?" He stepped between her and me. "Why would you do any of this?"

"I just explained that." Likosa scoffed. "I know you shadow men have a hard time listening, but this is bad, even for you."

"No, Likosa. I know there is more to it. I know who you are." As he spoke, the tattoos on his arms shifted like they were preparing for a fight. "You don't do things just because they feel good. You do things because they must happen. What did you see?"

"I don't owe you any explanation of my visions." She waved him off. "Don't come into my space and assume you know anything."

"You had visions about me?" I asked over his shoulder. "Is that true?"

"You are an important person. That's all that matters." She crossed her arms over her chest. "And that's why I helped you. Raymond is just paranoid because he's been running from his past for so long."

"What do you want with her? They told me you practically tripped over yourself to help us create those charms. Your eagerness surprised me, but there wasn't time to question it. Now, it turns out you already knew Jericha long before she got here, which means you knew I was near her, right?" His arms flexed more as he spoke, and something in the back of my mind told me this would not end well. "And what about everything that happened with Metice and Rayna? You knew all of that too. You did the same thing with her and that pool of water, right? Why are you so interested in these women?"

"Don't strain yourself trying to connect the dots of things you can't even fathom exist." There was a sharp cut to Likosa's voice that betrayed her previously sweet tone. "Watch yourself, Raymond."

"You're hiding something," he insisted.

"And you're getting on my nerves," she snapped.

"Wait, you said there are others you have found and helped? People like me." I stepped around Raymond and ignored the way he bristled. He had questions, but suddenly, so did I. "Is it just Rayna, or are there more? Are you connected to our bloodline? You said you're not from the Bane, right? Is that why you want to help us? To connect with us?"

"Why are you all so obsessed with this question? Can't you just say thank you?" She sighed, throwing her hands up as she walked away. "I got bored. Is that a good enough answer for you? I don't belong in the Bane. So, from time to time, I look out into the verses. I try to find something to entertain myself when it becomes too mundane around here. I found your people, the originals, in their home world. They were these intriguing beings with unique gifts, and I could not stop thinking about them. I thought of leaving the Bane and joining them, but before I could, something terrible happened: their world was all but destroyed."

She strode towards the opulent, tall seat that echoed her own bold energy and sat at the pool's edge like a throne. Her fingers gripped the armrest as her head dropped against the tall back.

"It took so long to figure out where they were, but I knew they still existed. That magic feels so unique, one of the few with a distinct texture. After a lot of work, I traced them to Earth. I don't know why, but I could not get the idea out of my head that there was something more there. Time moved so fast on that little blue planet. By the time I found them, most of them died out, but not all of them.

Some adapted. They lived in that dismal world, and they bred with the humans. Their babies inherited those magical genes, but over time, the sound of their magic became muted as it was buried within them. I thought it might have been lost, but I had a vision that it could be unlocked."

"So you made it your job to do so?" I asked. "Why did it matter so much to you?"

"Why, why, why?" She sighed. "Because such beauty should not be lost. It shouldn't quietly vanish. I've seen it happen—magic stolen, squashed out. I couldn't let that happen again."

"How many?" I asked, my throat tight with concern.

"How many what?" Her face twisted in confusion.

"How many others have you unlocked?" I looked at the water. "How many have you taken in there?"

"There have been a few others of your bloodline. They exist, but not all of them can be unlocked. Some are too resistant, but there are a few more. Now that your abilities are awakened, Rayna's as well, it may call to them. That's something you might want to keep an eye on."

She looked at me with this knowing expression, and I immediately thought of my sister. Could she also be awakened?

"You know the others," Likosa continued. "They are a little more resistant to the change, but you took right to it. You even got your first companion shortly after we met, right?"

"Yeah, yeah, I did." I thought of the little seed that turned into so much more. "Kaa."

"She's an interesting little thing, isn't she? Honestly, she's going to be amazing when she reaches her full potential."

"Her full potential?" I stepped toward Likosa. "What do you know about Kaa?"

"She's not from your world, so there's only so much growth she can do there. It would be wonderful to see what she's capable of if properly nourished. Maybe...hopefully, someday, that will happen."

"Okay." I glanced at Raymond, who shrugged.

"Sometimes, she's a little eccentric." He smirked.

"What about the cat?" Likosa asked, pulling my attention back to her.

"The cat? What cat? I don't have a cat."

"The cat. Black and full of attitude." Likosa explained. "He wasn't meant for you. He was meant to be given to someone else."

"Maverick?" My heart raced in my chest. I knew exactly what catch she was talking about. It was a cat I had given away. I told Jackie to be careful and made sure it got to my sister. "That came from you?"

"Yes, I sent it your way with a message." She sighed. "It can be difficult using the earthly witches to do my bidding, but I can't always go down there. It's too risky. So, I asked her to make sure you got it, to make sure you understood it had to go to someone special, someone who needed it."

"I can't handle this." I looked around for somewhere to sit, but there was nothing.

"Yes, you can. You're strong," Likosa said matter-of-factly. "Stronger than the last one who came here. Brand new. She didn't know a thing about who she was, and if I'm honest, she was a little annoying. How many times does one have to tell you what's going on before you stop questioning it? But I can already see you're way more receptive to all of this. You've been exposed to the magical world, and you've had time to adjust and understand there are things outside of your current understanding but not entirely impossible."

"Why did you want us here?" Raymond asked. "Cufio said you asked for us."

"Oh, well, about that. I don't think you're ready, so don't worry about it." She waved his question off. "My timing is off, which doesn't happen often, but no one is perfect."

"Ready for what? Don't play with us, Likosa." Raymond's jaw tightened. "There is too much going on for you to waste our time like this."

"The bond, obviously." She leaned forward in her seat. "Why else would I want you here?"

"What bond?" I asked.

"The marriage of souls." Likosa's lips stretched in a hopeful smile, like she thought I would jump at the sound of that. They quickly dropped when I stepped away from her.

"Excuse me?" Well, so much for that calming effect she had. Panic. It was time to panic. "I didn't come here for a marriage."

"We are not doing that," Raymond said. "That is not a favor you can ask."

"Oh." She paused, waving her fingers at us and twisting her lips. "I assumed."

"What did you assume?" he asked, jaw tight and voice laced with venom.

"Are you two...together?" She tapped her chin. "I couldn't have been that far off."

"No," I blurted, then shot a nervous glance at Raymond. "I mean, not like that."

"Right," she sighed. "I've seen, well...I guess I'll have to wait."

"Look, I am here to save my friend." I held my hands up as I cleared the air. "That's all. Whatever exists between me and Raymond is our business."

"Of course. I must just be losing my touch," Likosa said, but the strange lilt to her voice told me she didn't mean what she said. She believed I would marry Raymond.

"They said I owe you a favor," Raymond said. "What is it?"

"You? Oh no. *You* owe me nothing." Those pink eyes shifted to look at me. "She does."

I scoffed, placing my hand on my chest. "I do? When did I agree to that?"

"Yes," she said. "But it appears I've miscalculated things. I'll be here when you're ready. Besides, you have other things to worry about now. That friend of yours...she may not last long here."

"Natalie?" My heart skipped a beat. "What's wrong with her? What do you know?"

"I know she's human." Likosa sighed, a somber expression masking her face. "Most humans don't adapt well. They either die or they mutate. Either way, you'll want to get her back to Earth as soon as possible."

"Can you help us save her?" I asked desperately. "I don't want her to die here."

"My help comes with a bargain." She stood from the throne and took four deliberate steps. "What are you willing to do for me?"

Marriage. She wants you to marry Raymond.

"No, we can figure it out on our own." Raymond pulled my hand into his. "Keep your bargains for the next fool."

The shadow wall opened behind us, and he turned, pulling me with him.

"Wait," Likosa called out. She pulled the scarf from around her neck as she reached me. Then, with a cool smile on her face, she slowly wrapped it around my neck. "You'll need this. Keep it close."

23

Damn, I need a nap.

I opened my eyes from a quick call with Jackie, where I filled her in on everything. She, of course, clung to the idea of Raymond and me being married, and that was when I had to end it. Her head floated in front of me, fuzzy and unnerving, eyes filled with unspoken judgement.

"We're supposed to be focused on Natalie!" I fussed at her. If I could have grabbed her by the shoulders to shake her, I would have.

"Yeah, and then we can plan a wedding!" she teased.

"I'm leaving." I sucked my teeth then released the stone from my hand. My vision cleared, and I was back in the condo, sitting on the leather sofa next to Raymond. "So dang annoying."

I muttered, and Raymond's head snapped toward me. "You're back."

"Yeah, I am." I tucked the stone back into my shirt.

"What is it?" He sat next to me, a mask of concern twisting his expression. "Is something wrong back on Earth?"

"No, everything is okay. Just Jackie being Jackie. You know how she can be."

"Demanding more sushi?" He smirked at his lighthearted joke. "How much do you owe her now?"

"Not yet, but it's definitely coming." I rolled my neck. "I'm sure the longer we're here, the higher the tally grows."

He chuckled. "Don't worry. I'll cover the tab."

"You know, what I really wish is that I could have one of those little donuts right now." My stomach ached at the thought of the sweet treats. "I know they aren't the best thing for me, but neither is going to another world to face off against demons."

"Ask, and you shall receive." The corner of his lips twisted up into a half smile as he placed the little packet in my hand. "I told you I had plenty for the trip."

"Oh, thank you!" I snatched the little package away from him so quickly, I almost scratched him. "Sorry. That was a lot more aggressive than I planned."

"Don't worry about it." He chuckled as he watched me open the package and quickly devour the first sweet treat.

"What's that?" I looked up from the donut in my hand to see Cufio walking back into the room. They'd left us alone before I made the call to Jackie.

"Something to keep her happy," Raymond said as another packet of donuts appeared in his hand for me. "Did you find out anything useful while you were gone?"

"Actually, I did. I spoke with Punal," Cufio spoke. "He said Klougus is open to a meeting."

"How do we know they won't attack when we get there?" Raymond straightened next to me, the shadows on his arm lifted just slightly and swaying above his flesh. "Punal is a damned liar, and we all know that. I won't go unless we're sure what we're getting into."

"You know there are never any guarantees when dealing with demons. But hey, times have changed. People grow." He paused, looking at me, then returned his gaze to his brother. "You've definitely changed since you left the Bane."

"What else did they say?" Raymond asked.

"You might not believe this, but surprisingly, they are offering you a deal." Cufio sat in the leather armchair across from us and kicked his feet up on the stone table in the center of the space. "I don't know the details yet, but it sounds like there is something he wants from you in return for letting you off the hook."

"That sounds too good to be true," Raymond said. "Why would he ever just let me off after what happened?"

"Time passes, people heal and move on. There is definitely a catch, but what choice do we have?" Cufio sat down on the sofa across from us. "I mean, unless Likosa told you something different."

"She didn't. She wasn't much help at all, actually," Raymond muttered.

"That's not like her." Metice appeared, walking out of the kitchen with a glass in his hand. "What happened?"

"She gave her a scarf," Raymond answered.

"A scarf?" Metice looked at me. "Was there something special about it?"

"It's a long story." I held up the green scarf I'd stuffed into my pocket. "But it used to be mine. I lost it when I was a kid."

"It is always a long story with Likosa. She's the queen of playing the long game." Metice eyed the fabric in my hand. "But if she gave that to you, it means you're supposed to have it. I wouldn't brush it off as insignificant."

"So when do we leave?" I asked. With my stomach full of sweet treats, my mind was ready to do more, and listening to the men go back and forth sounded like a horrible idea. Raymond was clearly stalling, and his brother was doing nothing but antagonizing him. "I'm all for strategizing when we're talking about actual game plans, but that's not happening. Likosa said Natalie won't make it long here because she's a regular human. We need to get her home."

"She's right." Cufio nodded, leaning back further in his seat. "Which is why I already moved some things around. We have a scheduled appointment with the big guy, and Noville will be here in the morning with transportation for us to head over there."

"Transportation? Can't we just use the shadows?" I looked at Raymond. "Why are we making this take longer than necessary?"

"There are rules to our world. One of the biggest ones is that shadow walkers are not allowed to just pop up anywhere they want, not in private spaces and *especially* not in Klougus's place," Cufio spoke. "We need permission to do that. Since everything that happened...he's doubled down on security. Shadows can't just come and go like they used to."

"That gives you some time to rest. There is a lot that needs to be done, but none of it matters if you are falling over yourself." Metice pointed at me. "She needs it."

"No, I'm fine," I insisted. "I've eaten now. Plenty of fuel in those donuts."

"No, you're not. It takes time to adjust to being in this world, and that hardly counts as a balanced meal. You'll need more to eat than that." He looked at Raymond. "Make sure she rests. If she's anything like Rayna, she'll fight you on it. I have a few things to handle. I'll be back when you're ready to head out."

"Yeah, thanks." Raymond stood as if he needed to walk them to the door, but Metice vanished with that weird, pressurized feeling, and Cufio stepped into a shadow and disappeared.

"Are we really supposed to just take a nap or something now?" I stood from the sofa. "I don't think I'm capable of that right now."

"They're right." Raymond turned to me, his eyes softer than before.

What the heck was it about Metice that made him harden like that?

"I won't have you wearing yourself out here." He held his hand out to me. "Let's go."

It was pointless to debate him on it. I knew what would happen if I did: shadow hands. And honestly, after eating the sugary treat, I felt the ache of exhaustion creeping over my body. We had a plan. That was what mattered.

I followed Raymond into the large bedroom. It was simple—dark stone walls, flickering candlelight, one massive bed across from a large window overlooking a grassy expanse leading to the distant city lights. There was a fireplace, and just beyond the bed sat the luggage Jackie helped me pack. I'd been so worried about making it to Natalie, I hadn't thought about my things.

But Raymond had. I didn't know when he did it, but he'd considered me and my needs.

I noticed the zipper on one of the bags was opened, but before I could mention it, Raymond looked at me with eyes that made everything feel all too intense. Maybe I should have asked him what was on his mind. Maybe. But I wasn't sure I wanted to know the answer to that question, not after everything that had been said.

Likosa's words, that suggestion of marriage, hung between us like a neon sign, buzzing and blinding.

When I said nothing, and after it was clear he also wouldn't be breaking the awkward silence, I shifted my focus from his dark eyes to look out the window again. A quiet sigh slipped through my lips when I heard him moving around the room behind me.

"Come here." Raymond's voice was low and stern. This was his domain. He was in control.

Still keeping to the rules of our relationship, I turned around and found him with my nightgown in his hand. It was one Jackie insisted I bring on the trip. I walked over to him and held my hand out, expecting him to give me the garment, but he didn't. Instead, Raymond undressed me. Slowly, methodically, he pulled the t-shirt, sweats, bra, and panties away from my body.

My skin prickled, anticipating him to do so much more than undress me. My pussy tightened with excitement for something that wouldn't come. Because Raymond didn't kiss me, play with my pussy, or fuck me. Hell, he didn't even look at me, not in the way a naked woman would expect to be looked at by the man who claimed to want her.

He slipped the nightgown over my head, covering my body, and stepped away. Then, just as he had before, Raymond phased out of view and returned in black pajama pants that matched my gown. Silently, he pulled back the sheets on the bed, a dark red color, and called me over to join him by patting the mattress.

When I got into bed, he pulled the covers over my body as he slipped in close. His arm draped across my waist before he pulled me in close to his body. The moment my back pressed against his stomach and his warmth spread across me, I couldn't protest sleep anymore.

24

Demons Kinda Stink.

I woke up to the smell of fresh bread. Actually, my stomach growling woke me before the pleasantly nutty smell registered in my mind. I rolled over, reaching out for Raymond, but he wasn't there. Draped across his side of the bed was my robe, and I took that as an invitation to join him for breakfast.

With my robe wrapped around my waist, I headed back out of the bedroom to the front area, where I found Raymond sitting on the sofa. On the stone table was a platter of food, mostly pastries, but there were also some strange-looking fruits, colorful pieces with spots and fir. I only assumed they were fruit because of the seeds I saw in the pre-sliced bites.

Next to the platter was a separate tray with a large pot of coffee and one mug. I inhaled the scent and smiled. It smelled just like the kind I had on Earth, only with a hint of spice.

"This is a lot of food." I sat across from him and picked up a simple piece of bread. It was the safest looking thing on the platter. "Is it all safe for me to eat?"

"Yes, all of this is human approved. Eat up. You'll need plenty of fuel for the trip." He looked at me. "How do you feel?"

"Rested." I nodded. "Metice was right about the rest and the food. I'm starving."

"He has an annoying way of being right about things," Raymond muttered.

"One day, you're going to explain to me what's the beef between you two." I bit the bread and smiled at the fresh flavor. "How are you feeling?"

"I'm fine. Ready to get this over with and get you back to your world where you belong. You shouldn't be here."

"Right." I shouldn't have, but I took that comment personally. It felt like he was saying I didn't belong with *him*, and I didn't like that at all.

Girl, stop! One minute, you're blurting out to anyone who asks that you aren't with the man. Now, you're sitting here upset because he doesn't want you on his planet! Damn.

Instead of questioning him about what the comment meant, I focused on the platter of food in front of me.

"Did you make this?" I pointed at the little pastry with peach-colored crème on top. It called to me, but I was still hesitant.

"No." he laughed. "I purchased it."

"Hmm." My fingers hovered over the piece for a moment longer before I picked it up.

"You think I can't afford it?" He sounded offended.

"I didn't say that." I bit into it and sighed as the flavor, more like lychee than peach, filled my mouth. "Actually, how does that work here? Do you have money like on Earth? What's the currency?"

"Yes, we have a currency we use." He sipped from the mug next to him. "But people also barter. Actually, most people prefer bartering. Typically, money, as you would call it, is only used in the major cities."

"Interesting. And you still have money here?" I asked.

"Yes. It would seem after all this time, no one has taken mine." He reached over to pour me a cup of coffee, which I picked up immediately.

"Is it like a bank account?" I sipped the coffee and frowned. It smelled like what I was used to, but the taste was far more acidic.

"No." He shook his head. "Not an account."

"Well, how do you keep it safe?" I frowned. "What's stopping someone from stealing it? I doubt demons are any more honest than humans."

"Hey, let's not play the battle of the species," he joked. "But to answer your question, magic. Most people have pouches coded to their signature that only open to their owner. I have a vault hidden deep within the ground. Most shadows do it that way. Safest way for us."

"Hm, that's all so interesting."

"Is it?" He raised a brow.

"Yeah. And this is exactly why I asked you to put together a PowerPoint for me." I put the coffee down after another careful sip. "I wouldn't have so many questions now if you had."

"If anything, you would have more questions." He chuckled. "And I was never going to do that."

"Because you're no fun." I stuck my tongue out then jumped at the sound of knocking on the door behind me.

"Looks like they're here." He stood from the sofa. "You should go get dressed. Take your time."

I grabbed two more of the pastries from the platter and headed back into the bedroom. After devouring them while sitting at the foot of the bed, I got ready to go.

Near the back of the room was another door, and when I looked through it, I was relieved to find a fully-equipped bathroom. He said take my time, but I didn't want to make them wait too long, so I took a quick shower, nearly scalding my ass in the water, then dressed in the simple blue jeans and long sleeve shirt I'd packed. I pulled my hair back into a loose bun, and I was ready to go.

"Where is everyone?" I asked Raymond when I emerged from the room to find him alone.

"Outside. Are you ready to go?" He held up a small sack. "I packed more food so you can eat while we travel."

"Thank you." I smiled because I was still hungry. "Anything besides that coffee to drink?"

"Water." Raymond held up a glass bottle. "I have a few packed."

"Perfect. Thanks." I turned to look out the window, suddenly questioning if I really wanted to see his world. It was fine to sit back and imagine what was out there, but could I handle it?

Raymond's hands gripped my shoulders as he moved to stand beside me. He lowered his lips to my right ear and whispered, "It's going to be okay. I promise."

His hand slipped from my shoulder, and his fingers laced with mine. That gave me the courage I needed. We left the condo and headed outside. Raymond led me down a long flight of stairs. I realized then it wasn't a building full of different apartments, but one tall tower with a simple home at the top. Somehow, it fit, knowing it belonged to Metice. He didn't seem like the type to want to be bothered with neighbors.

"What are those?" I'm sure my eyes nearly fell out of my head as soon as I saw those massive beasts. They looked like horses, but their hair was fiery, and it looked like they had lava flowing through their flesh. Behind them was a carriage. It was dark, but it also had ruffled curtains that made me think an evil queen would be inside.

"Those belong to Metice." Raymond rolled his eyes. "So damn archaic."

"That's our ride." Cufio appeared and pointed at a vehicle that floated above the ground.

That odd-looking vehicle resembled a hybrid of a bubble and an antique train car. Large, curved windows were framed in brass, and through them, I could see four rows of seating all lined with plush cushions. Two large glass pipes at the back emitted steam. Though it floated above the ground, it also had wheels that looked like they could extend to the ground when not floating.

"Cool, huh? It uses a blend of hot air, static, and water to run," Cufio boasted as he headed over to the vehicle.

He reached up and opened the door, and a ladder of metal steps folded out and dropped to the ground, making it easier to climb into the vehicle that sat at least four feet off the ground.

"Impressive." I nodded, though a part of me wanted to ride in that carriage with the fire horses. Still, I knew that wouldn't happen by the way Raymond was already pushing me toward the hover vehicle.

"Let's go. We don't want to be late," Metice called as he stepped out of the carriage. Behind him was a little blue creature. It looked almost like it would be called a dog on Earth, the kind only millionaires could afford and would tote around like accessories instead of pets. It had enormous eyes and looked friendly, but something told me not to touch it. "What are we waiting for?"

"Nothing," Raymond responded. "We're all set. We'll ride separately."

"I figured as much." Metice nodded, appearing unphased by the comment.

"Why do you have a denati with you?" Raymond pointed at the creature.

Metice grunted, glancing down at the little blue one. "It's a long story."

"It's really not that long." Cufio jumped at an opportunity to tease Metice. "That thing belongs to his girl, and if he doesn't take good care of it, he's going to be in a lot of trouble."

"You know what? You're right—some things really do change." Raymond turned, put his arm around my shoulder and headed for the strange bubble car. A soft chuckle rumbled through his chest, and it was the first time I had seen him express anything but disdain for Metice.

We climbed into the car, and I sat next to the window. Raymond sat next to me, opened a bottle of water, and handed it to me.

"Where's Noville?" I asked when I realized the big guy wasn't with us.

"He's meeting us there," Cufio answered, sitting behind the controls of the vehicle.

Ahead of us, the horses roared and took off, carrying the dark carriage behind them. We pulled out behind them.

The ride was quick enough and smoother than any I'd had on Earth. We moved softly as we crossed through the hills, floating above the ground. As we rode along, I looked out the windows. It still surprised me how the Bane actually looked. If you asked me where I was, I probably would have said somewhere on Earth, maybe Scotland or Ireland, where they film all the big budget fantasy movies, but now and then, I would see something that would make it so very obvious this was not Earth.

Like fuzzy trees and birds with six wings, little critters running across the grass with strange ears, textured skin, and vibrant colors that weren't natural to my world. There are also beings the closer we got to the city, individuals who moved around. As I watched them, it felt less appropriate to call them demons.

Because passing them felt like driving through any city on Earth. They went about their days, doing the things it took to survive in their world. I told myself brief stories about all the quick flashes of interactions I saw. A breakup here. An engagement there. Someone just lost their job. Someone just had a new baby. A group of friends met up for a meal while a businesswoman cut a new deal. All these beings had lives they were living, completely unaware of the human driving by them on the way to save her friend.

When we arrived at the compound, I gasped at the enormous structure constructed of material that looked like bone. *God, I hope it only looks like bone!* I stepped out next to Raymond. He said nothing to me, but he pulled my hand into his, clutching it tightly. The first squeeze was a warning to stay close. The second was for encouragement, but I didn't know if it was for me or him.

"Noville," Cufio greeted the missing member of our group as he approached.

While they spoke, I continued to examine the building we stood in front of.

The entrance was a series of tall arches stacked on each other. From afar, the building's curved pillars ascended from the steps to the roof like a majestic crown. That was the way I chose to see it, anyway, because another description could be the skull of a dead giant. Those arches could definitely double as brow bones. And once the image was in my head, I couldn't get past the feeling of walking into a giant nostril.

Inside the building, accessed by a large stone door that slid to the side to allow us entry, there were so many different beings, and none of them had humanistic features. None of them appeared in a way that was comforting to me. They were large, bulky, slimy, gangly, all different shapes, sizes, colors, textures, and smells.

Oh my God, the smells. The one thing I hadn't considered was that not all demons were hygienic. I mean, Raymond, Metice, Cufio, even Noville, they smelled perfectly fine, like a shower and a toothbrush weren't unfamiliar concepts to them. These other demons, they stunk ass!

No one else seemed to notice it. I twisted my nose but didn't say anything. *That would be rude, even if we were on Earth.* It was like walking into the house of a person with a ton of pets. They became nose-blind to the faint smell of urine, but it felt like a punch to the face for anyone who didn't live there.

I clutched Raymond's hand and walked in the middle of the men, who I hoped would protect me if things went south.

We stood in the building's entrance, seventeen guards awaiting us. I counted each of them, noting the slight differences in their appearances. Some had gray skin while others had varying shades of the rainbow. Some were short and stocky while others were tall, slim, but still visibly strong. Their eyes, narrowed and intense, were fixed on us, promising an attack if we made a wrong move. The air crackled with their unspoken threat. The biggest two, the ones with horns in the center of their heads and faces that looked like a rhinoceros, stared at Raymond.

"Raymond. I can't believe you actually had the nerve to come back here." From the long, narrow hall that shot straight ahead, a tall figure approached us, his honeyed voice coming through a beak that curved down to his chin.

He had leathery skin the color of opals. On top of his head were three long antennae that hung down like perfectly formed wicks, and he had four horns. Two stood up from the front of his head and two shot out from behind his ears, curving down. They looked like they connected to the wings on his back, almost like a cape. He was bold and regal, and if I wasn't certain he hated Raymond, I might have even called him beautiful.

"Punal. It looks like you've done well for yourself in my absence," Raymond spoke in a confident tone laced with disdain. So, at the very least, their hatred for each other was mutual.

"Yes, despite your absence. Do you know how much your actions broke the trust among our people here? It took years to repair the damage you did." Punal threw hateful glances at each member of our crew.

"How bad could it really have been?" Raymond played it cool. "I'm being welcomed back here now with open arms."

"We'll see about that." He glanced at me for a moment. "Follow me. You know he doesn't like to wait."

I swear, if I could have, I would have climbed into Raymond's skin right then. Punal's eyes, thin slits in his face, left me feeling utterly repulsive. My skin itched, like his gaze was a slime covering me. It felt as though I'd need a dozen showers to wash away the feeling, but I did my best to keep all of that from my face as we marched down that long hall.

Entering the room, we found ourselves surrounded by the incredibly detailed, almost feather-like carvings on the walls. Strange plants sat in stone planters in the corners. The back wall, unlike the other three, was smooth and painted a solid taupe.

I also noticed the wall wasn't a solid structure. There were three distinct panels with a strange, muted glow around them. I wasn't sure if it was an art fixture or something more. Where we entered the room, there were seats, all narrow and curved like half cups, stiff and uncomfortable. In the middle of the room, there was one narrow table next to a massive seat. The thing had to be at least five feet across.

What the hell sits there?

The answer to my question came immediately when the door opened again and in walked an enormous beast. He was massive, with thick green skin, almost human in appearance, despite being bigger than anyone I had ever seen by at least four times. He had hooves that clunked against the ground as he walked past us and a tail that swayed, almost slapping my ankle when he turned to sit. It folded over the armrest behind him.

It was silent. No one said a word as they waited for him to decide what he wanted to say first.

"Mnuktilous." He addressed Raymond by his real name, the first one to do so since we'd been in the Bane. The thought tickled my mind when I considered no one else had done that. They had all used his human name for my purpose, even the Opal one. Why?

"Klougus." Raymond moved to the center of the room. It was the first time he had let my hand go since we got out of the bubble ride. I took that as a sign I was supposed to stay right where I was.

"You know, I told myself the next time I saw your face, you would either be dead, or I would be removing your head myself." He paused, gigantic eyes scanning the room, lingering just a second longer on Metice than anyone else. Then, he laughed, a loud, booming sound that echoed off the walls. "I guess that's why I'm no oracle."

"My brother said you had a deal for me." Raymond skipped the pleasantries.

"Straight to the deal. Hmm, not even an apology for what you did." Klougus's voice turned cold, all laughter completely removed. "Your actions led to the death of someone important to me, someone I can never get back. Yet, you don't even think to try to make amends."

"Would it make any difference if I did?"

I could only see the back of Raymond's head, but I noticed the way the shadows moved across his exposed skin. He was holding it together, just barely.

"You really haven't changed, have you?" Klougus grunted. "I used to like that about you. Focused, determined, sure of yourself. But that led you to ruin, didn't it?"

"What do you want?" Again, Raymond avoided the small talk the big guy tried to engage in.

"Well, it would seem your mistake actually turned out to be in my favor—not that any of us thought it would be. Your actions led to the death of my brother, and I was hell bent on making you pay for that. But as luck would have it, if you had not done what you did, my brother would have done it to me." Klougus's massive hand gripped the armrest as he leaned forward. "He was going to make a play for my power; waiting until I stepped down didn't seem to be enough for him. He was next in line, but I guess I was taking too long to get out of his way. It wasn't long after his death that his secrets were revealed."

"So that means we're even," Raymond said.

"Not even close." Klougus shook his head.

"Technically, I saved you," Raymond pointed out. "Sounds like a fair trade to me."

"But that wasn't your intention. You also ran away, which meant you were guilty of something." Klougus's eyes moved across every face in the room before returning to Raymond. "You and I both know what that was, so yes, you still owe me."

"What do you want?" Raymond repeated his question.

"Bring me Talkeen dead or alive, but alive is preferred."

Next to me, Cufio gasped. I looked at him to see his jaw tighten and his hands ball into fists at his sides.

"Why would you want us to do that?" Raymond's voice shook. It was a slight tremble, but if I heard it, I was sure everyone else did. "Talkeen was your main guy."

"He was also working with my brother in a plot to end my life. Now that my brother is gone, Talkeen wants his place and mine. I will not have it. *I* keep the order on this side of the Bane, no one else." He took a deep breath. "This is your choice. You can do this, or you can leave and the human will stay here, but I don't know how much longer she will survive."

Just then, the taupe wall behind him shifted. The color became a translucent window, and on the other side was a room. In the center of the space was a small bed, and on it, a woman. She lay there, and asleep next to her lay a demon. He looked a lot like Noville, only instead of stone, he looked to be made of bark. His flesh looked like they were branches woven together, and small green petals stood out from him in varying places.

"Natalie."

25

The Deal

"Oh, look how concerned she is," Punal said.

"It really is impressive how gruesome these humans can be, and yet, look at the compassion she shows." Klougus nodded.

"Don't hurt her," I said sternly, my voice tight with barely suppressed anger.

"Oh, you don't have to worry about that. You have my word. She'll be fine—for now." He shifted in his seat to point to the being next to Natalie. "That's Stalvin. He's a very special creature in that he can produce specialized atmospheres. In a way, he is acting as her own little ecosystem. But..." He snapped his fingers and Stalvin quickly left Natalie alone.

We watched in silence. At first, Natalie looked fine. She continued to sleep peacefully, but within minutes, she clearly struggled to breathe. Beads of sweat formed on her forehead, and her body jerked and twisted. Her eyes fluttered open before slamming shut. She clutched her chest and gasped for air.

"Okay!" I blurted out. "We'll do it."

"Jericha," Raymond turned to me as Stalvin reentered the room, and Natalie's fit ended.

"These Earth women sure are impressive, aren't they?" Klougus said, glancing at Metice, who gave a disgusted grunt at the comment. "That reminds me, where is Rayna? I had hoped you would bring her with you."

"Wedding stuff," Metice replied.

"I thought you two had already completed the marriage of souls."

"Not ours," he explained simply. "A friend."

"Man of few words, as always." Klougus sighed. "Well, since this Jericha has already agreed to my terms, I'll leave you to it. My daughter wants us to spend more time with each other, and considering how it is likely she will take over for me now that my brother is gone, I suppose that's important. Let's just hope she doesn't also plan to take my head."

We remained still as Klougus stood and exited the room, laughing the entire way. I could hear that booming sound minutes after he left. Raymond took my hand and held it tight as we walked out of the building.

The moment we were outside, he spun around to look at me.

"Why would you agree to this?" His voice was low but intense, and it made me uncomfortable, like a child being scolded by her father. "Are you really okay with this? Killing a person?"

"Are you really asking me that right now? What is your problem?" I looked around. The others had already piled back into the vehicles, waiting for us to join them. Metice was already closing his door because he knew we wouldn't get in with him. "Am I suddenly your child?"

I snatched my hand away, and he glanced over his shoulder at the others, something flashing across his face, bordering on embarrassment. His jaw tightened as he held his hand out to me.

When I didn't immediately take it, the shadows on his skin shifted frantically. I glanced at his arms for a moment before returning my gaze to his face. *I'm in control now. He is not about to treat me like some damn child. I don't care what world we're in.*

"Jericha." He looked at me, his gaze weighing more than the entire planet we stood on. When I didn't budge, he spoke again. "Please. Take my hand."

Looking into his eyes, dark and heavy, I couldn't protest anymore. There was something there, something he couldn't share with me in front of the others. "I thought you said you're not supposed to use your shadows here."

"I'm going, not coming. It's fine."

"Okay." I placed my hand in his and followed him into the shadows.

When we came out, we were back in his spot, the place he went when he wanted to be happy. His escape. So why would he bring me there when our conversation was clearly about to be a difficult one?

"Do you really understand what you agreed to do?" he asked as soon as the shadow closed behind him.

"Fight demons and save my friend." I nodded. "That's what I came here for. What's the problem?"

"Are you so comfortable taking someone's life that you don't even stop to question it? Even if they're not human?"

"Of course I'm not. But again, what choice do I have? Natalie is here because of me, and I'm not going to let her die. You saw what happened the moment that tree guy moved away from her!" I answered him. "Besides, he said we can bring the guy to him, dead or alive. Why do you jump to the conclusion I would choose murder over capture?"

"It's not going to be that easy. Even if we don't kill Talkeen, so many others will die in the process. He is an evil asshole, Jericha. You could get hurt!"

"I can handle myself, Raymond. I'm not some innocent woman who doesn't know how to take care of herself. I know you're not worried about Cufio or Metice." I stepped back from him. "So tell me, what's really going on? Why are you acting like this?"

"You don't know what you're getting into."

"Raymond, cut the shit. What's going on?"

"I don't want you to be like me!" he yelled, a sharp, piercing sound that made me flinch as startled birds erupted from the trees, their wings beating a frantic rhythm that matched my racing heart. The harshness melted from his tone when he saw my startled expression. "I'm sorry. I didn't mean to yell at you like that, but this isn't right. Jericha, I know you're tough. I get that, but this is different. This, taking a life, it changes you. You don't come back from that, and you're..."

"I'm what?" I asked as my heart raced.

"Better than this, okay? You're damn near perfect." He stepped closer to me, his hands tight at his side. "You're thoughtful, caring, and you don't mindlessly act. You want to save Natalie, I get that, but we can find another way, one that doesn't put blood on your hands."

"Don't do that." I shook my head. "Don't ruin everything by painting me as some perfect person. I am far from it. You can't put that on me, and I'm not about to try to live up to that. You don't know what I've been through or what I've done in my life, so don't. I will do whatever it takes to get Natalie out of this world and back to safety."

"I don't know every detail of your past, but right now, *your* safety is my priority." He kept his hands down by his sides, and I recognized the restraint it took for him to do that. "That means also keeping you from doing things you will regret. Jericha, you will regret this."

"It's happened before, okay? I've taken a life before. It was an accident, but it happened, and you're right. It changed me." The ground felt like it was trembling beneath me as I confessed to him. "It was the first time I realized the magnitude of my abilities, that I could use my gift to hurt others. A man lost his life. I won't act like I regret it. He stalked a woman with every intent to kill her, and if I hadn't taken a detour home that night, he would have. But the justification doesn't take away the way it altered who I am. If you think I'm some perfect person, that means perfection for you is someone who has taken a life, someone who will do it again if it means saving an innocent person. Am I suddenly different in your eyes now that you know that?"

Raymond said nothing. For a long moment, nothing. He stood in front of me, body gradually relaxing. The tension fell from his shoulders and arms as he reconsidered who I was.

"I'm sorry," he finally spoke.

"Why are you apologizing to me?"

"Because I didn't give you enough credit. I thought you could never handle being here and focused more on protecting you than supporting you. But I realize now you're okay without me." He smiled. "I feel like I'm seeing you for the first time all over again, and it's just as impactful, and not just because I face planted on the ground after you tripped me."

"Raymond, I know this is going to be difficult. I didn't step through a portal and walk into a new world expecting it to be sunshine and roses. Come on, I knew I was coming here for a fight. I got okay with the idea of having blood on my hands the moment they took Natalie."

"I knew what was happening," Raymond huffed.

"You knew they were taking Natalie?" I stiffened, hoping I misunderstood him.

"No, of course not." He shook his head. "You just shared something very difficult for you. You deserve to know the full truth if you're going to do this with me. I knew they were trying to kill Klougus. I was on his brother's side until I realized I had made the wrong choice. So, I defected."

The birds returned to their perches in the tree behind him, as if they also wanted to hear what he had to say.

"I thought I could just walk away from it. I hoped they would call it all off, but because I wasn't where I was supposed to be, an arrow meant for Klougus landed in his brother's chest. They coated the tip in a toxin that spread through him, killing him almost instantly."

"You were helping them?" I questioned as my mind processed his words.

"Yes."

"Why?" I looked him in the eye. "What made you think you should betray Klougus?"

"The why doesn't matter." He shook his head.

"Yes, the hell it does!" I scoffed. "You just told me we're here because you were going to help kill the person you worked for. I'm not going to pretend I completely understand how all this works, but it gives organized crime syndicate. I know damn well how messy things can get with those. You can't just drop that in my lap and not share the reasoning. I need to know everything."

"It's hard to admit." He took a deep breath then looked at the treetops.

"Yeah, well, it's not easy for me to be in the hellscape, but here I am. Suck it up and tell me what happened."

"Someone broke my heart." He scoffed at himself. "I hate to even think about it because it's a pathetic reason, but that's what happened. My life imploded because my heart broke, and I wasn't smart enough to just take a trip, go away, and heal."

"Is this a joke? Are you being serious right now?"

"No, it's not. I loved someone who chose someone else."

"So all of this is happening because your crush didn't like you back?" I didn't mean for it to sound so harsh, but there was something else there, something that stirred inside me, an ache almost like anger. I did not like that Raymond had loved someone before, and I particularly did not like that whoever that was, had broken his heart. But I didn't know how to express that to him, so I made a joke. "Male egos are so damn fragile, even in other worlds."

"Yes. I know how ridiculous that sounds, but that is why this is happening. I loved someone, and for a time, I thought she could love me back." His jaw clenched, and I could see him biting back embarrassment. "She chose someone else. I stepped aside, but every time I saw them together, that ache grew until it ate me up. And then, after all of that, he left her. He left her, and she came back to me—not because she wanted me, but because she wanted me to help her kill the man she chose over me."

"She sounds like a real piece of work." I rolled my eyes. "Maybe it was a blessing in disguise that it didn't work out."

"Oh, she is." He let out a hollow laugh. "The only way I thought I could get away from her was to help them take over. She would never join with the new faction if it worked. I hate to admit it, and I wish so often I could change it, but my broken heart led me down a really dark path. Eventually, I healed. I got over her, and I realized the magnitude of my mistake. It was too late, though. Everything was already in motion, and there was nothing I could do to stop it, so instead of playing my part, I just walked away. The next morning, the report came out that it was his brother who died, and I knew it wouldn't be long before they found us all out. I didn't want to face it, so I left."

"What happens now? Now that you're back here, in this world." I swallowed hard as I realized where that question came from. *Oh shit. Girl, is that insecurity?*

"What do you mean?" he asked.

"We're here, we're going to do this, and we are going to save Natalie." I chanted. "But then what happens? Do you keep running, or do you stay here and face the music?"

"I haven't gotten that far, to be honest." He scratched the back of his neck. "Jericha, I never planned on coming back here at all, so the idea of what happens next doesn't even register in my mind. I had firmly put this world and all those in it behind me."

"You can't think they are going to let you slip away after this is over. I haven't had much time to get to know Klougus, but he seems like the sort to want to keep you around." I frowned, remembering the brief encounter. "Just thinking about the way he looked at Metice makes my skin crawl. It's like he wants to claim him. Did they ever...you know? Get together?"

Raymond laughed, his body shaking with each boisterous sound. "I am definitely telling him you said that. But no. As far as I know, nothing ever happened between them. Klougus is like that—possessive. It's in his nature. If he had his way, he would keep us all locked up in little boxes, only letting us out when it was time for us to do work for him."

"That sounds pleasant." I frowned. "No wonder there were people who wanted to betray him."

"Yeah, trust me, there were valid reasons for it, including the fact that he has actually locked people away to try to keep their power for himself. Usually, it's people from other worlds. That was Metice's job. He went from the Bane across the universes, kidnapping the strongest people to bring back to Klougus, all under the guise that the people somehow owed him a debt. I'm not sure I entirely believe that part."

"Okay, so sticking around to go back to work isn't in the cards, but there has to be something else. Right?" I looked around us at the scenery. Gentle creatures, fresh air, peaceful territories—that was all I'd seen of his world. I knew there had to be more to it, but from my short exposure, I had every reason to believe he would want to go back. "What do you want to happen? Do you want to stay here? Go back to Earth? I hate to say it, but this looks like the better choice. Even the air is cleaner."

"Is it possible for us to figure that out later?"

Us? He said us. Not him, us. Oh, girl, stop it! So what? You're acting like a child!

"What's going on in there?" Raymond tapped my temple with his finger.

"What?" My eyes snapped back to his face.

"You get this far off look in your eyes whenever your inner voice starts to rattle off. What's it saying now?"

"My conversations with my inner voice are none of your business." I flicked his finger away from my face.

"Conversations? Hmm." He nodded, squinting as he teased me. "So it's a call and response. Do you talk back to it? Is this something you've shared with your therapist?"

"You think you're funny, huh?"

I dropped my eyes from his, and he put his hands on my shoulders and firmly squeezed them. He kissed my forehead and inhaled deeply, pressing his nose against the top of my head.

"Whatever decision I make, you'll know in full detail. I won't keep you in the dark again. Is that okay?" He tightened his hold on me. "For now. Is that enough?"

"Yeah...for now." I nodded against his lips.

"Thank you, Jericha." I could feel him relax more against me as he rested his head on top of mine.

"For what?" I dropped my head into his neck and rested on his chest. "You don't have anything to thank me for."

"Yes, I do." His arms slipped around me in a loose hug. "I have to thank you for sharing your secret with me. You didn't have to do that. I know it couldn't have been easy. I want you to know I appreciate the vulnerability."

"Well, you called me perfect, and I hate that word," I joked. "I'm not perfect. I'm flawed, and if you're going to be around me, I need you to know that."

"Technically, I said damn near perfect." He chuckled. "You snore. That takes away a few points."

"You don't have to sleep with me." I pinched his waist. "Telling me I snore like I forced you into my bed."

"Chill, woman. It was a joke." He batted my hand away. "Ouch."

"Ha ha." I rolled my eyes. "Next time, it will be more than a pinch."

"Look, I need you to know you can hate the world all you want, but even with the secret you shared, and the ones you haven't, you're still pretty damned perfect to me." He sighed. "But if you don't want to be called that, I'll use another term. How are magnificent, angelic, the epitome of excellence?"

"Stop it." I tried to move away from him, but he held me tighter.

Raymond moved his mouth right next to my ear, and in the deepest timbre, he whispered, "Make me."

The only thing I could think to do in that moment was kiss him. So, I did. I lifted onto my toes and pressed my lips against his. Raymond took that as his cue and wrapped his arms around me, lifting me from the ground. He growled low as our kiss deepened, and I moved my arm to wrap around his shoulders.

"Can we just stay here?" I spoke against his lips. "I like it here."

"No, but if you kiss me like that every time we come here, we're going to spend a lot of time beneath these trees." He slid his hand to my ass, cupping it with a light squeeze. "And not in all these clothes."

"I think the others would be mad at us if we did that." I smiled against his lips. "They're probably already annoyed we left like that."

"They'll be fine. All it means is that we don't ride back home with them. But you're right. We should get back. There is a lot to do. We need to plan, to figure out what support we'll have."

"Do you think Klougus will lend you any of his men to help? Looks like he has plenty of them still on his side."

"Honestly, no," Raymond answered. "He won't want his name to be associated with this if things go wrong. It's why he's making me do it. If I'm the one who gets my hands dirty, it doesn't matter. I was already a man on the run."

"And if it goes well, he gets the benefit, and he gets to boast about how brilliant he is."

"Exactly. I wouldn't put it past him to act like this was his plan all along, the long game to catch the enemy off guard."

"The politics here are just as dirty as they are on Earth."

"No, baby, they're a whole lot dirtier." He pulled one of my arms from around his neck and brought my palm to his lips to kiss. "And I'm going to do everything I can to keep your hands clean."

Behind him, the shadow opened again, and I sighed. "I guess that means we're leaving?"

"Yes," Raymond said as he carried me into the darkness.

We stepped out on the other side and were back inside our borrowed condo. The others hadn't made it back yet, so we snuggled up together on the couch.

Soon, after picking from the left-over pastries and making a comment about how I needed protein, I drifted off on his shoulder. I woke up when Raymond shifted beneath me.

"What is it?" I yawned. "Are they here?"

"I think so. Someone just knocked on the door." He got up and headed to the door.

"Oh." I sat up, straightening my shirt and making sure I didn't have a tit out of place.

"What are you doing here?" Raymond's voice had that edge to it, and I expected Metice to respond.

"That's no way to greet a visitor!" the cool, feminine voice spoke. "Besides, I didn't come here without an invitation. Daddy told me about what you were going to do, and I asked if I could help. I already spoke to Metice. Surprised he didn't tell you."

"We took a detour on the way back," I heard Raymond say as he stepped aside.

In walked a tall, slender demoness with green skin. She had an arm that looked like it didn't fully match the rest of her and tentacles that looked the same. I stood from my seat and prepared to give her a warm greeting when she opened her mouth again.

"Oh, so this is the human you replaced me with." She scrunched her nose. "At least this one is cuter than the last one."

"Last one?" My eyes shot to Raymond. *What the hell was she talking about? Was I not his first human? Why did that matter?*

"It's nothing." Raymond turned on her, finger pointed in her face. "Olian, stop it."

"First, Metice does it to me, and now you!" She threw her hands up like a damsel in distress. "How will I ever recover from this embarrassment?"

"Metice?" I shouted then slapped my hand over my mouth as all the pieces of the puzzle fell into place.

26

It was Olian?!

"We are not talking about this right now." Raymond looked at me after my outburst.

I still stood there, hand over mouth, eyes shifting between the two of them, all the dots connecting in my mind. This woman, this green demoness with mismatched parts, was the reason for all the chaos. Honestly, looking at her, it made so much sense. She looked like a handful, and when she opened her mouth, she proved my point.

"I think you should. Yes, talk it out." She swayed over to the room and sat on the sofa where we had just been cuddled up. "It's important for a healthy relationship to face the bumps in the road."

"Olian, shut up," Raymond grunted. "There is nothing to talk about."

"Raymond." She pointed at me, still there with a look of shock plastered on my face. "I think she would have a different opinion if she could speak right now."

"Come on." He grabbed my hand and took me into the bedroom. As soon as the door shut behind us, he spoke again. "Please don't make a big deal out of this."

"I'm not. It's just... That's the woman who broke your heart?" I could feel the enthusiasm creeping across my face, like finally reaching the itch you couldn't scratch. The revelation was so satisfying. "And she chose Metice over you. It all makes so much sense now. I kept wondering why you tense up whenever you're around him. It's because of her!"

"I do not tense up around him." He frowned. "And you don't need to sound so excited about this."

"Oh, yeah you do. And I'm sorry, but this has really been bugging me: I thought maybe you two had a fight, or he betrayed you. I was even beginning to think Metice was in on the plot to overthrow Klougus and you turned your back on him with all the others."

"So many theories," he grunted. "You could have just asked me."

"I do remember mentioning it but you ignored me." I reminded him. "You didn't even say he was the guy you got left for."

"It didn't seem important at the time." He sat on the bed. "Look, Olian isn't someone you have to worry about."

"I'm not worried about that woman." I waved my hand at him but lowered my voice when I continued because I didn't want to risk Olian hearing me. "Maybe you should be. You tried to kill her father."

"You're not worried about her?"

"Do I look that insecure to you?" I laughed. "I've never been the jealous type, and I'm not about to fight over a man, human or shadow. Yeah, it's a little uncomfortable meeting your first love, but I know who has your eye now."

"Damn, that's hot." He reached for me. "I love a confident woman."

"Hey, down boy." I stood and swayed back to the door. "We have company."

"I can kick her out!" he offered eagerly.

Break

Fortunately, it wasn't long before the others arrived. Luckily for me, Noville carried bags of food with him. I asked nothing besides if it was safe for me to eat before I dug into the steaks, vegetables, and sweet treats.

"I told you to feed her," Metice grunted at Raymond when he saw how I tore into the food.

"Oh, calm down," Olian teased. "Let him take care of his human. You worry about yours."

I raised a brow at the woman. So far, she hadn't missed any opportunity to bring up the woman Metice had apparently chosen over her. Every time he spoke, she spun it back to Rayna. And every time she did, it made me want to meet the mysterious woman even more. Because she had to be *bad* to have such a powerful demoness that stressed about her.

Even the little blue demon dog Metice called Piko was over Olian's snide remarks. When she tried to sit next to Metice, he plopped himself between them. His body expanded to double the size, damn near pushing her off her seat.

"So, which one of you is going to lay out the plan here?" Olian frowned at the food on her plate. "I have other things to do today."

"You can leave. No one wanted you here anyway." Cufio rolled his eyes.

Damn, does anyone like her?

"Maybe not, but you know you need me." She pointed at each of the men in the room. "Every last one of you has a target on your back. Talkeen knows Raymond is back. The secret is out. And if he's back, that means his old friends, and his big mouth brother, are clearly on his side. If you don't think his people are already looking for you, you're out of your mind."

"She's right," Noville spoke. "I went to the gathering before I met up with you at Klougus's place. The secret is out, and many of the people we thought would be on our side have chosen neutrality."

"Of course not. The cowards. Don't choose a side at all so you can pretend to have always been aligned with whoever comes out on top." Cufio shook his head. "They're all pathetic."

"Does that mean we are on our own here?" Metice asked.

"No." Noville shook his head. "We still have a few allies, and as soon as we decide how and when to move, they will be with us."

"Good." Metice nodded.

"When would be the best time?" Noville said. "I'll update them with the details."

"Early morning," Raymond said. "We're dealing with shadows, but lucky for us, a lot of them aren't the most skilled—unless things have changed during my time away."

"No, you're right. Honestly, I think Talkeen likes it that way," Cufio spoke. "He doesn't want anyone to be stronger than him. That's why he hated us so much."

"Good. So, first light." Metice nodded. "No sense in dragging this out."

"I have the layout of his place." Noville pulled out a large piece of paper and laid it out on the table between us.

I listened closely as they talked about the plan and memorized the layout. Lucky for me, I had a semi-photographic memory. After a few examinations of the map, I felt confident I wouldn't get lost once we were there.

The drawing was a blueprint of the layout from a bird's-eye view. The building looked like those simple drawings of Christmas trees, three triangles stacked. The top, the point of the structure, was marked as the main entrance. There were two dark circles at the center of the blueprint and four red marks in the corners created by the overlapping triangles.

"When did they build this?" Raymond leaned over the table, examining the map.

"Not too long after you left," Cufio sighed, "Talkeen did a money grab. He claimed all the resources for himself while Klougus was busy trying to figure out what happened to his brother. By the time everything came to light, this place already existed."

"What are the dark circles in the middle?" I asked.

"Shadow cores," Cufio answered.

"He has shadow cores?" Raymond looked concerned. "How?"

"I wish I could answer that." Cufio chewed his lip. "It's been centuries since we even heard of one."

"What's a shadow core?" I looked around the room, and I was the only one who looked confused.

"Something we banned a long time ago." Raymond spoke through a tightened jaw. "They're made of stolen power from fallen shadow walkers."

"You mean—" I started.

"He killed a lot of people to make that happen." Cufio nodded. "That's the only way to do it. Kill them and extract their power before their last breath. Do it enough, and you create a core. It makes your own power a lot stronger."

"Well, that takes away any hesitation to remove his head from his shoulders." Raymond's hand tightened into a fist on the table.

"When we're inside, make sure you don't touch that thing." Cufio pointed at me. "It's like an alarm system, but it will also suck you in and steal whatever magic you possess. It's not just limited to shadows."

"Got it." I nodded. "And what about the red marks?"

"That's where we enter," Noville said. "We've done some testing. Those are the weak points, actually created by the shadow cores. There are no security details there because his people are afraid of getting too close to the core for long periods. Also, the barrier is weak, with thin walls and loose soil. It will make it easier to get in."

"How many people do we have?" Metice asked. "We need to figure out who goes where, and we should enter from all points, spread out and split up their forces."

"Less than fifty, but it should be enough. Most of the guys who are joining us are a lot stronger than the average man."

"He built an empire of weaklings." Cufio scoffed.

"It makes sense when you consider the kind of man Talkeen is." Raymond nodded. "They're all desperate, probably can't fend for themselves, and none of them are strong enough to do to him what he plans to do to Klougus."

"Okay, so we have a plan. We'll meet here." Noville pointed at a spot just beyond the building. There were what looked like coordinates written there. "I'll let the others know we move at first light."

"Sounds good." Raymond threw his locs over his shoulder. He'd let them free of the bun for the first time since we left Earth.

"Everyone rest up." Metice stood, and Piko hopped down from the seat and shot a glare at Olian.

"Going to get your girlfriend?" Olian asked.

The question got her a serious growl from Piko while Metice said nothing. A moment later, they were both gone. The rest of them, Cufio, Noville, and Olian, left out the front door. I think it was because Cufio wanted to make sure Olian didn't linger and make things even more awkward than she already had.

"That was fun." I smiled at Raymond after he locked the door.

"Fun?" He sighed. "You have a sick sense of humor."

"It had to make you feel good, though, right?" I pointed behind him at the door.

He glanced over his shoulder. "What?"

"Watching her poke the bear and get no response. She's obviously still in love with Metice." I tapped my finger on my temple. "Any time she could bring up his new girl, she did. And the dog thing, Piko, was ready to bite her for getting too close to Metice."

"Interesting. I honestly didn't notice," he said, and from the confused look on his face, I believed him.

"You didn't?" I shrugged. "Well, I found it funny."

"I'm glad you were entertained, but my eyes were on you." He walked over and pulled me into his arms. "You know you do the cutest thing when you're concentrating. You roll your thumb across your fingertips, and it makes you look like an evil villain."

"You think evil villains are cute?" I pursed my lips. "I'm learning so much more about you now that you're home."

"If her name is Jericha, yes." He let out a low growl.

"Oh, you're being real sweet right now." I narrowed my eyes at him. "What's going on in that head of yours?"

"I want you." His voice was low, intense. "This might not be the time, but I don't know how much longer I can go without you."

"Oh." Suddenly, the room felt hotter, and my stomach clenched. "Where did this come from?"

"You bite your lip a lot." He kissed me gently, a soft peck that lingered just long enough to get my heart racing. "Every time you do, I look at your lips. I think about how your kisses feel against me, about how you taste. And my mind races with thoughts of tasting you—every inch of you."

"Raymond."

"Can I have you tonight?" he asked as he tightened his hold on me just a little, just enough for me to feel his desperation.

"You're asking?" I breathed against him. "I thought this was your domain. We're alone."

"No, not now. Not when there is so much happening. I need to know if this is okay with you. I don't want to confuse you or downplay the seriousness of our situation. Sex before a battle isn't really advised, so if it is too much for you, I'll shake it off."

I put my hands on his shoulders, feeling the tightness of his muscles. "You're tense. That's not good for anyone entering a battle."

"I'll do yoga," he grunted.

I scoffed. "Since when do you do yoga?"

"I'll learn it." He looked around. "I'm sure he has a book on it somewhere. I'm a quick study."

"I want to ask you a question, and I want you to be honest with me," I said.

"Always." He leaned his forehead against mine.

"Is there a chance we won't make it out alive tomorrow? Could we die there?"

His jaw tightened, and his brow stitched together. Then, he nodded slowly while keeping eye contact. "Yes, Jericha. There is a chance, but I won't—"

"No." I put my finger on his lips to stop him. "Don't make me any promises. Just pick me up, take me to the bedroom, and fuck me."

He pulled my finger away from his lips. Then, pressed his against mine as he picked me up and did exactly what I asked him to: he carried me into the bedroom. Before we made it to the bed, the shadows had removed all our clothing. I don't know how it happened, but I felt the pieces of fabric disappearing bit by bit until I was naked against him.

He lay me down on the bed, and this time, things were different. There weren't any extra tricks. The shadows didn't interfere. He kissed me gently, from the top of my head to the bottom of my toes. He took his time with me, and I let him.

When he put his weight on me, I arched my back to meet him. When he bit into my shoulder, I tilted my neck to give him better access. His hands traveled the length of my back. My hands cupped his ass, guiding him deeper into me.

In my mind, time and time again, I heard a word, one that scared me more than running into a compound full of demons and facing the possibility of my own death.

Love.

The words that came out of my mouth remained a surface level of encouragement for the man who ravished my body. But each time I spoke, a thought echoed in my head.

"Yes, please, more!"

Make love to me.

"Take me, yes, deeper!"

Make love to me.

"Oh, Raymond. Just like that."

Make love to me.

And even though I'd never said those words out loud, something inside me felt like I didn't need to. It was in the way he touched me, the gentle pressures and deep kisses. It was the long, slow strokes that lingered deep inside of me, my name moaned in deep, slow drawls.

It felt like his thoughts had echoed my own, his unspoken words tangled with mine.

It felt like Raymond made love to me.

27

The Early Bird...doesn't battle demons, let's be real!

We were up before the sun, but we lay in bed, holding each other for a while before we showered and dressed.

"This is for you." Raymond held out the hilt of the sword...with no blade.

"Am I supposed to throw this at the enemy?" I pointed at it. "I thought you wanted me to survive."

"Put it in your hand." He shook his head and pushed it toward me again.

I grabbed it, and he stepped back. A moment later, a long blade appeared, silver and wrapped in light.

"Damn, this is like something out of Star Wars." I swung it in front of my face, hoping for the cool, whooshing sound. There was none.

"I'll take your word for it." He nodded. "Open your grip, and the blade disappears."

I did as he said, and the moment I released my hold on the hilt, the blade vanished. "Nice."

"Be careful with that," he said as he stepped closer to me and wrapped a belt around my waist. It had a holster for the invisible sword. After securing it, he paused and pointed to the scarf I had wrapped around my neck. "Likosa's scarf?"

"My scarf, actually, and instinct told me to bring it, so I am."

"Good enough for me." He nodded, and the shadows opened behind him.

We made it to the meeting point at the same time Metice arrived. He appeared, the little blue demon dog with him. Those strange eyes found my face, and his tail wagged.

"Metice," Raymond greeted him as Piko settled at his feet.

"Raymond. You good?" Metice glanced down at the dog, and the corner of his lips twitched, like he was holding back a smile.

"Absolutely," Raymond answered. "Rested and ready for a fight."

"Glad you all made it here on time." Olian walked up. I wasn't sure where she came from, but she had a massive orange guy with her. He was one of the demons who looked nearly human, save for his alarming orange skin. The guy looked like a walking traffic cone! It also looked like he was actively flexing every muscle as he walked up.

"Why wouldn't we be?" Raymond asked.

"Figured you'd be," she pressed the tip of her tongue between her teeth, "... distracted."

"I don't even want to know what that's supposed to mean." Cufio stepped out of a shadow, followed by Noville. He rolled his eyes at Olian and the big orange guy.

"The others are already in their position," Noville reported, getting straight to the point.

"I'm going to join Noville and his men," Cufio directed. "Olian will have her own team, Metice will leave his own team, and you two stick together."

"I never thought I'd see the day you take control." Olian smirked, appearing impressed by Cufio. The big orange demon by her side flexed again.

Is he doing that for her? Is he jealous?

"Calm down, green girl." Cufio held his hand then nodded at the orange one. "Just because these two don't want you anymore doesn't mean I do."

"Oh, shut up." She crossed her arms over her chest, embarrassed. "That's the last time I give you a compliment."

"Focus," Metice said simply. "We don't have time for this."

"Metice is right," Noville spoke again. "According to my calculations, this entire thing should take no more than twenty-five minutes. If we're in there any longer than that, it's going to be bad for everyone involved."

"Make sure your people stay away from that shadow core," Raymond warned.

"They already know." Noville nodded.

"Is it a good idea to have that thing here?" I pointed at Piko, who remained by Metice's feet. His tail wagged the moment I acknowledged him.

"Uh, trust me, we're going to want him around." Metice nodded. "He's not as helpless as he appears."

"Alright, sun's coming up. Let's go." Cufio pointed at the sky where the dark blanket began to pull back.

In seconds, Olian headed off with her orange man, Metice popped out of view, and Cufio stepped into the shadows with Noville behind him.

Raymond grabbed my hand, pulled me over to him, and kissed my forehead before we crossed the shadows. When we exited, we stood in front of seven demons. Two looked like Noville, made of stone. There was a small furry one with large eyes and an innocent smile, and the others looked almost boring in comparison, two women and one man. They looked human, only slightly mutated with strangely textured skin.

Raymond addressed the team briefly, reiterating what Noville and Cufio had already told them. Then, we headed into the building. Raymond led us. He opened a shadow path tighter than any other he'd ever done before, and we all tiptoed through the weak point of the building.

On the inside, we stood against the wall of an angled hall. I expected an ambush, but the space was empty. In the distance, there was a strange whooshing noise, like someone had a powerful fan turned on. It was bright inside; the wide windows at the top of the walls let the sunlight spill in, and bright strips of light were fixed down the center of the ceiling.

"They really don't want any shadow walkers in here," the furry one commented in a soft, feminine voice.

"At least not ones who are against them." Raymond nodded. "Stay close. I can use shadows without darkness, but if you get too far from me, you'll be on your own."

"Understood," she responded.

They were effective. Having worked together for so long, they needed little communication to perform. I watched them closely, learning, and I couldn't stop myself from considering how I could get my own team to perform the same way—if I made it back home.

Um, no, girl. This is not the time to think that way. We're going to make it back, and we're going to buy Jackie so much damn sushi because I know those clients are driving her crazy by now.

Once inside, we had no direct way of communicating with the other teams, but we had our directives. Raymond and I were to find Talkeen, who happened to have his office stationed just below the most dangerous point of the building that could only be accessed through a shadow port—a door only shadow walkers could use—right beneath where the shadow cores sat.

The shadow cores we weren't supposed to get too close to. Yeah, those.

The others were there for one real purpose: distraction. While Talkeen's men attacked the other teams, we would slip in, face off with Talkeen, and hopefully drag his ass back to Klougus so the big guy could finish him off himself.

We made steady progress through the hall, moving closer together as the space narrowed around us. But then a blaring sound like storm alarms rang out around us, the lights above us turning red and flashing in furious alerts.

"Fuck. It didn't take them long to mess that up," Raymond said with annoyance.

"What happened?" I scanned the hall, bracing for an onslaught of shadow walkers, but nothing happened outside of that loud ass alarm. "Where are they?"

"I'm guessing someone tripped an alarm, or they got too close to the core," Raymond stated. "But it should have taken them at least a few more minutes before getting anywhere near the core."

"I'll check in." Furry's head vibrated, and then, when it stilled, she spoke. "Talkeen's guys spotted Olian's team. Couldn't catch the guy before he sounded the alarm."

"What do we do now?" I looked at Raymond, the official leader of our group.

"We head for the core. Our goal is the same here. Now, we just have to move a lot faster."

Moving faster meant more opportunities for mistakes, but we didn't have time to reevaluate things. Raymond ran, and I followed his lead. The sounds of battle quickly reached us. We weren't the only ones who decided to speed things up. As we exited the hallway, entering the open center of the building, we spotted Metice and his team.

Half of his men kept straight while he and the others turned left, heading for the front.

"You all go join the fight. We'll head for Talkeen," Raymond instructed the others, and they took off.

As the others ran, Raymond and I continued on our decided path. I couldn't see the entrance, but he could. What I could see were the flickering bodies in my peripherals. At first, I thought I was imagining things, but I realized it wasn't just phantoms caused by paranoia. They were shadow walkers, jumping in and out of shadows, getting closer and closer to us.

A minute later, we reached the center of the hollow hall. It sat behind a half-wall that wrapped around the two giant orbs floating in the middle. The orbs could be partially seen over the top of the walls that acted as a barrier, the only thing keeping the orbs in place as they performed a dangerous dance with each other. They weren't still like I had pictured them. And they felt like magnets. Huge magnets with fuzzy edges that called to me.

"Keep your distance," Raymond instructed me, as if he knew exactly what I was thinking. "I know how it feels. But trust me, do not get anywhere near that thing."

"Okay." I gripped the holster on my waist, making sure my weapon was still there.

"The door is just ahead." He pointed.

"Watch out!" a deep voice called out, and I turned just in time to see a man's fist coming straight for my face. I dipped down, dodging the hit and instead of meeting me, he met Raymond. My shadow walker grabbed the man by his throat and threw him back what looked to be at least fifteen feet.

"Are you okay? Did he hurt you?" Raymond was back by my side in a flash.

"Raymond, I'm fine. You know I can handle myself." I stood, pulling the hilt from the holder, and the blade appeared. "Eye on the ball."

"Right." He looked away from me. "Because we have company."

I turned to follow his gaze and saw several shadow spots opening.

"I thought they couldn't do that." I pointed at one of the spots. "They're supposed to be weaker? Right?"

"Clearly, someone got their shit wrong." He pulled his shirt off.

"What are you doing?"

"Taking the reins off." He winked. "Remember how hot I am now."

"Excuse me?"

"Trust me." He kissed me, and then the shadows lifted from his body. Those tattoos that danced across his flesh outlined his body like a visible aura, and he glowed! The man actually glowed as his shadows snapped out like flames dancing around him.

He held his palm out to me, and a string of shadow passed from him to me. It formed a ring around my midsection, spinning like an automatic hula hoop.

Then, he took off. Raymond danced in and out of the shadows. Every time he appeared, he had a different man in his clutches. Most looked close to humans, but some of them did not. I watched him closely, holding my position as he fought. But I couldn't stay there long because eventually, the shadows brought the fight to me.

A shadow opened to my left, and a hand reached out, but the spinning barrier around my waist shot out, slapping the hand away from me.

"Oh, shit." I watched as it pulled back to me, then I searched for Raymond again. Just ahead of me, I caught sight of his hair as he stepped back into the darkness. "Okay, let's do this."

It happened again. Another attempted attack, another defense from the shadow Raymond lent to me.

Let's get it, girl!

Something inside me clicked when I saw Raymond disappear again. He was holding his own, and I had to do the same. I wasn't going to let him or anyone else be distracted by the human on the field.

It didn't matter what came at me. If it attacked, I swung, I fought, I did whatever I had to do to survive. I hoped like hell I didn't accidentally hurt someone who was on my side. Even though I defended myself, I tried not to kill. Injure, take them out of the fight, sure, but never kill.

I couldn't say that for the other members of my team.

The shadow walkers danced in and out of the darkness, going in and out of view. But more often than not, when they returned, it was our men on top. The ones they fought no longer moved. Those who couldn't use the shadows fought in plain view, and it looked like the opponent had some non-shadow walkers on his side as well, because most of the demons I fought ran right at me. No shadows to assist them.

I cut through a purple guy with a golden fringe hanging from his face. As he ran at me, heavy fists poised to crush me, I shocked him and ran straight at him. I dropped to my knees, sliding across the floor and activating the blade. It lit up just in time to cut through his ankles.

He fell and cried out as he grabbed his ankles and realized his feet were no longer attached.

"Sorry about that." I shrugged and ran off. *Hopefully, he can grow them back. Is that a thing?*

My thoughts raced as I moved back to my position where Raymond left me. I don't know why, but it felt like I had to protect it. If it was the entrance to Talkeen's level, I couldn't let anyone get there.

As soon as I returned to my position, I saw flashes of Olian and her orange demon. They worked together in unison, like a pair who had been together their entire lives. If I hadn't known any better, I would have thought he was the love of her life. He supported her, protected her, even assisted her in her offensive moves. I appreciated it when he tossed her in the air so she could cut down a demon who flew above us, spitting down fiery shots that took out two of her men.

And at the farthest end of the massive room, where the main entrance was, Metice held his position. His body, it grew, and I don't mean he flexed. I mean the man literally expanded to the point where the clothes he wore ripped away from his body, and he stood there naked and fighting off everything who came at him.

He was a good fighter, though. He was almost too much for them. It seemed like every blow he launched landed harder, crushing those strange creatures beneath the weight of his force.

And Piko was right there with him, only he was no longer a cutesy little blue demon, instead a massive beast that honestly terrified me. He looked the size of an elephant and used sharp teeth to rip away at anything he could get close to.

All I could say was I was glad they were on our side.

It looked like we would win, like that full twenty-five minutes wouldn't be necessary. The opposition, while stronger than we had prepared for, was failing. I should have known better than to let that thought go through my mind, because the second I had, everything changed.

The ground beneath our feet shook violently, trembling with increased intensity, and then, with a guttural roar, massive stone spikes erupted from the ground. A thick, sticky orange slime that glistened in the light coated each one.

"Be careful." The furry one appeared, pulling me away from the spike that shot up next to me. "Those things are poisonous. One prick, and you're dead."

I nodded. "Thank you."

Simple enough—just dodge the daggers coming up from the ground and watch out for random creatures coming out of the shadows. No problem. I quickly noticed there was a pattern to where the spikes shot up. Faded spots marked the ground, and at first, I thought it was dirt or just a fault in the stone, but I was wrong. As I looked closer, I realized they were shadows fixed in place.

Once I noticed it, they were easy to avoid, but even that wasn't enough. Above us, the roof opened. A slit opened down the middle, and as the two halves slid apart, large stones like boulders fell into the room. So not only were we avoiding spikes shooting up from the floor, but now, we had freaking *bricks* falling on our heads.

And that's when the tide completely turned against us.

A large piece of stone damn near hit me in the head, but that shadow defense system Raymond left me with turned into an umbrella above me. The stone bounced off it and landed right on top of one of the spikes that shot up. I jumped away from it, nearly stepping on top of another spike. When I shifted my weight, avoiding it, I saw Metice drop. Several of the large stones fell on top of him, nearly burying him.

Piko quickly dug him out, but as Metice returned to his feet, smaller than before, he was far more vulnerable. He turned his back at the wrong time as a demon that looked like a bulldozer charged him. I screamed out his name, but when the impact landed, it wasn't Metice who took it.

It was Raymond.

He shoved the large man aside, the impact of the blow sending him sprawling as he took the full force of the hit. His body slumped to the ground with a thud.

28

Those freaky waters.

As soon as I saw Raymond down, I ran for him, forgetting about the pattern of the shadow markers for the spikes on the floor. And of course, I took all of two steps before I messed up. I heard the spike shoot up towards me and turned to see Raymond's shadow reach out to protect me, but it failed. As the spike ripped through the shadow, I flinched, preparing for it to cut through me.

But it didn't—because a body appeared in front of me. Phasing in and out of shadow was Cufio, the end of the spike, dripping in poison, tearing into his stomach.

"No!" I reached for him, but my hand went right through his body. "What? How? Oh, my God!"

I moved around him in a circle as I tried to figure out what to do. Cufio stood there, shimmering in and out of shadows, looking at me with wide eyes. His mouth moved, but I couldn't hear whatever he tried to tell me.

"Get to Raymond. I got him." Olian was there. The orange demon, her protector, stood behind her, watching her back.

"I can't just leave him."

"And you also can't help him, but Raymond can fix this," Olian said. "As long as he stays half in the shadows, he can slow the effects of the poison. But he won't be able to keep this up for too long. You need to get to Raymond. Now!"

Something in her voice, vulnerable desperation, kick-started me. I ran straight for Raymond, this time paying close attention to the markings on the ground. Just before I made it to him, I heard a loud metallic snap and turned back to see a cage closing around Olian and Cufio with the orange demon stuck outside.

Keep going!

My inner voice screamed at me. There was nothing I could do for them. I needed Raymond.

I reached him and fell to my knees at his side. With a grunt, Metice held the beast who hit Raymond against the wall, its claws scrabbling uselessly against the stone. He'd grown again and looked even bigger than before.

"What do I do?" I frantically touched Raymond's bloody face. His breathing was shallow, and his pulse felt weak beneath my fingers when I felt for it. "There has to be a way. There has to."

I felt a soft tingle around my neck and, through my teary eyes, I looked down to see the scarf I'd tied around my neck glowing. The trim around the edge shined, and as I blinked away the tears, I looked closer to see the threads moving.

That's why she'd given it to me!

Instinct kicked in. It twirled in my stomach and screamed little alerts in my mind. *Touch it! Think of her! Go to her! Take him with you!*

Never one to ignore that inner voice, I looked around at the chaos—bodies dropping left and right, Olian and Cufio still trapped, her orange guy trying his best to free them. It felt wrong to leave, but everything in me said it was the only way.

I took the scarf from my neck and pulled Raymond's limp hand into my right one. With my left, I wrapped the scarf around our laced fingers and thought of the cave with the pool of water and the woman with the pink eyes.

"Please, take us to Likosa," I whispered.

The surrounding room turned to fuzz, static like the connection to Jackie. I held on to Raymond, and though I wanted to close my eyes, I couldn't. I watched as the battle faded to nothing, and then, with a loud popping sound, we were in the cave.

Likosa stood in front of us, looking down at Raymond's body. "Well, I expected you to come back here, but not in such a dire state." She pointed at Raymond. "He doesn't look good at all."

"Can you help him?" I asked frantically. "Please tell me you can do something!"

"No, I can't," she spoke, and something moved across her shoulder. I thought it was a shadow at first, but it wasn't. It was familiar, a little snake-like body with pink flowering.

"Kaa?" I stood. "Why do you have her?"

"She stowed away in your bag. I'm surprised you didn't notice." She patted Kaa's head with her fingertip. "Found her way to me."

"You expect me to believe that?"

"I don't really care what you believe." She sighed.

"I—" I dropped my eyes to Raymond. "What am I supposed to do? Why am I here if you can't help him?"

"I said *I* can't help him, but *you* can." She sucked her teeth. "Why haven't you?"

"Well, if I knew how, don't you think I would have by now?"

"Maybe you don't like him as much as I thought," she said. "You did bristle when I suggested marriage."

"Look, he is hurt, and the others are in danger." I pointed at Raymond's body. "Cufio has been poisoned. There isn't time for this."

"I'm so tired of you all coming here and rushing me to help." She faked an exaggerated yawn. "It's like none of you have any manners."

"I'll apologize after everyone survives." I rolled my neck. "They all said you know what's coming, which means you knew we would be here needing your help. Please, you gave me the scarf. It brought me to you like you wanted. Tell me how to fix this."

"Well..." She kneeled, dropping her hand to the ground, and Kaa slithered down her arm. I watched as my pet stretched before planting herself into the soil. There wasn't time to question it. "Since you said please, I'll happily help. "

"Thank you." I glanced at Kaa, but again, I didn't question what she did. "What do I have to do?"

"The answer should be obvious, but I have to ask: why aren't you using your abilities?" She moved toward me and reached her hand out to touch my chin. "Hmm, interesting."

"What are you talking about?" I shied away from her touch.

"In the battle, you fought, yes, but you fought like a human. Why is that?" She scanned my face, took a step back, and looked my body over.

"It's safer that way," I said. "Besides, I'm not on Earth. My powers won't work here."

"Safe? You're fighting demons, honey. Someone's gonna have to die. They're not gonna hold back." She walked around me, continuing to look me over. "But that's not it, is it? Your power should work no matter where you are. You should be able to bond with whatever is natural there. No. You're blocked."

"Blocked?" I found her face again.

"Yes." She sucked her teeth. "I thought in all this time, you would have figured it out, but even Kaa looks depleted. You'll never survive like this."

"Can you help me?" I looked at Kaa, who swayed her head as if agreeing with Likosa's comment.

Likosa nodded slowly, her lips curving up into a grin. "For a cost."

"I know." I looked down at Raymond. "Whatever it is, I'll do it."

"I love it when they say that!" She clapped excitedly. "Undress."

"The water?" I looked over her shoulder at the pool.

"You know it." She grinned, and behind her, the waters moved with more rapid waves.

As I quickly undressed, Likosa explained what would happen.

"What I did before, it unlocked your abilities, showing you the way, but you haven't fully embraced them like I thought you had. So, we're going to have to push the envelope."

I didn't question it. I knew exactly what was coming, and I knew there was no time to get into a debate about things. Raymond was hurt, the others in trouble. Cufio was poisoned, and Natalie at any point could die.

As soon as I stepped into the water, it rushed at me. Like a hand wrapped around my waist, it pulled me to the center of the pool and lifted me. I looked down at Likosa, whose lips moved rapidly as the water worked. She stepped forward, putting only her feet in the water.

The encasing wave reached higher on my body until only my head was free. Then, a moment later, it covered my head as well. I couldn't breathe, but I didn't need to. It was an odd sensation, but it didn't last long. Humming, pulsing, energy moving through the water twisted and turned my body like it was investigating me. Then, everything stopped.

I dropped my eyes, hoping to find Likosa, but instead, I saw something far more alarming. Through the water, shooting at me like spears, were long stretches of brown and green. I squinted and realized they were roots from beneath the water. They reached me quickly and arrested my arms and legs. I struggled against the hold, but it made no difference.

"Accept it," I heard Likosa's voice in my mind. "Do not fight this. Embrace your power."

I tried to take a deep breath but realized part of my body no longer functioned. So instead, I went to my happy place. In my mind, I stood in my garden, naked, toes digging into the soil. I imagined my lungs full of fresh air and the plants reaching toward me, embracing me as they always did.

With that image in my head, my body relaxed, and I opened my eyes just in time to see the vines, long, snake-like, and covered in pink petals. In the center of them was Kaa. Her eyes bore into mine as she stopped in front of my face. She smiled at me, and instinctively, I nodded at her, giving her permission to do whatever she needed.

The vines that surrounded her face moved over to me, replacing the roots that held me in place. They snaked around my body from my toes to my neck and then fused with me. I cried at the feeling of light searing, like getting a full body tattoo all at once. I looked down to see my flesh covered in vines with pink flowers.

Kaa's face still hung in front of me. When I looked back at her, she swayed and then moved forward as if to kiss me. But instead of a cute little kiss, she jumped down my throat. *Literally*. And it burned like hell!

I screamed out in pain as I felt her moving beneath my flesh, but there was something else. I felt full. Not in the *I just ate my favorite meal and needed a nap* kind of way, but in the *I've always felt like something was missing and now I don't* kind of way.

The water swirled around me quickly before it halted and lowered to allow me to breathe again.

I gasped as Likosa stood there, no longer whispering her spell.

"Excellent! I—" she started but then abruptly ended whatever she was about to say.

Because as soon as I filled my lungs with air, something else happened.

Raymond's body, still laying at Likosa's feet, twitched. His eyes opened and then slammed shut, and then those dark strands, shadows that worked at his command, dove into the water. They followed the same path as the roots and shot up to me. Their touch was cool as ice, not with the usual heat when Raymond controlled them.

They pressed into my skin, settling behind the new vine tattoo like a cool drop shadow effect, making the vines look like they were popping out at me.

And then, it ended. The water moved me back to the edge of the pool, where I easily stepped out.

"Well, that was unexpected." Likosa hummed and handed me a towel I hadn't seen her obtain.

I half-assed drying my body and reached for my clothing. "What do you mean, *that was unexpected*? Didn't you plan this?"

"I realized Kaa would bond with you. She was quite literally a part of your soul removed. What I didn't know would happen was that shadow thing. You did that, not me. Somehow, you took some of his power, or he gave it to you—I'm not really sure which one." She smiled. "Oh, this is so interesting. I'm rarely stumped like this."

"What does this mean?"

"It means we need to think about that later, because you need to save your guy." She pointed at Raymond. "I'm assuming you know what to do now?"

"No," I sighed, and then that intuition screamed at me again.

Go to him! Hold him!

I lowered to the ground beside him and pulled his head into my lap. *Do what feels right.* I sighed and held his face in my hand. What felt right? What would be enough?

"Listen to me, because I know you can hear me. I know you're still here," I spoke as Likosa moved back from us. Maybe she wanted to give us privacy, or maybe she thought I would blow up the place. It didn't matter.

"All this time, you've been worried about protecting me, keeping me safe. And thank you for that, really, but I don't need you to protect me. You know how many times I told you that, but it doesn't mean I don't need you. Raymond, I *do* need you. I need you to challenge me, to keep me grounded. I need you to continue to be my safe space and allow me to be vulnerable enough to grow. You are so much more to me than my protector.

"I fought it, but I think I knew very early on that you were someone I could never live without again. Because in you, in us, I have found a part of me I didn't think existed. I've been able to let go in a way that should have felt uncomfortable. But because of you, it doesn't. I thought I was coming here only to save Natalie, but that's not true. I came here for you. A part of you was trapped here, stuck in the past you could not outrun. And just as you came into my life to help me be free, I'm here to do the same for you. So, listen to me when I say this. Stay with me. Fight with me. Live with me."

After I spoke, I kissed him. As soon as my lips touched his, a quiet energy moved through me into him. It returned to me warmer and then moved back to him. I felt that power move back and forth between us, pushing and pulling, each time stronger, different. His name repeated in my mind, sometimes in my voice and others in his.

And then, the vines lifted from my skin. They wrapped around him and me, back and forth, weaving us together like a cocoon. And then, his shadows did the same, intertwining, lifting from him, mixing with my vines.

And then, his eyes opened. I thought he would break the kiss, gasp, and question what the hell was going on, but he didn't. Raymond deepened the kiss. He pressed against me, his arms wrapping around me as he pulled me tighter than the cocoon already had.

He continued kissing me until the vines and shadows pulled back into our bodies.

"You're awake." I smiled at him as he reluctantly ended the kiss.

"I am. Because of you." His eyes flickered with something, a mixture of honey and emerald, and then they returned to that cool green I was used to.

"Well, that was really intense, wasn't it?" Likosa sounded like she was ready to cheer.

Raymond's eyes flashed over to her, like he had only just realized where we were. "What happened?"

"Battle happened. You got injured, others are hurt. She brought you here and saved you," Likosa reported shortly. "Boy, she really put on a show here. I wish you could have seen it."

"Who got hurt?"

"Cufio," I answered him. "He's poisoned, but he's in between the shadows, I think. Olian said you're the only one who can help him."

"We need to get back there. Now," Raymond grunted.

"You'll need this." Likosa pulled a small vial from her cleavage. She dangled it in front of us. "It's the antidote for that nasty poison."

"Shit." Raymond got to his feet and reached for the vial. "What do I owe you for it?"

"Oh, you've already paid this debt." She looked around at him and shot a strange look my way. "More than you know."

"Damnit." Raymond looked at me then held his hand out. "Let's go."

29

You ain't stronger than my girl.

Likosa's strange comment weighed on my mind as I followed Raymond through the shadows. How had I already paid her? Despite the unsettling feeling it left me with, I knew I had to put it out of my mind. I couldn't be distracted when we got back there.

Raymond stopped moving and turned to look at me. When our eyes met, that eerie wailing, sounds from the creatures in the dark stretches, quieted. "We have to split up."

"What do you mean, split up?"

"I need to go to Cufio. You get Metice." He paused. "I can sense it. They're in trouble."

"How am I supposed to do that?" I looked around but found nothing but more darkness. "I can't be here without you."

Raymond turned my hand over in his and rubbed my palm with his thumb. When he did, another path opened, branching off from the one we stood on.

"Looks like you can walk the shadows now." He pointed. "Keep straight until you reach the light, and I'll see you on the other side."

I almost panicked until I noticed the green webbing in my path. Seeing that and feeling the familiar pulses of the power that had existed in me all my life, I felt comfortable. When I stepped on it, it felt like walking into my garden. "Okay, yeah. I can do this."

"I know you can," he said confidently.

"Be careful." I kissed his cheek then turned and ran down my path. I couldn't watch him walk away first.

I reached the light, the doorway to exit the shadows quickly. When I stepped through, I was back in the building with the shadow walkers, surrounded by chaos. I glanced over my shoulder and saw Cufio still in the cage with Olian, but then he vanished from sight, and I could only hope that was because Raymond made it to him.

I turned my attention to the front of the building, where Metice was the last time I saw him. He stood back-to-back with Noville, both surrounded by demons and losing ground. The creatures encircled them, and while they fought, I could tell Metice was injured and Noville just wasn't as strong as the others.

"No more fighting like a human." I rolled up my sleeves to see the new tattoo moving. It shifted around and more pink petals formed, moving together into blossoming flowers, a visual cue that my new power had activated.

The vines moved from my arms, breaking through the stone surface beneath my feet and reaching into the ground. Soon, I could feel every plant and tree rooted for miles around us. They felt different from anything on Earth, and they made noises, sounds like coos and clicks, as they communicated with me. It was strange, but I quickly understood they would do what I needed.

The ground rumbled—this time, not because of the poisoned spikes, but for the answer of this strange nature as it responded to me. I ran to Metice, and, as I did, roots shot up from the ground and arrested the creatures that attacked them. One by one, they were wrapped up and pulled to the ground. Noville noticed what I was doing and instantly worked to secure the trapped demons.

He picked up the broken stone and threw it at them. The stone transformed mid-toss into traps that snapped down around them and blended into the roots.

It worked until one demon caught on and attacked Noville when he wasn't looking. A massive hammer landed against Noville's temple, and he fell out next to Metice just as I reached them.

"Shit!" I dropped to Noville's side.

"He'll be alright. Just taking a nap," Metice reassured me. "Going to need more backup, though."

Then, Metice whistled, and after the sharp sound cut through the air, Piko's massive, mutated form exploded into the area, knocking two demons over with his entrance.

"That'll do." I nodded at Piko, who wagged his tail like he was having the time of his life.

"Yeah, it will." Metice patted the dog's back. "Now, go to Raymond."

"He told me to help you," I rejected what he said. "I can't leave you alone."

"And he can't finish this thing without you," he insisted.

I looked over to where the cage sat, now empty. Olian had escaped, and Cufio was still nowhere to be seen.

"Get to the doorway." Metice said just as another demon targeted him, this one landing a blow before Metice responded by breaking his arm in half. "Go!"

"You need help!" I responded while shooting another branch to strangle the demon out on the ground. "I—"

BOOM!

An explosion sounded, and two demons splattered across the floor.

"Holy shit!" I screamed out.

"Oh damn, I forgot to adjust the strength of that." A woman with long, two-strand twists appeared behind Metice. She flexed her fingers and balled her hands into fists. "I love this shit!"

"Who are you?" I turned, ready to call the roots into action, but I paused when I realized the woman looked human.

"Jericha," Metice said, "this is Rayna."

"Oh, *your* Rayna?" I eased.

"Yes." He smiled, looking at her like she was his entire universe. The demon actually had a dreamy look on his face.

"Hey, I've heard a lot about you." She waved, and I flinched, afraid she might blow my head off. "Go on and get your man. I got his back."

Metice kneeled so Rayna could kiss his cheek, and Piko jumped over to Rayna.

Something about seeing them together like that gave me hope. They'd fought against the odds and survived. We could too. After a quick nod of confirmation, I turned from them and ran for where I knew the doorway was. The roots still shot from the ground, clearing my path of any demon who tried to attack me as I ran.

Just ten feet right of the cage that previously held Olian and Cufio was the marked spot Raymond had shown me—only it was different. I could see it! It was a tall, thin panel that rippled with energy. I searched the area for any sign of Raymond or his brother but found nothing.

"Jericha!" Olian called out to me.

I turned to find her slumped against the edge of the wall. She held her shoulder where she bled. "Olian, are you okay? What happened?"

"Yeah, I'm fine. Got cut by a dagger, but it wasn't poisoned, so I'll survive. I've had it worse." She groaned in pain as she readjusted herself.

"Where are they?" I scanned the area. "Raymond and Cufio. Have you seen them?"

"In the shadows. They haven't come out." She pointed to the spot where I saw the two brothers disappear. "They should have by now. I don't know what's going on, but I don't know how to get in there either. None of the shadow walkers on our side are here."

"Damn it." I looked around to assess the situation. She was right. There were shadow walkers, but they were far away, and they were all busy with their own fights. Her orange demon ran down the hall. I wasn't sure what he was doing, but he knocked out two others on his path.

That intuition yelled at me again and begged me to examine the cage. There had to be something to lead me to them. When I left Olian, she slumped to the ground and waved me off when I hesitated.

"Go. I'm fine."

Inside the cage, the door now hanging limp at the hinges, I almost gave up hope of finding anything until I caught the flash of something in my peripheral. I turned and squinted to see a small slit in the air. It took me a moment before I realized it was a shadow left open. There was a thread of darkness reaching from the slit in the cage and traveling back to the doorway to Talkeen's space.

My heart dropped into my stomach—I immediately knew what it meant. The brothers were still in the shadows, and they were in trouble. That instinctual voice told me I had to go in. It screamed at me that if I didn't, Raymond would not make it out alive.

I turned back to Olian and pointed down the hall. "Can you get your orange buddy back here to help you out? You need to leave. Now."

"What are you talking about? We can't just leave." She struggled to stand, stumbling back against the wall again. "This isn't done."

"It will be, but I have a feeling this place won't be standing when it's all over." I glanced at the two shadow orbs, but they moved more frantically, bouncing against each other, and every time they hit, there was another ripple, a shadow that passed through the space. "Look at those things, and that's before whatever needs to happen to take Talkeen down."

"What are you going to do?" She pulled out a device from her pocket and pressed a small button. "He'll be here in a second."

I nodded when I realized she had just called the orange one. *Dammit, I should have asked his name.* "I'm gonna do what I came here to do. Get the others and get out."

Without another word, I turned, a new magic humming within me, and silently called to the shadows, feeling their power stir. They responded instantly, widening the split in the space enough for me to enter.

On the other side, there wasn't a thin path for me to walk across. This was a massive field on checkered stone, and in the center of it stood Raymond. He faced off against a guy I had never seen before but could only imagine was our target. Behind him, slumped on the ground, was Cufio. He was breathing, but each inhale was a struggle, a ragged gasp for air. He clutched his side, and I could still see where the spike had stabbed into him.

"You think you can just come back here and do whatever you want?" Talkeen's voice boomed, and the domain we stood in trembled as he spoke. "I have worked my ass off to build what I have now, and I will not let you or anyone else destroy it!"

"You know how this works. It's just business." Raymond saw me, but he didn't acknowledge my presence. I took that as a sign to proceed with caution and started tiptoeing across the field, keeping my position behind Talkeen's back. "That's how you got to where you are, right? You took advantage of a situation that played in your favor. I'm only doing the same thing now."

"Neither one of us would be in this situation if you hadn't chickened out. I had the guts to do what needed to be done. I'm the one who's going to knock Klougus off his high horse. He doesn't deserve the power he has. He doesn't appreciate it. Look at him! He's become soft, and his grasp weakens every day because of it. Now he wants to hand everything over to his undeserving daughter." Talkeen's head fell back on a hollow laugh, and a wave of white hair fell down his back.

"I wonder how he would feel about her if he knew she was helping us all along. But of course, the second he said he would give her what she wanted, she turned her back on me. So, when I'm done ending you and your dumbass brother, I'm going after her. I'm taking everything. I'm taking what I'm owed, and everyone in the Bane will bow to me when I'm done."

"Wow, man, you really have been drinking your own Kool-Aid, haven't you?" Raymond laughed mockingly at Talkeen, who looked confused by the colloquialism, but it kept his rage focused on him. "I hate to be the one to burst your bubble, but none of that's gonna happen here."

As I got closer to him, I wanted more cover for my steps, afraid he would feel the vibration. So, I used my own magic. The vines slid from my skin, creating a moving platform that was eerily silent, unlike the sound of my feet.

"What makes you think you have any chance of surviving this? I'm stronger than you are now." Talkeen laughed. "I can feel it. You're weakened. Your time away from the Bane must have made you soft."

"You may be stronger than I am." Raymond dropped his head back as he pulled his locs up into a bun. "But you ain't stronger than my girl."

"What?" Talkeen laughed. "Even if that were true, she can't reach you here. Sad. I never thought you were the kind to let a woman fight for you."

"People change," I spoke from over Talkeen's shoulder, surprising him.

When he turned to look at me, I was ready for action. I told the vines to attack, and they did. They slapped him, hitting him in the chest. Talkeen, startled by the surprise attack, fell backwards, sliding across the ground. I took that moment to run to Raymond's side.

"You good?" I asked as I reached him, glancing down at Cufio, who clearly wasn't.

"Absolutely." Raymond looked at me proudly. "You?"

"Yes. Rayna showed up, so she's helping Metice. I told Olian to get the others out of here. Figured this place wouldn't be standing when we're done with him."

"Smart girl." He looked over his shoulder at his brother. "You heard her. Get out of here, find somewhere safe so you can rest up."

"I can fight," Cufio coughed, still clutching his center.

"Like hell you can. Go now," Raymond ordered him.

"I got his back." I nodded at Cufio, reassuring him we would not leave without each other. "Go."

He sighed, conceding, and a dark space behind Cufio opened. After one last glance at his brother, he fell back into it, disappearing.

"Let's do this," Raymond spoke as Talkeen got up.

I didn't think I hit him that hard, but the man looked like he'd already been through a war.

Talkeen said nothing. Once he dusted himself off, he attacked, and I realized pretty quickly that the space we were in belonged to him. Threads of shadows snapped at us furiously under his command. Raymond fought back, but Talkeen was right: he was stronger.

"We can't stay in here," Raymond said. "As long as we do, he has the upper hand."

"How do we get out?" I tried to ask the shadows to free me, but that didn't work. I heard a resounding *NO* in my mind.

"We work together." He blocked another strike from Talkeen. "When I open a doorway, use your vines to keep it open. He's strong, but he's struggling against them."

Talkeen realized what we were doing quickly. My vines threaded around the opening of the doorway Raymond created and pulled it wider.

"No!" He launched what would have been a brutal attack, but Raymond wrapped his arms around me, and we fell out the shadows back into the hall.

Most of the others had already left, but there were still a few who lingered. Unfortunately for us, they weren't on our side. Raymond and I had fallen onto our backs but made it back to our feet just as Talkeen stepped into view.

"Looks like you're all alone now." Talkeen smiled as if he was happy, but the tension around his eyes betrayed his mask. "Thank you for making this an easier task for me."

"Get over yourself," Raymond said. "I swear, it's like you're trying to *be* Klougus even though you claim to hate him."

"I am not!" Talkeen shouted, but the sound was borderline whining.

When he said it, I imagined him stamping his foot like a child, and it made Talkeen look a lot less threatening. Maybe that was Raymond's point. Let me see what we were really up against. A child mimicking more dangerous adults.

"Let's get this over with." Raymond glanced at the shadow cores. "Looks like your toys aren't doing too well. Do you honestly think you can fix that?"

"Yes, just as soon as I kill you and add your energy to my collection."

Another glance around the room to double check confirmed we were, in fact, alone. Part of me wished Rayna would pop in with her explosive powers, but that was selfish. It was better for them to be out of the way.

"I got you," Raymond spoke to me as the five shadow walkers circled us.

"You better." I winked at him. And when he laughed, the fight began.

Talkeen stood back and watched as we took on his men. His disappointment became obvious quickly as Raymond and I worked together like a well-oiled machine. He used his shadow hands, forming more than I had seen before, and I used my vines in combination with the roots from the ground. He would pin someone, and I would wrap them in the roots, dragging them deep down into the ground. It wouldn't hold them forever, and if they were stronger, they could have gotten out of it easily.

As we continued to arrest the members of Talkeen's team, I could feel them beneath me, struggling to get out, and made sure the roots reinforced their holds, threading into the shadows they hoped to use to escape.

When we disposed of his men, Talkeen had no choice but to face us alone. I thought more would come, but they didn't. Maybe his team wasn't as strong as he wanted everyone to believe. I'd hoped to make the first attack, shooting the roots from the ground to hit him in the back, but Talkeen had studied me. He anticipated the move and dodged the hit, retaliating with his own strike. A sharp slap of power hit me in the chest, knocking me over.

Raymond moved between us, blocking a follow-up hit.

"Guess she's not that strong after all," Talkeen mocked Raymond's previous bragging.

Raymond didn't respond with words. Instead, he raged. One look at me on the ground hurt, and whatever weakened him lost all effect. I heard the anger in his growl, and he called the shadows to him; they built around his arms and legs like armor. Then, Raymond took the fight to Talkeen. And I mean, he fought.

Talkeen tried to avoid Raymond, using his shadow techniques to protect himself, but soon enough, Raymond was on top of him, pounding away at a dark shield between them. I watched as the barrier cracked and Talkeen cried out.

Then, Talkeen held his hand out to the orbs, and thin strands of shadow started their path toward him. *Stop it!* intuition yelled at me, and logic went out the window. Yes, I know Raymond said to avoid contact with the damn things, and yes, I know I could have very well been running to my own demise, but I also knew I couldn't let Talkeen pull any power from those orbs.

And, like Captain Save-a-Ho, I jumped between Talkeen and those shadowy threads, and they slammed into my back.

"No!" Raymond screamed when he realized what I'd done, and Talkeen took that as his opportunity.

He punched Raymond in the jaw, knocking him down. Then, he turned his attention to me—only, I realized too late that I couldn't move. I looked down to see the shadows ripping at the fabric of my clothing.

"Fine, I'll take you out first." Talkeen was on his feet. He marched over to me, quickly wrapped his hand around my throat, and squeezed.

My lungs burned as I gasped for air, but the second I opened my mouth, a dark strand moved down my throat, aiding his attempt to strangle me. My eyes burned with tears and the edges of my vision darkened.

Just as I was about to lose consciousness, Raymond punched Talkeen in the side of the head, knocking him to the ground. He stood over him, shadows whipping from his form angrily.

"Don't you ever touch her again!" Raymond screamed, and the building shook. What was left of the structure crumbled around us. The threads from the shadow orbs left me alone, choosing a better target. They shot over to Raymond, and at first, I thought they would hurt him, but they didn't. They fed him, giving more power to his rage.

You'd think I'd be happy about it, but that intuition was telling me yet again to intervene. This wouldn't be good for Raymond.

As I gasped for air, I felt Kaa beneath my flesh. She moved frantically, angry I had been hurt. I could hear her voice, a snake-like sound stretching the syllables. *Release me!* Pressure formed in the center of my chest, and I ripped my top to see her face forming.

"Have at it," I told her, and Kaa shot out from my body in a massive expanse, larger than I had ever seen her before.

With her, the vines also lifted from my body, leaving my skin tattoo-free. Kaa coiled at my feet before she looked back at me. Our eyes connected, and in a moment, we had a full conversation, and I just knew what she wanted me to do.

Kaa went to Talkeen, and I went to Raymond. Before she reached him, three other shadow walkers appeared. It didn't matter, though, because she was ready. She entered the shadows, drawing his defense into the darkness, and I watched as the snake jumped from shadow to shadow. Each time she reappeared, her belly looked fuller until there was no more left for her to eat.

"Nice trick." Talkeen coughed, and he scooted back toward the shadow orbs.

"It's a new one. Thanks." I positioned myself between him and Raymond, who looked almost unrecognizable. Every time Talkeen moved, he shot another blast of power around me and into the man.

"I don't need them to kill you." The broken shadow walker spit, trying to convince himself he was still on top. "Besides, if he keeps absorbing that power, it will take him out for me."

I looked back at Raymond and instantly understood. Talkeen wasn't lying. Raymond's body bloated with power. The shadows covered more and more of him with each passing second.

What was I supposed to do?

"Raymond." I turned my back on Talkeen as Kaa started stalking him. "Listen to me. You have to fight it."

"I will not let him hurt you." His voice, a deep rumble that resonated with the power he'd absorbed, shook the space around us.

"Raymond, I'm fine," I spoke carefully. "Look at me, focus on me."

Gently, I placed my hands on either side of his face and forced his eyes, now pitch black, to look at me. "I'm okay, but I won't be if you don't fight this. I can't lose you here. Fight it, Raymond."

I saw a recognition flicker in his eyes, and then I could only think of one thing. It was cliché; it was corny; it was so dang sweet, it made my stomach ache. It felt right.

I kissed him.

And bippity, boppity, boop, the shit worked!

The shadows fell from around him, and Raymond returned to himself. He kissed me back, and I felt my entire heart flip. Damn it if I was going to be trapped in hell without him.

"Thank you," he said, voice heavy with something that made my stomach flutter.

"Don't mention it." I let him go. "Now, let's finish this."

"Shit." Raymond looked around me.

Talkeen had made it to the orbs. His hand was outstretched, and those shadows were feeding him the energy our attacks had depleted.

"We can't let him do this." Raymond moved to my side. "If he absorbs all that energy, it's over."

"What do we do?" I glanced at him.

"Act fast." Raymond vanished, stepping into a shadow and appearing right behind him.

He wrapped his arms around his neck, pulling back. Talkeen disconnected from the shadows, and the strings flung around, searching for a new target. Raymond rolled away with him, holding him down. Something in me said *help*, so I stepped forward, calling out to the roots in the ground.

They responded, breaking through the surface to help him. But as I was focused on directing the roots, I missed the dark thread flying toward my head. It slapped me in the face and, for a moment, snaked around my body.

Already hurt, I quickly weakened, but this time, Kaa wasn't trapped in the hold with me. She darted over and wrapped her body around me, fusing back into my skin. Then, instead of losing energy, I began to pull it from the shadows. Kaa took over, feeding off the power I wanted to avoid. Despite how eager she was, I knew I couldn't let it continue. It would kill me.

Control them!

That voice of intuition yelled at me.

Do not fear them. You are stronger!

"Right, I'm stronger," I said aloud. Then, with all my will, I told the shadows to do my bidding. I wanted them to save Raymond. They rejected me at first, but I gritted and issued the directive again, this time giving voice to the command. "Save Raymond! Kill Talkeen!"

The foreboding power moved through my body and out to Talkeen. It reached to him with thick arms, wrapping around him and starting to chew. It pushed Raymond away, answering my command, but Talkeen still had some hold. He fought, trying to regain control of the power as we entered a game of tug of war.

Raymond had tried to help, but there was nothing he could do. It was me and the enemy. I knew I had to end this, and so I opened my chest once again, calling to the soulmate who lived beneath my flesh.

I screamed as Kaa shot out from within me, blending with the shadowed arm and heading right for Talkeen. Before he could react, she snapped her jaw around his neck, releasing a venom that paralyzed him.

Talkeen fell to the ground, and so did I as the shadow core abandoned us both.

Raymond ran over to me when the connection ended. "We have to get out of here. That thing's going to blow."

"But Talkeen—" I said as we both looked over to where Kaa lay, happy and fatter than before, her mouth closing around Talkeen's head.

"I think we got him."

A furious shaking of the shadow cores caused their thin threads to morph into thick, trunk-sized ropes. They lashed out wildly, the spider-like tendrils ripping at the walls and ceiling. The sounds of cracking stone and the smell of pulverized earth filled the air as everything around us crumbled.

"What's gonna happen? That power, it can't just go out into the world, can it? Shouldn't we try to contain it?"

"I don't really know what's going to happen with that thing, but it's not our problem right now." Raymond scooped me up into his arms, and Kaa returned to me, blending back into my flesh. "We did what we had to do, and now we need to get out of here."

I nodded. "Yeah, okay. You're right." Raymond carried me into the shadows, leaving it behind. When we emerged, we were miles away with the others and turned just in time to see the building implode.

We all ducked for cover as the implosion sucked in debris from miles around, and then the entire building vanished with a loud boom.

30

Twerking on a Tree Demon

"Where is he? Did you get the job done?" Olian asked. She leaned on the orange guy, who supported her weight easily.

"Yes, but—" Raymond paused. "Fuck. We don't actually have any evidence to prove we got him."

"What do you mean, don't have evidence?" Cufio sat on the back of Piko, who happily let him rest atop his massive body. "We can't just go back there and promise him we did it. He's gonna want proof."

"I—" I was going to say something, but then I jerked when that pressure formed at my chest again. I looked down to see Kaa's head emerge. She didn't leave me entirely. Instead, she unhinged her jaw and regurgitated Talkeen's lifeless body.

"Oh, hell no! What was that?" Rayna jumped back, avoiding a wet splash.

"Well, at least we have proof now." Metice smirked.

I slapped my hand over my mouth as Kaa returned to her new home. "I'm going to be sick."

Olian slapped the orange guy's arm. "No! Get me out of here now. Damn Earth chicks can never keep their stomach contents to themselves."

"What?" I swallowed back the urge to vomit and frowned at her.

"Nothing!" she snapped, and everyone around me laughed at what was clearly an inside joke.

We returned to Klougus's home, and I slept the entire way. This time, we rode in Metice's fire horse carriage—not that I got to enjoy it.

When we made it, Klougus's right-hand man, Punal, met us at the door, and he was *not* happy we had been successful. He led us back to the room, where we waited for Klougus to address us.

"Well, I must say, I've heard the report of your escapades. Great job! Thank you for bringing that vermin back to me. His head will look great in my collection."

"Right," Raymond sighed. "The girl, please."

"Oh, right, Natalie!" he laughed. "That's what this was all about. Sorry, there is a lot going on these days."

"Where is she? Is she okay?" I asked.

"Oh yes, she is great. I had her moved to more comfortable accommodations." He sighed lovingly. "She really has grown on me in such a short time. Like a daughter."

"Ugh! Seriously?" Olian fussed by my side. "I'm going to the healer."

She marched out of the room, talking about how she didn't have to stand there and be disrespected.

"Excuse my daughter. Honestly, it's not her fault. I mess with her intentionally. After all, she tried to kill me!"

"You knew about that?" I shouldn't have said it, but I was tired, and my filter was shut off. "Talkeen told us."

"Right." He sighed. "Yes, I know about it. Everything done in the dark eventually comes to light. Isn't that right, Mnuktilous?"

Raymond nodded silently, and then Klougus clapped his hands again. The man really was expressive for someone who looked so intimidating.

"Punal will take you to the girl." He stopped, looking at the two of us. "Interesting. First, Metice finds his mate on Earth, and now you? I must pay my old friend a visit. I sense she has some hand in this."

After the cryptic message that kicked off that buzzing intuition inside me, he left us.

Punal then led us from that room to another deeper inside the compound. Only Raymond and I went. The others returned to the rides outside. After they handed Talkeen's body off to Klougus's team, we agreed we wouldn't need them anymore.

As we walked, bodies tired and sore, my initial nerves slowly faded. But they were replaced with a newfound sense of concern, because as we neared the room assigned to Natalie, I heard music blaring. This wasn't the kind of music I thought I would hear in a strange new world—rapid beats, flutes and strings, maybe a melody sung in a foreign tongue. No, this was rap music, as in rap music from Earth.

By the time we reached the door, I could feel the bass from the music and hear sounds of celebration on the other side. I threw a shocked glance at Raymond. "I know damn well she isn't having a party right now."

And right as I said it, Punal opened the door to the room, revealing my friend having a grand old time.

There were at least ten other demons in the room, all varying shades of what-the-fuck-is-that, and in the center of the bodies, Natalie. She threw one hand over her head while twerking on the tree demon who kept her alive. It wasn't the same one as before. This one had pink and purple flowers that fell from his head like braids.

"You have got to be kidding me!" I yelled, and like a needle scratching a record, the party stopped.

Whoever controlled the music lowered the volume, but it still played in the background as Natalie realized who had just crashed her party.

"Jericha! Oh my God, you're here." Natalie ran over to me, the tree demon keeping very close to her. "They told me you were here and that you would come to get me."

"Are you serious right now, Natalie?" I looked over her shoulder at the other beings, who were still vibing to the music.

"What?" She looked genuinely confused.

"Do you know what I just went through to save you?" I shook my head in disbelief. "I had to fight demons, literally cross realms, and when I get back here, you are twerking on the tree."

"*He* isn't a tree. His name is Keanu." Natalie frowned at me. "Well, actually, I can't really pronounce his real name, so we're going by Keanu now."

"You named him Keanu, as in the actor?" I choked back a laugh because I was trying to keep a serious stance.

"It fits him, don't you think?" She twirled her fingers in her hair and looked at the tree like she wanted to climb him.

"It's nice to meet you," the one now going by Keanu greeted me in a voice that sounded like he spoke through a mouthful of water. "Natalie has told me what a great friend you are to her."

"Uh, yeah, nice to meet you too." I pointed at Natalie. "Time to go."

"Do we have to leave so soon?" She glanced back at Keanu. "Can I have some time to say goodbye to everyone?"

"We're not even in the right world anymore." I threw my hands up. "It's not safe for you here. You do understand that, right?"

"Of course I do. That's why Keanu has to stay close to me, so I can breathe. If he goes too far, I start to choke and pass out." She waved her hand out. "But he's right here. I'm okay."

"Okay, pause." I took a deep breath. "Natalie. How are you so okay with this right now? I expected you to be panicked, upset, angry at me."

"Jericha, why would I ever be angry at you? You didn't do this to me." She shook her head. "And you know what my life is like on Earth. I've been craving something like this, something magical, something fun, and Keanu gave that to me."

"Keanu and his goons snatched you from Earth, thinking you were me," I corrected her.

"Actually, I wasn't there," he interjected in that dopey voice.

"Yeah, and once they realized their mistake, they were actually pretty nice about it." Natalie smiled. "They made sure I had Keanu so I would be okay."

"Fine. Take a moment to say goodbye, and then we can leave." I looked at Raymond, who stood silently by my side.

"I mean, do you think we could just spend one more day here?" Natalie asked.

"Is she serious right now?" I asked Raymond.

He nodded, looking at Keanu and not at us. "I think she is."

"Look, I know we have to go back. I'm not asking to stay here forever, but—" She looked over her shoulder at the tree guy, who pretended like he wasn't listening to us. "Can I just have one more night here with him? He told me once this was all over, he would take me to explore this world a little."

"Natalie, that's not safe." I looked around the room, afraid I was the only one with sense. "We don't know anything about the Bane. What if something attacks you?"

"I'm sorry, but unless I have misunderstood everything, you're literally standing next to a guy who is also some form of a demon. I know you want to protect me, but I'm a grown woman, and yes, you sign my paychecks, but you are not my mother." She sighed. "Look, I'm not trying to lose my job here. I need that. But can you, for a second, just be my friend and not my boss? Give me just one more night to have a little fun."

I grabbed her arm and pulled her just a little away from Keanu, who stiffened like he wanted to follow us but knew we needed space to talk.

"Are you telling me you...you like him? Seriously?"

"Why not?" She chewed the inside of her cheek. "He's sweet, and he's been so caring. I'm not saying this is my dream man. Never thought the guy for me would have leaves growing out of him, but I want to enjoy it for what it is. You know my track record with men. He is better than most of the scum I've encountered on Earth! Besides, how often do you get to explore another world?"

"A night here is a week on Earth. Did they explain that to you?" I asked. "Jackie is back home taking care of everything for us, and there are people depending on me."

"Jericha, please. Your world is full of magic. I only have this one night."

"Jericha, it can't hurt to ask." Raymond stepped over to me.

"Excuse me?" I looked at him. "You're on her side now?"

"I'm on whatever side allows me to rest soon." He rubbed the back of his neck, adjusting the weight of his locs. "Reach out to Jackie and see if she's cool with it. If she says no, we go home now."

"I can't believe this." After a deep sigh, I gave in. "Fine, I'll ask her."

I grabbed the stone that somehow was still around my neck, despite everything we'd been through. I held it, closed my eyes, and waited. Eventually, that static connection formed, and Jackie appeared in front of me.

"It's about time. Damn, are y'all okay?" A bonnet flopped over her head; I could tell I had just interrupted her sleep.

"Yes, we're good. Sorry, it feels like I just talked to you." I smiled because it felt good to hear her voice, even if she was on the verge of cursing me out. "We did what we had to do and got Natalie back. She's with us now."

"Hell yeah." She yawned, closing her eyes as if half listening to a phone call. "I knew my girl would kick demon ass!"

"Thanks for the confidence, but I'm actually here to ask you a huge favor. Not for me, but for Natalie."

"Natalie?" Her eyes popped open. "What does she need? Is she hurt? I can get medical staff here within the hour!"

"No, it's nothing like that." I reassured her. "She's good. Actually...she found a tree demon who she named Keanu, and she is asking if we can stay one more night so she can spend time with him. But of course, one more night here is seven there."

"Natalie's getting freaky with a tree demon." She laughed. "Ain't that some shit? Wait, Keanu? Like the actor?"

"Yes! Now, I can't confirm if they got freaky, but girl, when I got here, she was throwing it back on him while listening to Meg Thee Stallion!" At that, we both laughed. "She wants to stay. I'm against it and Raymond is playing neutral, so honestly, it's up to you."

"You know what?" Jackie nodded thoughtfully. "Let her have some fun. Everything's cool here."

"You know you can say no, right?" I tried to influence her decision. "I mean, you have a business to run yourself. And the other hunters, I know they're looking for you."

"True, but I have some vacation time built up, and honestly, I'm having fun here in your home. It's so much cozier than mine. Besides, I can run my business from anywhere. No one's missing me. Something's telling me Natalie isn't the only one who needs an extra night in the hellscape."

"Excuse me?"

"You and Raymond." Her head tilted, and she narrowed her gaze. "I know how these things go. This whole adventure solidified your relationship with him, hasn't it?"

I chuckled. "Maybe."

"Maybe means yes, and it also means you need to keep your butt there with that man. Because maybe he isn't ready to rush back to Earth either." She sucked her teeth. "Did you think about that? I mean, why else wouldn't he immediately be on your side when you insisted on running back home?"

"Damn, you're right. I didn't think about that."

"Of course I am. It's like you're new around here." She sighed. "So, take your time, spend another day there. I'll be here, keeping everything cool."

"I really appreciate this."

"I know, and I'm building my sushi order by the day, especially since you have so many pests here. If I wasn't so fly, I would be traumatized."

"What pest?" I freaked out. "Did you have to call an exterminator?"

"Not that kind. The kind with two legs and one itty bitty part in between. Men." She laughed. "First, it was a guy named Deonta. He came by asking for you, started ranting about how you having a new boyfriend wouldn't be enough to keep him away. So, I had Miguel drop him off with the pixies. Bet his ass won't be back now."

"Jackie!" I gasped.

"And then there was that Mitch bitch who came back here, asking if you were hiring. I slammed the door in his face so damn fast!" She rolled her eyes.

"You're a trip."

"Always and forever. Oh, also, I never found Kaa. I'm so sorry, girl. I think she ran away."

"Actually, she found me."

"She's in the Bane? How?"

"It's a long story, one I will explain when I get back."

"All right, girl. Talk soon."

I let go of the connection, and when I opened my eyes, Natalie, Raymond, and Keanu stood around me, looking at me with hopeful expressions, each for very different reasons.

I shook my head. "She said yes."

Natalie squealed and jumped into Keanu's arms. Raymond tried to look like he wasn't affected, but I could see the relief in his expression.

"I'll bring her to you in one day," Keanu spoke to Raymond.

"Not a second later, or I'll find you."

"Of course. You have my word." He held his hand out to Raymond, who accepted it.

Then, leaving Natalie to finish her party, Raymond took my hand and walked me back outside of Klougus's compound. He didn't say another word. When we were out in the clear, free from eyes and ears, he pulled me to him, opened the shadows, and took me back to his happy place.

31

Shadows v. Vines

"This is where you bring me." I looked around at the tree-covered plains. "I thought you would choose somewhere with a bed. Didn't you say you needed to rest?"

"I do, but we'll have plenty of time for beds." He placed his hands on my shoulders and massaged them in slow circles. "Are *you* okay? I just wanted to check in and make sure that after everything we just experienced, you're good."

"Yeah. I'm fine." I looked down at my body, assessing how I felt in my skin. "It's weird, though. I feel different, stronger, yet weaker at the same time. But I think after I get some time to rest and heal, I'll be perfectly fine."

He chuckled with a deep sigh. "You're too literal. I know your body is hurting, I can see that. I'm talking about mentally and emotionally, Jericha. You went through a lot—that was a lot for anyone to handle, especially someone not used to fighting creatures like that."

"It was a lot." I nodded. "But we survived it."

"And what about what happened between us?" His right hand slipped from my shoulder to my neck, settling just beneath my jaw. "We should discuss that."

"Yeah. We should." I looked into his eyes. "What was that? Please tell me that wasn't the marriage thing Likosa mentioned."

"No. Not quite the marriage of souls. Something different. We're bonded now. It's something that happens when shadow walkers care deeply for someone. We give them part of our shadows." He inhaled. "Now, I can feel you, wherever you are. It's like a tether."

"Yeah, I think I could feel you too." I nodded. "At first, I thought it was just the adrenaline, the heat of the moment making me feel things. But I could tell you needed me when you were in the shadows."

"How do you feel about that?" His voice was serious, the words deliberate, yet there was underlying compassion in his tone. "If you want, I can remove it."

"Do I have to know the answer to that now?" I chuckled. "Like you said, it's a lot to process, and I don't think I'll be able to do that until after I have a long shower and at least one good night of sleep."

"No, you don't, but I wanted to pause and ask the question. I don't want you to think any of this is permanent. If you want out at any point, you are out, regardless of whatever magical bonds exist between us."

"It happens when you care deeply about someone?" I swallowed. "How deeply?"

"Love." The word was heavy, like a boulder falling between us. "It happens when we love someone."

"You love me?" I asked, my voice nearly catching in my throat.

"Yes. Jericha. I do." He said with a simple weight that made my heart squeeze.

I paused, like he said, and listened. I listened to the strange calls of creatures around us, felt the breeze on my skin, and inhaled the sweet air. I paused and listened to my heart, to that intuition that led me to save him in the heat of battle.

It urged me to stay. I couldn't say the words back, because I wasn't sure if that was how I felt. But I was sure of one thing: I wanted Raymond in my life.

"And what if I don't want out?" The question came out on a shaky breath.

"Excuse me?" His eyes widened. "I don't think I heard you correctly."

"What if, after everything we've been through together, I don't want out? What if this entire experience has changed me in a way that makes me want all in with you? I'm not talking about marriage, but I like who I'm becoming with you."

"Oh damn, isn't that supposed to be my line?" he joked. "Wait, I'm going to start swooning!"

"Shut up." I slapped his arm but appreciated what he was doing for me, making the moment seem lighter. "You know how I like to take control."

"That I do." He lowered his hands to my waist and pulled me close. "But so do I."

Raymond leaned me back as a platform of shadows formed beneath me. A bed of his own making. He moved to lie next to me on the floating platform, kissing me as he did. Despite the ache in my body, I still responded to his touch. The shadows moved across my flesh, under my clothing, and I understood what they were doing: cleaning. Raymond was preparing our bodies to be together.

I couldn't help myself. While his shadows lifted the blood and dirt from my skin, my vines snaked through the grass. Just as Raymond's hand slid to my pants, his fingers working the button, the vines snapped from the ground.

They grabbed his arms and legs, pulling him back from me as they snaked around his body.

"What?" He looked down at the vines, not a lick of fear in his eyes.

I said nothing—I only sat on the floating platform and watched as the vines did for me what the shadows had for him, time and time again. They peeled away his clothing while I watched.

"What are you doing?" he moaned as the vines caressed him the same way I would have.

"In the bedroom, you're in control. That was our deal." I looked around. "This doesn't look like a bedroom to me, does it?"

"Oh, okay." He bit his bottom lip as the vines brushed against his balls. "I see how it is now."

The shadow platform shifted, moving me closer to him as he tried to pull me into the shadows. I knew what he wanted to do: take me back to the condo so I could hold up my end of the deal. Only this time, I countered it. Raymond was still weak, and while I had the upper hand, I took it!

I pushed the shadows back, and we were still in his happy place. The vines forced him to stand as I walked around him.

"Not this time." I kissed his neck then summoned a seat of woven vines and roots to sit on.

"Jericha," he grunted.

"Raymond?" I fluttered my eyes.

"You're being so bad right now."

"And I'll happily take my punishment later." I crossed my legs and leaned back in my new throne. "But for now, I'm going to enjoy the show."

"What show?"

I waved my hand purely for dramatic effect, and the vines did exactly what I wanted. They moved to his dick, which was saluting me, so I knew he enjoyed what happened.

"What's your safe word?" I asked him.

"Donuts." He raised a brow, but the smirk fell from his face as the vines stroked his dick.

They slid up and down his length, alternating levels of pressure and speed. I stood as Raymond edged to completion and the shadows fell away from his dick. They still held his arms and legs in place, restricting his movement.

He breathed heavily, chest rising and falling as I wrapped his locs around my hands and pulled him to kiss me. If he wanted to get away, he could have. Even if he couldn't transport me without my permission, he could phase out of the vines whenever he wanted. No, Raymond was right where he wanted to be.

I pulled away from the kiss, spit in my hand, then finished what the vines started.

"Oooh, shit!" Raymond called out as he came. His head fell on my shoulder with a deep chuckle. "Damn it, girl. You're going to be trouble."

"Yeah. And you're stuck with me now." I wrapped the shadows around us and took us back to the condo. Because this woman needed a shower, a nap, and then I was going to ride him until it was time to go back to Earth.

The End

A Favor.

"Did it knock your period out of whack?" I handed Rayna a cup of tea. It had been months since I last saw her, and we were catching up on things. "The first time, it didn't. But this last trip, I swear when we got back here, it jumpstarted my uterus."

"Oh, yeah, girl! It's so annoying, but if you do it enough, your body adjusts." Rayna paused. "I only get them once or twice a year now, actually, because of all the world-hopping we do. But when it comes, it's hell!"

"Great to know." I took a deep breath and made a mental note to order more pads.

"So, are you nervous?" She sipped her tea. "This is a big day."

"Yes. I mean, I know Whitney, or at least I knew her back when we were all in college. Even then, we barely spoke. I didn't want to accidentally reveal everything to her. But Jackie says she's ready now."

"Good. This will be good for you both, I'm sure."

"Yeah, I hope so."

"Listen, I don't care how much time I spend in the Bane—I'm not selling you my condo," Metice fussed as he and Raymond entered the room.

"You have twelve of them! Why do you need so many homes?" Raymond questioned. "Look, they burned mine down, and you have all the best property right now."

"The way you make enemies, any place you own will go up in flames." Metice chuckled. "Really, I'm doing you a favor."

Rayna and I shared a glance and both sipped our tea as we silently agreed to stay out of it.

The doorbell rang, and my stomach dropped when Rayna announced, "They're here."

"I'll get it," Raymond offered and headed out of the kitchen to the front door.

"It will be fine, trust me. We've worked with Whitney and Domino a few times now. She loves that monster hunter stuff."

"Thanks."

"Hey!" Jackie stepped into the kitchen, and following her was a woman who looked a lot more like me than I remembered. *Whitney.*

"Hey." Whitney looked as nervous as I felt.

"Hi." I stood.

"Oh God." Jackie huffed. "Whitney, this is your sister, Jericha. Jericha, this is your sister, Whitney. Now hug it out."

"You could give them two seconds to process this," the tall man with gold wired-framed glasses, the one I knew now to be a day-walking vampire, spoke to Jackie.

"And you could mind your business. I keep telling you, Domino, just because she's cool with you doesn't mean I am." She tapped the stake secured at her waist.

"Jackie, please stop threatening to kill my man." Whitney sucked her teeth.

"Maybe we should give the girls some space." Raymond suggested, and the three men eagerly headed out to the yard, where we could see them standing awkwardly together.

"So, Whitney. Jericha is going to be working with us now," Jackie spoke then turned to me. "Sorry Lena couldn't be here. Huge production thing going on right now. Something about a casting issue."

"No problem. I'll catch up with her next time." I nodded. "I'm sure I'll see her around the studio."

"You gave me Maverick?" Whitney asked.

"Oh, yeah," I started, and she hugged me.

"Thank you," she said as I hugged her back. "He saved my life."

"You don't hate me?" I asked her. "I was afraid you would be upset since I didn't tell you everything sooner."

"When Jackie told me everything, I was confused, but after all these magical revelations, I understand." She took a deep breath. "You wanted to keep me safe. I did the same for my sister. It involved wiping her memory, but she's safe now."

"You wiped her memory?" I gawked.

"Hey, it was the best thing we could do for the girl," Jackie said. "And we've monitored her since. She's mentally sound, and there have been no supernatural shenanigans in her life."

"I guess that's good." I smiled. "But about Maverick…"

"What about him?" Whitney asked.

"I-" I started to tell her the truth about Maverick and his ties to Likosa. I was sure it meant something more, but I didn't get the chance to.

The pressure in the room grew, and we all looked at each other. Someone was coming. I glanced out the window at the guys who were unaware. It didn't matter. If it was a threat, we could handle it.

The girls had the same idea, because when I looked at them again, they were all in a fighting stance.

Then, in a pink cloud, one done purely for effect, Likosa appeared.

"Well, now that we're all together." She adjusted the headpiece that made her look like royalty. "I have a favor to ask. And as far as I can see, you all owe me. BIG!"

Accidents Keep On Happening!

Continue reading more in the Accidents Happen Series.

I Accidentally Summoned a Demon Boyfriend

I Accidentally Hooked up with a Vampire

I Accidentally Hired a Shadow Walker

Thank you to our Kickstarter Supporters!

I want to give a special thank you to everyone who helped fund our Kickstarter for I Accidentally Hired a Shadow Walker! Thank you all so much for your help with making this happen.

Adrena Johnson

Adriane

Ai'Asia Williams

Akisha Burgett

Alayna Gazer

Alecia Watkins

Alexandra Corrsin

Alexis

Alexis Myers

Alexis Washington

Ali Finn

Alicia Hintzen

Allyson Lindt

Alonia Taylor

Alyssa

Amanda Balter

Amanda Hamilton

Amanda Lois

Andrea Gissentanna

Angelbelle

Anika

Anna Muhovich

Annait LJ

AnTia Thomas

April George

April Perrault

Arkia

Arne Radtke

Arricka Hickman

Ashara T.

Ashleigh

Aura Torres

Aylkaraemi

Brandi

Bri

Britiney

Cadijah Rogers

Caitlin Murphy

Camilla Sutton

Candace Bumpass

Candice Gary

Cassondra

Cecilie Steinsland

Cerissa Howard

Champrea

Chareece Madison

Charmaine Gray

Chavannah T McCann

Cheetara

Chelsea White

Cherelle Hopper

Cherry Atwood

China White

Ciara

Coco

Coco Fernandez

Courtney Haynes

Danielle

David Hankerson

Dazetrica Gray

Desi

Domii Perry

Dominique

Draconian Briana

Elisha Bryant

Elyse Thomson

Emily Soto

Erika Dawkins

Erin Buck

Famira

Florentina Nitschke

Fro Carducci

Gabrielle

Gabrielle Bauer

Georgia B

Gina Wohlgemuth

Glorimar Medina

Goddess Amber

Grace

Greg Burnham

Harmony L Gibbs

Hazel Stephens

Iesha Bree

India

Jackie Spradley

Jade Burns

Jaira-Traci Fiedler

Jasmin

Jasmine

Jasmyne

Jasmyne Lacy

Jellul

Jen (Fantasy girl)

Jennifer Milledge

Jessica

Jessica

Joyce & Benjamin Green

Julia Libby

Julius Lindsay

K

K.C. Cordell

Kaila Stovall

Kalia W

Kaneka Tenia Wilhoite

Katee Robert

Katie

Katie Daly

Katina Hill

Keaundray Osborn

Keema Osborne

Keia Joi

Kenja

KeyVonna Joyner

Kia Borner

Kimberley (Noriboo)

Kirstin Porter

KJ

Kosha

Kristen Williams

LadyJ

Lakea Leann Jones

LaKevion Trotter-Clark

LaQundra Hickman

LaReina

LaShaundrea Williams

Latisha Fray

Leah Phillips

Leslie Anderson

Lola Rock

Lorren Williams

Maddox Grey

Margaret

Marie Klassen

Marissa Krause

Mica Winchester

Michéle Thomas

Midnight August Moon

Mik

Mikah Harper

Miwa Williams

Monica M Render

Naomi D. Nakashima

Natalie Jess

Natasha Wadlington

Navonne Morgan

Nicole

Nicolette Andrews

Nikki

Norell Clemons

R.S. Kellogg

Rachel Schutte

Raechel Soicher

Rana Robinson

Raven McCandies

Rielle McGee

Rizing_1

Robert Barr

Rochelle Lowe

Runeda Scott

Rylie Van Court

Sabriya Joyce

Sangeetha

Sarah

Sarah Schultz

Sasha M Fountain

Shameka

Shanique Hyde

Shannon Bond-Cover

Shaunette Housen

Shavonna

Shaye Dente

Shenae

Sierra Wanzer

Sonya Bundschuh

Sophia-Symone Richardson

Stephleda

SUBSUME

Susan Hall Comrie

Tangela Williams

Tania Fernandez

Tee

Tenisha

Teralyn Mitchell

Tina Hawkins

Tisa Jordan

Tori Coke

Torri Long

Trenaye Trott

Twana Brunson

Tyesa Anderson

Tyrisha Hicks

Vesenia Lindsey

Victoria Chernecky

Whitney

About the author

ABOUT THE AUTHOR

ABOUT THE AUTHOR

Jessica Cage is an International Award Winning, and USA Today Best Selling Author. Born and raised in Chicago, IL, writing has always been a passion for her. She dabbles in artistic creations of all sorts but at the end of the day, it's the pen that her hand itches to hold. Jessica had never considered following her dream to be a writer because she was told far too often "There is no money in writing." So, she chose the path most often traveled. During pregnancy, she asked herself an important question. How would she be able to inspire her unborn son to follow his dreams and reach for the stars, if she never had the guts to do it herself? Jessica decided to take a risk and unleash the plethora of characters and their crazy adventurous worlds that had previously existed only in her mind, into the realm of readers. She did this with hopes of inspiring not only her son but herself. Inviting the world to tag along on her journey to become the writer she has always wanted to be. She hopes to continue writing and bringing her signature Caged Fantasies to readers everywhere.